FERRETT STEINMETZ

The Flux

ANGRY
ROBOT

ANGRY ROBOT
An imprint of Watkins Media Ltd

Lace Market House,
54-56 High Pavement,
Nottingham,
NG1 1HW
UK

www.angryrobotbooks.com
twitter.com/angryrobotbooks
You are not your fluxing khakis

An Angry Robot paperback original 2015

Cover by Steven Meyer-Rassow
Cover model Lyndsey Clark
Set in Meridien by Epub Services

Distributed in the United States by Random House, Inc., New York.

ISBN 978 0 85766 463 1
Ebook ISBN 978 0 85766 464 8

Printed in the United States of America

9 8 7 6 5 4 3 2 1

For Mom, who taught me calmness

And for Dad, who taught me curiosity

I hope I didn't put you through nearly this much trouble

PART I

Smart Patrol, Nowhere To Go

ONE
Not Rituals, But Love

Before Paul Tsabo brewed up a batch of magical drugs, he would demand $400,000 in cash from his financier, to be delivered along with the rest of his drug-making paraphernalia. The cash arrived in a great pallet of crumpled twenties, a shrink-wrapped parcel so big it took two of Oscar's drug runners to carry it into the abandoned auto repair shop Paul had designated as today's laboratory.

Paul checked the money off on the list.

Paul liked lists. Of *course* he liked lists, or he wouldn't have become a bureaucromancer. Lists were oases of sanity bobbing in Paul's increasingly chaotic lifestyle – maybe the King of New York would phone in a tip to the NYPD Task Force again and they'd have to flee the cops, maybe Oscar would finally get tired of Paul's inability to deliver Flex and quietly put a bullet in Paul's skull, maybe the magical backlash from brewing Flex would kill everyone in this sleepy suburban neighborhood…

…but by God, *Paul could ensure this list was checked off.*

So Paul checked off each delivery as Oscar's assistants, K-Dash and Quaysean, hauled them in. Paul ambled around the cracked, oil-stained floor unsteadily – years of physical therapy had gotten him almost used to walking on his artificial right foot. But when an insane 'mancer had lopped off the toes of his left foot two years ago, well, even a top-of-the-line orthotic boot hadn't helped him regain his former balance.

Still, he refused on principle to get a cane. The titanium rod that served as his right ankle drew enough stares; all of Paul's crisp suits weren't enough to hide the scrawny Greek man limping around on one metal prosthetic and one thick black boot. So Paul's legs trembled with exhaustion as he double-checked to ensure all his drug-making accoutrements were in place:

Fifty pounds of illegal hematite, the only substance on earth you could bind 'mancy into, worth hundreds of thousands of dollars? Check.

Valentine's battered *Pac-Man* machine, an antique cabinet from the original 1980 production line, used to detect dangerously shifting probabilities? Check.

Curling glass alembics and tubes to redirect the flow of 'mancy once Paul flooded the room with the power of paperwork? Check.

A desk with five fresh Bic pens, arranged above an untouched legal pad? Check.

$400,000 in cash?

His pen paused over the paper. That cash heap, big enough that Paul could use it as a futon made of Andrew Jacksons, made Paul's skin crawl. He *owned* that money now, a fragile stack of linen-cotton blend, to be loaded into a rented U-Haul upon completion.

If the brew went wrong, as it had so many times before, then this money would burn. And he would not be able to pay Oscar back.

Paul owed Oscar well over a million dollars for getting him all this hematite, and no amount of bureaucromancy could fill that gap. The universe disliked the way magic bent its rules, demanding the scales get balanced; if Paul rejiggered the paperwork to erase those funds from Oscar's ledger, then a million dollars' worth of bad luck would rain down upon Paul's head.

And if today went wrong – if the King somehow had informants seeded in this bankrupt rural town – then Paul would owe Oscar a million-four. Though Oscar was a patient businessman who played for the long game, Oscar was also a criminal. Paul's special Flex was a drug that made empires run smoothly, but Paul had to actually deliver some or Oscar would make an example out of him.

Paul's paperwork magic couldn't stop bullets.

Yet that wasn't what *really* worried him. There was no better 'mancer than he qualified to handle deadly loads of bad-luck flux. The NYPD Task Force was a threat – Paul wouldn't have had it otherwise – but he had inside sources that would alert him if the King somehow tipped the cops off to this remote location. And Oscar was slow to anger, especially with such rare and delicious material on the hook.

That $400,000, a terrifyingly large sum, was insurance against a much worse fate.

Paul stared at the cash, hoping it would not burn today. Hoping his friend Valentine's wards would hold.

Hoping his daughter Aliyah would not show up.

As usual, Valentine played *Pac-Man* while Paul checked in the equipment. Paul knew Valentine played videogames whenever she got nervous – and though Valentine's thrillseeking had gotten them in trouble before, even Valentine respected the danger of brewing Flex.

A glittery red eyepatch covered the hole where a military SMASH team had shot Valentine's eye out. She bobbed her head as she maneuvered Pac-Man along the maze, attempting to recreate stereo vision with a single eye, a strangely birdlike movement.

Her black crinoline dress jiggled; she played the game with her whole body, a fishbelly-pale pudgy girl in fuck-me red pump heels leaning into the console. Her long brunette curls shook as she slammed the joystick around, an Xbox controller dangling from the bandolier wrapped around her curvy hips.

"Some days," she said, "I'm tempted to warp into Billy Mitchell's home to show him who the *real* King of *Kong* is."

Paul flinched at the mention of the King before realizing Valentine was making small talk about someone else. "...who?"

She waved a tattooed hand at the machine, which froze. Old-school arcade machines didn't have pause buttons, but Valentine's videogamemancy tweaked reality in odd ways.

"Billy *Mitchell*?" she urged Paul, aghast. "The world champion *Pac-Man* player? First man to get a perfect score? Possessor of the world's most impermeable mullet?"

"...what's that have to do with King Kong?"

She spluttered. "Don't you pay *any* attention to the Twin Galaxies scoreboards, Paul? Billy Mitchell was the high scorer on *Donkey Kong*, too! Smug little snake. Kind of a bully. I think about dropping a life-sized ape on his house and making *him* run up the ladders! I bet his score would–"

She took in Paul's blank expression, then shook her head, radiating a terrible disappointment.

"Ah, Paul," she lamented. "You know every line in the New York State tax code, and yet your education features these tragic gaps."

"Can you keep Aliyah out this time?"

Paul hadn't meant to ask the question. It just squirted out.

Valentine blew a sigh through pursed lips. She noticed K-Dash and Quaysean, two leanly muscled Hispanic lovers who shifted nervously from foot to foot. Valentine jerked her thumb towards the garage's back door.

"Go look for the King of New York," she told them. "We spent hours covering our trail. If he drops the dime on us this time, that means he's followed us here somehow."

K-Dash frowned. "But we don't know what the King looks like–"

"Like *we* do? This neighborhood hasn't seen a paying customer in years – so if you see anyone lurking about, assume they're Kingish. But," she added, "just report back.

No…" She pulled an imaginary trigger.

They nodded and headed out, happy to give two of New York's most notorious 'mancers their privacy.

Valentine crossed her arms and leaned against the cabinet. For a plump goth girl dressed in striped black-and-white stockings and a cocked hat, Valentine looked like she meant business.

"Don't know if I can stop Aliyah this time, Paul. I'll try. But the kid plays by different rules."

"But you're both videogamemancers."

"And Aliyah plays different games these days," Valentine said. "I introduced her to gaming, but she's developed her own tastes: *Animal Crossing*, *Scribblenauts*, *Professor Layton*. Which means her 'mancy's got its own style. We used to be similar, but, you know… the kid's gonna be nine in two months. She's growing up."

"Can't you just play her games?"

Valentine looked like she'd swallowed a slug. "*Me*? Play *Cooking Mama*? Forgive me for having taste, Paul!"

Paul let it drop. Every 'mancer had a worldview that made sense to them, and them only. Valentine had asked a hundred times why Paul couldn't just conjure up a million dollars out of thin air, marshalling all sorts of arguments about how currency was an illusion perpetrated by society. Since the government printed money on demand all the time, why the hell couldn't Paul just – and here, Valentine always waved her hands in the air and made a "whoosh" noise – manufacture some damn cash to pay off Oscar?

But it didn't work that way. Bureaucracy's whole *point* was that it prevented fraud: without it, anyone could claim they had bought this car or this factory, and who was to say otherwise? Paperwork was what made the universe *fair*. Paul could launder money, hide its ownership, find the best investments for it – but taking stuff for free?

Hell, he had enough moral quandaries manufacturing drugs for a gang leader.

Valentine glanced over at the OfficeMax desk Paul would

brew the drugs on, propped across what used to be a repair bay.

"Look, I'm not saying this isn't the most fucked-up version of 'Take Your Daughter To Work' Day ever... But maaaaaybe instead of having me construct wards to keep your kid out, we should invite her along."

Paul clenched his fists. "You remember what Aliyah did to the last batch of cops, right?"

Valentine met his gaze evenly. "I do."

"And you remember what would have happened to her if I hadn't been her legal guardian, right?"

"Do *not* make this about 'who loves her more,' Paul," Valentine snapped. "I adore Aliyah like I squeezed that kid out of my own cooter. But 'mancy's a dangerous business."

"Which is why we hold classes," Paul shot back. "That's why we have Scouting Saturdays, and Sad Sundays. To *educate* her."

Valentine shrugged. "Not to suggest you have all the educational skills of a hungover substitute teacher, Paul, but... the kid's into videogames. She only cuts loose when she's challenged by real life. I don't want her hurt, but this profession has no training wheels. This is magic. She might die."

Paul wanted to get mad. Yet Valentine's reaction held the carefully chilled regret of all the nurses who'd told him, *Your daughter has third-degree burns over sixty percent of her body, Mr Tsabo. She might not survive*. They were not rejoicing in a child's death, were not ceasing their struggle... but they had a flinty awareness that everything within their power might not be enough to save Paul's daughter.

And in truth, though Paul had managed to save her through his bureaucromancy, Aliyah's scars had never truly healed.

"She'll be fine." Paul gritted his teeth. "She just needs to manage her temper."

"And where is she now?"

"With her mother, for the weekend. According to our

divorce agreement, Imani has custody until seven pm Thursday night."

"So the kid's stuck in a house with no videogames, with her douche politician of a stepdad and a mother who she has been instructed to lie to. She's pretending hard to be a normal kid, told if she fucks up this masquerade just *once*, then the entire US government will come down upon her head and wipe her brain. And you think the kid's not *already* managing her temper?"

Paul limped away in disgust.

"Where are you going?"

"Come on," Paul said. "Let's brew."

K-Dash and Quaysean arranged the Bic pens on the desk before stepping back, seeking Paul's approval.

Paul examined the pens, spaced perfectly parallel, then gave the boys a cheerful nod. They fist-bumped. Quaysean and K-Dash were nice, as criminals went: they held hands tenderly whenever they weren't hauling in goods. They were reliable, and Paul valued reliability. They had even taken to bringing donuts to the brews, as if this was some Monday morning work gathering.

Valentine tugged her cell phone out of her bra. "Eight pm, Paul," she said through a mouthful of vanilla crème donut. "If we hustle, we can finish this in time for me to hit the swing clubs."

Paul picked up the pen.

As his fingers brushed the legal pad, triggering a spark of bureaucromancy, the place's history flowed through him in one administrative flash: this had once been Patziki's Auto Repair Shop – a tiny two-bay garage founded in 2004 by one Samuel Patziki, age fifty-four.

He saw the credit reports the bank had run on Samuel before they'd approved him for the loan, noted the W-4 tax records as Samuel had proudly hired his first employees, tallied the dwindling orders to auto part vendors as business lagged. Paul groaned as the first notifications from collection agencies trickled in.

On May 14th, 2009, the bank foreclosed.

Paul looked at the high ceiling crisscrossed with rusted beams, the holes in the concrete where the car lifts had once gone, the windows on the two wide garage bay doors boarded over. All the equipment had long been stripped out; all that was left were rows of empty lockers, and a flyspecked calendar displaying a May 2009 pinup girl.

This place was a grave of ambitions, a bad location in a bankrupt town. That isolation made it perfect for avoiding the King – the King of New York's phoned-in tips had driven Paul to find a place so dismal even the homeless had stayed away – but though Samuel's failed business was convenient for Paul, Paul secretly hoped that Samuel Patziki was OK, wherever he was.

He could have followed the paperwork trail back to check in on Samuel, but... Paul needed the illusion of happy endings today.

Valentine spun a quarter between her fingers. "Ready to bring the thunder, Paul?"

Paul looked over at Quaysean and K-Dash. "You don't have to stay, you know," he said. "This gets dangerous."

"You always say that, Mr Tsabo." They interlaced fingers, kids eager to watch the fireworks.

As Paul turned back to the desk, he allowed himself one tiny smile. He loved having an audience. Maybe one in a thousand people had even seen 'mancy, and most of them found magic terrifying. 'Mancy was illegal because it could rip holes in the seams of the universe, letting buzzsect-demons spill in through the gap to devour the laws of physics.

But it also created unearthly beauty, for those with the eyes to see.

Paul snap-pointed at Valentine. "Ready, player one?"

She dropped the quarter into the *Pac-Man* machine. A jaunty eight-bit tune rang out. Paul glanced at the cash-pallet at the back of the garage, his insurance in case Aliyah showed up, then pushed all that out of his head.

He picked up the pen and drew boxes on the legal pad.

Do magic, Valentine had told him, back when she'd taught him to make Flex. *'Mancy isn't rituals, Paul. It's love. When you started, I'll bet dimes to dollars you didn't fire up 'mancy to do anything. You just… did it. And the 'mancy flowed from that love.*

Paul started making paperwork.

He started where he always did, sketching out the Universal Unified Form – the single form so comprehensive, it contained every single thing you could ever request, file, or catalogue. It existed only in his daydreams, but Paul's magic allowed him to open windows into his reveries and haul things back through.

He wrote the opening fields, same as always: *First Name. Middle Name. Last Name. Sex. Date of Birth…*

The tray of hematite rattled on the table, sending smoky green dust puffing into the air. The alembics rattled, their spiraled tubes swaying between them. Valentine played *Pac-Man*, glancing over at Paul between levels.

When Paul finished the basic fields, he drew the first thing that came to mind: a Psychological Assessment Report, adding fields for Test Administrator, Referral Question, Behavioral Observations – and the fields filled up with words…

Aliyah's mother has stated she has no friends and never initiates social interactions with other children, preferring to play alone on her handheld video game or sit quietly by herself. Her teachers confirmed this behavior, noting that Aliyah's classmates rarely approach her due to her aloof or aggressive reactions to their overtures…

The alembics vibrated, ascending in tempo until they shattered.

K-Dash and Quaysean ducked, looking fearful but not backing away. Paul touched his temple, pulled a shard out, blotted the blood away with a handkerchief.

"That's gonna make the brew harder, working without glassware." Valentine shook the glass from her hair, not looking away from her freshly cracked screen lest she lost her perfect score. "Everything copacetic, Paul?"

"You just concentrate on keeping Aliyah out." He bridged away from the psychological areas of the Universal Unified Form, shifting to another style of medical paperwork: emergency-room admissions.

The legal paper expanded to fill the desk, swelling as Paul added checkboxes, cross-references, signature fields, Paul's neat handwriting condensing into crisp Times New Roman font. The form overflowed the desk's edges in a vellum waterfall, crumpling as it unfolded across the concrete floor.

Paul kept writing, making space for the lists of prescription drug allergies once the patient checked in, the standard tests run upon fresh admissions, the work release forms for someone injured on the job...

"Pac-Man just went off the maze, Paul," Valentine said warily. "He's travelling through a hospital. Is that where he should be?"

"Yes," Paul confirmed. Pac-Man was their canary in a coal mine, telling them when the 'mancy got too dangerous. The raw 'mancy Paul summoned changed the odds, causing fantastic coincidences to happen around him. If the local odds got *too* wild, Paul couldn't rein in the magic enough to stuff it inside the hematite... and once you had wild magic ricocheting around, then Very Bad Things happened.

They'd once used a Bingo machine to calibrate the 'mancy-level, but Valentine said playing games gave more accurate readings. Any given *Pac-Man* game was confined to a single blue maze, with the monsters chasing Pac-Man in preordained patterns... but add in a dose of 'mancy to create bizarre glitches, and Pac-Man went on some very unusual trips. If Pac-Man died on his new adventures, then it was time to shut things down.

The frightening thing, Paul thought, was that after only two years of being a 'mancer, all this seemed *normal*.

The forms bunched up, folding as Paul's 'mancy ebbed. Paul had to focus. It was good to focus. It was *fun* to think about all the forms involved in the emergency room, not about his daughter who might teleport in at any moment to dispense mayhem....

Paul wrote in slots for the insurance preauthorization forms, the billing codes for each prescribed treatment, the maintenance records in the anesthesia machines, and there entangled in the forms was Samuel Patziki, now having his fingers sewn back on after a terrible accident at the garage he'd been working at.

Paul thumbed through the paperwork like a priest fingering his rosary. He pulled forms out of midair to list Samuel Patziki's impending medical expenses, compared them to Samuel's current income. Samuel Patziki had taken quite a pay cut, according to the IRS records, working a $22,000-a-year job to make the payments on his $47,256 mortgage at 8% interest.

"Pac-Man's in a shitty suburb now, Paul," Valentine said, looking worried. "Cracked streets. Not a lot of outs. Bankruptcy-ghosts are closing in on him from every direction..."

Paul flowed upstream, checking who Samuel Patziki's insurance holder was: Samaritan Mutual. Paul winced; he'd worked for them, once. Samaritan was the cheapest insurance provider, preying on the poor with the cheapest rates and even cheaper payouts. A few calculations revealed Samuel Patziki would pay $24,794 after Samaritan's claims were in.

That wouldn't do.

"Paul, what are you..."

Paper geysered out of the desk. K-Dash and Quaysean drew their guns, unsure where to shoot. Streamers of forms caught on the steel beams in the ceiling, filling the garage bays in gouts of documentation that shoved them against the lockers. Paul flipped through the paper, *swimming* through it, sorting through every possible combination of chargemaster prices, hunting for the cheapest available costs for poor Samuel Patziki.

"Paul, this is fucking *crazy*!" Valentine cried. "Pac-Man's chasing a hundred different fruits through a maze, and if he eats the wrong one he'll die! I can barely keep him alive! You need to–"

"I need to *help*," Paul muttered, recombining every line item until he found the right cost: $1,396 in bills to Samuel Patziki. Not free, but as cheap as humanly possible given Samuel's cut-rate Samaritan Mutual policy.

The paperwork crackled with green energy, sizzling like a summer lightning storm. Quaysean and K-Dash flattened themselves against the wall, waist deep in crackling paper files, not quite sure if the crumpled documents were safe to touch.

"Don't move," Valentine warned them, wading through the paper. She grabbed a fistful of paperwork in her hand; it struggled in her grasp, like an origami animal struggling to escape.

She squeezed the magic out of it, a dribbling stream of liquefied sunshine, until it landed skittering on the hematite.

"Dammit, Paul." She hugged another armful of glowing paper to her chest. The paper dissolved into ash after the 'mancy left dribbled into the tray, leaving Valentine's arms covered in ink smudges. "I don't know if Oscar gave us enough hematite to store this much 'mancy. Did you have to go all sorcerer's apprentice on me here?"

"Don't..." Paul pleaded.

Doing 'mancy had consequences; the universe wanted to balance out the unnaturally beneficial bizarreness with malicious coincidence. Paul needed to redirect this accumulated bad luck elsewhere, pushing the flux where he wanted it.

Under normal circumstances, an experienced 'mancer like Paul could hold the bad luck at bay for a day or two until he could find somewhere safe to bleed it off. Yet this flux crushed him like a garbage compactor. Paul felt the flux's pressure pressing in – *with the Flex comes the flux*, as the old saying went – probing for worst-case scenarios it needed to create *now*, an ear-popping pressure like an incoming hurricane.

Aliyah, it whispered. *Aliyah could show up.*

He closed his eyes, letting the thought float away. If he focused on his daughter, then some crazy chain of worst-case scenarios would bring Aliyah here, and for all the wrong reasons...

"You can't take these risks, Paul," Valentine chided him. "What if the cops had busted us in the middle of this brew? We'd be fucked."

The cops.

He'd braced himself against thoughts of Aliyah, but hearing about the cops was like telling Paul not to think about a purple elephant. The flux latched onto that thought, surfed through it; Paul felt that pressure flow out of him, a tide of misfortune racing westwards.

"Did you hear me, Paul?" Valentine repeated. "You can't back up a dump truck of 'mancy and unload it wherever you damn well please. Not with Aliyah sniffing around. And if you won't–"

She finally noticed the stunned expression on Paul's face, then dropped the paperwork. She balled her fists against her hips.

"...You just shit the bed, didn't you?" she asked.

By way of reply, they heard the *whup-whup-whup* of incoming police choppers.

TWO
Ready Player Three

"I thought you had, you know, kind of an *in* with the cops!" Valentine hissed. "Wasn't someone supposed to call you if the King snitched on us?"

Paul held up his dead phone's cracked screen. "It shattered when the alembics broke." *How the hell had the King found them?*

She flung up her hands. "Oh, that's great. Just *great*. I thought you'd mastered your flux, and here we are with the po-po about to kick down our door–"

"–if you hadn't interrupted me in mid-brew, I would have kept it under control!"

K-Dash cleared his throat politely. Quaysean glanced over towards the garage door, where the sound of the choppers beat louder against the plywood nailed over the windows.

Paul headbobbed an apology at Valentine. "...hug it out later?" he offered.

"Hug it out." She shot Paul a pair of jaunty fingerguns by way of forgiveness. Then she scooped up armfuls of paper and squeezed, raining gouts of magic down onto the hematite. Paul mashed the gritty green flecks and sunny 'mancy together, squeezing until they condensed into clear white crystals:

Flex. The most dangerous drug in the world. Magic a non-'mancer could use. Worth millions.

More than enough to repay Oscar for this hematite.

But by then, the choppers whirred overhead.

"Now what?" Valentine asked, her fingers curling around the Xbox controller she always kept at her waist. Oscar's meth labs had come pre-installed with secret exits, but they'd switched to a distant locale to try to avoid the King – which meant all this place came equipped with was obscurity. "Should I jack a car, go all *Grand Theft Auto*?"

"Civilians get hurt when you do that." Valentine's videogame magic was brutally effective at causing mayhem – her channeling a first-person shooter could slaughter any police force – yet Paul refused to hurt cops for doing their job. "Besides," he continued, looking longingly at the pallet of money, "we'd still leave evidence behind."

"So… we ask them to leave nicely?"

"You're damn straight we do." He grabbed a legal pad, rested it on a teetering stack of cash, and began scribbling.

Leasing agreements blossomed out from under his pen. Paul picked a name at random: Lemuel Galuschak. He inserted a birth certificate into the state records office in Menands, New York, then backfilled in several faked grade school records as Lemuel grew up in, let's say, the 1950s – Paul gave Lemuel unexceptional grades, preferring to have Lemuel be on the varsity sports team–

Sirens wailed, joining the chopper noise. Valentine made a circling motion with her finger. "Speed it up, Paul."

"Fine, fine." Paul blazed through, giving Lemuel Galuschak a spotty employment record until a fake uncle in Europe left him $75,000. That'd hold up to a cursory analysis, at least. Then Paul tracked down the building's owner, filled out forms showing Galuschak had purchased the building in an auction two months ago, for–

Oh, goddammit. He didn't have time to negotiate. Paul grabbed a thick stack of bills, $50,000 in cash. As he riffled through the stack, each bill evaporated into confetti snippets of shredded mortgage contracts.

That was $50,000 more than he wanted to spend, but the alternative was to have $50,000 worth of bad luck crash down now. Too much, with the cops setting up shop outside the door.

"There," he said, panting as he finalized the permits to store volatile chemicals. "We now own this garage. Or at least Lemuel Galuschak does, a sixty seven year-old man with a heart condition."

Valentine gave an exasperated gesture that encompassed the room, which consisted of ashen concrete, a desk, and a set of lockers – lockers lit up by flickering purple from the lights of the police cars outside leaking through the cracks in the boarded-up windows. "And when the cops bust through the doors, we tell them… what? Lemuel says it's *totes cool* to set up a magical meth lab in his empty auto repair shop?"

"Can you make it *not* empty? Can you make it look like we've actually set up shop in here?"

"…for Flex?"

"No," Paul said. "To repair cars."

"How do you propose I do that?"

"Don't ask me – you're the videogame queen. Isn't there some videogame-style way to populate this garage with fresh equipment?"

"Jesus Christ, Paul." The police cars screeched around the rear entrance, cutting off escape. "You come up with half a plan, then expect me to pull a miracle out of my ass?"

"…can't you?"

"Of *course* I can, but you shouldn't *expect* that!" Valentine clicked an imaginary mouse, and the police lights' flickering whirl halted. Quaysean and K-Dash stood petrified, literally petrified, their hands paused halfway towards reaching for their guns. Everything stood frozen in time.

A glowing white grid superimposed itself over the walls and floor, highlighting each individual square foot.

"First, we give it a fresh set of paint," Valentine muttered, selecting the walls so they pulsed gray. She flicked her fingers. Blocks of different colors appeared before her, a dollar cost floating below each shade: a palette.

She frowned, waving through various selections, until she settled upon a plain brick-red that cost $500. Valentine selected it; the flyspecked calendar vanished with a cash-register *ka-ching!*, to be replaced by a beautiful dry coat of paint covering all the walls.

"This is the only part of *The Sims* anyone gives a crap about," she squeed. "Buying crazy shit for your house!"

She pulled up a furniture menu, selected a countertop with a cash register, spun it into the corner. She scrolled through several categories until she found "Auto Repair," and began merrily dropping all sorts of repair equipment into the shop: spare tires, the car hoists, wheel aligners, engine analyzers....

Paul drew Valentine's attention to the depleting pallet of cash, which dwindled as she finalized each item. "Would you mind not buying *all* the top-tier equipment?" Paul asked.

"You've seen my Hot Topic frenzies, Paul," she shot back. "You should know better than to hand a shopping spree to a girl like me." But she guiltily highlighted the *Pac-Man* machine and the OfficeMax desk, sold them back with another happy register *ka-ching*! They popped out of existence. The tray of Flex resting on the desk clattered to the floor.

Paul sighed; if only Valentine could envision the proper videogame justification, she could have frozen time and teleported them all into another state. But Valentine's ability to bend physics stemmed directly from her intense vision of how videogame rules should apply to the world; Valentine couldn't teleport without a Portal Gun any more than Paul could conjure up free money.

Valentine finished up by purchasing a rusted Saturn and maneuvering it up onto the hoists. She squinted, double-checking her work, then purchased a large oil-stained tarp to drop over the much smaller pallet of cash.

Paul calculated; about $150,000 remained. Fine. The Flex was worth millions, it could pay off Oscar with money to spare...

With a satisfied nod, Valentine clicked an "Exit Build Mode" button. Quaysean and K-Dash's hands finished the grab for their guns; they whipped them out, then pointed them in confusion at a drum of antifreeze that hadn't been there a moment ago.

"What – what happened?" K-Dash asked, his voice cracking.

"Whoo, now *that's* a world of explanation we don't have time for," Valentine allowed, shoving them backwards towards the lockers. "Now be quiet while I make you look like mechanics."

"*What*?" Quaysean asked, "*How*?"

"Gonna reskin you," Valentine said, as calmly as if she'd told them she was going to get them a Coke. She snapped her fingers; two locker doors flew open, revealing blank TV static buzzing inside. She shoved the two boys inside.

They went in as two skinny Latinos with gun tattoos laced up their whipcord-muscled arms; they emerged as plump, bucktoothed white boys clad in mechanics' outfits. They looked in bewilderment at their bodies, spreading their now oil-grimed fingers before their faces.

Valentine patted them on the shoulders. "Just a character swap," she assured them. "You're still you underneath."

The cops smashed the boarded-over windows in, fired nerve-gas grenades through blindly.

"You work for Mr Galuschak." She coughed as the metal canisters bounced off the walls, spraying green gas everywhere. "Do *not* fight back. Act like confused mechanics."

She ducked into the locker herself, emerging as a lean black man clutching a wrench – and immediately vomited.

Paul held his breath, eyes watering, shoveling the Flex into a large plastic cooler. The fact that the cops had fired nerve gas without warning was a hopeful sign: that had been the NYPD 'Mancy Task Force's default strategy two years ago, signaling they still followed standard operating procedure. This meant Lenny Pirrazzini was heading up the attack – and while Lenny was dedicated to stomping out 'mancers, he had all the creativity of a brick.

Which meant Paul's plan might actually work.

Valentine-as-black-mechanic lurched over as Paul began to retch. The cops bellowed orders to *come out with your hands up*, not quite daring to charge headfirst into a 'mancer's lair.

Valentine shoved the Flex-cooler into the bottom of an auto-parts toolchest, then asked, "So what's Galuschak look like?"

"I dunno. Old and ethnic." She shoved him into the blackness. Paul felt the cold electron flow of being converted into reticulated splines, a process more disturbing than he could convey. His flesh was translated into essential mathematic formulas, recalculated.

He stumbled out of the locker, examining his hands to see what they looked like; they were wrinkled, liver-spotted. A walrus mustache tickled his lips. His watering eyes viewed the billowing gas through a curtain of overlong white eyebrows.

Ugly, but it hid his artificial foot and missing toes.

Paul's lungs ached. The garage door vibrated from the thump of shaped charges affixed to the hinges. He grabbed an imaginary pen, created driver's licenses for everyone, placed ID cards in everyone's pockets.

Lungs burning, he inhaled, and barfed all over his feet.

He'd only breathed in SMASH-grade nerve gas once before, and never wanted to again. The government had designed this anti-'mancer teargas to cause instantaneous headaches and vomiting – enough to jangle any 'mancer's concentration.

Paul fell to his knees.

The door blew open. Cops poured in, wearing gasmasks – *What if we'd worn gas masks ourselves? What would they do if we'd adapted to their old tactics?* Paul thought woozily, despairing at Lenny's total lack of strategic forethought.

The cops took no chances: they zip-tied the four of them, ankles and wrists, hauled them outside. The two choppers swooped around overhead, focusing spotlights on them, their rotors' air wash dispersing the gas.

The cops deposited them before a skinny Italian man in black armor who loomed over them, hands on hips. He smirked, wrinkling a wispy pube-stache that any man with a scrap of sense would have shaved off – but Lenny Pirrazzini was as overconfident about his marginal looks as he was everything else in life.

"Four 'mancers," he preened. "We got *four* of these fuckers. SMASH has been riding my ass for two years 'cause we hadn't caught a one – but now four, in the basket!"

One of the cops looked at Paul – who was, to all appearances, an elderly heart patient. "Uh, Lieutenant...."

"I'm gonna shove this right down their damn throat," Lenny continued, licking his lips. "Call 'em up every damn day and say, 'Hey, you remember that time I rounded up four 'mancers in one shot? Without a scrap of your fuckin' Unimancy to assist us? Maybe you guys could learn from us...'"

"Sir!" the cop interrupted, extracting the driver's license from Paul's pocket. "I don't think – I don't think these are 'mancers."

Lenny blinked, an oddly squirrel-like action. "Of *course* they're 'mancers. We got a call from the King of New York. The King is Midas, 'cause his information is *golden*."

Paul shivered: it *was* the King who'd turned them in. Somehow. "With all due respect, sir," said the cop, "The – the 'King' is an anonymous informant. And I think – I think he gave us the wrong address..."

Lenny looked at the fully-stocked garage, the four mechanics, the total absence of anything resembling a Flex lab. He frowned in confusion. Paul almost felt sorry for him; Lenny hadn't had much success since he'd been promoted to second-in-command of the NYPD Task Force.

"I'm just–" Paul said, then coughed when he realized he still spoke in his own voice. Fortunately, the projectile vomiting had roughened his usual tones, so Paul adopted a fake German accent. "I'm chust a mechanic. I bought ze shop two months ago…"

That was all Paul could get out before he dry-heaved again.

He hoped Lenny would buy it. Lenny *had* to. Paul's head spun like a Tilt-a-Whirl, making it impossible to summon more 'mancy. If Lenny decided to haul them all in for questioning, Paul's fake ID would hold up, but the hastily assembled driver's licenses he'd given to Valentine, K-Dash, and Quaysean would fall apart once they got booked.

But Paul knew that Lenny *hated* looking bad in front of other people.

Lenny stomped into the auto repair shop to investigate. Puzzled, he kicked one of the hoist's steel beams experimentally, then looked around for evidence of Flex-making equipment. There was none; Valentine had sold it all off.

A smarter man would have scoured the garage, knowing 'mancy could do bizarre things – and would have discovered the cooler full of Flex and the $150,000 in the lockers in short order. But Paul knew that Lenny, sweating, must have been thinking of the press that would come down upon him for a false bust, the potential lawsuits over assaulting a small businessman over an anonymous tip.

And Lenny, as noted, had no ability to improvise.

He hurled his helmet at one of his subordinates.

"*You dumb fucker!*" He stepped over Paul's still-zip-tied form to get to his fellow officer. "*You got the King's address wrong!*"

"I got nothing wrong!" The officer thrust out a Post-It note. "I had him repeat it! Patziki's Garage, 584 W Lark Street."

"Well, the name on the sign says *Galuschak's Garage!*"

Paul allowed himself a grin; one of Valentine's touches. A risky thing to do with the Task Force's black opal 'mancy-detectors parked outside the door.

"But this *is* 584 West Lark Street."

Lenny grabbed the paper, crumpled it. "Has the King ever given us a bad lead?"

"No, sir. But we don't know a thing about him. We don't even know how he gets his tips. Maybe he's just… wrong."

Lenny fumed. Paul knew why: the King was Lenny's only reliable information. If the King had started fucking up, then Lenny was dead in the water.

Valentine chuckled, then moaned thanks to the gas-induced migraine. Paul shushed her – even whispering sent shooting pains down his neck – but inwardly, he whooped with elation. If they could escape the cops *and* cast doubt on the anonymous King of New York in the process, then this would be a red-letter day.

Paul gurgled, affecting the same German accent. "I bought ze shop two months ago… check my records…"

"You phone that in?" Lenny asked a cop sitting in the cop car, running traces.

The cop held up Paul's faked driver's license. "His ID checks out, sir. Lenny, I think…"

"You don't tell me what to think," Lenny snapped. He grabbed Paul by the scruff of his mechanic's outfit to haul him to his feet – or tried to. Lenny was almost as skinny as Paul, and couldn't quite manage it, so a fellow officer rushed in to help. Despite his chubby reskinning, Paul still weighed a hundred and sixty pounds – but Lenny was so furious, neither of them noticed.

"All right, you motherfucker." Spit flecks flew off of Lenny's wispy mustache, landed on Paul's pseudo-skinned cheeks. "You say you're a mechanic. And these guys *think* you're a mechanic. So… I'm gonna let you go back to work, because I'm generous that way. But if I ever find any – *any!* – evidence of you harboring a 'mancer, especially that Psycho Mantis videogamemancer, I will rip you a new asshole and piss in the slit."

Over the chopper's dull roar, Paul made out a mechanical *chunk-chunk-chunk* videogame noise coming from the garage.

But Valentine got rid of the Pac-Man *machine*, he thought, dazed.

Then: *Valentine's wards have dropped*.

"You have to get out of here," he muttered.

"You don't give me orders. I give *you* orders."

"No." Paul tried to summon his 'mancy; the piercing headache smothered it. "Evacuate *now*, while you can...."

Lenny shook Paul. "If you're holding back information, you dumb motherfucker, I will–"

The twin bays of the auto repair shop filled with flame, looking for all the world like the nostrils of some great and terrible dragon.

"What–?" Lenny said, puzzled.

The cops turned, readying their guns, but it was too late. Several bowling ball-sized wads of fire, like miniature suns, came bouncing out of the entryway, searing straight through the metal of the cop cars–

Lenny Pirazzini flung his body over Paul's to protect him. The patrol vehicles clustered outside went up with an ear-splitting *whump*.

Fortunately, the flame balls shot low, sending the explosions straight upwards. The helicopters juked left to avoid the obliterated cop cars, their rotors sucking up great columns of burning smoke.

The Task Force was in chaos now, some firing into the garage, some checking in with the other cops, others grabbing more tear gas. Lenny examined Paul for injuries.

"What's going on?" Lenny was shell-shocked, trying to shield the civilian. "What *is* that?"

The ground rumbled. The flames in the burning garage roared, parting to reveal a tiny silhouette, maybe four feet high, wearing an inexplicably jaunty cap with wild tangles of hair stuffed underneath. A little black girl, dressed in a

Super Mario outfit complete with blue overalls and puffy white gloves, strode out – a look that might have been ludicrous, if she hadn't been weaving another sphere of fiery plasma between her hands.

Paul remembered the first time he'd watched her become Fire Mario, the first time Aliyah had ever killed a person, and wished with all his heart Valentine had never introduced her to that damn game.

The girl's words were a quavering shriek of betrayal, of long-dampened fury finally given voice:

"You hurt my Daddy!" Aliyah cried, and flung flaming death straight at Lenny Pirrazzini.

THREE
I Am Become Mario, Destroyer of Worlds

Lenny leapt off Paul, the fireball missing him by inches –
but the heat still blistered Lenny's skin. The fireball bounced
down West Lark Street, leaving bubbling cauldrons of
asphalt behind.

The remaining cops – some had already bolted –
regrouped behind the smoldering wreckage of a car, tossing
nerve-gas grenades over the top in Aliyah's direction. They
didn't dare make themselves a target – but the two copters
did, whirling around to bring their snipers to point in
Aliyah's direction.

She's an eight year-old girl, Paul thought, horrified – but
the cops didn't realize that.

*Every act of death and destruction I made will rob someone
of something they loved*, Anathema, insane and powerful
Anathema, had told Paul as she held the spear to his throat.
*It will cause someone, many someones, to retreat into misery.
Withdrawal. Obsession. 'Mancy.*

Anathema had burned his daughter as part of an
experiment to create 'mancers all across New York. 'Mancers'
obsessions usually didn't solidify into magic until they were
in their late twenties at the earliest, a lifetime's worth of
mania congealing into universe-contorting willpower.

But touched by Anathema's 'mancy, Aliyah had become

a 'mancer at the unthinkable age of six.

I said burn! Aliyah had shrieked, as she'd roasted Anathema alive for daring to hurt her father. *'Mancers burn! Bad people burn! All the bad things in the universe* burn!

Two years after, her rage at a world that wanted to kill her father had never ebbed.

So the cops did not see a little black girl. They saw a videogamemancer who could reskin herself into any identity at a moment's notice, someone who slipped effortlessly between Psycho Mantis and Tommy Vercetti and Ryu and a thousand other videogame characters.

More importantly... they saw 'mancy. And when most people saw 'mancy, they stomped it dead.

Paul grabbed Lenny by the ankle; the sudden movement sent sloshing waves of pain up his neck. "You have to..." He coughed, remembering his German accent, then held up his cuff zipties. "You must cut me loose. Before she hurts someone."

"I think she's the one who's going to get hurt, pal." Lenny looked at the copters.

"*She doesn't want to kill*!" Paul pleaded. "But if you back her into a corner, she'll – she'll..."

The snipers fired.

Aliyah flicked her fingers in their direction; the bullets vaporized in mid shot, bursting into sprays of white-hot fireworks.

She spun in a circle, taking in the nerve gas canisters hissing around her, the cops closing in. No one paid attention to her burn-scarred face, not between the bright red cap and the leaping flames. But Paul saw Aliyah's puffed cheeks as the forces closed in, the confused look of a scared little girl about to throw a temper tantrum.

This tantrum would kill cops.

"*I said get out!*" Aliyah shrieked, "*Get away from him! He can't protect himself, but I can!*"

The choppers swooped low, angling for a better shot among the flames. Aliyah reached improbably deep into her pocket to pull out a bright yellow pencil as large as a baseball bat.

Aliyah grabbed it; a large tan banner unfurled out. She wrote on the banner, her handwriting a panicked schoolgirl's scribble:

Large Air Vent

I introduced her to gaming, Valentine had told him, *but she's developed her own tastes:* Animal Crossing, Scribblenauts...

And just as in *Scribblenauts*, writing the word caused a gigantic air vent to pop into existence. Except in the game, the objects you created when you typed were cartoonish, adorable: this was a black wrought-iron creation, sharp and seething with tetanus. It howled, a fetid hurricane blowing the gas back towards the cops.

Is that what Aliyah's imagining these days? Paul wondered, grateful he'd never allowed her to play M-rated games....

The snipers waved to the copters to get closer to the ground; the pilots steered in, setting up the shot. Aliyah whipped out another tan banner to write on, except this time were the words:

Black Hole

"*No!*" Valentine screamed, then vomited Vanilla Kreme.

The gas whirled into a pulsing void that opened up between the two copters, sucking in the firelight's flickering brightness so the entire street *dimmed* like polarized sunglasses. Both copters got yanked towards the hole, as abruptly as a drunk being hauled away from the bar by a bouncer.

"*Jump!*" Valentine shrieked at the pilots. "*Touch that shit, and you won't leave bodies for us to bury!*"

Paul couldn't be sure whether the pilots had heard her – but they bailed out regardless, eager to flee that roiling nothingness. Pilots down from the sky, landing with bonebreaking *thud*s on the parking lot's hard asphalt.

The copters bumped against the hole, then crumpled in midair as they contorted to fit through a space the size of a washing machine.

The pilots twitched. Thank God; they were alive. Aliyah hadn't killed anyone new today: just Anathema, still, and Paul knew that one murder was more than Aliyah could bear.

He started breathing again.

"*You're bullies!*" Aliyah stepped towards the injured pilots, gouts of flame dancing between her fingers. "*He's helpless! You think every 'mancer is... is powerful, but some aren't! All you do is pick on people who can't fight back! Make us ashamed of stuff that's not even our fault! And someone—*"

She sobbed, looking at the remaining cops setting up to fire at her again. Her dark eyes went wide with sorrow.

"Someone has to stop you," she whispered, and raised her hand to incinerate them.

"*Cut me loose!*" Paul screamed. The old man pseudo-flesh housing his body hadn't so much blistered as half melted. Lenny stared at Paul's runnelled fake skin in horror.

Paul dropped the pretense. "I'm trying to help you, Lenny."

Lenny cocked his head, examining Paul. "...Your Majesty?"

Paul almost contradicted Lenny – he wasn't the King, nobody knew what the King looked like, the King had been out to get him for months. And to call some anonymous informant "Your Majesty" was a terrifyingly asskissing move for a municipal cop.

...But whatever it took to get Lenny listening.

"Yes, Mr Pirrazzini. Zis is ze King. And if you do not cut me loose, you vill all die."

German accents, Paul found, were fantastically good for delivering death threats.

"All right." Lenny whipped out a twelve-inch knife – far too large to be practical, but traditionally Lenny – and sawed Paul's cuffs open. "I've trusted you this far, sir. But – I need to know who you're working for..."

"*Go.*" Paul clambered to his feet as Lenny retreated. Aliyah's face squinched up as she grabbed at her head.

The cops had dug in deep, ignoring Lenny's cries to unload full-automatic gunfire on Aliyah, the bullets bursting into fireworks as they bounced off Aliyah's videogame shields...

...*the flux*...

Paul staggered towards Aliyah, feeling the pressure rising around her. Paul had sat down on Sad Sundays and forced her to do tiny spells, holding her flux for as long as possible before bleeding off the bad luck with stubbed toes and head colds. Driven by panic, Aliyah had done all this 'mancy – *vulgar* 'mancy, *sloppy* 'mancy, vast acts of destruction the universe could not overlook. And...

...Tears streamed down Aliyah's molten cheeks, evaporating into clouds of steam. She hated all these men, the men who'd hurt her daddy... she didn't want to kill them. Not yet. She *would* want to, in time, if Paul couldn't find a better way to teach her...

But for now, Aliyah was still a good kid.

A good kid stuck in a war zone.

"*Sweetie!*"

Aliyah turned to face him, somehow recognizing him even trapped in this stupid Galuschak-skin. Seeing his fear triggered hers. She'd done so much 'mancy that she was carrying a near-fatal load – and there were so many things that could go wrong now. A bullet would break through her shields, and when it did it wouldn't just kill her, oh no – that bullet would sever her spine at the worst possible location, leave her trapped in a comatose shell for the rest of her life, aware and paralyzed...

"*Daddy!*" Aliyah cried, reaching out to her father to save her.

And under normal circumstances, nothing could save her. 'Mancers had tried their best to hand their flux off to other people, to push it away, but no; you had assaulted the universe's laws, and the universe would only accept your bad luck as payment. The bullets would find their mark, taking their toll for Aliyah's careless use of power, and Aliyah would be the youngest 'mancer-suicide.

Except Paul was a bureaucromancer.

Paul was her *father*.

Paul was her *legal fucking guardian*.

Paul flipped his hand open. A contract unfurled from his palm – and the sick wash of the nerve gas pushed back, filling his body with 'mancy-suppressing queasiness.

But his daughter's life was at stake. Again.

The contract was a million words of legalese, too much to read, yet it all boiled down to this:

Universe, I have the right to take my daughter's pain.

He stabbed himself with a Bic pen, raining blood spatters down onto the paper – the oldest and most binding of signatures.

The universe scanned the contract, found no loopholes. The pressure lifted from Aliyah, who sucked in a great whoop of air, then turned and blew up another police car, sending the squad's remnants fleeing. Lenny waved them back, directing them to fall back to the abandoned mall across the street.

The flux squeezed Paul, hunting for the worst things in his life that could go wrong. But Paul had prepared his answer long before Aliyah had shown up:

The cooler. In the auto repair shop. Burn it.

The flux siphoned out away; the auto repair roof caved in, sending the glowing embers of Paul's borrowed cash flying high into the night air. Two million dollars' worth of Flex burned up, the crystals popping in dazzling blue twinkles. They dissolved into wisps, along with all the remaining good grace of mob boss Oscar Gargunza Ruiz.

Aliyah had been profligate. It wasn't enough.

Paul collapsed as the flux slithered off somewhere else, following its own pathways, pushing bad luck into an uncertain future...

Aliyah pressed her palm to Paul's forehead to make sure he was OK. She looked over at K-Dash and Quaysean, still in their mechanic white-boy skins. They'd grabbed guns, firing over the heads of the retreating cops.

A pixelated aura of 'mancy surrounding Aliyah soared after Lenny Pirrazzini and the retreating cops…

Paul grabbed her foot. "Stop."

She plunked back down to the ground. Aliyah looked at him in disbelief, her near-dreadlocked hair poking out from under her Mario cap.

"Daddy, you're *sick*." She cupped his face, frowning at what the gas had done to him. "They want to kill you. I'm not always here to protect you. *They have to burn*."

"We can't kill them. They're just…"

Just what? Paul wondered. *Doing their jobs?* What kind of explanation was that to give to his daughter – that all the people in the world who wanted to trap and brainwash her were just following orders?

"…they don't understand," he finished lamely.

"How can I *show* them?" she cried. "I can't show anyone what I do at school! I can't tell my teachers! I can't even show *Mommy*, or she'd lock me away!"

Paul felt a stab of guilt. Probably *lock you away*, he almost corrected her, but swallowed it back. His ex-wife Imani loved Aliyah as fiercely as Paul did, but they'd never seen eye to eye on the proper way to raise her. Imani's hatred of 'mancy had been the finishing blow to a harsh marriage.

Paul couldn't risk Imani finding out. Because merely *being* a 'mancer was illegal. The penalty was to be abducted by SMASH, the government's brainwashed troops, and converted into a Unimancer. If Imani decided that was best for Aliyah, he couldn't stop the troops from finding her.

Even if the secrets Aliyah locked up were corroding her.

"If all they ever do is hurt us when we do 'mancy, then…" Aliyah flailed her arms. "They're *never* going to understand!"

"You're right," Paul admitted. "I don't know how to show them how… how beautiful our gift is."

He'd given Aliyah some blunt truths in her short life. Too many. Yet somehow, his daughter never stopped believing Daddy could make it all better.

"So we have to *stop* them, Daddy," Aliyah said, her innate fierceness rising to the fore, staring at the ground as if she wanted to stomp Lenny Pirrazzini. "We have to hunt them down before they hunt you down, then kill them until they're so scared they don't dare come *near* us...."

"Maybe we do need to kill them," Paul allowed.

Aliyah stopped, astonished that reasonable old Dad would agree with her. Paul held her, letting her contemplate all the things she'd have to do to make the world safe her way, and then asked:

"The question is, do you want to be the person who does that?"

Aliyah's eyes welled with tears. She grabbed him tight, burying her face in his shoulder so no one would see her cry. But cry she did, copiously, the tears of a girl who never wanted to hurt anyone, yet was coming to the conclusion that maybe she would have to.

Paul held her, let her pour her anguish into him.

There would be time for fighting later.

FOUR
Layers Peeling

K-Dash emptied clips over the cops' heads, keeping them at bay, while Quaysean poured a huge Thermos of sweet Dunkin' Donuts coffee down Valentine's throat. The quickest way to recover from a nerve-gas hangover, they'd discovered, was to boost the blood sugar.

Aliyah trailed behind Paul, no longer Fire Mario, just a scrawny scarred eight year-old kid with wild hair. She refused to let go of her daddy's hand. Paul led her among the smoking wreckage, ensuring Lenny's men couldn't get a clear look at her.

"Valentine," Paul said. "You got enough juice left to go *Grand Theft Auto*?"

"Tall order, Paul. I feel like a squadron of trolls just bukkakked in my brain."

"What's 'bukkakke', Daddy?"

"It's like snot. They snotted in her brain."

Valentine snorted. "Don't *lie* to her, Paul." She turned to Valentine. "It's a sex thing. I probably shouldn't have said it in front of you."

Aliyah brightened. Aunt Valentine was a reliable source for all the secrets grown-ups wouldn't tell her. "But what's that *mean*?"

"A) Don't you *dare* tell her, and B) We need to get you

out of here now," Paul snapped. "Push through the gas. Get her home. But don't drop her back at Imani's house by yourself; the last thing I need is more evidence for my ex-wife to think we're shacking up."

Valentine looked like she'd licked a cockroach. "You're Ken-doll smooth down there as far as I'm concerned, buddy. Actually, you might be. When was the last time you had a date?"

"Just get Aliyah somewhere safe and wait for me."

"Where you going?"

"This will be a PR fiasco. Lenny can't cope with this mess on his own. And if Lenny goes down…"

She adjusted her eyepatch, covering the hole where SMASH had shot her eye out. "Then the creampuff local Task Force goes down, and Big Bad Federal SMASH starts patrolling town again." Valentine groaned, getting to her feet. "I had a hot date at the swingers' club with two firemen. *Bisexual* firemen, Paul. They told me they were good at sliding down each other's poles. If you put that much 'mancy out again without checking with me…"

"I don't think I'll get the chance. Oscar's at his limit."

"You had to burn our Flex to save her? Jesus *fuck*, Aliyah!" Aliyah hung her head. "How many hours have I spent teaching you how to keep your shit pent? You can't keep using your dad as some kind of fucked-up flux-diaper, you have to manage your own–"

More choppers sounded. More sirens.

"You and I *will* continue this talk in the car," Valentine said to Aliyah, who cringed. Valentine gestured at a smoking car, which flipped over and turned into a sleek Maserati. "Get in."

K-Dash and Quaysean leaped into the back seat. Aliyah grabbed Paul's hand as Valentine hauled her into the vehicle. "*No!*" she cried. "I'm not leaving until Daddy's *safe*!"

Paul looked around at the burned repair shop, the shrapneled cars, the chunks of rotors embedded deep in the asphalt. He tried to imagine how all this would look on the

evening news, and realized what a total catastrophe this
night had been.

"We'll be a lot less safe unless you let Daddy clean up this
wreckage," he said sadly.

Aliyah, confused, looked to Valentine for confirmation.
Valentine nodded, buckling Aliyah into the seat before
pulling a pair of driver's goggles down over her face that
hadn't been there a second ago. Aliyah spread her fingers
against the window, sniffling back tears as she let Valentine's
'mancy take her away.

The windows tinted. Valentine skidded out of the parking
lot, going zero to sixty in the blink of an eye, swerving to
knock over a couple of streetlamps because that's what you
did in these games.

Paul retreated, gouts of pain thrumming through
his body. He kicked in the plywood of the abandoned
convenience store next door, feeling the ache in his stump
as his metal foot hit the wood, then pushed his way through
sodden tiles to find the bathroom. Those were Valentine's
stupid videogame rules: you could only change back to your
original skin by entering a dark room.

Why? Paul had never understood videogames. But it
made sense to Valentine, and Valentine's obsession shaped
her magic.

He emerged as Paul Tsabo, his normal self – a small,
neatly dressed man with a crisp tie and a power suit, an
effect only slightly dampened by his metal ankle on one leg
and his clunky orthotic boot on the other. His balance was
wobbly to begin with, and the nerve gas's residual effects
made it even harder to walk; maybe he *should* get a cane.

No. He felt crippled enough, most days.

His left arm dribbled blood. That was nothing new. He'd
incurred one wound the last time he'd fought SMASH in a
magical battle so intense they'd punched a collective hole
through the laws of physics, allowing extradimensional
buzzsects to pour through a broach in space. Paul had
managed to heal the gap before it had torn itself out of his

control – but the buzzsects had eaten a groove in his left forearm that could never heal, could not be stitched up.

He also had a bleeding head wound from the shattered alembic. But Paul's extradimensional wound was a constant, oozing reminder of why he could never let SMASH have jurisdiction in New York again.

He crawled out of the convenience store, ready to ensure that would never happen.

He headed for the terrified cops holed up across the street – debating whether to approach the garage now that the 'mancers had apparently left.

Paul strode across the street. They aimed rifles at him.

Then they grinned as they recognized him.

"*Mr Tsabo!*" Lenny cried, flinging out his arms. Paul could never tell whether Lenny was genuinely grateful when Paul showed up at fiascos like this, or if Lenny was self-deluded enough to think blatant routs were somehow successes.

Then again, Paul would never have hired an *efficient* man to be the person who hunted 'mancers in Manhattan.

"What kept you?" Lenny asked as the cops well enough to walk surrounded Paul, shook his hand. "I sent you a text an hour ago. The King tipped us off again!"

"Phone broke." Paul held up his shattered screen. "So what happened?"

"We had a little incident here." Lenny shrugged off the rubble around him. "But... I met the King! I think he's working with Psycho Mantis, feeding us information from the inside! Legitimate fucking intel at last!"

Paul scowled. "How many injured?"

Lenny's mustache wilted. "Nine."

"Any deaths?"

"No. The copter pilots broke some bones. But... I think they'll be OK."

"Oh, thank God." Paul sighed in genuine relief. He'd have to visit each of the officers, make sure their insurance covered the damage. Despite Aliyah's hatred of the police, everyone on Paul's force were good men, dutiful, having joined to make the world better.

They'd just been convinced the world was better without 'mancy – and in that, ninety-nine percent of New York agreed with them.

If only he could tell them he was a 'mancer.

"I'm sorry, Mr Tsabo," Lenny said. "I just... I got a tip, and you know how damn slippery Psycho Mantis is..."

"So you sent the whole team in. Without making a plan. Or scoping the territory. Just... sent them in." Paul mentally tallied up the cost of the wrecked patrol cars, of the two helicopters, of the hospital costs of the injured cops. He glimpsed the incoming news choppers, envisioning how the blackened rubble must look from overhead.

If I could only tell them who I am, Paul thought guiltily, looking over at the moaning men waiting for ambulances. *If Aliyah wasn't at stake, I* would *tell them. They trusted Lenny to lead them because they trusted me...*

As a drugmaker, Paul had been grateful for Lenny's limited bag of tricks. But putting on his other hat, Paul was starting to realize the flux hadn't just impacted his drugmaking career.

"So who got the call this time?" he asked.

"Wieczniak," Lenny jerked his thumb in Wieczniak's direction.

"And the trace?"

"To yet another pay phone. They're seeing if there's surveillance video in the area, but... there won't be. When the King doesn't want to be seen, he *won't* be."

Who was turning them in? Paul thought. He'd isolated the location this time, which meant there was a mole in Oscar's organization. The obvious targets were now K-Dash and Quaysean – but no, he trusted them. Oscar wouldn't set the cops on him to try to take him out, would he?

Fact was, Paul didn't know who the King was, or what his motivations were. Unknowns always scared Paul.

"Cut the admiration, Lenny. He's another informant. We don't know what his motivations are."

Lenny blushed. "Yeah. Yeah, Mr Tsabo. It's just that...
you know we've had a dry streak."

The burning garage collapsed inwards, sending sparks
high into the air. News vans peeled around the corner,
reporters jumping out with the eagerness of men who'd
found juicy footage to fill tomorrow's broadcast.

"Time to polish this turd," Paul muttered.

Lenny sagged. "Yes, sir."

Paul straightened his tie. The reporters thrust their
microphones out, calling out to Mr Paulos Costa Tsabo, chief
of the New York Task Force For 'Mancer Control, asking for
comment on this most recent fiasco. The remaining officers
surrounded him, pushing the reporters back, buying Paul
some dignity.

Paul tried to think of something noble to say to put a
good face on today's rout. There wasn't much. So instead,
he went on a clichéd defensive – the usual stew of "setbacks
will happen" and "'mancers are a danger that can surprise
even trained professionals" and "I promise you, we are
closer than ever to catching Psycho Mantis."

Which was a lie. His best friend was Valentine DiGriz,
aka Psycho Mantis. They'd hidden in plain sight for almost
two years, Paul abusing his privilege to steer investigations
away from his door – which had all gone perfectly until the
King of New York started dropping anonymous tips that led
Paul's forces straight to every brew site.

As Paul watched the reporters practically get into
fistfights over who got to ask the first question, he realized
this latest flux might have shattered his life more than any
arrest.

FIVE
Love Is The Plan The Plan Is Death

By the time Paul finished handling the press conference – which did not go well, and would lead the eleven o'clock news – he was ready to collapse.

But first, he had to return Aliyah to Imani's custody.

He didn't dare have Valentine bring her back – Imani loved her daughter deeply, but she'd had a plan laid out for Aliyah from the moment of Aliyah's birth. That plan began with getting her daughter into the right preschools and ended with a *summa cum laude* Yale graduation as a lawyer. (Not coincidentally, Imani was a Yale alumnus and a high-powered corporate lawyer.) Imani saw videogames as time-wasting pursuits that siphoned precious hours away from Aliyah's inevitable climb to respectability.

Imani had managed to keep Aliyah free of videogames' taint until Aliyah was six, when Anathema had roasted Aliyah. Valentine had met Aliyah in the hospital and, sensing a wounded child in need of distraction, handed Aliyah a Nintendo DS.

Aliyah had most sincerely strayed from Imani's plans since then. So whenever Imani spoke Valentine's name, it was with the chill malice of a parent about to reopen up her court case for sole custody.

Imani wasn't a threat to Paul – his beloved paperwork

would never let Imani take Aliyah away from him – but she *did* make him feel eternally guilty. Imani and he both wanted the best for Aliyah; they just disagreed on how to make that happen. And maybe Imani was prone to looking for people to blame whenever something bad happened, but....

Paul had once loved Imani, and even now he would not hurt her.

If he was lucky, maybe Imani hadn't realized Aliyah had slipped out again. Imani nervously joked that her little girl was part ninja, not realizing Aliyah had 'mancied into Sly Cooper stealth mode to sneak past her.

So Paul took the subway back to his apartment complex, then let himself into Valentine's place. He'd used his bureaucromancy to get them side-by-side apartments, wanting his best friend next door to him – but not too close.

He could accept living next door to Valentine's sloppy black hole of an apartment, but not *in* it.

The door opened partway, bouncing off a trashbag packed full of Valentine's endless supplies of second-hand clothing. Paul picked his way among the discarded Subway wrappers and flattened videogame packages and dried condoms that festooned the kitchen floor.

What he heard in the living room was not Valentine and Aliyah playing videogames, as he'd expected, but Valentine talking to Aliyah. Paul could just peer around the corner to see them in the living room, sitting cross-legged, side by side on a broken futon.

Paul paused.

He should have announced his entrance. But Valentine and Aliyah had created their own dynamic: they made playdates with each other, laughed at in-jokes they didn't bother to explain to Paul, ate sloppy fast-food meals together. Imani would have had a heart attack, had she known her precious daughter was eating processed sugar. Even now, Paul saw the crumpled Shake Shack bag where Valentine had treated Aliyah to an extra-large peanut butter milkshake.

Their bond didn't make Paul jealous. Aliyah needed friends, and Valentine always relayed the important details back to Paul.

But... Valentine related what *Valentine* thought was important.

As he looked at the old skirts Valentine had tossed to hide the used sex toys on the kitchen table, Paul wondered whether Valentine understood what a normal parent needed to know.

He hated himself for eavesdropping. But if Aliyah was telling Valentine something – particularly after Aliyah had nearly gotten herself killed tonight – then didn't he deserve to know? As a father?

He couldn't help himself.

"No!" Aliyah squealed, giggling. "I told you to dip the fries in the *shake*!"

"...nod pud them ub my dose?"

Aliyah let out a disgusted squeal. "You are *inhuman*."

Valentine plucked two fries out of her nose, wiped her face with the back of her hand. "It's salt and fat: two of the best things in the universe. They're delicious no matter what orifice you put them in. And what else could make a French fry better but sugar?"

"...bacon?" Aliyah suggested.

"Goddammit, your genius means we're gonna have to haul our ass back to Shake Shack and swirl some bacon all up in this shiz. All the deadly flavors, swing-dancing in my heart. I won't last a minute."

"Don't worry," Aliyah said. "We'll stock up on medi-packs."

Aliyah munched her fries – a silence that lasted so long, Paul almost gave up and walked in. Then Valentine sighed.

"So why'd you bust in on us, kiddo?"

"I didn't mean to."

"OK."

Paul would have pointed out how Aliyah had been battering at Valentine's shields for hours, highlighted just how unlikely it was that Aliyah would have *happened* to wind up at their exact address at the exact time they were brewing by *accident*, a chain of events that indicated clear intent. Paul would have dissected her excuses, a lawyer flensing lies on the witness stand, until Aliyah was forced to admit the truth.

That was what Paul always hoped would happen, anyway. In practice, when Aliyah was presented with facts that contradicted her story, she denied the facts. Then she fell silent, and no force Paul had discovered could get her to open up again.

Yet Paul was fascinated: here, Valentine went silent. Her casual agreement was the discussion's end: Aliyah had told her it was an accident, Valentine accepted that, which left nothing more to say.

Aliyah pushed a fry around in her shake, making patterns in the ice cream.

"...I don't like staying at Mom's place."

"Of course not," Valentine snapped. "Your Mom makes GlaDOS look like a well-adjusted human being."

Paul didn't get the reference; he assumed, as with most of Valentine's non sequiturs, that it somehow related to videogames. Aliyah clearly got the reference, looking shamed and uncomfortable at Valentine's insult.

Which warmed Paul's heart; Aliyah shouldn't hate her mother.

"Sorry," Valentine apologized. "What don't you like about being there?"

"I'm a freak."

"You're not a freak. Would a freak beat my best time on *Mario Kart*?"

"Mom doesn't let *Mario Kart* in the house. There's... books. Mom has a library for me. She picked them out to read to me, and... they're *good*, Valentine. They're such wonderful stories. They're about girls who live in the woods and have happy families and date boys and do chores, and..."

"And?"

Aliyah went silent again. Valentine matched her silence. Paul stayed hidden in the hallway, shifting from foot to foot; Aliyah's quiet times always made him nervous.

"...I'm never having that," Aliyah whispered.

"So you snuck in to watch us do 'mancy, so you could feel normal."

Paul winced at Valentine's bluntness. He'd always been careful to let Aliyah come to her own conclusions, afraid parroting back interpretations of her feelings would just create some sad, rubber-stamp version of himself.

Valentine, however, ricocheted through a life based upon snap judgments. And gauging from Aliyah's reluctant nod, Valentine had summed up Aliyah's feelings.

She clasped her milkshake to her chest. "Dad said there would be other 'mancers to talk to! *Tons* of them!"

"That's... what Anathema told him," Valentine allowed. "And she was kiiiinda crazy."

Aliyah's face went grim. "I know."

Aliyah had never spoken of the day she'd burned Anathema alive, though Paul and Valentine had done everything they could to get her to open up. Aliyah had committed murder for all the right reasons: Anathema was a psychotically focused 'mancer who'd already killed hundreds, and had in fact had just severed Paul's toes with a spear when Aliyah had come to his defense. And Aliyah had never done 'mancy before, had no control over what happened aside from her literally incandescent rage.

But Aliyah had never expressed remorse over the killing. That flinty unwillingness unnerved Paul.

"I know Anathema said she'd seeded New York with 'mancers..." Valentine began.

"She said there'd be hundreds!" Aliyah interrupted. "And it took two months for her to... to get *me* started, so where *are* all my 'mancer friends? Who's going to protect us?"

"Trust me, kid, you don't want them to show up," Valentine said. "'Mancers, well... they're like ice and fire.

We believe, and believe *hard*, that the universe works a certain way. Usually when we meet, we kill each other."

Aliyah gasped. "But you and Daddy…"

"We get along. But if it wasn't for our love of magic, we'd never be friends."

Paul wanted to debate that – then looked at the fuzzy mold of rice deliquescing in Valentine's sink, and thought of the scalding hot decontamination showers he always took after spending the evening at Valentine's place.

"Maybe I can make friends at school," Aliyah said. "This one girl liked *Mario Kart*…"

Valentine grabbed Aliyah's shoulder. "Kid, you're a 'mancer. Your dreams bleed out of your head and turn into reality. That means *you will spend your life alone.*"

Had Valentine really *said* that? Paul froze. Aliyah trembled in Valentine's grip.

"I'm sorry," Valentine continued, emphasizing her words by shaking Aliyah. "But you need to understand. What you have now? Me and your dad to talk to? This is the most social support you'll ever *get*. Your dad's absorbing your flux for you, so you don't understand. But… the bad luck goes after whatever you fear losing the most. So even if you *found* someone who somehow wasn't 'mancy-terrified to confide in, you'd…"

Valentine slumped back in the futon. "I had a boyfriend. I liked him. I liked him *too much*, Aliyah. And when I singlehandedly fended off a battalion of SMASH agents, which is *exactly* as exciting as it sounds, the flux got away from me, and… it asked, 'What would reach into Valentine's chest like Kano's hand to tear her beating heart right the fuck out?' And bam. Poor Raphael got skewered.

"So I'm not gonna lie. I *can't* lie. You need to embrace loneliness, because your magic's going to kill all your friends."

Aliyah set down her milkshake, sickened. "Even Daddy?"

"Maybe." Valentine sighed. "Look, kid, SMASH and the Task Force, they're… they're out to get us. And… you've got to be *prepared*, Aliyah."

Aliyah stared at the blank television screen, eyes flinty. "I *am* prepared."

Paul thought back to that counsellor's report:

Aliyah's mother has stated she has no friends and never initiates social interactions with other children…

Now Paul knew why.

"That is *bullshit*."

He stepped forward, swept Aliyah into his arms; Valentine froze like she'd been caught raiding the cookie jar. Aliyah looked up, beaming, at her father.

"Daddy," she said, delighted. "You swore!"

"I'll swear whenever Valentine is that wrong." He released Aliyah, whirled on Valentine. "Just how many 'mancers had you met before we started working together, Valentine?"

Valentine glowered. "Enough."

"Two! You met two! That whole speech, Aliyah, was based on Valentine's experience with two 'mancers. Imagine if you'd met two Chinese people and extrapolated behavior based on that sample size!"

"Paul," Valentine warned him. "We don't have to have this discussion in front of her."

"There's no discussion to be *had*, Valentine. You and I have forged a great friendship. Who's to say we couldn't join forces with other 'mancers?"

Valentine raised one plucked eyebrow. "…all the dead people in Europe?"

"That was in World War II," Paul said, undeterred. "And that accident happened when the whole *world* was at war."

"Thank you for clarifying that, professor."

"And yes, warring 'mancers ripped open broaches to the demon dimensions, but the Allied 'mancers – a volunteer squadron! – worked together quite efficiently until then."

"That's like saying the *Titanic* sailed beautifully until it hit an iceberg, Paul."

"I'm not saying things can't go wrong, Valentine. I'm

saying that if we can find the new 'mancers Anathema promised, well... maybe some of them could help us."

"And some could be new Anathemas."

Aliyah clutched her milkshake to her chest as though it were a teddy bear. Paul gave Valentine an icy glare. "Can we talk in the kitchen?"

"What, you mean that conversation I *told* you we shouldn't have in front of her suddenly seems like a bad idea?"

"*I* don't conceal the things I say to her from *you*!"

Valentine rose from the futon, hands grasping imaginary game controllers. "And maybe *you* should think before you promise her–"

"*STOP IT!*"

Aliyah flung something at them; Paul heard a whoosh and a triumphant *ching!*, then the world condensed around him, turning tight blue and spherical. He struggled for freedom as he lifted off the ground, floating into a glimmering icicle sphere that held him tight. Valentine wriggled for freedom next to him as they were bound back to back.

"...Did that bitch just throw a *Pokeball* at us?" Valentine asked, her voice rising in admiration – before the ball dropped to the ground and rolled under the futon, carrying a now-shrunken Paul and Valentine with it.

"You do *not* fight!" Aliyah cried. Paul saw her crouching down to look under the couch, brandishing her milkshake at them as their Pokeball jail rolled back to bump against the wall. "It's bad enough when Mommy and David fight! We all have to be friends! So you–"

In her anger, Aliyah forgot her training. The flux took her by surprise. Her milkshake cup sagged; ice cream spattered all over Aliyah's shoes.

"*Fuck!*" Aliyah screamed.

Paul felt Valentine's shoulders tense apologetically against his.

Aliyah flung the milkshake against the television; sticky cream oozed down the blank screen. "*You're all I have! So you – you* get along!"

She opened the closet door, which, with a glimmer of 'mancy, now opened into her room at her mother's place – a large space as neat as a landlord's showcase, a tasteful duvet spread across the bed, the vacuumed carpet, a box of *Good Housekeeping*-approved toys against the wall. A picture-perfect space for a normal little girl.

Aliyah slammed the door shut, leaving Valentine and Paul trapped in Pokespace.

Paul had the distinct feeling he'd been put into a timeout.

Neither spoke for a very long time. Then Valentine cleared her throat.

"…I just don't wanna *lie* to her, Paul."

"And I don't want her to lose hope."

Valentine nodded. "Yeah," she said. "I get that."

"I know you do."

The argument settled, they both relaxed. Paul was more comfortable with silence, anyway.

"I spy with my little eye," Valentine said, "Something beginning with 'M'…"

It was a long several hours before the Pokeball dissolved.

SIX
Bold and Infeasible Stances

Paul usually loved riding the subway. As a man with one artificial foot and a toeless half-foot jammed into a clunky orthotic boot, people stared at him when he walked by. Yet on the subway, jammed shoulder to shoulder with the Saturday morning crowd, Paul was just another commuter.

Except on days when Paul's face was on the front page of every newspaper.

A little old lady looked up from her knitting, starting the recognition cycle. She glanced at Paul's face, seeing a scrawny middle-aged Greek man.

She checked his ankle: Paul's signature black carbon ProPrio™ artificial foot.

Her eyes flew open.

Paul raised his newspaper, blocking eye contact. The local headlines had not been kind: the *New York Post*, flippant as always, had a picture of Paul at the press conference, with the smoking garage Photoshopped in behind him, along with the bold words "TSABO TSTRIKES OUT AGAIN." The *Daily News* was slightly nicer with "PSYCHO MANTIS PSLIPS AWAY," but they still had a goofy picture of Paul, baffled by the escape.

Paul wrinkled his nose. He hated the way the local papers treated him like a crazy superhero – *yes*, he'd lost his right foot killing an illustromancer, a handful of mundane men who'd taken down a 'mancer single-handed. And yes, he'd lost the toes on his *other* foot in a showdown with Anathema the paleomancer, which made him the greatest 'mancer-hunter alive, but...

...he didn't *want* to hunt 'mancers.

To read the papers, you'd have thought Paul only got out of bed on the off chance he might get to strangle a 'mancer. The papers made 'mancy seem like a toxic hazard that any good American wanted eradicated from the earth.

Furthermore, the papers spoke as if punching Psycho Mantis in the face would be the greatest thing Paul could do for humanity. Paul found that idea repellent; true changes weren't created through violence, but through thousands of tiny kindnesses and efficiencies.

Paul didn't contradict the papers, though. In fact, he'd let the mayor's office play up that dumb 'mancers-versus-mundanes angle... because it had helped keep his job.

And now, after years of holding his nose to court the media, the news had turned against him. Which was why he was commuting into the mayor's office on a Saturday morning.

The subway screeched to a stop. Paul's replacement phone rang: it was Imani, his ex-wife.

They'd been divorced for almost three years, and still his heart stuttered whenever she called.

"Paul," she said, "We have to talk."

Paul had never once seen Imani cry – not when she'd come to him after thirteen years of marriage asking for divorce, not when their daughter Aliyah had been so burned the doctors feared she might not survive. Imani worked at the highest tiers of corporate law; women who broke down under high pressure didn't last long.

But her voice quavered now.

He scurried off the subway, huddled under a steel support beam to scrape up some privacy. "What'd she do this time?"

"She mouthed off to David when he told her it was

bedtime – told him *he* didn't get to tell her what to do, Daddy did. So I sent her to her room. Then I found her on her bed with milkshake all over her dress, hours later. We don't allow processed sugar in this house, Paul. She must have snuck out again. But I don't know *how*."

Imani hadn't called last night. She must have stayed up all night, deciding whether to confide in Paul.

Paul heard Valentine's voice: *Why do you even* talk *to that frigid clamhole, Paul? She sued the courts for exclusive custody! If the judges had sided with her, you'd never have seen Aliyah again. Why don't you just let her rot in the sewage of her own awful choices?*

"...because she cares about Aliyah as much as I do," Paul muttered.

"What?" Imani asked.

"I said Aliyah loves you."

"A little girl! Eight!"

" – almost nine – "

"A *nine*-year-old on the streets! On her own!" Imani cried. "Where anyone could... *take* her. All because I gave her a timeout for swearing at my husband."

Paul hated hearing Imani talk about her husband, as though they'd never been married. He also hated himself for not being used to that by now.

"You did nothing wrong," Paul reassured her. "A timeout is – it's pretty generous if she used the F-word."

"She used the MF-word."

"Oh Lord." It was increasingly difficult to raise Aliyah, even with Paul and Valentine's 'mancy to keep her in line. Teenagers started rebelling once they got a taste of power – growing large physically, getting jobs, finally gaining alternatives to circumvent their parents' punishments. But Aliyah, not quite nine, had almost infinite magic power at her disposal.

She was rebelling early. Way early.

Poor Imani had no clue what was about to hit her.

"I tried to get her to open up when she got back, Paul.

I talked about how inappropriate she'd been, like the psychologist suggested. I asked her what David had said that angered her; she said nothing."

That was the flip side to Aliyah, Paul thought. A normal little girl wouldn't have been able to keep a secret like "Being a 'mancer" for long – but Aliyah had locked her emotions deep inside long before her 'mancy. That secrecy kept her safe from the world.

But when Paul wanted her to open up about killing Anathema, Aliyah's stubborn refusal to share slammed shut like a door.

"I asked her where she went," Imani said, "*Still* she said nothing. Not a word. I hugged her, and begged her, and did the active feedback thing, and… and…" She pulled back with a dispassionate sniff.

Paul could imagine her now, in a crisp corporate attorney's outfit designed to complement her dark brown skin, sitting regally with ruler-straight posture at the edge of the bed, brushing off the hem of her dress rather than allowing tears to ruin her makeup's subtle enhancements.

"It was like talking to a doll," Imani continued. "I made an emergency therapist appointment this morning: she sat silent for a full forty-five minutes!"

"You know our girl, Imani: she'll talk on her time." That was the theory, anyway.

"And I have done *everything* to keep her safe. I moved to a new apartment with no windows. I set burglar alarms. David and I, when she's home, we…" She swallowed, as if debating divulging this information to her ex-husband. "We take shifts. Watching. So she can't slip past us. And still she *got out*. David said it must have been something I'd done. Then he stormed out. And…" She swallowed. "I don't know what to do, Paul."

"David will be back," Paul reassured her, wanting her to feel better, wondering, *when did I sign up to support my ex-wife's relationship with the man she cheated on me with?* "Even if he hated you," Paul joked, "He wouldn't risk the headlines of a bad divorce. You've got friends in the court and the press. You'd make his life hell."

"Very funny." The suppressed bemusement in her voice made him smile.

"And Aliyah's bold, but she's not stupid. If she's out on the streets…" Paul winced, hating to tell Imani even a half-truth. "I'm sure she's playing it safe. Some mothers even let their kids take the subway at this age."

"But how do I stop her from getting *out*? How do I get her to *talk*?"

"I don't know, Imani. She doesn't do that at our house."

"That's because you give her those damn videogames. As a pacifier."

"No, we play them together. They could be quite a social activity, if only you'd–"

"Can you honestly tell me," Imani shot back, her voice glacial once again, "That you think videogames are *improving* her life?"

It's not the videogames. It's the 'mancy. And she can't stop doing that.

Paul rolled the words on his tongue, wanting to say them as he had so many times before. If he could just tell Imani, then everything would be easier. He hated watching Imani's leonine confidence eroded. And Imani loved Aliyah, would almost certainly help Aliyah in ways he and Valentine could not…

Then Paul's eyes settled on today's *Times* op-ed: "Why Reprocess 'Mancers When We Could Execute Them?"

Paul remembered the dead eyes of the Unimancers he'd fought. They had all been 'mancers like him once, each obsessed with model trains or baseball or death metal – and someone had reported them. SMASH had rounded them up, shipped them off to the Refactor out in Arizona, brainwashed them until they all thought the exact same way as their commander.

They could use magic only if the group hivemind allowed it. Their individual needs: erased.

They barely remembered their names.

Paul had drawn up endless pros-and-cons lists, crunched numbers: he gave it a ninety percent chance that Imani would accept the news that her daughter was a 'mancer with compassion. He'd seen Imani go to great lengths for charity – after she'd canvassed her neighborhood to help get Aliyah her reconstructive surgery, Imani hadn't stopped after Aliyah's face was rebuilt to the best standards that modern medicine could provide. Imani turned those initial donations into a full-on foundation, managing fundraiser events that helped get other burned kids their necessary treatments. Imani might see Aliyah's videogamemancy as just another special need, and adapt to it. Aliyah had picked up her stubbornness straight from her mother; if any non-'mancer could get Aliyah to master her flux, it was Imani.

But that ten percent chance....

We don't allow processed sugar in this house, Imani had said. *I moved to a new apartment with no windows.*

As much as Paul wanted to give his ex-wife the benefit of the doubt, it was also possible Imani would react to the news by instituting *greater* control. Imani had always believed in outside help – sneering at the parents who suggested Aliyah might benefit from home schooling, sending Aliyah to endless battalions of psychiatrists and pediatric trauma experts despite Aliyah's shrieking protests, interrogating teachers to get their recommendations.

And the federal troops were the only experts. By law.

He tried to push the image away, but it kept recurring: Imani, picking up the phone to call 1-800-SMASHEM. Aliyah, tear-gassed and hooded. Aliyah, out in the Arizona desert, tortured until her spunky rebellion leaked away.

Paul mouthed the words, figuring out how to tell Imani what was really happening. And as always, he imagined a doctor holding up a hypodermic needle that contained an experimental cure:

We think this treatment has a ninety percent chance of curing Aliyah's psychological problems, the imaginary doctor told him gravely. *But if we're wrong, this shot will destroy your daughter's brain beyond repair.*

Are you ready to risk that?

His phone alarm buzzed. It wouldn't do to be late to the mayor's office when he was being called on the carpet.

"I have to go," Paul said. "I promise I will call you later."

"All right." She breathed in through her nose, regaining composure. "Thank you, Paul. It's not fair to dump this on you, I know. And… you're a good man. I just wish we could have…"

Paul hung up before she could finish that sentence. He stormed off to the mayor's office, swallowing back frustration. Paul hated lying. He hated *liars*. Yet Imani had divorced him because he'd had to lie about his love of 'mancy to her.

And now, to save his daughter, he had to layer falsehoods on top of falsehoods….

Paul's tension rose as the mayor's office came into view. All the paperwork flowed through City Hall, New York's beating heart, where things got catalogued and approved.

Politicians, Paul thought, were fatty clumps sticking to the walls of an aorta – clogging the flow from time to time. But the strength of bureaucracy and good records kept New York City functioning. Paul had read histories of the time before building codes, when cheap landlords built wooden fireplaces and uninspected meat markets had sold horrific surprises…

Bureaucracy was the best tool humanity had to fight dishonest men.

But aren't you dishonest, Paul? a voice at the back of his head whispered. *They'd lock you away if they knew what you really were. You don't try to fight City Hall, you slither in and subvert it…*

He'd do anything to protect Aliyah.

A secretary escorted Paul to a small meeting room. No one was there, but he'd expected that; Paul had learned that in City Hall, some people waited for you to arrive, and others you waited for.

The meeting room was furnished in a way Paul could only describe as "stately": leather upholstery on polished wood chairs, gilded frames with oil paintings of New York's turn-of-the-century skyscrapers, a cut-glass pitcher of ice water waiting for him. A cozy place, designed to impress.

Paul closed his eyes, summoning up the strength to face down the mayor himself.

The door opened.

"...David?" Paul spluttered as his ex-wife's new husband, David Giabatta, entered the room.

"I *am* a senior member of the mayor's cabinet, Paul," David said coldly. That chilly tone was unusual for David. He turned everything into a joke, that politician's trick to transform vindictive insults into jocular ribbings. Paul couldn't remember a time when he hadn't seen David smiling that salesman's grin.

David was not smiling.

Well, Paul thought, *at least I know why he's not at home with Imani*. The mayor had summoned his hatchetman to talk to Paul.

David sat down across from Paul, as far across the table as he could get. He straightened his tie – Imani had once confided in Paul that David had his tailor cut his suit specifically to display his muscular form. He looked presidential, solemn, disappointed.

He lowered his face into his hands.

"You could have had it all, Paul." His palms muffled his voice. "You could have made this office look magnificent. Instead, you pissed it away."

"It's a setback, David," Paul said.

He glared at Paul. "The fact that you do not realize how bad things are, Paul, shows me *exactly* how ill-suited you are for this job."

Paul squirmed. "It's one bad fight. But catching 'mancers is what I do. We'll get there."

"And if your job was to *catch* 'mancers, I would be reassured."

"My job *is* to catch 'mancers. That's right on the paperwork."

"No." David shook his head. "Your job is to make the mayor look good. Which you do by making New York's citizenry feel safe. You have failed at that job, time and time again."

"...you're telling me that I'm a figurehead?"

"No. Though that *is* why we appointed you to the job – a man without a scrap of political savvy who nevertheless made headlines. Imani assured me you could pick up the skill of *making connections*."

Paul winced. He'd disliked lying to City Hall, assuring everyone how bad 'mancers were, how he took great satisfaction in tracking those universe-warping bastards down. So he'd skipped the meet-'n'-greets, hoping sheer efficiency would keep him in the role.

"But no," David continued. "We've gone almost eighteen months with no 'mancers. *After* Anathema promised we'd have a tide of magicked-up freaks storming our bastions. You could have claimed credit, told the news of the horrible things that would have happened had not Mr Paulos Costa Tsabo scared the 'mancers away. But no! You expressed bafflement – *repeated* bafflement – that Anathema's dire predictions weren't coming true. You asked for more funding to investigate this strange quiescence. Truth be told, you sounded a little *disappointed* more 'mancers hadn't arrived."

Paul *had* been disappointed. Anathema had told him all sorts of 'mancers would be popping up all across New York. That's why he'd taken the job, even though he'd known the politics would be interminable: as the first responder to any 'mancer incident, he'd planned to shunt the helpful 'mancers off to safer places, playing a sort of Oskar Schindler.

Paul had anticipated moral dilemmas, sorting out which 'mancers were worth saving.

What he hadn't anticipated was no 'mancers at all. None.

"Don't you think it's a *little* odd?" Paul asked, leaning

forward. "*No* 'mancer activity for eighteen months? In a city *this* size? Not so much as a single bookiemancer? Hell, Los Angeles averages ten 'mancer incidents a year, Chicago twenty–"

"And we are *safe*, Paul!" David spread his hands. "That's *good* news! Why couldn't you tell the media that was the result of your fine preventative work?"

"Because it's not true?"

"How do you *know* it's not true? Maybe they're terrified of your manly presence. Christ, Paul, I'm not asking you to lie, I'm just asking for good *spin*."

"You know I don't like talking to the media, David."

"Yeah, well, that's
a strange allergy for someone who's in fucking *politics*."

"Politics," Paul shot back, "often stops shit from getting done."

A cold silence.

David reached for a glass of water with the aggrieved air of a man cutting Paul some major slack. It was all Paul could do not to remind David that *oh, yeah, remember how you slept with my wife while we were still* married, *and I haven't brought that up even once*?

"It sounds," Paul said stiffly, "Like you'd be happier if Lenny hadn't gone after Psycho Mantis at all."

"No." David planted his index finger on the table's dark-wood surface. "We should scour the city for *all* 'mancy-related threats. Yet Psycho Mantis was not a risk *at the time*. Lenny didn't scout the zone, and he endangered lives – all on an anonymous *tip*."

Paul winced. David had a point.

"The media wants someone strung up," David continued. "Lenny Pirazzini seems like an excellent target. Well, him and – well, let's say you suspend your five weakest officers without pay for a week, just to show the papers we're taking it seriously. I expect Lenny's resignation in time to make Monday's headlines, and then you and I will discuss what, exactly, you are supposed to do as a Task Force Supervisor."

"No."

David tilted his head. "No?"

"Lenny's cock-up is... it's my fault as a manager. I should have been working more closely with SMASH, training my force in the newest anti-mancer tactics. I should have been riding Lenny's ass; everyone knows he's a hothead. And his men, they were... they were following orders."

And, Paul thought, *I don't talk to SMASH because I'm worried they'll figure out what I am. I don't trade tactics with them because I don't want our Task Force to be that good at capturing 'mancers. It's unfair that the squad gets punished when I set up them up to fail.*

"Paul," David said prissily, then paused, as if that one word should have been warning enough.

"I'll reprimand Lenny. Officially. A month off, no pay. But the man doesn't deserve to lose his job."

"*Someone's* going to."

"No," Paul said, digging in. "We had one major goof-up against a very cunning opponent. But we got some more information on this 'King of New York' fellow. The papers are making this look bad, that's their job, but... it's not a rout."

"Paul," David repeated. "I'm here with orders from His Fucking Honor himself. I don't have a lot of love for you. You spoil your fucking kid, and I have to clean up the mess. You make my wife neurotic that she's a bad mother. And if I, a man personally authorized by the greatest fucking power in New York City, tells you heads will roll, then you fire Lenny Pirrazzini and suspend some officers... or you turn in your resignation right. Fucking. Now."

Oh, we've gone personal, have we? Paul thought.

"I will not." Paul got up from the table. "I'm not going to sacrifice good men so we can lie to the newspapers. This will pass. And when it passes, we will have a stronger and more diligent Task Force, and you will thank me for not caving in to simple politics."

SEVEN
Yup

Of course they fired him.

EIGHT
The Woman In The Shy Castle

On Sunday night, just in time to make Monday's headlines, the mayor proudly announced David Giabatta would be taking over the Task Force.

The man who'd stolen Paul's wife now had Paul's old job.

Paul decided to allow himself precisely four days of self-pity, ending when Imani dropped Aliyah off at his apartment on Thursday. He took to it with gusto.

Of course, Paul's "gusto" consisted of managing the tiny details that went with being freshly unemployed. He called up the firm that held his unemployment insurance – not Samaritan Mutual – to ensure that everything was handled. He cut back on all his unnecessary expenses, canceling his cable and renegotiating his cell phone plan; paying for both his and Valentine's side-by-side apartments would be tricky on sixty percent of his old salary, even with the rent-controlled deal he'd gotten. He compiled a list of potential future employers, ranked them by potential, culling a sub-list of people to call come Friday morning.

His former employer Samaritan Mutual was conspicuously not on that list.

And all the while he did not shower, he did not shave, he did not sleep. He did not change the bandage on his ever-bleeding left arm. He ignored all incoming calls. (Though he did send a text to his drug overlord Oscar saying "We'll talk soon" before locking his phone away in a drawer. Thankfully, the King either had no ability, or no interest, to track Paul down when he wasn't brewing Flex.)

Occasionally Paul would take the Scotch down from his liquor shelf and weigh the bottle in his hands, imagining precisely how drunk he could get given the number of ounces of alcohol compared to his own meager body weight.

Then he would put it back, and make some more lists.

And at 4:35 Tuesday afternoon, when Paul was happily lost in comparing Internet service provider plans, there came the videogame *chunk-chunk-chunk* noise of Aliyah teleporting into her bedroom.

Paul felt the surge of bad luck lunge after Aliyah – a dangerous surge, one that indicated Aliyah had done magic she felt conflicted about. He grabbed for his legal pad, scribbled a notification of legal guardian status onto it; the surge changed course and slammed into him with such force that the Scotch tumbled off the shelf.

The flux squeezed in all around him; it was like being shoved into a closet full of rubber balls, a soft probing from every angle, asking *What could go wrong? What could go wrong?* And Paul, unprepared for this, didn't have a good answer. He could normally hold his flux for a day or two until he could direct it towards some bad luck he was prepared for – but this wave hit him when he was already distracted by worries about incoming bills, bad credit ratings, what would happen to the men on the Task Force–

The flux wriggled away, leaving Paul to wonder what whammy he'd triggered.

He pushed himself away from the desk, feeling shamed. Aliyah shouldn't see him like this – covered in sweaty stubble, clothes in shambles, stinking of freshly splashed Scotch. Paul buttoned his stained shirt, trying to regain some semblance of authority.

He stormed into Aliyah's bedroom. "*Aliyah Rebecca Tsabo-Dawson!*" he bellowed, in his best angry dad voice. "You do *not* do 'mancy without warning Daddy!"

Aliyah sat on her bed, surrounded by three suitcases; she must have teleported them in with her. She gazed up at her father, unruffled.

"Valentine's in the maze," she said.

Oh crap.

He had forgotten about Valentine.

The door to Valentine's apartment had been transformed into a flat sticker pasted onto the wall, an image of a door so lifelike that Paul was fooled until his key skidded off the hole-less lock. It was one of Valentine's standard-issue privacy tricks; there were plenty of unopenable doors-as-scenery in videogames.

"All right," he told Aliyah. "Get us in."

They walked back to Aliyah's bedroom in Paul's apartment next door. Aliyah unpacked her Nintendo DS from her suitcase – which, Paul noted, had all her favorite dolls from her mother's house neatly arranged inside.

Before he could ask further questions, Aliyah plugged in the *Super Mario Bros* cartridge, flicked on the game, and curled up in Paul's lap. She twisted her neck around to interrogate him.

"When was the last time you went in?" Aliyah asked.

"Last month," Paul admitted.

"*Daddy!*" she cried. *She's chastising me?* Paul wondered, amazed how easily Aliyah could trigger his guilt reflex. "What if you forget?"

"I've committed the levels to memory. I don't forget."

"Do you remember how to squash the turtles?"

Paul sighed. His daughter was a tiny drill sergeant when it came to videogames. "My reflexes aren't as good as yours."

"You take lead, Daddy." Aliyah thrust the Nintendo DS into his hands. "You *always* have to be able to find us."

Paul pursed his lips. She had a point.

He hit the start button. *Super Mario* started up; Paul felt the subtle tingle of Aliyah's 'mancy connecting her world to Valentine's.

Paul manipulated Mario through the opening level's blocky cartoon world, his fingers feeling fat and clumsy. He'd never liked games, but Aliyah had insisted he master at least *one* videogame.

So over the past few years he'd dedicated an hour each evening to play *Super Mario*. It was like swimming laps in the pool for Paul's physical rehab classes; a tedious, necessary task that brought him no joy.

Playing also involved a surprising amount of memorization, as the levels were packed with "hiddens," as Aliyah called them – secret paths uncovered by breaking this particular block, or crouching in a certain pipe. Aliyah quizzed him on the hidden locations, even though getting to her secret area in Mario took one circuitous route.

Aliyah perched on his lap, vibrating with excitement as she shouted suggestions: "Jump now, Daddy! Don't forget the bats! That bomb's about to go off. YAY! You did it, Daddy, you did it!"

At the end of each level, she gave him her "princess's reward": she kissed his cheek. That was a better reward than any imaginary gold coin: seeing how thoroughly Aliyah was rooting for him.

He *liked* that she was better than him at this, that it took him hours to finish the game while she could have whipped through it in minutes. There had always been something immeasurably wild about his daughter – and where Imani had wanted to lock that rebellion down, Paul treasured Aliyah's stormy enthusiasm. It made for rocky days as a parent, but he secretly adored how you couldn't force her to do anything – you could only convince her to agree with you.

He gave her free rein because he saw how strong she'd be when she grew up. Society took all the traits that a kid needed to be a successful adult – independence, a questioning spirit, a ferocious drive to satisfy your own needs – and then quashed them relentlessly, so thoroughly suppressing those urges that some adults never figured out how to be happy again. Paul needed to protect Aliyah's free spirit until the time it would serve her well.

So playing *Mario* with Aliyah, feeling her deftly thread her 'mancy into his videogame, hearing her cheer him on? He would never have chosen to have his daughter become a videogamemancer, but with her riding his shoulder as he played, he saw the raw joy she took in gaming – a joy she went out of her way to share with him.

It wasn't enough for her to game; she needed him to see what she loved about it.

That good feeling lasted until he got to the lava levels.

Sweat prickled Paul's face as he dropped onto a blackened stone platform. The screen, once the size of his palm, had inched open as wide as the far wall, a window through which he could walk. The graphics had upgraded themselves – finely detailed cartoon shapes, Mario himself a full-sized man made of Legos, the whirling fire traps turned three-dimensional.

The castle was dark, cavernous, saturated with death. Any single misstep could kill you. Paul wondered, not for the first time, *How could anyone relax under all this pressure?*

Yet he could see from Aliyah's smile how much she loved it. She was a magnet, drawn to danger.

The lava burbled, hissing pixelated holes in the living room carpet.

"Keep going, Daddy! Just a few more steps. You can do it!"

"Are you sure she's on *this* level?"

"Auntie Valentine's never anywhere else."

And sure enough, through the gaping portal they'd opened up, Valentine stood on *Super Mario*'s final level – fighting Bowser on a tightrope suspended over a deadly volcano. Bowser hurled stone hammers at Valentine; Valentine dodged them. In the real world, plump Valentine got out of breath jogging down the street to Dunkin' Donuts – but in this world, she was an acrobat, the twirling hammers whizzing by so close they ruffled her hair.

She was topless.

And fighting with both arms clasped behind her back.

Paul had never gotten used to walking into Valentine's apartment to find her walking around half-naked, though Valentine never minded. She *liked* clothes, changing outfits three times a day, but didn't see a *need* for them, comfortable in her own stretchmarked skin. She was fifty pounds overweight, but those pounds accentuated her curves – curves that unnerved Paul. He was old-fashioned enough to believe you shouldn't see someone naked unless you were at least a little in love with them, and Valentine was utterly not his type – so as always, he covered his eyes, censoring her with his fingers.

Valentine landed badly, wobbling on the tightrope. She almost let go of her wrists, which she clutched to keep her arms locked behind her spine – but with an effort of will, she struggled to find her balance without releasing her grip.

As she jerked away from one stone hammer, another smashed her in the face.

Valentine tumbled towards the lava – and everything froze.

"Restart," Valentine muttered, her face pale as though in a fever dream. Her nose leaked blood.

Valentine upended herself from the lava, tumbling upwards in a reversal of gravity and time, landing on the rope. She landed on the far ledge, across from the switch that would send Bowser plunging into the lava.

Her breasts were bruised hammer-black.

This was what 'mancers did, when the world upset them; they retreated to their own reality, creating a safe place where they endlessly acted out fantasies of better worlds – except Valentine's retreat was bloody and bitter.

Paul wondered how the flux didn't kill her, but that was every 'mancer's trick: though creating a lava pit with an animated villain would have destroyed Paul, Valentine believed in a videogame-based escape right down to the roots of her heart. So the universe didn't complain too much, just as it didn't give Paul too much guff for summoning apartment leases out of midair.

Valentine cracked her neck, then clasped her arms behind her back again and stepped out onto the tightrope.

"Valentine?" Aliyah called.

Valentine frowned at them, as if to ask, *What the hell are you doing here?* – and freed her hands. Her full balance regained, she darted across the rope in one smooth motion, tumbling under Bowser's great horned feet, jamming her elbow into the switch before Bowser tossed his first hammer. The tightrope snapped, sending Bowser tumbling into the lava below.

Paul realized Valentine had been toying with Bowser, could have finished this whenever she desired.

She only relaxed when challenged.

Valentine panted, blood dripping from her nose onto her bare breasts, glaring maliciously at them.

"What do you want?"

Aliyah stepped forward, not quite entering the level. "You haven't slept in three days, Auntie Valentine. I'm worried about you."

"Are you *spying* on me?"

"I'm taking *care* of you," Aliyah said, hurt.

Valentine choked on laughter. "Nobody cares for us. You're too young to understand, and he–" She gestured violently in Paul's direction "–He's too naïve."

"Too naïve for what?" Paul asked.

"You–" She wiped off her face, then massaged her temples. "Oh, for Christ's sake, I came here to stop *thinking* about this shit."

"What shit?" Aliyah asked, then looked intensely guilty as Paul glared at her for swearing.

"You haven't *done* this," Valentine spat. "You don't know what the end *looks* like. But me, I've been through it before: the bad luck piles up until you can't recover. You lose your job, then you lose your home, then you lose your boyfriend, and... and..."

She scrubbed tears from her face.

"We're gonna lose each other," Valentine whispered. "One 'mancer's flux load is bad enough. But three? God, Paul, these years with you and Aliyah have been the best years of my life. You don't know what a balm it's been, having friends, having a place to live, this *stability*…

"But you've lost your job," she continued. "Now it's just a matter of time. Eventually SMASH will take Aliyah, or you'll die like Raphael, or… or something terrible. That's how 'mancy works. And you gotta *brace* for that crash. You gotta start pushing stuff away, before…"

Her tears sizzled into the lava below. "Goddammit, Valentine DiGriz doesn't *do* tears."

"Does she hug little girls?" Aliyah asked.

"Always," Valentine promised, stepping out from the lava-filled castle to embrace Aliyah with the fervor of a woman trying to freeze this moment in time forever. "Always."

Valentine shook as she held Aliyah, trembling with – rage? Terror? Sadness? Paul couldn't tell.

Paul was reluctant to join in, mainly because Valentine was topless, sweaty, and bleeding. But he drew in a breath and embraced them both.

After a long time, Valentine stopped trembling.

"…this isn't the end," Paul told her.

"You don't know that."

"Neither do you. You were alone when things were bad."

Valentine jerked away. "And how is it going to get better with *more* 'mancers bringing their flux load crashing down on us? Hell, Aliyah goddamned near killed us all with her last trick."

"It's not my fault," Aliyah protested. "They hurt Daddy! And you! Those stupid mundanes deserved to be punished!"

Paul scowled. "Where did you hear *that* term?"

"…punished?"

"*Mundanes.*"

Aliyah seemed startled by her father's anger. "In school…"

"That," Paul said hotly, "is a *bad word*. It makes it seem like we're *better* than they are."

Aliyah thrust out her lower lip. "We *are* better. Mundanes are *mean*."

"Sweetie. I know the police are... a problem, but–"

"*Mommy's* a problem."

Paul exchanged a quick glance over to Valentine: *can we put your concerns on hold to discuss the kid's issues?* Valentine nodded and grabbed a towel, blotting the blood off her nose.

"Aliyah," Paul warned. "Do not talk about your mother like that."

"She wants to kill me."

"What? Your Mommy loves you. More than anything."

Aliyah shook her head. "She was at the table, talking with stupid *David*. And David was talking about how close he was to finding the 'mancers you couldn't catch. They were *laughing*, Daddy! Laughing at how he was going to find us! They toasted to him finding you!"

"Sweetie, that's–"

"And then I was so mad, I asked if I could go play my Nintendo so I didn't start yelling, and Mommy said if I didn't stop playing, then I'd become a videogamemancer and David would have to hunt me down."

Oh no, Paul thought. Imani had probably meant it as a joke. But to Aliyah, in these circumstances...

"I didn't hurt David," Aliyah said. "I *wanted* to. Instead, I'm moving in with you and Valentine, and never talking to mundanes as long as I live."

"Aliyah. You must talk to your mother."

"*No*. She *acts* nice! But I can't *trust* her."

This would all go so much easier, Paul thought, *if I could tell Imani what was happening.*

Then he remembered what Valentine had said: *It's the beginning of a slide into a deep abyss. SMASH will take one of us...*

Paul wondered what that load of flux squirming away had already done to them. Yet he was strangely grateful Aliyah had generated a big load of flux; 'mancers got more bad luck whenever they felt like they broke their own personal rulesets, and Aliyah must have felt guilty indeed about running away from home.

"You're not moving in with us full-time, Aliyah. The court order says we alternate weeks. When you're twelve, if you feel the same way, we'll get you a lawyer."

Aliyah stomped her feet, and the apartment complex shuddered. "You can't stop bullets with your stupid papermancy! This is the one thing you can do! You *fix* this!"

"I *could* change that, Aliyah. But I won't."

"Then you break Mommy and David up!"

Aliyah crossed her arms, braced to dismiss whatever counterargument he made. Going head to head had never worked out well.

Paul took another tack.

"Do you know what happened after Daddy lost his foot, Aliyah?"

Predictably, Aliyah softened. She craved that intimacy of being let in on grown-up talk. "...No."

"Do you remember *how* Daddy lost it?"

"You–" Her eyes widened as she remembered. "You killed a 'mancer. But before she died, she hurt you."

He nodded. "She hurt me in more ways than one. Because I didn't want to kill her. I'd never seen 'mancy before, and she was an illustromancer–"

"A what?"

"A 'mancer who loved art. More specifically, this poor girl loved a painter called Titian. She had posters of all his art tacked up in an alleyway. Daddy only found her because she was selling Flex, trying to make enough money to buy Titian's paintings. Not that she could have, poor thing. She was crazy to think she could buy paintings from the museums, like a shopping mall.

"But crazy as she was, she loved those paintings. And they came alive for her. Angels soared overhead, warriors thundered on horseback, sea serpents writhed in the oceans..."

Aliyah hugged her knees, looking troubled. "And that...."

"Yes, Aliyah. It all went away when I killed her. But Daddy was a mundane back then. Daddy thought all magic was bad. That's why I hunted her down. I was just as stupid as Mommy or David." Paul sagged. "And when she saw me, all *she* saw was a mundane. Someone to be killed. So she sent her painted horses after me, and I shot her."

Aliyah frowned, uncertain. "...so?"

Valentine gave Paul a confused look. *Yeah, Paul. What's your moral here?*

Paul felt like he'd been leading up to something. But there *wasn't* a moral to be taken away. They *couldn't* be honest.

"I isolated myself, Aliyah. I... I pushed your Mother away, and she never understood. Even if I... well, I *couldn't* tell her about the 'mancy, but once I started walling that part of my life away from her, the rest of it just... well, it died."

"David wants us all dead," Aliyah whispered – as though shamed to say such a thing out loud. "And Mommy? Mommy *agrees* with him."

Paul wanted to say that David was just following the polls and Imani was just going along with David, that of course Imani didn't want all the 'mancers locked away – especially not Aliyah. But Imani *did* hate 'mancers. She'd hated them ever since the illustromancer had crippled Paul, hated them so hard that Paul couldn't even tell Imani that he blamed himself for the accident.

That *almost*, that granule of doubt, seized his tongue for a critical second before he stammered out a "no."

Aliyah nodded, as if that settled things.

"I love Mommy. But... we can't trust her. So I won't go back."

Paul fishmouthed. He looked to Valentine for help; Valentine shrugged.

"No, Aliyah," he said. "No. You can't abandon–"

Someone pounded on the door.

Paul realized the portal to the Super Mario lava level

was still open, filling the room with the stink of hot metal; Valentine slammed it shut, locking her personal flux-load tight so it wouldn't seep out.

Aliyah looked at Paul as if to ask, *See how much you trust the mundanes?*

The pounding continued, now accompanied by a muffled voice: *"Paul! Paul! It's Lenny! Open up!"*

Paul gestured at Valentine to take Aliyah to her bedroom. Lenny wasn't the brightest bulb on the marquee, but if Lenny met Paul's friend with the videogame tattoos all over her body...

Paul unlocked the door. Lenny Pirrazzini came bounding in, excited as a puppy.

"Paul!" he cried. "You–"

He took in Paul's uncharacteristic stubble, Paul's blood-soaked bandage on his ever-bleeding arm, the reek of Scotch in the kitchen.

"Whoah." Lenny wiped his sleeve across his forehead, wiping away a prickle of sweat; the apartment must have been at least a hundred degrees. "Now I see why you weren't picking up your phone, buddy. I guess a little pity party is justified, but – whoah. Didn't see you as a drinker."

Paul was too tired to argue. "What's up, Lenny?"

"I got news that'll get you back on the case, Paul. It's David! He had a brainstorm to find Psycho Mantis!"

"Have I...." Paul had never minded Lenny's blatant adulation, but he'd never encouraged it, either – and Lenny seemed like a man who, once he'd broken the seal, would have dropped by at odd hours. "Did I give you my address?"

"Looked you up in the records," Lenny said, sticking his head in Paul's refrigerator and waving the cool into his face. "I know, I know, 'confidentiality' and all that happy crappy, Paul, but damn! We are on the *case*!"

Paul's terror grew. "...You realize I'm not on that case anymore, Lenny."

Lenny looked heartbroken, then rallied and punched Paul in the shoulder. "You kidder! Guy like you *hunts*! Even if the mayor takes you off the case for a little collateral damage, will *that* keep you away? It sure didn't stop you when you tracked down Anathema! Nah, you'll find these magic-slinging psychos wherever they cower! You *hate* 'mancers!"

"...what's David doing?"

"He had a brainstorm an hour ago!" Lenny held up both hands, as if framing a picture. "He told us to *follow the fake IDs*."

Lenny grabbed a stunned Paul and shook him.

"Don't'cha get it?" Lenny cried. "We've got all four fake IDs on record from the Lark Street bust! Someone put a *lot* of money into getting all the right certificates filed, to create the illusion of a working garage!"

"But Psycho Mantis, he's... he's a videogamemancer..."

"A videogamemancer with *backing*. Someone's doing his grunt work. David, that prick, he's hired a team of analysts –" And here, Lenny beamed, acting as though he'd handed Paul the greatest of gifts "–but who's better suited to track down white-collar crime than you, the Master of Paperwork?"

Paul sagged against the counter as Lenny rummaged around in Paul's fridge. He understood something Lenny did not:

Bureaucromancy did not conjure up certifications and fake IDs out of nowhere; it was more like a supercharged form of money laundering. Everything Paul did was on record. He could bury the request underneath a trail, he could masquerade behind a series of faked IDs, but if someone was determined enough then Paul's name would turn up *somewhere* downstream.

"We *got* the bastard, Paul!" Lenny cried, thrusting a celebratory beer into Paul's hands. "And we'll pitch in – the guys on the force know who had our backs when the press wanted our heads! You point us at this cocksucker, and we'll do the rest!"

Paul eyed the beer blearily, then swigged it down in one gulp. *At least I know where the flux went,* he thought.

NINE
Donutmancy

It's just an insurance company, Paul told himself. *You worked there, you got a better job, you quit. It's not like they're mad at you or anything.*

But still, Paul felt powerless standing before Samaritan Mutual's great glass tower. He'd have to walk back in there and ask for his old job.

He needed that job – not just for the money, but for the ability to request forms. His bureaucromancy, he'd discovered last night, was hampered. Back when he'd been an insurance agent, he'd had the legal ability to request police dossiers, which he could chain upwards into phenomenal requests. When he'd been the New York Task Force leader, he'd had almost unlimited access.

But Paul Tsabo, unemployed civilian?

As a man with no particular legal standing, his power was much, much lessened. He could file requests for information, but no one was obligated to grant them – and though his bureaucromancy could still force people's hands, it also increased his flux load dramatically. In obfuscating his paper trail last night, what had once cost him a stubbed toe now required the theft of a credit card.

Paul frowned. The credit card had been stolen at Paul's favorite diner, where they'd taken Aliyah out for a late-night supper. She'd refused to place her order with the mundane waiter, instead pointing to the items on the menu.

In an ideal world, his daughter's decision to move in with them would be his first priority – followed closely by tracking down the King – but the government was hot on his tail.

Fortunately, Imani had been understanding when he'd told her Aliyah wanted to stay at his place for a few days. He'd heard David yelling in the background as Imani shushed him, bellowing she had every legal right to demand her daughter back…

But Imani had simply asked, "Is this what she needs, Paul?"

Paul hadn't been sure. But he also wasn't sure how to keep his videogamemancer daughter at her mother's house if she didn't want to stay. So he'd said, "Give her a couple of days, Imani. Let me see if I can talk some sense into her."

"I know I should make her an appointment for a psychiatrist – she's young for medications, but…" Imani sighed. "I just… I don't know how to talk to her anymore."

Neither do I, Paul had thought. But Paul knew of no psychologists qualified to rein in daughters with unlimited cosmic power – and if they did exist, then SMASH employed them.

He took the elevator up to the Samaritan Mutual offices, twitching with reluctance. He had to fix things before Aliyah's next flux-load complicated things. He'd considered setting himself up as a private investigator, but the licensing process would have taken weeks. He could certify himself in seconds, but with David poking around, Paul didn't want people asking how he'd punched through the paperwork with supernatural speed.

No. Paul needed instant access, in order to cover his trail against David Giabatta. His old job as an insurance claims investigator would get him there. He could make requests in Samaritan's name; they'd grant him temporary access until his official paperwork came through.

So why was he so nervous?

The elevator doors creaked open. Paul ambled in, looked over Samaritan Mutual's offices – as ever, a strangely antiquated workplace. Lawrence Payne, Samaritan's CEO, infamously despised computers. He didn't mind data analysis, but thought the "frippery" of email led to needless miscommunications, wasted time spending fifteen minutes writing memos that a two-minute conversation could handle. Emails weren't *dis*allowed, certainly, as many customers expected them, but... if you sent emails to your superiors, your promotion chances sank.

So the phones always rang at Samaritan. People bustled from cubicle to cubicle, tugging each other aside for impromptu meetings. Everyone was in open-air offices, so the managers had nowhere to hide when Payne stormed through. There were typewriters, honest-to-God *typewriters*, where underpaid secretaries read information off computer screens and typed claims onto paper forms, all because Mr Payne didn't trust printouts.

Paul had taken to typing up his own forms directly, just in case Mr Payne needed them – an inefficiency his co-workers thought crazy, until they saw how many of Paul's claims went through.

Reflexively, Paul scanned the offices for Mr Payne's presence. You learned to watch out for the old man – the gray Marine buzzcut, the squared shoulders, the old sour face, striding through the office as people practically flung themselves out of his way. Payne still walked with a soldier's vigor, though he was pushing eighty.

Mr Payne dropping by your office was like a military invasion. He ensured no claims were paid unless they hewed perfectly to the paperwork he himself had designed. If he showed up, it meant you had approved an imperfectly filed claim and cost him money.

People who cost Lawrence Payne money got fired.

Paul tightened his tie. Already, he felt the tension returning.

Yet it wasn't tension that made his hands tremble.

He looked at the beleaguered secretaries, hammering keys into paper on antique machines, all so Mr Payne could find a way to refuse more claims. And Paul put a name to this feeling:

Guilt.

Paul had discovered his skills as a bureaucromancer at Samaritan – fixing forms for claimants so Samaritan's stingy claims department couldn't deny them. Hell, Old Man Payne had denied Aliyah's plastic surgery claims, sniffing that reconstructive facial surgery wasn't life-threatening…

Mr Payne had only hired him because he was good at tracking down evidence of 'mancy, and 'mancy was cause for refusal on cheaper insurance plans. Paul's entire *job* had been to find ways to negate claims, which he'd counteracted by staying late and filling out forms to ensure others would *get* their money, and…

His leaving had hurt people.

Samaritan's forms were needlessly specific and baroque; there were forms to handle damages caused by meteor showers, forms if you slipped in the shower, different forms if you slipped at a pool. Yet that paperwork had felt like a living organism to Paul, each form serving a specific and perfect purpose…

And Paul had been its heart.

When he'd left, he'd taken Samaritan Mutual's kindness with him. People who didn't know the difference between the *wasp* hive injury form and the *bee* hive injury form might as well have had no insurance at all. That challenge was fair on some objective level – if you had the time to devote to navigating their thousands of forms, eventually Samaritan Mutual had to pay out. But who had the time?

Paul had, once. If he just filled out the right forms, he'd save people.

He'd saved people so often, it had become magic.

And in taking the job at the Task Force, Paul had abandoned his duty.

Nobody at Samaritan blamed him, he realized; he was mad at *himself*, for allowing a cold company to freeze into permafrost. Mr Payne had always run a skinflint operation, but Paul's absence had allowed Mr Payne to rip even more people off.

Now he had to kiss the old man's muscled ass until the skinflint gave him the information he needed....

"Mr Tsabo?"

Paul didn't recognize the cheery voice – but as the Mundane Who Killed 'Mancers, strangers often greeted him enthusiastically.

Paul didn't know the woman – a Samaritan Mutual secretary, to judge from her prim, 1960s-style dress – but the tray of Dunkin' Donuts this cheerful Asian woman carried was all too familiar.

"A gift from an old friend," she said. She grinned as she handed Paul the donuts, the excited smile of someone happy to be in on the gag.

Inside the lid, on a Post-It Note: "CALL ME, YOU YUTZ."

"Tell the old rascal we miss him," said the secretary. "The company's just not as interesting without his stories."

"Will do." Paul dialed his old friend Kit's number, holding the phone away from his ear so he wouldn't be deafened.

"*Boychik!*" Kit's voice was scratchy but boisterous, an old Jewish man who'd worn his throat raw extolling various pleasures. "*Finally* you call! What, is the toll call to Florida too expensive for your unemployed ass?"

"Kit, who the hell talks about 'toll calls' anymore? You're going senile in retirement."

"I am going mad with boredom in retirement. No magical cases to investigate. The beach is nice, but it's not the same as being on the hunt."

"So you gossip."

"It's what old men do. And Valentine, she likes to blab once in a while. Good kid. A little low on the self-control, a little too into the Vanilla Kremes – speaking of which, what's your choice?"

Paul looked down at the donuts, plucked out a chocolate glazed. "I'm taking a glazed today. Do you ever stop with the donut psychoanalysis?"

Kit grunted, displeased. "Chocolate glazed isn't your style, bubbie. You changed to a Boston Kreme, after Anathema. From sweet and gooey to crisp and chocolatey. And a man switches donuts when he's on the cusp of a major change."

"My donuts have nothing to do with my state of mind."

"Really?" Paul practically heard Kit raise an eyebrow. "So with the firefight and the firing and the fights with your daughter, you deny you're on the cusp of a major change?"

Paul swallowed his donut.

"As I thought," Kit concluded. "You're running hot. And you're going to blow this interview unless you listen to your old friend Kit."

"I'll just kiss that rat bastard's ass until my lips turn brown."

Kit sighed. "He knows you hate him, boychik. He'll push your buttons to see where your loyalties lie."

"My loyalties? What about *his* loyalties!? He–"

Kit clucked his tongue in loud mock sympathy. With a shock of shame, Paul realized he was practically shouting into the phone.

Maybe Kit had a point about him running hot.

"Yes, he refused the surgeries to repair Aliyah's face after she got burned," Kit said sympathetically. "Yes, he tried to fire you when you started making waves. But... that's not personal to him."

"Not *personal*?" He cupped his hand over the phone. "He would have left Aliyah *scarred*! For God's sake, Kit, it sounds like you *admire* the bastard!"

"Admire? No. But I respect him. Because he lets me live in Florida."

"'Lets' you? Are you under Samaritan Mutual House arrest?"

Kit laughed. "No, silly. But I have a nice pension. It's pricey, living on the coast. How many companies do you know that haven't tapped into their pension funds these days? Not Payne, though. He wouldn't allow it."

"That's sweet, Kit, but... he was going to let Aliyah die."

"Die? No. He paid for Aliyah's hospital bills to keep her alive – he just wouldn't foot the bill for her to be pretty again."

"So you're saying Payne is..." Paul swallowed. "*Good people*?"

"I'm saying the man has his own morality. You think he owes you for the hell he put you through – but Payne won't see it that way. Payne won't hire you for your old job. Payne doesn't need *me*, and *I* was your manager."

Paul grabbed a cruller. This was becoming a two-donut day. "So what do I do?"

"Offer him something he needs. Something he can't get anywhere else. Something profitable."

Paul wished he could hug Kit over the phone. The old man had always been good at refocusing him when he got too angry. "But what if what Payne needs is more than I'm willing to give?"

"Then give it to him. Because I gotta tell you... even from here, I can tell Aliyah needs some help, and fast."

TEN
Manufacturing Benefactors

Even now, Paul had to quell anxiety about pressing the silver button up to Mr Payne's office. Long-time Samaritan fellows called that elevator "the guillotine," as when it descended, heads rolled.

He braced himself as the elevator rose. Kit would be proud: Paul would do anything, anything, to keep his daughter safe.

Even if that meant shackling himself to Payne.

A bell chimed.

The doors opened.

Lawrence Payne's lobby was frugally impressive: just enough flash so bankers wouldn't think the organization was going broke, but not a penny more decoration than necessary. Payne's office lay safeguarded behind a large bank door in accountant's-visor green, imposing enough to send the message: *this is where the money lies*. The Samaritan Mutual logo was engraved on the door in tasteful gold.

Payne's name, famously, was not on the door. He had no ego when it came to his company.

Payne's secretary looked up, coiffed in a 1960s-perfect beehive hairdo and a tight red dress. "Mr Tsabo," the secretary said. "Right on time."

She pressed a recessed button under her desk. The door glided open.

Paul remembered to breathe.

Mr Payne's office was a narrow space lined with steel filing cabinets, jutting all the way up to the ceiling, blocking out the walls. Here, there was no hint the world had advanced beyond the 1960s. A long, narrow meeting-room table was topped with antiquated relics, which carried out their functions inexpertly. There were old typewriters, and mimeograph machines with their pink papers to make copies, ticker-tape machines that still rattled off spools of Morse-code-like stock prices.

It's more a museum than anything else, Kit had once reassured him.

Are you sure he doesn't *use the ticker-tape machines?* Paul had asked.

...no.

Paul stepped in, balancing on his bad legs as he made his way through the narrow spaces. The tight squeeze comforted Paul, reminded him of his old office; he'd liked having everything he needed at arm's reach.

At the far end sat Mr Lawrence Payne, who sat stiffly yet welcomingly – the old-fashioned lord of the manor receiving guests. Payne's stiff white hair was cropped close, his skin so pale and age-thinned it looked like papier mâché plastered across a bullet-shaped skull. He was dressed in a tweed suit, his hands crossed, a thick stack of forms beneath his slender fingers.

Behind Payne stood a tall black man, his cheeks branded with tiny spirals. He stood with a stiffness that spoke of an upbringing in some distant country that disdained American excess – and as if to accentuate that contempt, he took a deep pull on a gigantic cigar, inhaling until the tip burned a cherry red, savoring the taste of smoke.

Then he exhaled – not *quite* in Paul's direction, but rather up towards the center of the room, a huge and thoughtful stream of burned tobacco that seemed in some way to be marking territory with his lungs. Paul's eyes prickled from the scent – a hot, forest-fire smell.

Payne did not acknowledge the smoke cloud above him as it drifted down across the desk, flowing onto the floor. His iceberg-blue eyes swept across Paul like a lighthouse beam, as if to ask, *do we have a problem here?*

Paul did. He knew all the regulations about smoking in the workplace. Smoking was not only a health risk, but a fire hazard in an office so crammed with paperwork. Perhaps that foolishness might have seemed wise back in the 1960s, but today?

Instead, Paul took the closest chair to Payne's desk, and bowed.

Payne interlaced his fingers, pleased that Paul had passed the first test.

"So. The prodigal son returns." Payne's voice had a movie narrator's plummy tones, with the white-mustached tickle of an English accent dropped in. "Oh, Paul. Paul Tsabo. Would that you had bent the knee sooner."

"…sir?"

Payne spread his hands, as if offering the world to Paul. "I was overjoyed when I heard you had been picked to spearhead the New York Task Force. *One of my boys, placed high in the world!* I'd always taken a special pleasure in signing off on your claims, Paul. It was as though I'd filled out those forms my very self."

Paul tried to quell his blush. He was praised so little, these days.

"So when you moved up, as talent should, I thought, *well, here's a man who will keep New York safe.* You'd always found evidence of 'mancy, Paul. If it was there, you furrowed it out."

Payne made a violent digging motion with his fingers to accentuate the "furrowed it out." Paul's embarrassment grew: he'd always *found* the evidence, but hadn't always *reported* it.

"I waited for you to come to me, Paul. You and I, Paul, we're rare coins: living New Yorkers with direct evidence of how deadly 'mancy is. My mother fled from Europe – back when the first broaches ripped across Germany. My poor sisters, devoured by demons – *worse* than devoured. I saw buzzsects, pouring out of the broaches, eating... eating laws. Of *physics*. They... they ate *gravity*, somehow. They chewed away cause and effect. And my sisters, Lisa and Anna, they... they screamed in reverse as the buzzsects devoured the time from their bones. And I... I..."

Payne's taut face slackened with memory. Paul felt a glimmer of sorrow for the old man. He could envision a young Lawrence Payne, carried by his mother to safety, shrieking as he watched the world unravel.

Paul squeezed the Maxi pad taped to his left forearm, blotting up fresh blood. Payne was right; Paul had once healed a broach, but it had left an empty furrow though his skin that would never heal. Those seething buzzsects had gobbled SMASH agents, chewed away magic, devoured an entire factory before Paul had finally driven them back – what must it have been like to be a mundane, watching entire cities consumed by swarms of extradimensional mouths?

No wonder you went into insurance, Paul thought. Insurance battled life's chaos with actuarial tables – you couldn't choose *which* houses would burn, but could turn that destruction into a predictable percentage.

"I'm sorry that happened," Paul said.

Payne seemed startled to see Paul there. He flicked his fingers, dismissing years of history.

"No need for sorry, Paul," he said gravely. "You were there at that botched SMASH operation – the one that broached. You know how bad it would have gotten, don't you? If SMASH hadn't... sealed it?"

Paul had sealed that rift himself. But yes. He understood just how close New York had come to being the focal point for an invasion from an alien dimension.

"Oh, Paul." Payne sagged. "I thought we'd clasp hands to stamp out this world-rending threat. Instead, you snuck in my back door. *Stole* information I would have given. I had to force poor Kit into retirement when I discovered he fed you the information. How can I reward you for that?"

All Paul's sympathy vanished. Kit hadn't told Paul the reason for his retirement.

I gave you eight years of my life, and when my daughter got burned, you tried to fire me so you wouldn't have to pay her claims. The whole reason I fought SMASH forces is because you wouldn't cut me a check to restore Aliyah's face. So how dare you lecture me about loyalty?

The black man removed his cigar and leaned in, sensing Paul's anger. A faint smile curled on his thick lips: *No, please, Mr Tsabo. Tell us what's on your mind.*

"...When did you hire a bodyguard?" Paul asked.

Payne chuckled. "Mr Rainbird is not my bodyguard. He is my head of special HR. He vets all of my specialty hires."

Paul looked up at Rainbird. "How am I doing?"

Rainbird wrapped his lips around the cigar again, inhaling. The tiny scar spirals on his dark cheeks glistened; he seemed to grow larger as he savored the heat within him.

Then he exhaled at Paul, engulfing him in such a torrent of ash-stinking smoke; Paul choked. Eyes watering, Paul remembered feeling around for Aliyah in the scorched apartment, the burning carpet sending toxic fumes into the air, Aliyah shrieking for Daddy in her bedroom...

"Comically," Rainbird said.

Paul stiffened. He didn't know *for sure* that Rainbird had intended to summon up those memories. But Rainbird's toxic grin that told Paul how badly Rainbird hoped to push him into saying something regrettable.

"Mr Payne," Paul ventured. "I'm sorry I didn't contact you earlier..."

"I would have mentored you, Paul. I could have guided you through New York's political snakebeds. Together, we could have equipped New York to ward off any magical threat, and instead you..." He grimaced. "Well, to be honest, I'd have to say you've *weakened* this city."

Paul bristled. "One bad incident does not make a career."

"A bad incident caused by a loose cannon you did not control. By poor staffing. By poor *authority*."

Paul clenched his fists. This was no interview: it was a humiliation conga line. He was tempted, *so* tempted, to tell the old windbag just why the New York Task Force had been ineffective...

But no. He had to get David off his trail. Off *Aliyah's* trail. *Offer him something he needs.*

"I'm not...." Paul swallowed. "Perhaps I am not a natural leader. But as a follower, I saved you millions in claims. I found evidence of 'mancy at sites no one else even *suspected*. And I'll save you *more* money, if you'll hire me. Sir."

Payne's thin lips compressed into a contemplative scowl, a father who wanted to believe his begging son was responsible enough to take the car for the weekend.

"...I'm sorry, Mr Tsabo. No."

"No?"

He spread his hands. "New York has been magically quiet over the past two years. Truth be told, in such peaceful times, there's a reason I felt comfortable demoting Kit to a part-time consultant. Sadly, I run a business. As such, I only cut checks to people who'll benefit me."

You anticipated this, Paul reminded himself. *Now offer him something he can't get anywhere else.*

"What if I told you *why* New York was so damned quiet?"

The regretful look vanished from Payne's face. His nostrils flared, as if he'd scented something particularly tasty. Even Rainbird had paused in mid puff.

"*Do* you know, Mr Tsabo?" Payne asked, arching trimmed white eyebrows.

"It all comes down to Anathema."

"The paleomancer you killed a few years ago. The last time New York faced any serious danger."

"She had access to some deep, *deep* 'mancy. 'Mancy that we still don't understand."

"You *say*." Payne's leatherbacked chair creaked as he leaned back. "You've *claimed* she boasted she'd raise new generations of 'mancers. But we have only your word for that."

"No. I've fought 'mancers before. She was different." *She made Aliyah into a 'mancer twenty years earlier than any 'mancer I've ever heard of.* "If she said she seeded New York with 'mancers, then... she did. And something's *blocking* that."

"Do you know what that 'something' is?"

"No."

Payne snorted through his nose. "So you have a theorem. A–" He whisked his fingers across his desk, as if sweeping everything away. "A sense of a counterforce."

"A counterforce that's kept New York clean of 'mancy."

"And I..." Payne gave a taut little *you're kidding, aren't you?* laugh, looking at Rainbird. "I should pay you to track this... force... down? When it's keeping us so safe from harm? Why would I–"

"Because we could make *every* city as safe as New York."

Payne's laughter wilted. Rainbird froze, still bent over, focused on Paul. Paul drank their confusion in, then reached out to lay his hands on Payne's desk – violating Payne's space.

"Hire me. As a full-time 'mancy investigator. Hire me to find out what makes New York different from all other cities. If I'm right, and I find what's protecting New York, there'll be no more broaches, no more Europe, no more poor Lisas and Annas hurt in magical crossfires."

Payne flushed. "I did not ask you to weigh in on personal matters–"

"And I could give you access to something other insurance companies would pay *billions* for."

Payne squinted, balancing money lust against trust. "Why not get it yourself, if it's worth so much?"

"I have a child to take care of. I need a salary now, or I lose my apartment." That was bullshit – what Paul needed was enough Samaritan Mutual access to throw David's investigators off the scent – but it played to Payne's worst impressions.

"Huh," Payne said. "I thought of all people, *you* would be good with money."

Paul shrugged: *I have many surprises, Mr Payne*.

Payne glanced up at Rainbird, who looked uneasy; Rainbird shrugged.

Payne then hunched over his desk, resting his chin in folded hands, glaring at Paul with an X-ray intensity.

Paul straightened, feeling an insane confidence washing over him: he was the 'mancer-hunter. Every newspaper headline touted his deadliness.

Paul glared at Rainbird, as if to ask, *how am I doing now?*

Rainbird lowered his cigar in confused surrender.

"You might find nothing," Payne said.

"It's true. These last two years may be a statistical fluke."

"Why would I pay you to hunt for something that might not even exist?"

"You risk a little money now in the hopes it pays off big later on," Paul said. "You probably know something about that."

Payne laughed – a rich and luxurious noise, a true laughter Paul hadn't been sure the old man had, a genuine amusement that lasted until Rainbird produced a handkerchief from his suit pocket. Payne's laughter dwindled to chuckles as he dabbed a tear from his eye.

"Very well, Mr Tsabo." Payne squeezed Paul's hand hard enough to remind Paul that Payne had once been a soldier. "Welcome back to Samaritan, my boy."

Paul breathed in cigar smoke, wishing this felt like triumph.

ELEVEN
Unbreakable Bonds of Interlaced Flex

Paul sketched out plans on his legal pad as he rode the subway back home. The car held the usual mid-morning weekday crowd, a motley mixture of students, late businessmen, and weary retail workers heading into their late shifts.

He'd gotten the job. That was step one. Step three was covering his tracks. Step two, however, involved tracking down the King of New York – no sense scrubbing his trail if the King would just drop another dime on him – and *that* was the tricky part.

Step four was Aliyah. But he wasn't going to deal with that right now.

He brainstormed solutions for the first three, writing them down. The pad twitched in Paul's hands. A new sheet flew up, and neat handwriting appeared on the yellow paper, as though written by an invisible pen:

The party of the first part wishes guaranteed confidential access to the party of the second part.

A notary seal indented itself into the paper, waiting for Paul's signature.

Paul covered the legal pad, worried someone might see him – but of course, everyone around him had their faces planted in their cell phones. Oscar's artificially induced good luck stretched out to protect his Flex supplier.

Paul clicked his ballpoint pen and signed the request. A surge of 'mancy left him, but no flux came back; he'd paid for that when he'd brewed that Flex for Oscar a year ago.

"Good," Oscar said from behind him.

Paul jumped; he hadn't even seen Oscar enter the car. "I hate it when you surprise me."

"Ssshhhh." Oscar placed a thin finger over thinner lips. He leaned back in his seat, looking towards the subway doors with the serene air of a man expecting a grand show.

Only the thin ring of crystals around Oscar's nostrils told Paul that Oscar was flying high on Flex.

Paul watched Oscar, an unassuming man who did not look like a grand crime boss, but rather a henpecked accountant. Oscar did not acknowledge Paul's attention; his face was strangely merry, though that might have been the Flex talking. It also explained why he'd left his bodyguards at home; on Flex, the odds were ever in Oscar Gargunza Ruiz's favor.

Oscar tapped his ivory cane expectantly against the subway floor, adjusting his Panama hat. His olive skin had a stylish tan that Paul envied; he wore a custom-fit suit that reeked of tasteful wealth. He could have been at the opera, waiting for the show to begin…

…and one stop later, dreadlocked college students stormed in, wearing sleeveless Che Guevara shirts. A willowy woman brandished a cardboard sign: THE BREAKDANCER BEAT.

"Ladies and gentlemen!" she cried. "May I have your attention? You may think we are ordinary breakdancers, looking for spare change – but no!"

The woman flipped the sign over: THE BREAKDANCER POETS.

"We are here to blow! Your! Minds!"

Grinning at each other under the assumption that they were blowing people's minds, two launched into a series of voluminous slam poetry; two more spasmed on the floor in a mockery of dance moves. The others wriggled their way through the crowd, thrusting self-published manuscripts at people.

This didn't happen often on New York subways these days. But Oscar's Flex-luck had ensured these students had thought this was a perfectly fine idea right now, and Oscar's Flex-luck ensured no policeman would arrive to chase them away until Oscar's conversation with Paul was completed.

"There," Oscar said, content. "Now no one will overhear our conversation."

"*Must* you find me without warning?"

Oscar raised an eyebrow. "Preauthorization before making contact wasn't in the contract. Though I might *make* appointments, if you'd care to manufacture some restriction-free Flex for me…"

"No, that's all right." Paul wouldn't give Oscar a magical drug that could allow his gang to commit the luckiest of murders – so he'd forced Oscar to pre-authorize any usage of the Flex. Oscar had accepted that, only requesting certain drug runs went without a hitch, or that meetings with rival gangs were ambush-proofed. Not things Paul was *comfortable* with, but nothing violent.

Still, Oscar chafed at restraints. And he was smart enough to make his first request *The party of the first part may, at any time, use the drug to locate the party of the second part no matter where he may be* – a clause Valentine had referred to as "lightly ominous."

Fortunately, Oscar ruled with a light hand.

"Mr Tsabo, I must insist you report in to me after any Flex-brewing failure. I dislike getting my information from the headlines. Though you *do* tend to make headlines these days no matter what your identity."

"I'm sorry," Paul said – and he *did* feel sorry. Oscar had always treated Paul with respect. "It's just – there's been a lot going on…"

"*I* understand." Oscar tapped his temple. "The issue is my fellow compatriots."

"It's…" Paul wrung his hands. "I know $1.4 million is a lot, but I'll pay it back…"

Oscar threw his head back and laughed – a loud, generous sound that the poets' beat-boxed verses about government abuses in Guantanamo Bay drowned out.

"You… you don't want me to pay it?"

"No, Mr Tsabo. $1.4 million is *not* a lot. You're a penny-ante slot machine with a Lotto-size payoff. Have you any idea what one batch of Flex does for my business? As investments go, Mr Tsabo, you're among my cheapest."

Paul brightened. "So… you don't care?"

"I didn't say that."

The poets began doing a dance, accidentally jabbing subway riders as they whooped in a bad imitation of Native Americans. Paul tried to read Oscar's face, but those leathery features were impenetrable.

"Well," Oscar said, relenting. "To be clear, *I* don't care. Not much. I like you, Paul. You go out of your way to keep our agreements. You could go to war with us – your bureaucromancy could track us down, Psycho Mantis could rain meteor showers down on our heads. And yet–" Oscar shook his head, looking at Paul with unmistakable fondness "–with all that power, you treat this debt not as an inconvenience, but as an obligation to be settled."

Paul was so relieved, he almost passed out. "Thank you," he whispered.

"Don't." Oscar held up his cane. "The issue is, I am not a single entity."

The poet-dancers started throwing Xeroxed dollar bill confetti.

"I represent a loosely held cabal of conflicting needs. I have bodyguards who covet my power, subordinate dealers longing to best me, superiors who fear my competency. So when I put my faith into someone who doesn't deliver… well, I begin to look weak.

"Your Flex is worth quite a bit to me, Paul," Oscar continued, looking grave. "It keeps accidents from happening. But I need results. Soon. Or people will think I'm your bitch. And when *that* happens... well, are we clear?"

Paul shivered. Valentine had told Paul not to worry about Oscar, telling him she could take that "little punk" if she had to – and she *had* bested Oscar once already. Still, something about Oscar's calm, contemplative nature made Paul tremble.

Valentine's splashy violence looked good in a videogame cutscene, full of gratuitous shrapnel-filled explosions. Oscar's pinpoint violence involved silenced guns, never-to-be-unearthed quicklime pits in construction lots.

"How much more credit do I have?" Paul asked.

Oscar unleashed a crooked grin. "You have a plan! Is it a cheap plan?"

"Somewhat. I need another lab – not a big one, but with a decent-sized bag of hematite – and an opal. *A good* opal. Top tier."

"Top-tier opals are not cheap." Oscar waved a gloved hand to indicate no expense was a problem for him. "Will you be making Flex for me, with this lab?"

"I'll be trapping a King."

Oscar nodded. "I was wondering when you'd get around to that."

Oscar's approval convinced Paul that whatever else Oscar was up to, he was not calling in tips on Paul. Which meant Oscar was not the King of New York – which was good, because Oscar made Paul feel strangely content. Oscar was reasonable. He delivered. He made the rules clear. And it was ridiculous that a criminal should serve that purpose in Paul's life – but by making 'mancy illegal, the government exposed Paul to unthinkable dangers.

In an ideal world, 'mancers would be working for a reliable organization overseen by professionals, properly regulated. Something to help them manage their flux, keep civilians safe.

A school, to teach Aliyah.

A place both Imani and Paul would feel comfortable sending people to.

Instead, Paul had to ally himself with criminals, worry about his own protection. As a 'mancer, no law could shield him.

Oscar contemplated the costs. He watched as the breakdancers did the Worm up and down the car, while the poets donned priests' collars and wore paper manacles of Xeroxed cash, shrieking, *"The power of money compels you! The power of money compels you!"*

"I'll get you the equipment on one condition," Oscar whispered.

"And that is?"

The pad twitched again. Paul read the additional clause.

"I think we can manage that," Paul murmured, signing off on the new agreement. He felt a tingle as a surge of newly authorized luck flowed from Oscar's Flex-fueled body somewhere further down the subway line.

The car jerked to an abrupt stop. The people seated were *almost* flung forward; the people riding held on to their straps. But the subway poets, who were not at all paying attention, were flung bodily into the back door.

Oscar raised his white-gloved hands and applauded.

TWELVE
Garbage Angels

Valentine had insisted on driving them all to the Flex lab, and had made a conscious effort to clean up her beater of a car. She'd removed the usual tide of crumpled Burger King bags from the floor, and had even bought a Donkey Kong-shaped air freshener to hang off the cracked rear-view mirror.

What she had *not* done was vacuum the seats. There were dead ants on the car seat that had gotten mired in an old milkshake stain.

Valentine looked at Paul. "Everything OK?"

Paul contemplated what that sticky mess would do to his suit.

Then he got in the car.

Paper and plastic crunched behind him. There was no *seat* visible any more, just garbage so high that Aliyah spread herself out in it, thrust her arms into the detritus, moved her arms back and forth.

"Look!" she cried. "I can make garbage angels!"

Valentine started to laugh, but muffled it when she saw Paul's disappointed stare.

"You couldn't clean out the back seat, too?" he asked.

"Hey, I didn't think we'd have kidtacular company today. Hasn't been SOP to bring the munchkin along to our drug brews before."

"But you went to the effort to clean out the front seat," Paul spluttered. "Why not just keep going, and... and do the... do the whole..."

His argument wilted under Valentine's oblivious gaze. She squinted her remaining good eye, trying hard to follow his argument, but not quite getting there – it really *hadn't* occurred to her to clean beyond the absolute minimum of what she had to.

Paul looked in the filthy back seat. Valentine had lost her apartment to flux, doing 'mancy to try to save Paul's ass from an incoming SMASH team, and then she'd slept in that garbage-strewn car for three weeks while she'd hunted Paul down to save him.

So Valentine's car was a little dirty.

He reached back and peeled a desiccated Twizzler out of Aliyah's hair.

"Thanks for the ride," Paul said.

Valentine brightened. The embarrassment vanished, replaced with bonhomie.

She stuck one bruised elbow out the window as Aliyah felt around for the seatbelt – and then turned on the *Halo* soundtrack and pulled out into the street.

Paul never asked how Valentine managed to afford a car in New York City, a place infamously hostile to vehicles, but he suspected some usage of videogamemancy. They drove, the engine seizing up sporadically, to the place Oscar had designated as today's Flex lab.

Paul wished he'd rented a nice car for the occasion. Normally he shrugged off Valentine's sloppiness, but today required scientific rigor.

If they couldn't track down the King of New York and neutralize him, then David would utilize the King's hints a lot better than Lenny Pirrazzini had.

Paul would have felt better in a nice rented Lexus. Something *professional*. Valentine's cheap car reminded him all their efforts were a ramshackle improvisation.

"Surprised you didn't set up the location yourself,"

Valentine said as Paul consulted his notes for the address. "Usually, you're all about getting your control-freak on."

"I'm isolating variables. If this turns up nothing, then I'll choose the next lab."

She winked at him jovially, then screeched out of the way of a delivery truck.

"Whoo," she said. "Winking and driving when you have one eye is *not* recommended."

They pulled up next to an abandoned pharmacy. Paul pulled the key out of the envelope he'd sealed last night and marked, "SITE KEY." They let themselves in and waited for Quaysean and K-Dash.

Aliyah puttered around the shop for a bit, bringing back everything the old store owners had left on shelves, winding up with a pile of dusty candy bars and crumpled Ex-Lax.

"I need my Nintendo."

Paul didn't look up from his checklist. "I told you, Aliyah. No videogames today. No 'mancy at all."

"I don't *want* to do 'mancy. I just might *need* to do 'mancy."

Valentine took a bite of one of the dusty candy bars, spit it out. "You don't get your Nintendo. But if you practice, and get very good like your Aunt Valentine, then you can do videogamemancy *without* holding a controller in your hand."

"I said I don't *want* to do 'mancy!"

"You won't have to today," she said, taking Aliyah's hand and leading her away. "This is just like that *Walking Dead* episode – the one where they were holed up in the pharmacy, all the zombies ready to rip their tender flesh to pieces?"

"You let her watch..." Paul said.

Valentine looked aggrieved. "I wouldn't let her watch the *show*, Paul. This was the *game*. Anyway, Aliyah, let's play hide-and-seek. *Tag!*"

"That's not the way hide-and-seek–" Aliyah protested, then ran off, giggling, after Valentine.

Paul watched as the two darted through the aisles, giggling madly, just another girl and her crazy aunt playing on a lazy afternoon. Paul ached to join them; as a 'mancer family, they had so few moments of fun. Imani had loved this raw joy, making up games with nothing more than two hands and an imagination...

...and the kind that Aliyah could never have as long as Imani didn't know what was going on.

Then he remembered he was here to cover his trail so Imani's husband couldn't track him down.

Before he could ponder that too much, Quaysean and K-Dash pulled into the abandoned strip mall's parking lot. They kissed in the front seat of the U-Haul before hopping out, and though Paul was doubtless not meant to see that, the gesture still somehow made Paul happy. At least *someone* had a love life.

Paul went out to meet them. "Did you get all the paperwork?"

Quaysean handed over a thick manila folder, rubber-banded to keep everything together. "The U-Haul truck rental forms, the ownership forms for this store, the receipt from where we bought the desk, the receipt from the alembics and the silver knives–"

"Each bought at a different store?"

"Yes, Mr Tsabo. The only hitch was the, uh..."

"The hematite."

Quaysean scratched the back of his head. "Yes."

"Because you didn't buy it."

"It's, uh... no legal transaction, to be sure, Mr Tsabo. That shit is guarded."

"Our hematite always arrives in factory-sealed bags. It fell off a truck somewhere, correct?"

"Yes."

"Then you'll need to write down everything involving the truck it came off of. The guard you bribed to look the other way, the company you retrieved it from, the day and time of the transaction, how much you paid."

Quaysean paled. "I'm not... Oscar doesn't like paper trails the way you do..."

Paul squeezed Quaysean's shoulder. "Don't worry. I'll burn the evidence once we're done. I just need it for today."

It was gratifying, to see the trust Quaysean had in Paul. It reciprocated the trust Paul had put in Quaysean. The simplest way of checking Oscar's organization for a mole would have been to tell Oscar to assign different bodyguards to the next brew, leaving K-Dash and Quaysean in the dark – but that would have implied that K-Dash and Quaysean were untrustworthy, and Paul didn't want Oscar to think poorly of them. Paul suspected that once someone instilled a doubt in Oscar, that doubt never faded.

No. He would try literally every other approach before he tested their loyalty.

Paul turned his attention to K-Dash, who was removing the opal from the dashboard.

"You kept that glued to your odometer the entire time, correct?"

"Yes, Mr Tsabo. No breaks yet." K-Dash flashed a gold-toothed grin from behind the windshield and held up the opal –it was top grade, came in a small adhesive case you could stick to any 'manceable surface. Its silver-flecked surface, polished flat, was intact.

"And it's unbroken?"

K-Dash stuck the black-and-gold case out the window, offering it to Paul; Paul estimated its worth around $50,000. Opals themselves weren't rare, but ones pure enough to crack in the presence of 'mancy were. Uncracked ones were rarer still, as angry 'mancers often went after opal manufacturers.

"But," K-Dash said, clambering down from the U-Haul, "I brought the most important thing of all."

He proudly displayed a tray of Dunkin' Donuts.

Valentine lunged for a double handful of Vanilla Kremes. Paul took the chocolate glazed, smiling despite himself.

K-Dash knelt next to Aliyah, holding the tray in her

direction. It looked absurdly incongruous, this lean-muscled, tattooed gangster with a do-rag offering a tiny girl a donut, but it was also somehow heartwarming.

Aliyah snorted through her nose.

"If you're giving information to the King," she said, "I'll hurt you."

K-Dash cringed. He knew Aliyah had once murdered a 'mancer in order to protect her father, and that danger rolled off her in waves. Quaysean moved to stand behind his partner, and Paul saw the absurdity of the situation: a professional enforcer, moving to protect his lover from an eight year-old girl.

But that eight year-old girl, almost nine, was very very dangerous.

"...the *fuck*?" Valentine wrenched Aliyah around to look her in the eye. "How *dare* you talk that way to our friends?"

Paul was relieved: Aliyah still had the decency to be shocked.

"*Someone's* tattling on us," she explained, hurt that Valentine wasn't on the same page. "Why couldn't it be them? They're mun–"

She bit her lip, remembering at the last second that Daddy didn't like that word.

"Because if *we* get busted, so do *they*!" Valentine roared, her face covered in fading bruises. "And those 'mundanes,' little girl, have done more to help us than *you* ever have. They bring us equipment. They protect us. They bring us... they bring us donuts, for Christ's sake."

Valentine thrust a glazed donut into Aliyah's hands. Aliyah quivered, not quite willing to cry.

"Whereas *you*, Miss Prissypants 'mancer – all *you've* ever done for us is get your goddamned Daddy fired. You won't listen when we tell you not to dump flux on us! You've hurt us more than they *ever* will!"

Aliyah turned to Paul, wanting Paul to deny Valentine's words, and Paul... couldn't.

Valentine mouthed at him: *Good cop time?*

Paul hated the way Valentine roughed up Aliyah emotionally and then handed her to him for cuddles. He especially hated how effective it was. In the absence of friends, Valentine's anger was as close as Aliyah got to peer feedback.

"Valentine," Paul warned. "Back off."

Valentine held up her hands in surrender, instantly abandoning the approach. As always, Paul wondered how much of these outbursts were theater.

Aliyah, however, looked stricken by guilt. "…did I really get you fired, Daddy?"

"'Mancy has a cost," Paul reminded her for the ten millionth time. "When you do it, it hurts Daddy. And Auntie Valentine. Do you understand?"

She nodded, looking quite studious. But like any child, Aliyah didn't understand reality. She could merely recite facts.

Valentine shot Paul a steely glance, blaming him for Aliyah's ignorance. Paul looked away, not wanting to face her down now. *I don't want her hurt, but there's no training wheels in this profession*, Valentine had said – except there were, when Paul was around. By siphoning away her flux, he kept her from experiencing the consequences of her decisions. As he watched Aliyah's uncomfortable confusion, it occurred to him that maybe he should let her experience a full blast of flux. Just once.

Then he remembered Valentine's words: *This is magic. She might die.*

'Mancers were rare, simply because most of them got killed by the backlash of their own 'mancy.

He'd find some other way to teach her responsible magic use. He had to.

"And not only is 'mancy dangerous," Paul continued, "Aunt Valentine is right about something else: K-Dash and Quaysean are our friends."

Both raised their eyebrows as if to ask, *We are?* Followed by a prideful inhalation: *We are*.

Aliyah shot a mortified glance at K-Dash and Quaysean – then crept close to her father.

"Daddy," she whispered, pushing her face into his shoulder to hide her embarrassment, "I thought they *worked* for you."

"I worked for Uncle Kit. Some people you work with are friends."

She frowned, as if filing this new revelation away somewhere in a large cabinet marked "ON JOBS." Then she turned to K-Dash and Quaysean – who backed away from her.

"Sorry," she said.

K-Dash shrugged, a casualness that filled Paul with gratitude. "Ain't nothin', little girl." He extended the tray again, tilting it so it pointed at the glazed donut Valentine had pressed into her hands. "That the donut you want, sweetie? You can take another one, if you want."

Aliyah took a cruller off the tray.

But when K-Dash and Quaysean headed back to the truck, Paul watched as Aliyah chucked the donut into a sewer grate.

THIRTEEN

The First Fracture

"I'm *bored*," Aliyah said, kicking her heels against the old pharmacy counter.

"Sorry, kid," Valentine said. "I played tag, and *Walking Dead*, and *Call of Duty*, and… without 'mancy, I'm fresh out of games."

Aliyah whistled. "Mommy knows lots of games."

Valentine bristled. "Yeah, well, that's why I'm your aunt."

Aliyah tensed. Valentine reached over and squeezed Aliyah's foot, as close as Valentine ever came to apologizing.

"Look, you wanna go watch Paul work? There's gonna be some crazy 'mancy going on soon."

She tensed. "Really?"

"Well, Daddy-'mancy."

"Oh." Aliyah slumped. Paul quelled indignation at this quiet insult; Aliyah had never respected his magic. It was, he supposed, the way of all parents – children never seemed to respect their parents' strengths – but he resisted an urge to explain that "Paying the rent" was a power greater than any *Grand Theft Auto* rampage.

But Aliyah had enough to feel guilty about. And the poor girl was in for a long day. By sunset, Paul thought, he hoped to have a lead on the King of New York.

Paul phoned up Lenny; the last thing he wanted was to

spend the day loading and unloading equipment, only to find Lenny had dropped his end of the deal.

"Yo, 'mancer-hunter," Lenny said on the third ring. "You ready to bust some bewitching bitches?"

"Can you keep it down?" Paul asked, remembering how Kit had gotten busted at Samaritan Mutual. "I'm not on the force. You're not even supposed to talk to me."

"Relax those britches, I'm on the snitches. Our grand ol' boss David is up to his nostrils, chasing that paper trail to figure out who bought the Patziki garage. He's *miles* from my department."

That failed to reassure Paul in any meaningful way. "So you'll call…."

"…the moment we hear from the King, Paul. I'll get you timestamps and everything. I know you love precision. You wanna share your reasons, though?"

"Thanks, Lenny."

Lenny's voice overflowed with admiration. "You are the most secretive son-of-a–"

Paul hung up. Quaysean and K-Dash leapt up as Paul glanced at them; they were as bored as Aliyah.

"Just one more thing," Paul said, double-checking his list, which contained each piece of equipment they used to brew Flex. The columns waited for Paul to record the proper information: when the equipment was hauled in, when they were first used, who brought them in.

Bureaucracy was like science: it only worked when you collected the correct data.

"You have the opal on properly?" Paul asked.

"Yes, Mr Tsabo."

"All right. Haul in the desk."

Aliyah perked up a bit as K-Dash and Quaysean brought in the new OfficeMax desk, then slumped again as Paul brought out a stopwatch – aside from a burner cell phone Paul had picked up at the mall, nothing digital was allowed on site – and clicked off an hour's waiting time.

"What's the stone, Daddy?" Aliyah stared at the silvery

rock stuck to the cheap desk. "It's pretty."

"The opal? They shatter in the presence of 'mancy."

Aliyah touched it, then jumped back. "It didn't break!"

"That's because you didn't do 'mancy." Her eyes narrowed mischievously. "And if you do 'mancy here, Ms Aliyah, I will break your butt. That opal is worth more than your Mommy's car."

Aliyah poked at it again, seeming relieved. "So I'm not magical."

"Not until you do 'mancy," Paul explained. "And even then, most opals aren't that accurate. You have to target your 'mancy directly at the person wearing it before the opal breaks. Most people think opals are a safeguard against all 'mancy – but honestly, the ones I could get for the Task Force–"

" – you're not *on* the Task Force any more, Daddy! – "

"–Yes I know, Aliyah, I was using the past tense there, and the ones I *could* get *back then* were government grade. We wore them, and had them placed all around our office, but there are all sorts of ways to cast 'mancy that don't affect people directly."

"Like Valentine changing the furniture in the garage?"

"Good answer, Aliyah. Yes. Those weren't cast directly on anyone, so they didn't crack the government-grade opals.

"But this," Paul said, polishing the opal with a handkerchief, "is a very expensive opal. It shatters in the presence of any 'mancy, no matter how subtle. They have to ship it a special way, routing all the way around Europe so nothing breaks it. If anything magical happens, anything at all… This will break like a mirror."

"You think the King is a 'mancer?"

"I think we need to rule that out."

Paul waited a half an hour – long enough for the King to call in – and then opened up all the drawers, using the desk just like he'd use it to cast 'mancy. Nothing.

"Bring in the legal pads," Paul said.

The rest of the day went like clockwork, which was to

say not particularly interesting when you had to stare at it for hours straight. The legal pads were brought in, and opened up half an hour later. Then the Bic pens. Then the alembics. Then the silver knife.

"Nothing's *happening*, Daddy," Aliyah cried.

"That's science for you. Sometimes things don't happen for long periods."

"But I'm *bored*."

He chucked her on the chin. "It builds character."

"*Ghod*," Valentine huffed. "That is the daddiest thing you could say *ever*. Don't listen to him, Aliyah, all boredom ever builds is naps."

They brought in the sack of hematite, a $50,000 opal pinned to the burlap, put it on a shelf. Half an hour passed. Paul recorded the time. Paul ripped the sack open...

The opal shattered.

"Well," Paul said, satisfied. "That's progress."

FOURTEEN
He Sells Sanctuary

Later that night, Paul spread out the paperwork on the desk in his bedroom. Sure enough, the King had called seven minutes after Paul had ripped open the hematite – just long enough to get to a pay phone. And the 'mancy surge had been small, *very* small; only years of tracking 'mancers had attuned him to this 'mancy.

Someone had tagged the hematite bags, and used them to trace Paul's Flex operations.

Paul closed the bedroom curtains, ensuring privacy, then stacked K-Dash's notes into piles. This was the tricky part. Somewhere between the time some underpaid worker dug this raw hematite from the earth and the time K-Dash bribed a guard named Annabelle Leckie down at a plant in Long Island to look the other way, a 'mancer had gotten his hands on this.

Which was, supposedly, impossible. Mage-grade hematite was closely regulated, guarded by multiple levels of government anti-'mancer protections personally designed by SMASH agents. Yet someone had clearly infiltrated the supply chain to do some extremely subtle 'mancy.

Fortunately, subtle 'mancy was Paul's specialty.

Paul spread his fingers across the receipts, then breathed out; his fingers lengthened and sank deep into the papers, disappearing into a fathomless sea of recordkeeping. The vouchers riffled apart as his fingertips probed through receipt after receipt, extending with a crackle of bone, pushing deep like questing tree roots.

He infiltrated the records, the endless storage web that tracked *this* bag of hematite from the pay stubs of the workers in Australia who had unearthed it, to the freight invoices where it was loaded onto the docks, to the duty taxes from the ship that'd hauled the hematite in to New York, to the truck mileage records when it had been delivered to the processing plant in Albany, to the sampling records taken at the hematite preparation facilities...

Paul reached out with fingers that stretched across continents, in a bureaucratic daze, tapping each invoice to check for that hollow ring of magic. He'd hunted 'mancers for years. 'Mancy had an unmistakable feel he could never quite put into words.

He tapped gently, because something was hunting *him*. But Paul didn't think the King of New York expected Paul to follow him back home.

Paul frowned. He'd been reluctant to attribute the snitching to 'mancy – too slow. He loved magic, and had prepared a safe haven for other 'mancers. He didn't want to believe he'd have to fight a fellow 'mancer, but Paul had been convinced to take the initiative.

He rippled his lengthened fingers; they split at the knuckles, budding into new finger-growths, each finger following its own trail through dusty files and backup computer tapes. Paul was dimly aware of his vine-like curtains of digits combing through the global networks, a probing entity growing through the information storehouses like fingernailed kudzu.

There. Something at the preparation facility glimmered with 'mancy – evanescent enough that Paul almost wrote it off as a hallucination.

The samples as the hematite was refined.

Paul wasn't sure what that meant, but that was

bureaucracy's beauty: you never had to wonder for long. He pulled up the other sampling records, seeing how many had this 'mantic tinge, pressing out gently with his millions of fingertips so as to avoid the government-grade opals studded around the plant.

This was so easy, Paul thought, grinning as if in a pleasant dream, his wrists weighed down by the miles of flesh he'd extruded into the paperwork. Most 'mancers were like Valentine – producing vulgar gouts of 'mancy that twisted the world into something violently different. The government wasn't prepared for whisper-quiet intrusions that changed a few lines on a piece of paper.

He riffled through the records, checking them each in turn for that strange, familiar magical tinge. The plant's records were saturated with this elevator-music 'mancy, so quiet you barely noticed its presence, an insidious thread worming its way through every crevice in the hematite processing plant.

This 'mancy – it had started almost three years ago. Right after Aliyah had killed Anathema. Yet this wasn't Anathema's 'mancy; her magic had made him sick. This 'mancy practically curled up in Paul's fingers like a kitten, a comforting correctness…

He shook his head. The pleasant nature of this 'mancy distracted him. What had happened two years ago? What had been the inciting incident that had tainted this hematite?

Paul wrists were sunk deep into his desk. He wrapped his distorted fingers around the records, sinking deeper into the information. Many things had happened at the plant shortly after Paul had been appointed to the Task Force – the usual promotions, new hires, government regulations – but the most notable was when the plant had changed hands to a subsidiary of a larger mineral processing conglomeration.

Even *that* transaction bore a tinge of 'mancy.

He heard muffled explosions, followed by cheers; Valentine and Aliyah, playing some game with the volume turned up in Valentine's apartment. His throat was dry. How long had he been investigating, anyway? Maybe he should stop...

No. He was close. He clenched his fingers, and his millions of fingertips split yet again, slithering into thousands of small businesses that tried to obfuscate an owner. That sense of comforting magic got closer as he sifted through, somehow familiar as he tracked this thread of 'mancy through shell corporation after shell corporation back to its owner...

Lawrence Payne.

Paul rocked back in his chair, stunned. He would have fallen off, were he not rooted to the desk by his infinitely long fingers. But his flesh tendrils knitted together to tell the full story – the shell corporations were owned by Samaritan Mutual, and Samaritan Mutual was owned by Lawrence Payne, and oh God the King of New York was Lawrence Payne.

And as he realized this, his distant fingers accidentally brushed across another 'mancy-node embedded in Samaritan Mutual. Something within the miles of paperwork flared to life, a buzzing electricity coursing up Paul's dendritic fingers, tracing its way back to him.

Paul yanked away, trying to sever the connection. But bureaucracy was in his blood. And flesh, and bone. He was literally bound to the 'mancy. He could not unknot himself from this paperwork Gordian knot...

"*Valentine!*" he yelled. "*I've figured out who the King is! It's Payne! It's Lawrence Payne! Payne is the King of New York!*"

More explosions. Giggling. They couldn't hear him. And speaking Lawrence's name seemed to accelerate the process. The tracer-'mancy climbed up the knuckled nets of his hands, crawling spiders locking him into place.

He'd used Samaritan Mutual's authority to gain access, and that access homed in on him.

Despite everything, Paul admired the magic's subtlety: Payne was a master. And why not? He must have been doing 'mancy for decades. Why hadn't Paul seen it before?

The reliance on totems in Payne's office: the filing cabinets, the antiquated mimeograph machine, the stock ticker.

They weren't just old equipment; they were *loci*, the tools Payne used to summon his version of bureaucromancy.

Paul had hunted 'mancers for years. But Payne had used Samaritan Mutual to hunt 'mancers for *decades*.

And Paul realized why. It was so simple, why hadn't he thought of this *before*…

The tracer-'mancy finally clambered up to his wrists, signaling its location in a burst of GPS coordinates. The curtains caught fire, a flicker at first, then rippling into flame.

"*Valentine!*" Paul screamed, rattling the desk. "*Valentine!*"

The curtains burned away, revealing the window – but instead of New York City's skyline, Paul saw an endless portal of white-hot fire. It shone like the sun's interior, a swirling flame vortex speckled with black sunspots…

…one of the spots grew larger.

Paul's body prickled with a sheen of sweat; the room heated up like an oven. He stopped screaming. He'd vowed long ago, back when he first met Valentine and thought she'd murder him, that when he died he would do so with dignity.

Though Paul wasn't sure he would die today.

The black spot swelled to take the form of a well-dressed man in a suit, wearing a burning-wood mask. He expanded to human size, then stepped out of the window, his footsteps setting fire to the now-burning bed, puffing on a cigar.

He paused, removing the cigar from the furnace of his mouth.

"Rainbird," Paul nodded in Rainbird's direction, as though Rainbird had shown up to a scheduled business meeting. The dancing flames on Rainbird's oaken mask obscured his face – but he halted in mid-step, rattled by Paul's calm.

"You'd given me a job," Paul said. "You didn't expect me to find you, did you? You planned to… mislead me."

Rainbird flicked ashes off the end of his cigar, not quite acknowledging Paul. But nor did he incinerate Paul – an excellent start.

"And I wouldn't have found you." Paul directed Rainbird's gaze down to his distorted hands, the green-glass shimmer of Paul's bureaucromancy still glimmering across the desk. "Not without my own 'mancy."

Rainbird glanced back through the portal, as if searching for fresher orders.

"You're not killing 'mancers, are you?" Paul asked. "You're *saving* them. I wanted to make a sanctuary for 'mancers. To protect them from a world that would hunt them down.

"The only thing I hadn't considered," he finished, "was that someone might have done it first."

Rainbird sighed, exhaling black coal-smoke, shoulders slumping. He removed his mask; the sigils on his cheeks glowed like burning embers.

"I was assigned to remove the evidence of whoever had tracked Mr Payne's business dealings back to him," Rainbird said. "Normally, Mr Payne does not brook having his orders countermanded. Yet these are special circumstances..."

Rainbird rolled his cigar between his lips, pondering. The flames danced across the bed as he stood, unconcerned, in a raging bonfire, the curtains engulfed in fire, the room filling with smoke.

He was not immune to flame, Paul saw. Rainbird's skin crinkled into burnt ash, consumed, but his flesh regrew around the embered sigils, endlessly renewing itself to stoke his beloved flames. Rainbird's now-naked face was set in a grimace of exultant pain, his cheeks dripping fat as holes opened up to reveal blackened teeth, then healing over once more, pulling strength from the fire that consumed him.

Rainbird's eyes, however, never burned. They were glazed in rapture.

Rainbird shook a caul of fire off his right hand, spattering flames across the carpet. The gesture looked threatening, until Paul realized he was extinguishing his fingers to reach into his pocket for a phone.

Thank God, Paul thought. *Sanity*.

"*Step off, fucknuts!*" Valentine cried. Paul felt a surge of 'mancy as Valentine's magic filled the room – then everything froze. The flames halted in mid-flicker. The smoke clouds turned solid, immobile. Rainbird's hand paused, fingers wrapped around an ancient Bakelite black plastic phone from the 1950s, clublike, the kind that couldn't make a call without being attached to the wall.

The entire world froze within a block of glass, like a picture.

Then the tableau shattered like a broken window. Cracks shivered through reality, crystal shards pulling free, jagged chunks of curtain and fiery bed and smoke tumbling down into an endless void, revealing an empty TV screen.

The world spun as Paul tumbled down into the television...

FIFTEEN
Kick Extreme Super-Bahamut-Style Ass

A green HP bar hovered over Paul's head.

Moments ago he'd been chained to his desk by miles of questing information fingers – but now he bounced on the toes of his artificial feet, back and forth, back and forth.

He willed himself to stop bouncing, couldn't. He was a pixelated game sprite, cycling through the same animation.

The room was transformed into a blocky recreation of his bedroom. Though the bed remained on fire, the flames no longer grew as they consumed the bed. Instead, the same two pillows cycled through identical fire animations, exuding a pillar of smoke that always dissipated as it reached the ceiling. The fragile curtains, which had been blazing away into ash, now rippled with endless flame – threatening to ignite the room, but never progressing beyond their programmed destruction.

Valentine had transformed his bedroom to be as large as a gymnasium – big enough for two teams to face off. She stood off to Paul's left, raising her fists pugnaciously, occasionally pausing to pop a double-barreled middle finger at Rainbird.

Rainbird stood before the fire portal, cycling through his own animation – a man in an asbestos suit, snapping his fingers, generating sparks of flame. He looked supremely irked.

Paul tried to say something. His mouth refused to open. It wasn't his turn.

Valentine's mouth moved; no words came out. Instead, a small blocky menu unfolded over her head, her dialogue appearing one letter at a time:

Paul! We are in a Japanese RPG now! Act as master support while I draw fire!

A pause, as the window stayed long enough for Paul to read it, then unfolded itself the moment he finished the words. Then, another dialogue window appeared over Valentine's head:

...get it? "Draw fire?"
Hee hee hee hee hee.

She snapped her fingers. A menu appeared as she scrolled through the options:

Kick ass
Kick extreme ass
Kick extreme super-Bahamut-style ass.

She chose "Kick extreme super-Bahamut-style ass" without hesitation. Rainbird frowned as an orange diamond appeared over his head. Valentine confirmed her target with a nod, and then did a swirling dance, her diaphanous dress flowing as she summoned something huge from the earth.

Wait, Paul thought. *When did she get a diaphanous dress?*

The apartment floor burst apart as a dragon exploded out from caverns deep underneath New York.

The dragon, whiskered and silvery and baring sharklike teeth, shrugged the roof aside to soar high into the night air, whizzing across a preternaturally black New York skyline before posing next to the full moon.

But it's a waning moon tonight, Paul thought, before going with Valentine's videogame logic.

"*Kiiiiick – assss!*" Valentine shouted, her words echoing across all New York's skyscrapers. The dragon grinned as it heard her command, plunging down from untold heights to smash into Rainbird.

The dragon hit Rainbird like a nuclear bomb detonating.

The world went white.

Small numbers coalesced out of the blackness – **165,739 damage**. Paul was always disconcerted by the way Valentine's games somehow instilled rules knowledge into his head. That damage was tremendous, an *end-game* amount, damage that would obliterate most normal bosses.

But as the light dimmed from the dragon's nuclear fury, Rainbird was still standing.

He adjusted his collar. A dialogue box popped over his head.

My turn....

Valentine's eyes went wide. A dialogue box appeared over her head.

...crap.

Rainbird summoned his own menu, selected from his own list:

Conflagration
Inferno
Supernova

He selected "Supernova," then moved the orange targeting reticule to over Valentine's head. He breathed in, his lungs sucking in all the flame from the apartment – which was completely healed from all the dragon damage as though the Bahamut attack had never happened. Rainbird's chest glowed an ominous blue-white, his body armored in flames, the room thrumming as Rainbird smashed a fist into the floor and opened up a channel to the Earth's fiery heart.

He lifted his hands; a tide of magma smashed into Valentine, burning her flesh to blackened bone. Paul strained against his animation, trying to scream – but it wasn't his turn to react.

Valentine's body appeared from nowhere, seemingly unhurt despite having burnt to ashes a moment before. Numbers popped above her head: **888,888 damage**. The eights were little skeletal heads, crumbling to ash as Valentine wobbled unsteadily.

Then she collapsed, unconscious. A glowing red status

appeared above her: **VALENTINE is down!**

Then it was Paul's turn.

A menu appeared above Paul's head, which somehow he could read despite it hovering over him:

Papercuts

Analyze

Item

Dammit.

Paul bounced from foot to foot – this damnable sprite form left him no choice but to bounce from artificial foot to orthotic boot, an activity both painful and pathetic. The strange little dance, the menus, all accentuated the fact that Paul wasn't any good in a one-on-one physical confrontation. He'd hoped for an option like "Sword Swarm" or "Mantis Attack," but no.

Papercuts.

Without Valentine or Aliyah to back him, a mugger could take Paul down, let alone some fire-touched phoenix avatar – and Valentine was down.

He scanned the options again. No "retreat" option. No "dialogue" option, either; he wished he could tell Valentine they didn't need to fight, that Rainbird could be negotiated with, though maybe the attack had changed Rainbird's mind. Paul flicked back and forth through the menu, examining his three options, uncertain which to use.

Paul wasn't sure, so he selected "Analyze." The menu buzzed and flashed red.

Are you sure you don't want an item?

What item could he possibly want at a time like this? He selected "Analyze" again. Another buzz.

Are you sure you don't want an item, Paul?

Paul looked over at Valentine, who, though unconscious, seemed to be pointing to the items. He chose that option, which opened up a submenu with sorts of items: healing potions, speed potions, status removal effect potions, Phoenix Down....

He moved the cursor over the Phoenix Down potions.

"Revives any one character," said the description.

Hint hint, Paul.

Paul selected the Phoenix Down. A golden feather shot out from between his palms to hover over Valentine, showering her in golden sparkles that tugged her to her feet. Her HP bar refilled itself as she steadied herself, then cracked her knuckles.

You're one hell of a boss monster, Valentine's dialogue box said. But I am the game. And you are going down.

Rainbird struggled to speak, but it wasn't his turn. Yet before Valentine selected from her menu, a chime of triumph sounded and someone ran into the room in a puff of smoke:

ALIYAH has joined the party!

Even in sprite form, Aliyah looked nervous. Paul knew why: all her worst moments had happened in burning rooms. Anathema had trapped her in a blazing fire, burning her horribly, and when she'd become a 'mancer she'd incinerated an apartment building in the process.

It was so brave, for Aliyah to enter the flames. She must have hesitated outside, working up the courage to fight for her father – but now Aliyah was in *real* danger.

Yet Rainbird... stopped.

The room thrummed with 'mancy – and Rainbird's endlessly shifting sprite paused, stooping down to examine the tiny, scarred child who'd entered the battle. The sigils on his cheeks burned bright with admiration.

He took an experimental step towards her. Aliyah held her ground, her cheeks puffing out, refusing to give way to the blazing figure before her.

The flame... Rainbird said in a dialogue box. It has forged you, little one.

Aliyah cocked her head, not giving him ground. Instead, she raised her Nintendo DS high, ready to strike him down with gamefire.

The apartment shuddered as Valentine tried to regain

control of her game, but Rainbird broke free to bow to
Aliyah. He turned, ambling away despite Valentine's best
efforts, to disappear back into the fire portal. The window,
now a molten pane of glass, shattered in the cool night air.

RAINBIRD has fled!

Valentine, as scripted, did a ballerina twirl and shook her
hips lasciviously before holding up an Xbox game controller
in triumph. The room faded back to real life – still on fire,
the flames stoked by the fresh inrush of oxygen from the
shattered window.

Aliyah screamed, getting out her Nintendo DS and
screaming *"ICE! ICE! ICE!"*, scribbling it on the pad as if
she wanted to stab it. The flames crystallized into dripping
icicles.

Valentine flopped down onto the burnt mattress, not
caring that it was still smoldering.

"That guy..." She wiped the sweat from her forehead.
"He fought like he didn't know what flux was. What the
hell are we gonna do against that, Paul?"

Paul looked at the shattered window, the soaked plaster,
the ruined bed.

"Well, first we're going to call in the super to clean up
this mess," he said. "Then we'll talk to Rainbird's boss."

SIXTEEN
No. There is Another.

Valentine lied and told the superintendent that the curtains had caught fire due to a candle, and they'd thrown buckets of water at it until it had gone out. Which earned her a stinkeye, but the super got some plywood from the supply cabinet and hammered it in over the empty windowframe until they could call in a window repairman.

"You just lost your deposit," the supervisor told Paul.

Paul thought of Rainbird's inferno. "Coulda lost more than that," Paul replied.

The inspections took a couple of hours, as did the paperwork, which allowed Paul and Valentine to carefully bleed off their stored flux from the fight: the elevator broke down as they took it to the super's office, the fire inspector fined them for leaving an open flame in a hazardous area, part of the wall pulled out as the plywood was nailed in.

Once everything was fixed as well as it could be, and their flux level was nice and empty, the doorman called.

"There's a... a limo waiting for you," the doorman said, confused. Paul knew he was, in the doorman's estimation, a mild up-and-comer in New York's political field, but certainly not a limo guy.

"Thanks, Maurice," Paul said, pleased to bollix expectations. "We'll be down shortly."

Valentine scratched the backs of her hands, a boxer preparing for her next fight. "So that's…"

"Payne. I'm sure of it. Once Rainbird saw I was a 'mancer, his whole demeanor changed. I think they've been working to protect 'mancers the whole time."

"If you're right, *Payne* is the King of New York! If he's so protective of 'mancers, why'd he call the cops on us?"

"I'm pretty sure he's going to explain once we get into that car."

"Yeah, and I'm sure the limo has FREE CANDY stenciled on the side. I'm questioning the wisdom of locking ourselves inside a limo with, you know, a crazy pyromancer."

"And a bureaucromancer – I mean, *another* bureaucromancer."

"Oooh!" Valentine bugged her eyes out. "Maybe he'll revoke my W-2s!"

"You can't revoke a tax form, you can only–"

She flicked gloved fingers at him. "Whatever. I'm a little more worried about the guy who can *barbecue my bones*, Paul."

Paul should have bristled at how Valentine shrugged his 'mancy off – but instead, he felt lessened. He hadn't had time to fathom what Payne's existence meant, but…. Until now, he'd been the master of his own unique magic.

After seeing the immense complexity of Payne's spells, Paul realized he was a second-rate bureaucromancer in his own city. Worse, he couldn't shake the feeling that maybe he'd somehow inherited his powers from Payne – he hadn't become a 'mancer until he'd worked at Samaritan Mutual for years. Had he absorbed something from Samaritan's atmosphere?

Paul felt a mild depression coming on. He shook it off. Now was not the time for an identity crisis.

"We have to talk to Payne," Paul said. "Would you rather chat with New York's oldest bureaucromancer at his office? Surrounded by his forms and typewriters?"

"All right, yeah, yeah, we can't exactly negotiate our

safety through text messages. Especially when Payne's got a guy who can teleport through fires. But…"

She glanced over at Aliyah, who stood halfway behind a door, making only a token effort to pretend not to listen.

Paul knelt down to grasp her shoulders. "You understand coming with us is dangerous, right, honey?"

Aliyah trembled, but her face was grim. "I protect my Daddy."

"If I told you to stay home," Paul asked, "Would you listen?"

"If I told *you* to stay home, would *you*?"

Valentine laughed. "OK, points for Gryffindor."

"I think we should take her. It's not safe, but… I don't even know what safe *is* any more. I suspect Payne has access to a lot more 'mancers than just Rainbird. If Payne *is* out to get us, then leaving Aliyah at home might make him send a couple of, I dunno, ninjamancers after her. At least this way we know where she is…"

Valentine brushed her hair back angrily. "This is *just* like the *Walking Dead* game. Reams of shitty options packed with risk, none good."

"So we bring her?" Paul technically had the last word on all matters Aliyah, but he never felt right unless Valentine agreed.

"I think if things go tits-up, it's the call I can most live with. And…" She knelt down, got the Xbox controller she wore on the bandolier around her waist. "It's not like my girl didn't, you know, take down an entire squadron of cops by herself the last time someone pissed her off."

Aliyah raised her Nintendo DS somberly and bumped controllers with Valentine.

They all changed clothes – Paul always felt more authoritative in a crisp blue power suit, and Valentine's dress had been ruined in the fight. She showed up in a Bad Religion newsprint T-shirt with a ragged cut-off plunging neckline, and faded skin-tight jeans with fluffy claw marks showing patches of pale skin all up and down her thighs.

Aliyah, however, dressed in her best school uniform – a bright burgundy shirt, a plaid skirt, sneakers, her Nintendo DS strapped into her backpack. It was, Paul realized, the closest Aliyah had to business wear.

"All right," Paul said. "Let's go."

They walked down to the lobby, holding hands the whole way, where Maurice the doorman looked anxious. They followed his gaze to the obscenely long black limo on the street. Such cars were common out by the UN, but a rare sight in this district.

The car's silver trim gleamed, familiar to Paul for no reason he could name. It looked imposing and old-fashioned, a classic build; the window whirred down to reveal Payne's sour soldier's face looking out at them.

Then a sunny smile broke over the old man's face, a smile that Paul would never have guessed hid inside those old, crusty features.

"*Paul!*" he yelled, opening the door to wave them in, thrilled as a kid at Christmas. "*You clever bastard! You rooked me! You completely rooked me!*"

SEVENTEEN
Invite to the Prom

They clambered into the limo, which seemed as large as a nightclub – an effect further bolstered by a low bar filled with cut crystal glasses that sat between them and Payne. The minute Rainbird pulled the door shut, tinted windows blocked out the light, leaving the limo lit by dim pseudo-gaslight lamps attached to the red velvet walls.

Payne tapped the partition. The driver, obscured by smoked obsidian glass, pulled into traffic.

Paul wiggled back in the seat to slump against the window, sprawling more than he'd like; this limo was slung low so that you had to lean back in a kingly fashion, spreading your legs out for balance. Aliyah curled protectively at his side, shooting dark death glares at Rainbird.

Paul squinted at the interior.

"I know this car."

Payne winked. "Bet you do."

"This is… this is the limo I took Imani to prom in."

Payne clapped his hands merrily. "Not *the* limo, Paul – I'm not that powerful – but the same model. The same memories."

Paul suppressed a goofy grin, then squeezed Aliyah's hand. "Your mother, she… well, she liked making an impression. And for prom, sure, I mean, *any* limo is impressive to a teenager, but Imani wanted the finest limo in New York. She dreamed about it. She never asked me, but... I knew how important it was to her. I remember scrimping, and saving, and..." Paul sighed.

"When she emerged from that limo, she was the most beautiful thing I had ever seen. The other girls wore these puffy abominations that made them look like pastel-blue marshmallows, but your mother – she'd sewn her own gown. Pure gold. She looked like an empress. I knew I'd propose to her the minute I got on the force."

"A grand and glorious future, Paul," Payne said solemnly, reaching across to deposit a bubbling glass of champagne into Paul's hand. "And you, my friend, have just received an invite to the greatest prom in New York City. The secret dance, if you will."

Valentine snorted as she took the champagne.

"Come on, Valentine," Paul asked, reaching over to nudge her. "You didn't go to prom?"

She clasped the glass to her chest with a frown, conspicuously not drinking it. "Boys didn't ask girls like me to *prom*."

"Young boys are notoriously stupid." Payne toasted Valentine with his champagne. "They overlook uncut diamonds in pursuit of colored glass baubles. But you, my dear – you've got *power*."

Valentine smirked, flattered – then pulled back angrily. "Then why were you trying to *kill* me?"

Payne chuckled, embarrassed, covering his mouth. "Oh, I wasn't trying to kill *you* – I was trying to undermine *him*!" He tipped his glass towards Paul.

"That's supposed to make me feel better?"

"Not *Paul* Paul," Payne explained, making little fluttery gestures in Paul's direction. "The *other* Paul. Paul Tsabo, famed 'mancer-hunter. Paul Tsabo, leader of the New York Task Force – a man who, if he was successful, would encourage the mayor to pour more money into local 'mancer suppression. A man who could potentially be more effective than SMASH." Payne gave the amiable shrug of someone caught with his hand in the cookie jar. "*That* man,

I admit, I wanted to ruin. That's why I only fed clues to his squad when Lenny – the least competent person on Paul's team – was on duty, and *only* when Paul was off duty. I was trying to goad the Task Force into a confrontation against Psycho Mantis – something big and splashy, knowing they would get *pureed* going head-to-head against the violence of a videogamemancer... providing New York with front-page-friendly proof that Paul Tsabo wasn't up to the task..."

Paul doubted Valentine even realized she was reaching over to protect Aliyah. "You put us in *danger*!" Valentine said. "What if they'd gotten us?"

Payne produced a legal pad. With a flare of magic, he pulled up a list, then licked his thumb and began going down it. "Two helicopters damaged, worth $600,000 apiece. Seven squad cars totaled. Thirty broken bones, at least $340,000 in hospital bills, and that's not counting the inbound therapy for PTSD." He whistled, arching his eyebrows at Aliyah – who refused to acknowledge him, never taking her gaze off of Rainbird. "And that's *the child*. Am I to believe her mentor can perpetrate *less* mayhem?"

Valentine wriggled in the seat, secretly pleased. "All right. I *do* bring the noise."

"I admit, I disliked endangering a fellow 'mancer – but Psycho Mantis had already taken down a squadron of SMASH agents. I was equally confident she'd wreck Paul Tsabo's career."

Payne clapped his hands, excited. "Still, how was I to know the man who ran the Task Force – a man famed for killing 'mancers – was, instead, trying to save them? How could *you* have known the man who ran this tight-fisted insurance company only did so because insurance was one of the first places people notified when something odd happened? We couldn't have been more at cross-odds, Paul, because we were *both* playing for the long game!"

Paul blushed. "I guess that's what happens when you have two bureaucromancers in the same city."

Payne pursed his lips. "...Bureaucromancy?"

"What do *you* call it?"

Payne sipped his champagne thoughtfully. "*Bureaucromancy*. That's a good name for what we do, Paul. Far better than mine. In fact, if you don't mind, I think I'm going to steal that. Rainbird!" Rainbird pulled his eyes away from Aliyah. "Mental note: from now on, it's bureaucromancy."

"Very good, sir." Rainbird lowered his gaze to watch Paul's daughter again. There was something about the way he took Aliyah's discomfort as a spectator sport, taking long luxurious draws on that omnipresent cigar, that rubbed Paul the wrong way.

"...would you mind not staring at my child?" Paul asked.

Rainbird winced, sullenly taking his cue from Payne. He lifted his cigar into the air, drawing smoky spirals in the air with the tip; Aliyah's gaze moved to match it. "My apologies, Mr Tsabo. But I'm afraid it's your daughter who is staring intently at me."

"Aliyah. Don't *glare* at him." Aliyah ignored Paul. He moved to shake her.

Rainbird leaned across the bar to grab Paul's wrist. Rainbird's fingers felt like hot plates fresh from the oven, not quite hot enough to sear flesh but enough to hurt.

"She's *terrified* of the flame," Rainbird said. "Watch her face, Mr Tsabo; where other children would hide behind their mothers' skirts, your daughter refuses to give ground. Show her what she fears, and she digs in."

Paul had that bewildered feeling he often got with Valentine, that there was some interaction here he wasn't quite equipped to get. "Regardless. She's my daughter, and you will stop."

Rainbird drew closer. Paul flinched. He couldn't help himself. Rainbird had the dull gaze of a man who'd have no problems extinguishing his cigar in Paul's eyeball....

Paper burns, Paul thought, frightened. Valentine's hand dropped to her controller. Aliyah swung her backpack around to yank her Nintendo DS from the webbing...

Payne snapped his fingers. "Rainbird! Put it out."

"But–"

Payne's cold blue eyes glared. There were now two monsters in this vehicle, and the old man was scarier. "*Extinguish it.*"

Rainbird hissed, scowling, and stubbed the cigar out in his palm. He curled his fingers around the wound, which glowed, and glared ferally at Payne.

Payne clucked his tongue. "I didn't tell you to hide your flame, Mr Rainbird. I told you to *extinguish* it."

Payne unscrewed the cap on a water bottle and held it out to Rainbird.

Rainbird breathed through his teeth – teeth that were now blackened ash – and pried open his wounded hand, revealed a smoldering pile of sizzling flesh. He took the bottle, eyes closed in terror, fingers quivering like a junkie.

As Rainbird poured a splash of water in, it caused a hiss of steam like a bucket over a campfire. Aliyah made a strangled noise and hugged her Nintendo.

"It's all right, child," Payne assured her. "There's no shortage of fire where we're going. If he has to ride home without his precious burning, well, perhaps he should learn to be polite to his superiors."

Aliyah pulled away from Paul, pressing her fingertips into her cheek scars. She traced the patterns on the ridges of her old burns, brow furrowed, as if trying to solve a vexing puzzle.

Paul reached over to squeeze her foot. She kicked his hand away.

"I don't think you understand the magnitude of what you've uncovered today, Mr Rainbird." Payne sounded reasonable, once appeased – but Rainbird was nearly insensate, rubbing his hand against his neck to sop up the last of its residual warmth. Rainbird looked smaller, boyish. "Paul, if you wouldn't mind showing Mr Rainbird who he's dealing with?"

Payne leaned over to proffer Paul a legal pad. It buzzed with 'mancy, faint lines jiggling on formal yellow paper. Paul took it, turning it over in his hands.

"...I'm afraid don't know what you want me to do here, Mr Payne."

"Call me Lawrence. And we are on a journey. Our driver has a destination. I'm not intending to surprise you with the location. Nor do I intend to tell you where we are going."

Valentine shifted in her seat, as if plotting the easiest methods of blowing out a door. Paul held up a hand.

"It's all right, Valentine. I know what he wants."

She arched plucked eyebrows. "You do? Because I kinda feel like I'm drowning in a sea of hidden intentions."

"Hidden to you, maybe." Paul studied the pad, taking the mechanical pencil that Payne offered him. He tilted the pad towards Aliyah so that she could watch, if she wanted; she turned away, disinterested as always in Daddy's 'mancy. "Know how I complain whenever you put me in some game and I don't know what the hell I'm supposed to do?"

Valentine winced. "Ugh. Is *this* what it's like for you?"

"I'm assuming, yeah."

She sat the champagne glass on the bar, looked out the darkened window. "Whoo, I owe you a *boatload* of retroactive apologies. Mental note: add more tutorials."

But Paul was already delving into the layers of shell corporations that swirled around Lawrence Payne. When he looked up, he saw Payne wreathed in cold blue numbers, stock market tickers circling protectively around him.

Now that Paul knew what to look for, he slipped through Payne's defenses effortlessly, shucking aside the false trails.

Paul squeezed his eyes shut – and when they opened, his eyeballs were white as ledger paper, inscribed with small dollar signs scrolling up his eyelids.

"You own a private mental hospital near Hudson Valley that hasn't accepted an outside request in ages," Paul said, his voice booming like a CNN anchor. "You don't advertise – also rare for a private institution. The Peregrine Institute isn't even ranked on US News and World Report's list of mental health care facilities. All your staffing records list people who don't work on-site – except for a few discredited psychologists you list as 'consultants.' Yet you funnel *millions* in charitable contributions to it."

Rainbird, startled, looked over at Payne's smug grin.

"So," Paul finished. "When we get to the Peregrine Institute, how many 'mancers will I find under your care?"

"*That's it!*" Payne cried. He launched himself halfway across the bar, spry for an old man, to grab Paul's bleeding arm.

"I told you how you and I were one of a handful of people in New York who'd witnessed a broach." Payne squeezed the blood-soaked Maxi pad strapped to Paul's left forearm as if to emphasize just how dangerous the broach had been. "But reality only tears when 'mancers are *at odds*. Germany is cut to ribbons because mundanes feared us, shoved us to warfare, made us fight – so when I got to America, I vowed I would make a haven for 'mancers. So we could live in *harmony*."

He released his grip, his face hollowed. Paul saw the strain it must have taken to create a hidden sanctuary and *keep* it hidden for the past half a century.

"Let's be honest, Paul: I'm pushing eighty. Rainbird is effective at what he does, but most 'mancers – well, they're either not as powerful as you and Valentine and your darling daughter, or they're not suited for leadership. I thought when I died, this – it would dissolve. But now I have someone who can catalogue everything I have, maintain it…"

Valentine straightened. "So OK, you've got millions of dollars, a huge company and a mysterious wonderland at your disposal."

"Yes."

"That makes you Willy fucking Wonka, doesn't it?"

"It does."

She whistled. "And that makes little Charlie Bucket here…"

"Indeed, Ms DiGriz. Mr Tsabo here is the best candidate to be my rightful successor. Assuming the 'mancers under my protection accept him, of course."

"Fuuuuuck." Valentine downed her champagne glass in one gulp.

EIGHTEEN
The Masque of the Red Tape

As the limousine pulled up the winding driveway to the Peregrine Institute, Paul felt a great tension unclench in his chest. The gatehouse had an attendant in a crisp white uniform who checked their papers before allowing them in. Groundskeepers raked leaves off the vast lawn and stuffed them into bags. A delivery truck sat out front, with a cook signing in a load of fresh groceries.

"We have seventeen 'mancers in residence." Payne's voice took on the plummy tones of a tour guide. "Most of my employees here are unaware of who they're taking care of. They're told – correctly – that these are special-needs patients on a retreat from the world. We imply my clients are celebrities who value their privacy – which, as far as I'm concerned, is true. They're paid well to maintain our clients' confidentiality. Only a trusted handful know who they're really dealing with."

Aliyah, however, bolted halfway out of her seat. She had the joyous beam of a kid waking up on her birthday. "Seventeen 'mancers?"

Payne laughed indulgently. "Yes, my sweet girl. Not quite the hundreds that Anathema promised, but her assault on New York *did* create an uptick. We save as many as we can, but it's difficult – they're such helpless creatures."

"Helpless?" Valentine asked. "I held off a SMASH squadron by myself. Seems like–" She counted on her fingers "– seventeen 'mancers, *plus* your bureaucromancy, would let you take over NYC at will."

"If only every new recruit was as powerful as you," Payne lamented. Valentine preened despite herself. "Most 'mancers we find are low-key, possessing only a trick or two. Useful in the right circumstances, but don't expect them to destroy the Institute with a wave of their hands."

Valentine sized up the Institute – a sprawling two-wing, three-story marble building covered in ivy. The crenellations up top were made from fine white marble, the bushes below were trimmed into playful dog shapes tussling in leafy abandon, lending a festive air to the grounds.

But hints of the Institute's true ability poked through, if you knew where to look. The Institute's entryway had large steel gates, ready to be slammed shut in case of emergency – necessary reinforcement in case the cops came knocking. All the windows had thick steel shutters ready to drop into place.

And if you peered *very* closely, you could see sniper holes carved into the crenellations.

Yet the Peregrine Institute's forbidding nature calmed Paul. It had size. It had scope. It had *staffing*. The built-in defenses spoke of planning.

Up until now, Paul had been on his own, guessing the best way to try to raise Aliyah. Here, there were protocols. Payne had run this place in secrecy for years; there would be regulations formed from experiences.

The Peregrine Institute had professionals who knew how to train 'mancers, and that thought filled Paul with glee.

Aliyah bounced on her tiptoes, pressing her face against the window, vibrating like Paul had only seen her on Christmas morning. And not even recent Christmas mornings. Paul hadn't seen her that eager to be anywhere since – well, since before the fire.

She waved him over, whispering into his ear so the others wouldn't hear.

"Is that my new school, Daddy?" she asked.

Paul's throat hitched. He would finally have help, raising Aliyah. He nodded.

She hugged him.

"Thank you." She leaned in closer, wanting to make her gratitude a private present to her father. "Thank you, Daddy...."

"I *could* destroy that with a wave of my hands," Valentine boasted, polishing her fingernails on her dress's shoulder. "A big mansion like this goes boom in every cutscene."

"Which is why we're *quite* glad to have you, believe you me," said Payne. "It's all fine and well to have a culinomancer make you a grilled cheese without a scrap of trans fat, but that's useless once the guns come out. And besides...." Payne pursed his lips, evaluating Valentine. "If you're as good as I hope you are, perhaps you'll be one of my trusted agents who rescues the poor dears before SMASH gets to them."

They cruised to a stop at a set of bulkier gates, this one with tire spikes embedded in the ground. A trio of uniformed guards, wearing holstered guns, emerged from a security booth to wave them through. The limo pulled around towards the rear entrance.

Here, at the Institute's rear, looking over the sprawling green fields, the shutters were rusted shut and covered with dead ivy. The friendly topiary gave way to NO TRESPASSING signs. Shadows fell over the limo, cast by overhead trellises, and Paul guessed that's what stopped any satellite imagery from picking up anything odd here.

The limo cruised to a halt before the shallow marble steps leading up to the Institute's rear entryway. This one had a single steel door just wide enough for one person to enter at a time, rimmed with heavy automated bolt locks and a metal box mounted at the side of the door at water-fountain height. It took a moment for Paul to identify the box as a retinal scanner.

"Is that them?" Aliyah's voice was a high-pitched squeal

of delight. Payne gave her an indulgent smile. "Is that where the 'mancers are?"

"Yes. We just have to go over the rules, and then you can meet my 'mancers."

"All seventeen of them?"

"Sixteen. You've met Rainbird," he allowed. "And... well, Mr Rainbird may be the only 'mancer you meet today. Most, well, they keep to themselves. And that's the second most important rule here, Aliyah – not just for you, but for Ms DiGriz and Mr Tsabo as well. Your room at the Peregrine Institute is your own. No one else may enter your room without your permission – or you theirs. Your space is *sacrosanct*."

Paul could see Aliyah's eyes narrow. She'd be looking that word up later. But Valentine gave Payne the stink-eye. "...we get rooms?"

Payne spread his hands in a gesture that hovered somewhere between *dear me, I forgot!* and *what a surprise!* "Luxury suite. Though honestly, the 'no trespassing' rule is for your safety as much as theirs – that's where they do their 'mancy. Things *change* in there. So as much as you'll be tempted to open Mrs Liu's door and pet her kitties, well..."

"You might be pulled into a hallway full of infinite cats and never be seen again," Rainbird finished.

Aliyah gave Payne a deeply suspicious look.

Payne regarded her evenly. "It's no joke, Aliyah. Our spaces are sacred. It's where we create alternatives to this world's laws. If you stumble into someone else's space without knowing their rules, well... bad things can happen. And speaking of bad things...."

He unhooked a microphone from the car door. "This is the King of New York, confirming the airlock is cleared. We have unmasked with us. This is not a drill."

"...the airlock?" Valentine asked.

"The internal staff are not allowed to fraternize." Payne tapped his temple; his wrinkled cheeks puffed out, turned angular, his sagging skin hardening into the glossy sheen of a lacquered mask. His hair fused into a solid wavy mass, turning dark brown. Within seconds, Payne's harsh ex-Marine face had become an art deco art piece: a young, handsome warrior with bright red dots in the center of both cheeks, sporting a lion's mane of a beard and a golden crown.

"Cool," Aliyah whispered. Payne leaned forward, his porcelain lips curling up in a geometric grin, offering up his newfound face for exploration. Aliyah pressed her palms against Payne's forehead:

"It feels like glass!"

"It is glass," Payne said. "Well, porcelain. Mrs Vinere, our masqueromancer, makes them quite comfortable. You forget you're wearing them – which is good, for you may never be in the Institute without a mask."

"We gotta be masked?" Valentine asked. "How many rules are there, anyway?"

"Well, we *are* bureaucromancers." Payne gave Paul a chummy punch on the shoulder. "So quite a few. Yet I assure you, they're all time-tested rules, proven to ensure safety."

Valentine glanced over at Rainbird, who now wore the burning tree mask he'd worn when he'd teleported into Paul's place – that anguished expression carved out of twisted bark, the eyes glowing with hellfire, the mouth contorted like a damned soul. "How's making the world's creepiest Halloween party keep us safe?"

Payne turned to Aliyah, a teacher giving a class.

"The biggest problem in hiding 'mancers is SMASH's Unimancy. Do you know what the government does to you if they catch you, Aliyah?"

Aliyah shivered. "They take you out to the Refactor. And they… they torture you."

"Government psych-ops professionals put you in isolation cells and run batteries of stress tests on you, forcing you to escape into whatever fantasies you've constructed. In our case, our fantasies are our power – so if you *can* do 'mancy, the government *will* drive you to do it. Once they uncover your true nature, the brainwashing begins."

Valentine coughed, directing Payne's attention to how miserable Aliyah looked. "I'm not sure the kid needs to hear about the Refactor."

"She's a soldier, like the rest of us," Rainbird interrupted. "The more she knows, the smarter she'll be. Keeping a child in a war zone uneducated is tantamount to murder."

"Quite so, Rainbird," Payne said, pleased. "You may reignite yourself."

Rainbird fumbled eagerly for a Zippo lighter, lit his cigar, sucked in a deep breath with supreme fulfillment. With great satisfaction, he mashed the lit cigar into the circle of blisters in his palm. They burst apart, trickling magma onto the limousine carpet, filling the car with toxic smoke that made Paul cough.

Rainbird stiffened, the sigils on his cheeks glowing like a lit furnace, his face a paroxysm of ecstasy.

Aliyah balled her hands into fists, took a deep breath, and inched closer to Rainbird's burning suit.

Show her what she fears, and she digs in, Paul thought.

The radio crackled. "Clear for entry, Your Highness."

Payne grabbed the microphone. "Confirm camera shutdown. We have unmasked with us."

"Shutdown confirmed. Entry at your command."

Payne preened. "You see, Paul? Like clockwork."

Payne exited the car quickly, walking with the brisk pace of a man giving a factory tour on limited time. He bent over and glared into the scanner, which flashed a blinding green. Rainbird handed Payne a handkerchief as Payne dabbed the tears from his eyes.

A whirr came from the box as it confirmed Payne's identity. The doors unlatched with a harsh explosive sound. Rainbird pulled the door open, revealing a long corridor of polished gold-flecked marble, tastefully recessed fluorescent lights, and oil portraits of Mr Payne's King-of-New-York mask peering sternly down. Both sides were lined with keypad-locked doors – an upscale institution somewhere between a college dormitory and a banking lobby.

Aliyah ran in, then skidded to a halt, looking in befuddlement around her.

"A few more rules before you can see the other 'mancers, Aliyah," Payne said, taking her hand to lead her down the hallway. "As you can see, every employee here – well, the internal staff, anyway – has their own changing room, to prevent unwanted camaraderie. The less they know, the better. Come on, let's bring you to the trainee room, we'll get you masked up."

Valentine backed up against the entryway, not budging from the doorway as Payne and Aliyah walked down the hall.

"'Masked up.'" Valentine flattened herself against the entryway. "Christ, this antiseptic hallway's already a *Resident Evil* level as it is. Throw in the Red Death, here, and we're approaching *Silent Hill* levels of fuckimosity."

Paul sighed. "I suppose you think I get that reference? Or, in fact, *any* of your references?"

Valentine beamed. "Nope! I make 'em to amuse me."

"Come on, Valentine. I know you're not big on regulations, but..." He lowered his voice, grateful Payne had given them a moment alone. "Aliyah. She needs some guidelines. And we–"

Valentine poked Paul's chest. "I *know* what this means to her. That's why I'm doing it. But I reserve the right to say this isn't for me."

He held up his hands in surrender. "I know. I know. Just... give it a chance, OK?"

She lifted her hands before her eye, like a magician unveiling a trick. "Look at my face, Paul. You see this dubious resignation? This. This is my 'giving it a chance' face. What I want from you is your 'I understand that Valentine's not big on creepy white guy fiefdoms' face."

Paul bugged his eyes out and gave her a wan smile. "Is that the face you need?"

She hid a smirk, pushed him gently away. "God, no *wonder* you're single."

She put her arm around him and sauntered down the hallway, catching up with Payne and Aliyah.

"...I don't do it to be cruel to our employees, Aliyah," Payne explained. "Keeping them separated is necessary to the Institute's safety."

"How's that work?"

"The trick is, once SMASH brainwashes you to learn Unimancy, your thoughts become theirs. You *want* to tell them everything you know – including the names, faces, and powers of every 'mancer you ever met. One of the reasons 'mancers can't band together to fight the government is because the more 'mancers you network together, the quicker they fall once one is captured."

Satisfied, Payne stopped to unlock a door – a door that, to Paul's eyes, seemed like every other door in the facility. Except this one led to a tiled locker room lined with luchador masks and green nurses' scrubs. Each luchador mask had a different name embroidered on the forehead: SKIMMER. ARTICHOKE. HYMNAL.

"...the *fuck*?" Valentine said.

"Standard procedure for mundanes." Payne shut the door, locking it. Another locked door with a card reader stood at the far end of the narrow locker room, marked with a bright orange sign: "AUTHORIZED PERSONNEL ONLY. PSYCHIATRIC PATIENTS WITHIN. TRESPASSING WILL BE PROSECUTED."

That's where the 'mancers live, Paul thought, giddy with anticipation.

Payne consulted a clipboard, running his finger down it. Muttering, he plucked a bright orange, full-faced wrestling mask off a brass post, then knelt down to speak to Aliyah with ritual solemnity.

"This," Payne said, snapping the mask open briskly between his hands, "is how we fight SMASH: anonymity. None of the nurses know what the residents look like. None of the *residents* know what each other looks like. None of the employees know each other's names, just the names on the hoods. If someone betrays us, they can only tell SMASH so much."

Except for us, Paul thought guiltily. *We figured out who Payne was.*

"Even Rainbird is not his true name." Payne jerked his chin over towards Rainbird, who glowered at the revelation. "I chose it out of a book. He left his name behind to become something stronger in here… and I ask you to do the same."

Payne held the mask out to Aliyah; it had glittering swirls of flames running up its cheeks. Paul wondered if Payne had unconsciously chosen it to mirror Aliyah's burn scars.

"Jesus, she's looking at that mask like she's choosing her first Pokemon," Valentine muttered.

"HOTPLATE," Aliyah read off the mask, in a daze.

"The names are chosen at random for staff," Payne explained. "Once you choose your own name later, Mrs Vinere will find a perfect mask to fit your personality. But for now…"

"*No.*" Aliyah pulled it on over her face, then turned to face Rainbird. "I'm Hotplate. I can be Hotplate."

Payne chuckled, then tied the back of the mask tighter, trying to fit an adult-sized mask to a child's head. It was a fatherly gesture; Paul suppressed a pang of jealousy.

Instead, he reached out with his own bureaucromancy, interfacing with Payne's records to see which masks here had already been assigned so he could choose a free one. The act felt foolish, slightly redundant: after all, his 'mancy was Payne's.

Still, he plucked a blue-sky mask off the rack, one with white clouds sewn into the leather and bright lightning-bolt rims around the eyeholes. "I'll be MONGOOSE for now. I see you're not taking your 'random' names from old CIA case files."

"Good eye, Paul!" Payne said, thrilled. "I like a man who can catch me out."

Paul pulled the mask on, feeling detached from the world. Looking through the eyeholes felt like looking through a camera lens; it wasn't *him* participating in this bizarre scene, he was watching it happen to someone else. He tied the back tight, pressing the leather taut against his face, feeling as though if he pressed it to his skin it would root him to this reality.

He turned to Valentine, curious to see what mask she'd choose – but Valentine wasn't there. What *was* there was a shifting nightmare of oily tendrils in roughly human form, like a dark snake orgy at midnight, drooling wet saliva from a million tiny teeth.

Paul leapt away. The thing reached out for him apologetically, a bundle of organic cables in the mockery of an arm – then the squid-like blackness flushed pink, coalescing into a fully human hand.

A mouth sagged open, spoke in Valentine's voice. "Hang on there, Paul."

The hand rippled with colors and patterns, convulsing up the body, black leather scabbing across its greasy surface. When the transformation finished, a slouched angry man in a leather jacket stood before them, a sullen face shadowed by a hoodie, examining its hand as though it might burst into an octopoid shape again at any moment.

"Ta da!" said the man; Valentine's merry tone was completely at odds with her angry-white-boy skin. "Call me Alex Mercer."

"...Is that a videogame guy?"

"It'd be hysterical if you got the gag here, Paul, but let's be honest: all my best jokes involve Wikipedia research."

Rainbird held out a mask to her, letting it dangle off the end of his finger. "You can't choose your own shape, Ms DiGriz. You need a mask. Or an official 'mancy chosen by Mrs Vinere, our masqueromancer. Something *stable*."

"The hell I can't." Something slithered ominously under Valentine's leather jacket. "I've already lost my peripheral vision after SMASH shot out my eye. I'm not putting a goddamned Mexican wrestling mask over my head."

Rainbird made a strangled noise; Payne made a calming gesture. "Let it go, Rainbird. For now. It's time we–"

Payne looked around in confusion. "…Where's Aliyah?"

A thunderclap sounded from the doorway. "LET'S PLAY!" Aliyah cried, her voice echoing across the complex, a high and joyful sound.

"Oh no," Payne muttered, "Oh no." But Paul was already running towards the door where all the 'mancers lived. Valentine burst the door into splinters with the press of an imaginary "A" button, letting Paul rush through first.

Aliyah stood atop a circular nurses' station in the center of an ornate atrium. The sun shone down on the nursing station through a vast polarized glass canopy overhead. The atrium was so large that Aliyah's voice still echoed back and forth when Paul and Valentine burst in.

Paul limped across the atrium's gold-flecked marble floor, trying not to trip over the squares dug into the ground where pruned trees had been planted at erratic intervals. The 'mancers couldn't be allowed outside all that much, Paul realized, so Payne had made the space to mimic some Greek pantheon, a place where they could stroll in the sunshine and savor what snippets of nature they could. Even as Paul vaulted over the statues of slender goddesses, bolting in a straight path for the nurses' station in the center, he knew it would take him a few minutes to cross the vast floor and reach Aliyah.

The atrium itself was ringed with gold-flecked marble pillars, modelled after a grand hotel lobby. Twenty gold-trimmed doors faced inwards – the luxury suites Payne had spoken of, their majestic entrances set into the walls' circular sweep, the atrium shaped like a great compass with a room in every direction.

The doors cracked open, heads peering out to see what the commotion was.

Aliyah held her Nintendo DS high, ready to summon more lightning down through the circular skylight three stories above. A glowing pillar of pixelated light limned her slim form. An attendant in a black and yellow luchadore mask cowered next to her, unsure what to do.

Aliyah did a slow 360, eyeing each of the doors. *"My name is Aliyah!"* she boomed, her luchador mask glimmering with power. *"I am almost nine years old!"* She hesitated, as if she wanted to say more, then burst out with: *"Who wants to play with me?"*

"No," Payne muttered. "No, no, *no*. I'm supposed to introduce them, some of these 'mancers haven't been out of their room in *years*..."

The doors around Aliyah opened wider.

Sixteen 'mancers poked their heads out. Most were pale; some looked positively sallow. They were mostly whip-thin with bodily neglect or pudgy with comfort eating, peering out to look at Aliyah with the vague confusion of someone who'd crawled into a hole and had asked not to be disturbed.

"Any of you?" Aliyah asked, looking heartbroken.

An emaciated Chinese lady crept cautiously out of her room, followed by a trail of well-groomed tabby cats in an orderly queue. Behind her, Paul saw a room crammed full of pacing cats.

An obese jowly black man with sweat stains chewed on his cigar, then scribbled notes on an immense leather ledger he carried like a small infant in the crook of his arm. He opened the ledger; a buzzing swarm of black numbers soared out to explore the room ahead of him, swirling to investigate this small black girl standing on the table.

A beet-faced woman in sauce-splattered chef's garments emerged, holding a sizzling saucepan filled with pure 'mancy, the bottom of her pan red-hot and continuing to cook her magical food.

A stylish woman with no face at all, just a blank caul, clutched the doorframe and aimed her empty face towards Aliyah – then vanished inside to reemerge as a willowy socialite, her face reshaped into a friendly abstract mosaic.

"I thought there were seventeen of them," Paul muttered.

"You're forgetting me." Rainbird jerked his chin towards a room that glowed lava-red.

One by one, the 'mancers came out, each trailing some indication of their own obsession: a glowing lightsaber, bloodied ballet slippers that never quite touched the ground, a duffle bag of plush raccoon dolls.

They converged on Aliyah, cocking their heads, groundhogs being called to rouse themselves after a long and shadowy winter. They clutched their fingers, summoning 'mancy, as the orderlies ran for the hills...

"Orders, sir?" Rainbird asked.

"...hold."

Aliyah stood in the center of the 'mancers, looking at them earnestly. They shuffled to a halt, sizing her up with curiosity.

She spun in the air once, twice, three times, rising as she twirled, then came down with a golden sword clutched in her hand. "It's dangerous to go alone!" she recited, a solemn oath. "Take this."

Kneeling, Aliyah split the weapon into sixteen smaller swords, each carved from shimmering 'mancy. She fanned them out and offered a sword to each politely.

The crazy cat lady laughed.

The bookie applauded.

The chef kissed her fingertips.

They stepped forward, smiling, thrilled to see a small child so eager for their company. They each took a sword from Aliyah's hands, and transformed it – the ballet dancer made it into a graceful golden swan, who she did a *pas de deux* with. The woman with the blank face plucked a sword with fine grace and, stripping her old face away to drop it on the ground like a shed snakeskin, plunged the sword into her cheekbones to become a radiant being of golden blades.

Aliyah giggled as the cat lady turned the sword into a laser pointer to turn her cats into a wild circus of tumbling whiskers, and the bookie split the sword into two and handed it to two 'mancers to show Aliyah what the odds were on their fighting, and the Lucasmancer engaged Aliyah in a great Jedi fight, his lightsaber against her sword, in an epic battle that scarred the walls with lightning and elicited a thunderous roar of approval from all the 'mancers when Aliyah finally won victory to a great swell of "Duel of the Fates."

"Daddy!" she cried, exultant. *"I'm home!"*

NINETEEN
EULA

The dazzling shows of 'mancy went on for a while – well past Aliyah's bedtime, but Paul felt no urge to end such a perfect night for her. Eventually the orderlies crept back out, adjusted their luchador masks, and brought out beachfront chairs for Paul, Valentine, and Payne to watch the show.

"I should order in pizza," Payne mused. "As a reward for their kind welcome."

"You'll annoy Julia," Rainbird said. He stood at attention behind Payne. His wooden-mask eyes were blazing treetrunk gashes, but he never took his gaze away from the 'mancers exchanging barrages of 'mancy with Aliyah.

"Quite right. Rainbird, when it's calmed down a bit, see if our resident culinomancer won't do her loaves and fishes trick for us."

Paul looked over to Valentine, who he expected to complain – Paul spent more time trying to get Valentine to eat her vegetables than he did convincing Aliyah – but Valentine bent over her own Nintendo DS, conspicuously ignoring the sixteen-'mancer party.

He considered saying something, but didn't want to have that conversation in front of Rainbird. So instead, he watched his daughter, who now fed and maintained a living stuffed-animal corral, courtesy of a pallid plushomancer with a pink kitty face. The other 'mancers sat in a circle, waiting their turns to play with her. Paul understood why – Aliyah was enthralled by the slightest 'mancy.

Even though all the plushomancer could do was make his toy raccoons waddle about a bit, Aliyah treated him like royalty. She joined her 'mancy with his, had the raccoons sit up and bow to him.

Occasionally she'd gallop back to grab Paul's hand, shouting *Daddy Daddy come see this*, and would make a great show of something new she'd figured out how to do with her powers. Paul would applaud, and Aliyah would smother him in more kisses, whispering more thanks for bringing her where it was safe.

Then she'd dart off to the next 'mancer to entwine her magic with theirs.

The other 'mancers filed by to thank Payne, bowing one by one; he waved them away graciously. Each had delicate masks, affixed by 'mancy, obscuring their identity but displaying who they wanted to be.

Paul couldn't remember the last time he'd relaxed.

"You've given your girl a special gift, Mr Mongoose." Payne nudged Paul to remind him of his code name. "Most 'mancers find other 'mancies to be – well, a little offputting. Proof the universe isn't entirely on their side. Joining to *combine* spells is like getting Israel and Gaza to negotiate. But your daughter – she's been casting spells with you all along, hasn't she?"

Paul straightened his tie. "She has."

"And you and Mr Mercer over there." He lifted his drink to Valentine, who did not react. "That's how you avoided the police – by combining your strengths?"

"Yes sir."

Payne toasted him. "You did so much with so little, Mr Mongoose. Your resourcefulness, it's... well, I wish I'd had you at my side when I brewed Flex in upstate New York."

His words quenched a thirst Paul hadn't known he was starved for. Raising Aliyah, alone, with no one but

Valentine and Kit to talk to, well... It had been stressful. Paul knew every parent worth their salt worried how they were screwing up their kids, but at least those parents could compare their experiences with the other parents at school.

Aliyah's 'mancy, though – no one else was raising a child 'mancer. How could he tell how well he was doing? Tears welled in his eyes as he realized how badly he'd needed to hear *You're doing OK*.

Then he realized: though the 'mancers had been playing for hours, there had been no flux.

He bolted up, ready to... well, he wasn't sure how to protect Aliyah, but he would. Payne pressed him back down into his seat, surprisingly strong for a septuagenarian.

"Relax. The flux is handled."

"But..." Paul sensed the 'mancy in the area, tried to figure out where the flux was going. "You can't erase flux." He remembered the one time he'd done that, back when he'd saved New York with magic forged from perfect conviction. "I mean, not unless you're absolutely convinced what you're doing is right..."

"When Hotplate there assaulted the Task Force – how did you stop the flux backlash from obliterating her?"

"I signed her bad luck over to me."

Payne clucked his tongue, the bemusement of a student who'd figured out the answer before you did. "Oh, Paul. You were so close. Another year or two, you'd have figured it out."

"Figured *what* out?"

Payne held his hand out. Rainbird deposited a smartphone into it; Payne tapped an app open before offering it to Paul. "I'd like to introduce you to my friend Eula."

"Eula? That's..." Paul sent tendrils of inquisitive 'mancy into the phone, which showed Sami R, the Samaritan Mutual Incident Reporting application – a cute little 1950s cartoon businessman ready to take your information. Except Paul detected a tiny dollop of 'mancy stashed away somewhere in the code.

"My End User License Agreement," Payne said with satisfaction. "Now me, I like paper. Paper can be locked away safe, unlike all these hackers chipping away at my domain. I enjoy the feel of paper in my hands. And if I *had* to open up my forms to the Internet to remain competitive, well, I thought, those mundanes damn well *owed* me."

Paul punched the signup button, which gave a little popup window: "Before you can use Sami R, you must agree to the following terms and conditions," followed by seventy pages of eye-wateringly small text. The touch of a button scrolled to the bottom of the page, which said "Agree" – but his 'mancy informed him of a clause buried deep in the legalese, abstracted and dense.

"The agreement," Paul said in wonder. "They agree to absorb your leftover flux."

"We process five hundred claims through that app each month. Our bad luck is distributed across a pool of almost twenty thousand people. If my clan generates excessive heat, well, everyone who's filed an electronic claim stubs a toe."

Valentine looked up, sour-faced. "So you just dump all your shit on your claimants?"

"I said 'excessive.' Much of what I do here is focused on training novice 'mancers to manage their flux load – early on, as you know, is the time when SMASH is most likely to catch them. This is merely a bleed-off mechanism to help the untrained."

Paul sighed. "And the perfect safety mechanism to teach Aliyah."

"You mean Miss Hotplate, don't you? And yes. We'll get her doing 'mancy responsibly. And–"

Rainbird's phone buzzed. "Sorry, sir – you told me to interrupt you when things were ready?"

Payne's kingly face brightened. "So soon? Excellent." He clapped his hands to get the 'mancers' attention; only Aliyah ignored him, still playing with the stuffed animals. "Pardon me, friends! I'm afraid it is time for tonight's gathering to end."

Disappointed groans.

"That's all right! You still have your apartments to play in. If you wish further company, well... I don't suppose you'd care to come back, little Hotplate?"

She's not Hotplate, she's Aliyah. Paul quashed an irrational surge of jealousy. Imani had picked that name out for her, naming Aliyah after Imani's favorite singer. Calling her anything else felt like... well, like she wasn't his daughter.

But here, she was Hotplate. She needed to be, for safety's sake. Hopefully nobody remembered her using her name when she'd called out to them.

Yet he'd *think* of her as Aliyah.

The thought felt oddly rebellious.

Aliyah – Hotplate – looked up, eyes wide through her mask. "You couldn't *stop* me from coming back!"

The 'mancers gave a cheer, before slinking back into their lairs. The cat lady led her cats back inside to the cluster of felines waiting for her return, the culinomancer opened the door to a bustling kitchen, the bookiemancer opened the door to a room with seven widescreen TVs tuned to sports networks. Crackles of magic fizzled as the doors slammed shut.

Valentine slouched in her hoodied Alex Mercer-skin. "Wow, are they recluses or what?"

"We build them places that are comfortable for them." Payne extended his hand to help her off the chair. "Speaking of that, I have something I think you'll all enjoy."

Valentine frowned, but let Payne guide her on. He led them under a well-trimmed tree, around a huge Roman column, headed towards three doors ringing the lobby's huge circle.

"Thing is, it's not safe for 'mancers to be out in public. So we encourage people to stay here. That way, if they get the urge to do a little 'mancy – and I think we all know it spills out of us as we daydream – it won't alert anyone. But if I ask them to commit to living in a single space," Payne said, unlocking one of the rooms with a great golden key, "then I should provide the proper incentives, shouldn't I?"

He swung open the door to reveal a spacious, three-story apartment with polished mahogany floors and a twisting spiral staircase that rose up into a cut-glass chandeliered ceiling. The floors were lined with the plush oriental rugs Paul had always preferred, the walls lined with neat brass filing cabinets packed tight with forms.

Paul stepped towards the great black desk in the room's center, an altar to forms. That wooden desk held everything he'd ever wanted – a green ink-blotter, a rich leather deskpad, a brass lamp.

Payne reached into his breast pocket pulled out a small bouquet of four jet-black fountain pens. "No more Bic pens for you, my friend."

Paul twirled in circles to take it all in – three stories of beauty for him to collate, fill, and organize.

"Here's the best part," Payne said.

He nudged an electronic pad with his elbow. The smooth, rhythmic tones of Snoop Dogg pulsed throughout the place, Paul's favorite music, the easy flow of his teenaged years thrumming through the carpets.

"With our 'mancy, it's easy to look up your favorite iTunes tracks," Payne told him.

"This – this…" Paul trailed off, gaping at the wonder.

Aliyah gave it the cursory inspection of a bored kid wandering through a museum. "It's pretty, Daddy," she allowed. She looked up at the single bed, placed artfully high up for privacy. "But where do I sleep?"

"Oh, we have a special place for you, little Hotplate! And you, Alex." Valentine shrugged sullenly. "If you two will come next door? You both have similar 'mancies – why, you're almost sisters! So I figure I can show you both at once."

Aliyah darted out of the room, bouncing with excitement. Valentine shrugged, her body rippling with uneasy black tentacles, and followed. They all walked over to the next room, and Payne produced another golden key.

"Now this – this, I think, should be enough to win any videogamemancer's heart."

He pushed the door in to reveal another three-story apartment – yet where Paul's library had been all golden lamplight, Aliyah's room was lit a bright and welcoming game-store white. The walls were decorated with colorful *Pokemon* mosaics, formed from bright plastic pixel tiles.

Huge flat-screen televisions dominated every story – each with a comfortable couch and a library of games, still in their original packaging, lined up neatly on shelves. Periodic snack food stations were slotted into the walls – a Slurpee machine, a Dunkin' Donuts rack, a popcorn cart.

But the rows of game cartridges dominated all.

"There's a space for every video game system we could find, from Vectrex to the PlayStation 4," Payne explained, leading in Aliyah, who muffled a squee with both hands. "We cobbled together as complete a library as we could muster in a day – we'll get more, of course."

Aliyah ran over to the Nintendo DS section, which had every game on her Amazon wishlist. She took them off the shelves, comparing them to each other – then pulled them all down, a waterfall of cartridges tumbling to the ground. Aliyah scooped them up, clutched them to her chest.

"This is Hotplate's room, so the games are rated appropriately for her age," Payne said. "Yet if you'll allow me to escort you to your room, Ms Mercer, the selection is – "

Valentine stood in horror, her arms flopping black pseudopods.

"You..." Her face rippled in distress. "You think I can do 'mancy in *this* corporate shithole?"

TWENTY
Schisms and Spasms

Aliyah dropped the cartridges, concerned, then ran over to take Valentine's hand – and kept it there, even though Valentine's hand was a squamous mass of cilia.

"Aunt Valentine, this is everything we need." She looked terribly hurt.

"Oh, bullshit. Look, I..." Her face drooped into her old Valentine self. "I can't talk to you guys when I'm shapeshifting."

"Ms Mercer, if anyone sees you–"

"*Can* it, G-Man," Valentine said, whirling on Payne. "This is between me, Paul, and the kid. *Not* you."

Payne held up his hands. "Then I'll leave you to discuss this amongst yourselves." He exited the room, Rainbird trailing reluctantly behind him, closing the door.

Aliyah pressed a spanking new Nintendo DS into Valentine's hands. "Aunt Valentine, this has all the videogames we ever need! We can play whatever we want! And you and I, we can..." She looked shamed for reasons she didn't quite understand. "We can sit on a *comfortable* couch, like at Mommy's house, and play in a clean place..."

"Oh, no. No no no. You..." She swallowed, raising the new Nintendo DS. "This is a door prize. Some rich asshole gave it to us. It cost us nothing and it means nothing." She reached over to pluck Aliyah's old Nintendo DS from her hands. "This, Aliyah – this, I saved up for weeks to get, working a minimum-wage job, putting away my money, sneaking into GameStop to play snippets on my lunchbreak. *This* was four months of labor and longing, brought into this world like a child, and when I finally got my hands on one, well, you bet your ass I treasured it."

"But you gave it to me."

"Yeah." Valentine knelt, getting down on eye level with Aliyah. "When I saw a burned little girl in a hospital, I gave her my best toy ever, because that kid needed some love." She clutched the Nintendo DS, touching it to Aliyah's forehead as if trying to bestow a blessing. "This *is* love, Aliyah."

She took the new Nintendo, cocked her arm back, and pitched it like a fastball into a *Squirtle* tile decoration. "*That*," she said, "is marketing."

Aliyah flushed with anger. "You broke that! That was mine!"

"Who the hell cares? Hang on a sec." Valentine flung open the door. "Hey, Flameface! Our Nintendo DS is broken! Can you req us another one?"

Rainbird did a double-take. "Of course. I'll–"

She slammed the door on him. "You see, Aliyah? It means nothing to him. So how can it mean something to you?"

Paul felt like he should interrupt, just to reassert his status as a parent, but as usual he wasn't sure how to disturb the flow of Aliyah and Valentine's relationship.

Aliyah swept her hand out, encompassing the three stories' worth of games, the television sets, the hammock of plushie Pikachus. "Aunt Valentine, we don't have to play the same game over and over again. We can try anything."

"Oh, sweetie." She clutched Aliyah's shoulders. "When I grew up, all we had was one cartridge. It's all my parents could afford. That's how I found the magic in it – I played it over and over again. We're not playing the same game because we can't afford it – we're playing it because you only find the awesome secrets when you keep investigating the old things."

"Well, *I* get bored!" Aliyah said, huffing behind her mask.

Valentine clenched her fist between her breasts, as if Aliyah had struck her.

I introduced her to gaming, Paul remembered Valentine saying. *But she's developed her own tastes.*

"Valentine," Paul said. "Can I talk to you for a moment?"

Valentine held Aliyah's gaze, but neither broke. They both seemed to expect some sort of apology. Then Valentine sniffed haughtily, and walked away with Paul.

"Look, Valentine..." Paul stopped. The space he'd ushered her to had a blinding spotlight shining down and a 60" television blaring *Dragonball Z* cartoons in their face. "Hang on, let me shut this off–"

Valentine snapped her fingers; all the electronics in the area sizzled and went black, giving them a shadowy respite. Aliyah had curled up in a *Spongebob Squarepants* chair, pointedly playing a new game.

"You didn't short out Aliyah's–"

"I'm not gonna fuck up her room any more. I just pulled the plug. And take off that fucking luchador mask, Paul. This is close enough to a Mexican soap opera as it is."

Paul tugged it off, feeling blissfully cool air prickle his scalp. "OK, look. I know this isn't your comfort zone–"

"You can say *that* again."

"But you know, this is just what Payne thought you wanted. If you want to buy your own stuff, well, great, *do* that. You never have enough space in your closets, so... why not customize this big space until you're happy?"

She dangled Paul's mask in front of him. "And when I bring some new guy home to fuck, what am I going to tell him? Mexican wrestlers are my kink?"

Paul sagged. "...oh."

"Maybe the other 'mancers here have abandoned their earthly pleasures, Paul, but me? I've got a few itches I need scratched. Not that the swing clubs are any place to find a boyfriend, but I... even if I can't have a lover in case I kill the fucker – again – I need something more than a Hitachi. I need warm flesh. I need to feel *needed*."

Paul rubbed his temples. "Hoo boy."

"'Hoo boy' as in you think I shouldn't do that?"

"'Hoo boy' as in, 'I think you of all people shouldn't have to live as a nun.'"

She closed her eyes, gave Paul a pained smile. "*Thank* you, Paul."

"But it's past eleven, and it'd be a two-hour ride back to our apartment, and you're always a little crabby after you've fought a battle for your life."

She held up a finger to interrupt him. "I would have *clobbered* that soot-streaked asshole, Paul. That's what I do. You need some firepower to back up your management skills, and I? Am your firepower."

She trembled with pride. Though Valentine was a pain in the ass, her protective belligerence sprang straight from her love for them both – and her insistence that Paul needed so much protection filled Paul with an uneasy mixture of love and helplessness.

He hugged her. She patted him on the back, stiffly; she'd once likened Paul's hugs to being slowly encased by a mantis.

"All right, Tsabo, break it up, break it up," she muttered, pushing him away.

"Just... let's give it two weeks here. Can you go two weeks without sex?"

"I can go two weeks without food, Paul. Doesn't mean I *want* to."

"I know. But... did you see how happy she looked? Playing with the other 'mancers?"

Valentine looked over her shoulder at Aliyah, half asleep in the chair, refusing to stop playing her Nintendo even though she kept nodding off between changing game cartridges. A reluctant grin crooked across Valentine's mouth. "...yeah."

"And you know she'd be heartbroken if you left, right?"

Valentine winked her good eye at Aliyah. Aliyah *hmpf*ed and turned away, but it was proof Aliyah hadn't been paying nearly as much attention to the game as she'd have liked Valentine to believe.

"All right, you silver-tongued bastard. Two weeks."

"Who knows? Maybe you'll find love here."

Valentine shivered. "If that plushiemancer makes a move on me, I'll teleport his ass into a game of *Resident Evil*."

"Thanks." Paul squeezed her shoulder, then went over to Aliyah, who thrashed to protest that she hadn't been sleeping. "Hey, sweetie. I think it's time I tucked you in."

"OK." Aliyah got up, shambled towards the door, dragging the Nintendo DS with her.

"Wait. You don't want to sleep in your new room?"

She rubbed sleep from her eyes. "I don't like sleeping away from you."

Paul almost lectured her on how his room was right next door if she needed him... But the days when Aliyah still wanted to cuddle up with him were coming to an end.

He stood, transfixed by that bittersweet realization that one day she would not need him, and – maybe within the year, at the rate she was progressing through the rebellion of her prematurely-accelerated adolescence – one day she'd retch when he tried to accompany her in public.

And it was their first night here, he mused. Safer to stick together.

"Come on, sweetie." And though it always hurt his stump to pick up Aliyah's weight, he scooped her up in his arms and teetered over to his new and glorious apartment, ready to curl up next to his precious little girl.

TWENTY-ONE
What the Fire Knows

Rainbird's room is three stories of slotted metal catwalks, each crisscrossed over an industrial cauldron of molten iron. Breathing the superheated air here cooks Rainbird's tongue into brown hamburger, but his body draws strength from the heat and heals into living flesh again. He spends hours examining his fingers as he dips them into a sluice of processed lava, watching his fingernails sizzle and peel back...

He sits on a throne of red-hot rebar, and watches what burns on the brick fireplace before him. Sometimes it's wood. Mostly, he straps his wriggling fuel into place before he ignites it.

The door opens.

Aliyah enters.

She stands on the catwalks, wearing a tiny suit of power armor, all curves and shiny orange plating: the Varia suit from *Metroid*. Underneath, she still wears the pajamas she wore when she used 'mancy to put her dad to sleep and sneak away.

Slowly, she removes her helmet and shakes her dreadlocked hair out.

There are a thousand ways to protect yourself from lava in videogames; Aliyah could have taken the form of Charizard or written "snowstorm" in *Scribblenauts* or extinguished this room in a variety of ways.

She wants Rainbird to see her face.

Rainbird doesn't get up.

"You burned," he tells her. "You almost died in your father's apartment. The smoke blistered your lungs."

"Yes." Her burn-scarred face is determined, not showing any fear – or, at least, not any fear of *him*.

"You dream of fire every night."

"Yes."

"You know he can't protect you."

"I have to protect *him*," Aliyah says, a note of childish – petulance? urgency? – in her voice. "Anathema would have cut him open if I hadn't stopped her. Then, the police had him on the *ground*. Tied up. Nerve gassed. Almost dead. And if I hadn't come when I did…"

She shakes her head, trying to clear the image. That is what Aliyah dreams of – fire, dead fathers, mothers with husbands who want to kill her, and no one in the world strong enough but her.

Maybe we do need to kill them, her father had told her. *The question is, do you want to be the person who does that?*

Someone has to be.

She squeezes her eyes shut, locking the tears tight. And when she opens them, Rainbird stands next to her. He keeps a respectful distance. She watches the flesh on his ribs burn away, opening up a latticed glimpse into the blackened cinder of Rainbird's beating heart.

Tiny glowing faces peek out, grimacing with each heartbeat, shrieking silently before going quiet again – all the men and women Rainbird has burned alive. He pulls his ribs open, affording her a better look.

Though Aliyah shudders at the sight, she refuses to look away from the tiny souls trapped in that ashen heart.

Rainbird nods, sympathetically. "You want to be strong."

"I killed only one person. And I… I think about her *all the time*. She *cried* when I killed her. I took away everything from her. And if I feel sorry for some murdering buh-*b*-word who was going to... she was stabbing my father with a *spear*! And even then, if I had to do it again, I don't know if... if I..." Aliyah swallows. "So I *can't* be sorry, can I?"

Rainbird pulls flesh down over his ribs as though tugging a shirt over himself. When he grins, the nerves in his teeth are glowing filaments. "No. Of *course* you can't."

"But Dad, and Valentine, they... they keep trying to *stop* me, and if I listen then who's going to protect them?"

Rainbird smiles as though he understands completely. "They're afraid of what you could be, Aliyah. Whereas *I* think people should be like fire. They should consume everything they can grasp to grow strong. And never you fear, Aliyah, for I know fire's most cherished secret..."

Aliyah gazes up at him, trembling with relief. The door closes, pushed shut by a waft of burning gas.

"...I'll teach you how to regret nothing."

Part II

Suburban Robots to Monitor Reality

TWENTY-TWO
Tikka Masala

Paul hated the way he always felt nervous whenever he had a lunch date with Imani. She was his ex-wife, for God's sake. Whatever they'd had, it was over. They only got together to discuss issues like Aliyah – which, of course, was precisely what they *would* be discussing today.

So why did he feel like he had to impress her?

He'd chosen a nice little Indian restaurant that had opened last week to good Yelp reviews – not someplace well known yet. Imani liked fine dining, but more than that, she liked the thrill of discovery, and in that Paul had always been happy to indulge her. And the place was well kept, trimmed with fresh green plants and the gaudy red and gold wallpaper that Paul was never sure was actual Indian tradition or just what New Yorkers expected of an Indian restaurant.

Then Imani came in.

Paul forgot all about the restaurant.

She dressed stylishly as always, shrugging off her long tan coat, revealing an Egyptian goddess clad in a gold and tan sheath dress that showed off her long legs.

She paused in the doorway, troubled, looking for all the world like a dame in some 1950s detective novel about to hire a private investigator. Which was ridiculous, he reminded himself: she was a corporate lawyer, working ten-hour days, had squeezed the space out of her schedule for a lunchtime talk.

Then she smiled as she saw Paul, striding towards him with both arms open, as though his presence had chased her fears away.

He hated hugging her. Not only was it awkward standing up with his prosthetic leg, not only did he worry about smearing blood on her fine dress with his ever-bleeding left arm, but that flash of casual intimacy always reminded him of the tenderness they no longer shared.

He hugged her anyway.

"Good choice for lunch, I think." She brushed off her dress, picked up the menu. "Though I'm going to win this time."

"Who says I'll let you?"

She rolled her eyes; between that and her coiffured mop of hair, the gesture reminded Paul very much of Aliyah. "You'll let me."

He chafed at her announcement, but knew he would let her.

She picked out her meal, then crossed her hands across her lap, politely; table manners ran deep in the Dawson family. But that worn, sorrowful look had returned to her face.

"So." She whispered so the waiter couldn't hear her. "Does she still hate me, Paul?"

"She doesn't *hate* you, Imani. She's just... she's a very confused girl right now."

She clutched her fingers once, twice, as if trying to grip something to calm her nerves. "She hasn't answered my calls in ten days."

Paul cringed. Aliyah had been caught up in playing with the other 'mancers, she'd done 'mancy all day and crashed into bed at night. Though even with a full night's sleep, she still dropped off into naps throughout the day. *Did* doing new 'mancy tire children? It never did him, but...

"I didn't realize it had been that long," Paul apologized. "I'm sorry, I should have made her call…"

"It's fine, Paul. It's just… you said you had something to tell me about her?"

Paul braced himself. "Oh yeah." He fished out a brochure from a manila envelope. Here's the part where Paul lied. "I've found a school for Aliyah. It's upstate. A dorm school. Specializing in girls with post-traumatic stress disorder. Which, honestly, is what I think Aliyah has."

"That's what her therapists say, yes."

Imani reached over and took the leaflet, perused it. The brochure had been printed yesterday. The LisAnna Foundation For Children's Post-Traumatic Stress Disorder hadn't existed until two days ago. Hell, it hadn't had a name until yesterday, when Mr Payne had decided to name it after his sisters who'd died in the war.

The site for the school had been purchased four days ago – a location Aliyah had insisted be *very* far away from the Institute, because she didn't want Mommy and stupid, stupid David to know where she *really* lived.

But on the Internet, this newly minted school was a venerable institution. Payne had demonstrated to Paul how the Internet was a large storehouse of bureaucratic records. Paul had infiltrated ICANN's opal-secured servers to insert records so the LisAnna Foundation had apparently created a website in 2004, inserted reviews into hundreds of web pages from various parents, rearranged Google's database entries so the LisAnna Foundation would come up as a hit if Imani Dawson searched for it.

That's what he'd been doing with *his* time, and Paul felt guilty he hadn't checked in on whether Imani and Aliyah were talking.

Imani folded the leaflet. "Can you afford it?"

"There are government programs to help assist."

She hid an exhausted smile behind the brochure. "Of course *you'd* get funding."

"Now, it's a ninety-minute drive away," he said, holding

up his hands to ward off her aggravated interruptions. "So you'd need to rent a car. And they're set on creating structure for their students, so you can't visit without making an appointment in advance. I know you–"

She slid the brochure into her purse. "It's fine, Paul. They're professionals. We need professionals." She trailed off into a defeated silence.

The waiter came by. Imani ordered, having forgotten about the food game – but as usual, she'd unconsciously homed in on the one dish on the menu Paul was dying to order: the tikka masala.

He could have ordered something else. But how could they have a mealtime battle if they both had the same thing?

According to the rules of the game, Paul had arrived first and so had the right to order first. Yet Imani looked so dejected over sending Aliyah off to the Foundation that he ordered the tandoori chicken instead.

Once the waiter shuffled off, Paul said: "After the court battles for custody, I thought you'd go balls to the wall to stop me from putting her in a private school."

She rearranged her fork and knife to be perpendicular, an oddly shy gesture. "I don't know, Paul. Maybe I should. But... I don't..." She gave the plate a rueful smile. "Oh, God, Paul I thought *you'd* be the bad parent. You'd been distant those last few years, working late, never coming home – then Aliyah gets burned and you all but commit suicide, leaving her in the hospital to go fight 'mancers."

Paul felt sick. He *was* the bad parent. He'd charged after Valentine to save her, gotten kidnapped, and in the weeks he'd been held hostage, well... that was when Aliyah had played videogames over and over again, sick with pain, trying not to think about her maybe-dead Daddy.

If Paul had been a better father, Aliyah wouldn't be a 'mancer.

Imani straightened her napkin. "But I keep thinking: *If I'm such a good goddamned mother, how come Aliyah is getting worse?* And I've rounded up all the help I can get, every therapist and teacher and consultant, and... she only seems content when she's with you. So maybe you should..."

She took a long sip of her water, embarrassed.

"Maybe *you* should hire the people to look after her," she finished.

It would never occur to Imani to help Aliyah without assistance.

"It's not like I won't visit," Imani stressed. "I'm not giving up on her. I'm just... I need to shift strategies."

Paul's stomach clenched with guilt. How could he help her be a better mother to Aliyah without telling her everything? If SMASH captured Aliyah now, that would lead them straight back to not just Paul, but Mr Payne and all the 'mancers at the Institute.

Paul reached across to take Imani's hands. She let him, which inspired a wave of almost terrifying gratitude.

"She thinks you're a little scary sometimes," he told her. "Telling her SMASH might haul her away if she won't stop playing games?"

She stiffened. "She knows 'mancers don't start until their mid-twenties. I know lots of kids love videogames, but... why take a chance? Who knows what could happen twenty years down the line?"

He almost told her about Aliyah; didn't. "Yet when you tell her she could become a 'mancer, well... Aliyah gets scared."

She closed her eyes, breathing through her nose; her old trick to calm herself before she yelled. Her hands tightened, grinding his fingers. "*I* get scared, Paul. Those fuckers are running around loose in the city, and nobody can catch them. A 'mancer almost burned my daughter to death. *Twice.* A 'mancer crushed my husband's leg. A 'mancer ruined *our marriage*, Paul. Those fucking 'mancers, Paul... they've hurt us *so much*."

The 'mancer didn't ruin our marriage, he wanted to tell her. *I fell in love with magic. And I couldn't tell you.*

Imani's fingers traced a light circle in the air, a half a

shrug, then tossed her anger away. "But you're right, you're right. If it scares her, I need to back off. I suppose all the dinnertime conversations with David weren't helping."

"...what's David doing?"

She leaned forward. "Oh, you'll be interested in this. You love hunting 'mancers. He's got a lead on some real advanced hardware for finding 'mancy – hi-tech Israeli stuff. SMASH doesn't have the jurisdiction to use that kind of tech but the Task Force? They'll be unleashing some advanced stuff *very* soon."

Paul prickled with fear sweat. "Where'd he get the money? The mayor never gave *me* black-book funding."

"David's squeezed all his connections for this operation. This is... well, you know what a high-profile position it is." She coughed politely, overlooking Paul's traditional allergy to politics. "If he can get Psycho Mantis when you couldn't, that puts him on an upwards trajectory. He's aiming to head up SMASH."

Paul froze.

Paul remembered what Payne had told him to do with the faked identification, to hide them forever from David: *Make the trail lead back to SMASH, Paul. Force him to start requesting records from the bureau he's in competition with. A proud man like David would sooner die than work with people who might steal his thunder.*

If David wasn't jealous of SMASH, he might have found Paul already.

"But David's not military," Paul spluttered.

"Won't matter if he shows enough results. And he is hell-bent on getting Psycho Mantis."

The waiter brought their lunch. Imani took a dainty bite of the tikka masala and did a happy wiggle dance in her chair. Paul took a mouthful of a decent, if unexceptional, tandoori chicken. She offered him her bite, which he took, and felt the tasty heat of turmeric-laced tomatoes.

"You win," he admitted.

"Sometimes you lose," she shrugged, scooping half her

masala onto her bread plate and pushing it towards him. "But I wouldn't worry, Paul. David's driving himself hard, because, hardware or no, he knows no one's better than you at hunting 'mancers. And if *you* couldn't catch Psycho Mantis, what hope does David have?"

Paul imagined a competent Task Force run by people determined to catch him, and thought David had a very good chance indeed.

TWENTY-THREE
Mrs Liu's Infinite Kittens

"Hello, Mittens!" Mrs Liu picked up one of her cats. "Hello, Trouble. Oh, you're a *mischievous* little devil! And my sweet little Lickums…"

Paul perched on a chair as a sea of ragged tails bobbed to and fro beneath him: clusters of cats purring on the stove, tangles of cats squabbling beneath the kitchen table, rows of cats staring down at him from the cabinets with the grace of queens.

The 'mancy here *looked* mundane, but Paul had watched for hours, fascinated, trying to figure out how it was done.

Mrs Liu looked quite kindly as she hugged each of her cats, an elderly Chinese lady with a thin chuckle and a staunch disregard for the way the cats knocked her teacups off her table – yet she'd hugged a new kitty to her breast every minute or two for several hours, and had not hugged the same one twice.

This was a large apartment, but it held infinite cats. And Paul had eventually realized Mrs Liu's secret:

There was no litter box.

No cat never escaped out the front door.

It had taken him days to figure this out, but… Paul was pretty sure Mrs Liu's cats didn't actually exist.

The Institute's records said she'd been brought here with

three cats, all spayed. She'd created a litter of kittens that were completely unremarkable aside from the fact that they'd coalesced out of midair.

He felt a vague temptation to tug on a cat's 'mancy and see what was left once Mrs Liu's spell unraveled. But Paul had been informed that one word from Mrs Liu and the place would turn feral, wherein he would be dragged by cat-induced peristalsis down the hallways, torn to shreds and never seen again.

He preferred not to die wearing a gaudy luchador mask.

He didn't want to upset her anyway. One of the joys at being at the Institute was watching everyone's different magics. After he'd done the necessary paperwork for Mr Payne, Paul would relax by flitting from universe-bending joy to universe-bending joy – dropping in to see Natasha the culinomancer whip up a magical flan, or trying to figure out what Juan the bookiemancer saw as he plucked predictions from the buzzing swarms of numbers, or watch Idena the origamimancer crease a single typewriter-sized sheet of vellum into a table-sized paper forest, every leaf and branch meticulously outlined.

He just wished they would *talk* to him.

The Foundation was legally designated as her full-time school now, and Aliyah – sorry, *Hotplate* – had the run of the place. Here, she was everyone's favorite godchild. Even now, Aliyah made a magical mask with Mrs Vinere. Aliyah taught her how to make Majora's Masks, where each mask let you bounce around the room like a pinball.

Without Aliyah, the best Mrs Vinere could do would give you a new face. But with Aliyah, all the 'mancers seemed… amplified.

Mrs Liu, like all the other 'mancers, had been skeptical of Paul. She'd cracked open the door when he mentioned Aliyah's name – he shouldn't have confirmed he was Hotplate's father, it broke Mr Payne's SMASH-thwarting information barriers, but he needed to introduce himself with the proper authority. And even then she eyed him warily, as though at any moment he might reveal he did not like cats.

It was funny; all his life he'd been attracted to 'mancy, had lost his foot because he'd had to watch the illustromancer work, had become a bureaucromancer because he loved magic.

Here he was, with all this 'mancy, and still no one to share it with.

No Foundation 'mancer made eye contact. They had their own fiefdoms; his visits perplexed them. They paid attention for precisely as long as he spoke to them, looking away as if they longed to get back to their kitchen, or their football game, or their stuffed animal caves.

The culinomancer had baked amazing dishes of grilled purple cauliflower couscous – but left them stacked by the ovens, shrugging when Paul asked for a bite. The origamimancer had completed her forest and then chucked it into the garbage.

They created beauty, but felt no need to share it.

Their tiny magics made him itch with guilt. He loved bureaucracy, but... he had a daughter he loved, and Valentine, and an ex-wife he still had dinner with. *Still* his 'mancy was stronger than theirs.

Their lives had been consumed by their obsessions, yet they'd been rewarded with magics barely more than coincidence.

It was unfair. Valentine could destroy buildings, and she wasn't half as devoted to her games as that lonely little plushiemancer who sat for hours, trying to teach his befuddled stuffed animals to dance. They only rocked back and forth.

But when Aliyah dropped by, his animals did musical numbers. They loved Aliyah because her videogamemancy could be anything – a cooking game, a basketball game, a little farm with plushie horses. They didn't have to pretend to like anything else, because Aliyah loved what they did. They could plug into her 'mancy.

Paul was proud of Aliyah. They both needed to socialize these poor recluses.

Which was why Paul had brought Mrs Liu a bottle of cream, and tried to make conversation.

"So… why *is* Trouble such trouble?" he inquired. "What's the little scamp get up to?"

"Piddles," she murmured, nuzzling a new kitty nose-to-nose. "Aww, Piddles."

Maybe he should have brought cat treats.

A brisk knock on the door: Mrs Liu straightened. She stood up, brushing clumps of cat hair off her dress, then slicked back her hair. She flung the door open wide, then crouched almost as if to bow.

Mr Payne pushed a dolly heaped high with canned cat food through the door, sunny as a sour man like Payne could be. "Here you go, Mrs Liu. The cleaners will be in to take out your garbage later today."

She bobbed her head, trembling, as if wanting to get the words right. "Thangew."

Payne cocked his head. "What was that, Mrs Liu?"

"Thank you, King." Her words had the stiff ring of a practiced speech. When she curtsied, her cats stretched out, miaowing respectfully in Payne's direction. Payne nodded curtly, a general acknowledging his troops' marginal effort.

"All I need." He turned to Paul. "Mr Mongoose! Good to see you. Come with me."

By the time Paul remembered his code name was Mongoose, Payne had left. Mrs Liu stayed frozen until Mr Payne was gone, then unloaded her cat food with shivering gratitude.

Paul picked his way through the swarming cats and left; no one seemed to notice.

Payne had already strode to the next room. Two luchador-masked orderlies pushed pallets of supplies behind him.

Paul caught up just as Payne was unloading bundles of paper into the origamimancer's room. The origamimancer – a woman as pale and angular as the paper she worked with

– bowed and presented a sculpture of Payne to him.

"Wonderful." Payne turned, pleased, to deposit it in Paul's hands. "What do you think?"

The origami was a sternly angled version of Payne, with a blank face and a stiff twisted-vellum crown. Even cupped in Paul's palm, it seemed to loom over him.

"It's quite nice," Paul lied.

"We'll put it in my antechamber." Payne whisked it off Paul's palm and handed it to an orderly. He shut the door on the origamimancer. "So, Mr Mongoose. What do you think of your fellow 'mancers?"

"They seem a little…" Paul didn't want to sound cruel. Payne had found a way to keep seventeen 'mancers working together in secrecy. Hell, Paul had juggled three 'mancers, and *that* had come close to disintegrating at times.

"They're not the friendliest people," Paul finished.

"They're not," Payne admitted. "Though you mustn't let that get you down. Truth is, I don't encourage them to mix much."

"…you don't?"

"I don't *prevent* socializing – but frankly, each 'mancer represents their own worldview. It's quite stupid, honestly, but I've seen the evidence with these old rheumy eyes: get two different 'mancers talking, and they forget the world is out to get them! They forget they're a precious few blessed enough to bend physics with mere willpower, and start squabbling over which hobby is superior. Next thing you know, you've got a magical war on your hands."

"You really *do* think 'mancy is a blessing, don't you?"

"Oh God yes. You've felt that fervent glory, haven't you? That sense the universe has lined up behind you?"

Paul had, once. He'd saved New York City with it. The rest had been doubt and concern.

Payne slugged him on the shoulder. "It's a wonder any of us can do – well, any of this. But we forget what we have in common. I'll tell you, sir, there were some real catfights back in the 1970s before my psychologists perfected 'mancer integration. That's why there's so many regulations here."

"I'm happy to be here," Paul demurred. "And Aliyah is so content. But..."

"They're hothouse flowers."

"What?"

Payne swept his hand to encompass the pillars, the lobby, twenty doors with a 'mancer secluded inside each one. "The 'mancers. They're hothouse flowers, sir. I know you want them to be as witty as Ms Mercer and lovable as little Hotplate, but... not everybody gets to be charming."

"I didn't expect..."

"No. You came here expecting company. You were hoping to find others to... what term do you children use these days? 'Geek out' over your love of 'mancy?"

Paul slumped. "Maybe I did."

Payne nodded in sympathy. "I did once, too. But... in truth, I've come to realize doing 'mancy is the real beauty. I didn't bring them here to socialize them. I think it might even be an insult to see them as broken. What we do here is to foster a little demesne for them to follow their bliss. That's our job, Mr Mongoose – to create a place where 'mancers can thrive. Together."

It was funny. There had been a time where Payne's voice would have set him to trembling. Now, somehow, Payne reassured him.

"In fact," Payne said, pacing the lobby's rim, "There's only one person who does not fit in."

And he stopped before Valentine's door.

"No," Paul whispered.

Paul cracked open the door to check in on Valentine. She was curled up in the wreckage of all the ripped-down *Mario* mosaics and smashed display racks. She'd kicked the videogames – still in their packaging – into a gigantic heap in the corner. The shattered fluorescents sputtered overhead.

She hunched over, sullenly playing her old videogames on her old Nintendo DS, looking like Valentine.

Paul shuddered. She wasn't wearing her Alex Mercer

skin any more. A bad sign, considering she had only three days left on her promise to stay here.

Payne closed the door. His orderlies, sensing the incoming storm, had scattered.

"She hasn't left us yet," Payne said, exasperated. "Which is good. I don't know what I'd do if she left, considering all the intel she has on our operation. If the Task Force picks her up and hands her to SMASH, we're good as dead."

"Mr Payne – "

"King. It's *King* here. You of all people should understand the need for obscurity."

"Look, Mr King. What are you suggesting?"

Payne flung up his hands. "Who knows, Paul? You're her supervisor. I brought her in here because I supposed you ran a tidy operation. Do you?"

Payne stepped closer, almost bumping chest-to-chest with Paul; all his old fears came rushing back. That terror that Mr Payne might check in on you today, and take away your job.

Paul tried to envision Valentine, checking in at 9:00 every morning, and saw the impending disaster in Payne's Institute. Payne could *not* think of Valentine as just another employee.

"She's no hothouse flower," Paul explained. "She's my enforcer. Just like you have Rainbird. And *he* doesn't stay cooped up in here."

Payne harrumphed. "Rainbird's won special privileges."

"And Valentine's won mine. She needs real-world challenges in addition to illusory ones. So what do you have?"

"Paul, I can't give her an assignment without knowing she's with us…"

"She's with me. That should be good enough."

Payne shifted his weight. Paul remembered Payne was a six-foot-tall ex-Marine, and he was a scrawny man tottering on a fake ankle.

"You wanted a second-in-command." Paul forced an

unnatural jolliness into his voice. "But you're not hiring us, Mr Payne. This is a merger. That involves adjustments on *both* ends."

"A merger," Payne snapped, "assumes the other company was successful in its operations."

"It *was* successful. Until you and I accidentally went to war."

The only person who Paul had ever seen go toe-to-toe with Payne was his old boss Kit. Kit had defused Payne's managerial explosions with cool logic. Paul stole from Kit's playbook, driving Payne right up to the edge by dismantling his assumptions.

Once again, Paul thought, *my daughter's wellbeing depends on Mr Payne not firing me.*

And just as he did whenever he faced down Kit, Payne broke. He gave Paul a sickly smile.

"I suppose you're right, Paul. 'Mancers, we– we mustn't fight. There's too much at stake. If we can't bring everyone onto the same page, well... well, then we're back to Germany, and the broaches, with physics raped in its still-warm grave...."

Payne's eyes dimmed, his hands shivering, and Paul almost asked what horrors Payne remembered. They had to be grim. Decades had passed, and he'd still been driven to honor his dead sisters by naming the PTSD school after them...

It seemed kindest to let the memories pass, without digging them up further. Sure enough, Payne squeezed back the tears.

"I can offer you a training run. Which I am not thrilled about, mind you. Your successor David has installed a fortune's worth of opals around his relevant servers and filing cabinets, making it *much* harder to see what he's doing at the Task Force. You've told us he's ordering in more equipment from foreign militaries; his new budget is concomitant with that. Under normal circumstances, I'd *never* let a novice out with the NYPD hunting for us."

"...but?"

"But there are still 'mancers being created in New York. If I don't miss my guess, we've found one we need to get to before David Giabatta's cursed Task Force gets their hands on him. I was going to assign this one to Rainbird, but... I suppose my best investigator can do the job just as well."

He squeezed Paul's shoulder affectionately. Paul felt almost shamed by the intense pride the old man's compliments inspired. Paul liked having his work graded. Running his own illegal 'mancy business had meant forever having to bury his greatest triumphs.

Paul hadn't realized how desperately he hungered for appreciation.

"But," Payne added, jerking his head towards Valentine's room, "keep her in line. I know a loose cannon when I see one. If this is truly a merger, Paul, then you must get her on our side."

Payne placed a gentle emphasis on the word *our* as he swept his hand around the great stone rotunda.

Payne's extended fingers pointed at Aliyah.

He didn't recognize her, at first. She was hidden behind ivy-covered columns, shouting as she sparred with a fellow 'mancer. She held a pair of wickedly curved daggers, chained at the hilt, the chains wrapped around her forearms, lashing out with such force that her blade nicked stone off of a fluted pillar.

Streaks of fire arced into the air. Rainbird, then. She was playing with Rainbird.

Aliyah pressed her advantage, backing him back up against the lobby's central desk where – for the hundredth time this week – a luchador-wearing receptionist dove for cover. Rainbird had summoned blazing swords in his blistered hands, thwarting Aliyah's wild attacks with precise defenses.

And for a moment, Paul wasn't sure if it *was* Aliyah. Her pretty little-girl smile had crumpled into a glowering old man's goateed scowl. Her keloid burn scars were reduced to a single puckered scar cleaved down through her right eyebrow and cheek. A sweeping red tattoo covered her left eye, looping over her bald head, around ears now studded with gold pirate's loops.

It must have been some videogame character. It didn't look like Aliyah, at least not the Aliyah he knew.

But then Aliyah darted past Rainbird's defenses, nicking Rainbird's long coat with her daggers – and though her face was an old male warrior, her triumphant shout was purest Aliyah.

Rainbird chuckled, patting her on the head.

Aliyah shook his touch off, clutching her daggers.

"Again," she commanded.

Rainbird grinned around his cigar and fell into another defensive stance as Aliyah went after him. "Bleed it off before it gets too bad."

Aliyah pressed her attack, squeezing her eyes shut as she unleashed a flow of flux. Sure enough, one of her chained daggers shot wild, chopping a thin birch tree in half; the tree toppled towards her, threatening to tangle her up in thin branches. Aliyah leapt away and continued the assault.

"Good," Rainbird murmured. "Now keep your feet together. I could push you off balance."

Aliyah adjusted her feet, but never stopped advancing. When she wanted something, Paul thought, she'd never held back. And she wanted to beat Rainbird.

Rainbird smiled serenely the entire time, as if he was certain she would beat him some day.

Paul just watched them. Aliyah had stopped playing with the other children. She'd been terrified to. But here, swinging blades, accidentally chopping trees in half, she could hurt no one.

"What a lovely little girl," Payne said, content, then excused himself.

Aliyah had lost so many things, Paul thought: her parents' marriage, her normal looks, her ordinary childhood, her innocence. He couldn't let her lose the Institute; not so soon after finding it, anyway. Valentine threatened to get them all ejected from this new-found – well, the Institute wasn't paradise, but it was stable. Safe. A place for Aliyah to master her 'mancy.

And if Valentine couldn't get on board, well... no. She'd learn to love it here. Or at least find something tolerable. With Payne's wealth, there had to be *something* here to appease her.

He looked back at Aliyah. She swung her daggers with such force that she almost gutted Rainbird. He'd reminded himself to tell Aliyah to hold back when she played; Aliyah got overexcited, but Paul knew she didn't want to kill anyone, not really.

Then Paul opened the door to talk to Valentine.

TWENTY-FOUR
New Sheriff in Town

"I came here expecting a briefing." Valentine looked around in confusion at the small beige meeting room. She squinted at Payne, who'd entered carrying a manila folder.

"This *is* a briefing," Paul explained.

"Where's the big oval seats we sit in while a computer voice narrates our next mission?" she asked. "Where are the billboard-sized screens that zoom in on our target? Where's the staff of data analysts in dark gray Samaritan Mutual uniforms, huddled over computer terminals as they sift for data?"

"Um… we never had those. Not even on the police force."

"And so reality disappoints *once again*." Valentine plopped her ass into a swiveling computer seat. She turned to Payne. "Can't you whip up a PowerPoint presentation or something?"

Payne frowned, taking his place at the head of the table. "That's nonsense frippery the Internet has encouraged. We need no frills. Just data."

Valentine reached into her skirt to pull out her Nintendo DS, propping her stiletto-booted feet up on the table. She conspicuously played while Payne laid out the contents of his manila folder upon the table's clean white surface.

Paul almost asked Payne to just make a damn PowerPoint slide for once. He'd spent the last hour convincing Valentine that rescuing 'mancers could be a grand adventure, full of the excitement she was distinctly not getting being cooped up in a room "surrounded by weeniemancers," as she put it. And he'd gone *far* out of his way to imply – though not promise, Paul would never lie to her – that tracking down 'mancers wouldn't be more boring Paul stuff like reading through files.

Now Valentine and Payne were on edge, jockeying for Paul's attention.

Not a good start.

It didn't get much better when Rainbird walked into the room.

Valentine leapt out of her chair. "What the fuck is Creepazoid doing here?"

Payne rearranged the papers Valentine had knocked out of true. "I said you could investigate. I did not say unsupervised. Not with this elevated threat level."

"This fucker tried to burn me."

"That 'fucker' burns whoever I aim him at, Ms DiGriz. I authorized him to burn anyone who attacked him."

"I–" Valentine looked at Paul, who pleaded silently for her to go along. Rainbird swept by them to sit next to Payne, examining Paul and Valentine with the faint amusement one would give to watching two birds fighting over a scrap of bread. He turned his scarred hands over upon the table, palm-up, as if to ask: *Well? Are you going to leave?*

Valentine slapped her hands on the table hard enough to make the waterglasses rattle. "Right," she said, leaning over to scour Payne's compiled evidence. "Let's see who's better at wrangling some goddamned 'mancers."

Paul could breathe again. If they could get through this mission, maybe he could make this…

"First, these." Payne handed out a silver Samaritan Mutual badge to each of them, folded inside a leather case. "Keep these touching your skin at all times."

"Not sure I want you rubbing up against me," Valentine said.

"Those badges are the flux dumps that allow me to redirect your bad luck out to my risk pool. Without them touching your bare flesh, when you do 'mancy, your bad luck comes down on one person: you. I'd consider going solo to be fairly risky behavior, given that David Giabatta's task force have vowed to take you down – but that's your decision, Ms DiGriz."

Valentine turned the heavy badge over in her fingers, not quite willing to give it back.

"No?" Payne asked archly. "Then clasp it to your bare breast and thank me."

"What?"

He turned away to rifle through a folder, uncaring. "That's how it activates."

Valentine fumed, then pressed the thick curves of the badge against the swell of her left breast. The badge's ridges squeezed shut, a tick affixing itself to her skin. Feeling queasy, Paul tucked his badge into his pocket, wanting to distance himself from the metal's skin-warm touch.

"Thank you, King," Valentine said between gritted teeth. Paul felt a flow of 'mancy open up between them. Payne nodded.

"Some day I'll make you mean that, Ms DiGriz. But we have a case to investigate." Payne touched the papers, assuring their proper order, before clearing his throat. "This one's very unusual. He's an ex-employee. In fact, I'd almost overlooked him… but recent evidence has shown Samaritan Mutual may be proficient in generating 'mancers."

He gave Paul a broad wink, an actor trying to simulate warmth.

"Where are the pictures?" Valentine asked, shuffling through the papers. "He worked for you, so you must have ID. All you've got are these blurry shots of a guy with… shit, looks like someone's roughed him up. All I can see are bruises." She leaned back, closing her eyes in bliss. "Mmm, bruises. You know what bruises are? Makeup for men."

Payne sniffed. "Those *are* his employee IDs. Which have somehow been blurred. Furthermore, his fellow employees don't remember what he looked like. They remember catastrophic injuries, yet... he never filed a medical claim, despite some coworkers remembering him with broken cheekbones."

Valentine wrapped her arms around herself and rocked. "Sexy, sexy bruises."

"So... what happened?"

"We fired him, of course. Yet he *had* investigated some of Anathema's terrorist attacks for us in years past, and we know Anathema's attacks were designed to create new 'mancers. That, in conjunction with the fact that we don't know... well...."

Payne hesitated, embarrassed. Rainbird drummed his fingers on the table sympathetically. "It's 'mancy, sir. Odd things come with the territory. You can't be expected to have all the facts."

Payne nodded, appeased. "Thank you, Rainbird."

"So what's this dude's name?" Valentine said. As Paul spread the case files across the table, he noted thumbprint smudges of sickly brown blotted across the files. All the fields that had once contained the man's name had bloated, swelling up from water damage and dissolving into mold – though the rest of the papers remained the same crisp eggshell-white they'd been when they'd been extracted from Payne's immaculate records.

"That can't be right." Paul frowned, reaching out with his 'mancy to pull up the file on a computer. A flickering static haze obscured the field where the man's name should be. Paul scrolled down, but sure enough, the haze fizzled and reappeared in front of the name before Paul could read it.

"That's the problem," Payne said. "As far as we can tell, he's erased his name from the world."

TWENTY-FIVE
The Strongest and Smartest Men Who've Ever Lived

"Not a problem." Valentine scooped up the papers. "We've got his last known address. We'll walk it over."

"It's not quite that simple." Rainbird tugged the papers out of her grip. "We should pinpoint what kind of 'mancer he is. Or determine whether he is, in fact, the 'mancer at all. Perhaps he's the victim of another man's obsession."

"You think some crazy 'mancer's erasing people's injuries *and* their names? Tchuh."

Paul held out his hand for the files. A nod from Payne, and Rainbird deposited them into Paul's palm. "A little advance groundwork wouldn't be amiss here, Valentine. Fact is, when *I* bureaucromanced Payne, I tripped his wires. Yet someone was so good they waltzed in through Payne's records and deleted himself, and Payne didn't even *notice*."

"The old boy's oblivious to a *lot* of things." Valentine headed for the door, yanking the paper out of Paul's fingers. "This is a wild goose chase to keep me distracted anyway, so tell you what, Paul – we're gonna do this the Valentine way. We're gonna go pound on his door, hope this game is structured so the clues are lying on the ground, and skip all this Samaritan Mutual overcautious bullshit."

"That's–"

"Tut-tut-tut." She held up a hand. "As much as I appreciate

how y'all are trying to engage my sense of mystery, we all realize this comes down to one thing: *will Valentine be satisfied, trading in a healthy sex life for chasing random 'mancers around Brooklyn?* Frankly, we either find out I like the hunt, or we have a real uncomfortable conversation about what happens next. So I'm not presupposed to doing a lot of legwork here, capiche?"

She paused by the door, daring Paul to contradict her.

"All right, Valentine," Paul said. "This is your show."

Payne's shoulders were stiff with disappointment.

Three hours into the investigation, Paul allowed himself a smidgeon of hope.

Valentine was proving surprisingly good at investigating. She was conspicuous as all hell, of course – a stocky woman with a glittery eyepatch, wild black hair tied up in a bow, and wearing crinoline dresses with zombie-blood stockings was guaranteed to stand out – but she'd knocked on John Doe's landlady's door, claiming to be his cousin dropping in for a surprise visit.

The landlady – an old Mexican woman with a prominent Bronx accent – couldn't remember what John Doe had looked like, but when prompted did remember "the man with those horrible injuries." She told tales of his terrible insomnia, the way she heard him clomping around in the apartment above her, talking to himself. She'd spoken with him, but the problem had gotten worse; he'd taken to coming in at all hours, drooling blood from his gashed mouth, clapping steaks to his blackened eyes, frightening her other tenants.

"That must have been horrible," Valentine said, sipping the tea the landlady had made for them. "Did you kick him out?"

"Oh, no. He blew his apartment up."

Rainbird leaned forward, eyes gleaming.

Valentine put the tea down. "He blew it up?"

The landlady shook her head. "He sealed everything off and filled it with bug bombs. Blew his Ikea furniture to flinders. Oh, he claimed his stove's pilot light went off by mistake… But his security deposit wasn't enough to rebuild the room. Haven't seen him since."

"Oh, man. How much did my cousin cost you?"

"Haven't been able to repair the damage. My insurance company hasn't paid me yet."

Valentine waved Paul into action. While Paul magically hacked her paperwork to get a check on the way, Valentine asked about a forwarding address.

"I don't know where he's gone," the landlady apologized. "His records burned up in the fire. Otherwise I would have called the cops on him."

Valentine thanked her, walked out into the hallway, and twirled on her toes. She extended her index finger, rotating around with a surge of 'mancy, and followed her fingernail out to the complex's back alley. It was piled high with burned garbage – old glass dishes with tiny bubbled imperfections, sooty Eurotrash shelving units, ashen armchairs with faint green stripe patterns.

Something glowed in the detritus.

Valentine kicked aside an old film reel to find a damp receipt for a sale of soap stuck to the ground. The receipt was limned in a pulsing emerald shine, encouraging Valentine to pick it up.

"Quest item," she explained, squinting at the address written on it before looking it up in her phone. "Next stop: our crazy-ass bug-bomb-o-'mancer."

Rainbird drove them to the destination, piloting the limousine, giving them some privacy in the back. But Valentine was uncharacteristically quiet, staring into her Nintendo without the usual stream of commentary she gave whenever they drove together.

"Thanks for going along with this, Valentine," Paul said to clear the silence. "I know it's giving up a lot…"

"Where do you want to live, Paul?"

She'd placed the Nintendo in her lap, stared evenly at Paul. Paul had never been comfortable making eye contact, especially not with Valentine.

And the truth was, he *wasn't* sure he wanted to live at the Institute. He'd been trying to make friends, hoping to find interesting talks like he had with Valentine, but the other 'mancers had nothing to say.

It had been fun for a few days, living in that glorious library, but... His office back at Samaritan Mutual had been cramped, the cabinets rusty, stuffed underneath a staircase. Yet he'd acquired every book of regulations personally, his macaroni pen cup made by Aliyah, his desk blotter stained with his own ink. He'd reorganized his new digs, but it seemed–

–well, he didn't want to say "soulless." It had a feel. It just wasn't *his* feel.

But when Paul had told Aliyah he was leaving to investigate a 'mancer, she threw a temper tantrum: Daddy was *not* going out without her. Then Rainbird had appeared, promising to keep Aliyah's father safe. Paul had expected Aliyah's usual skepticism – she followed up every one of Paul's promises with a "really?" – but Aliyah had nodded and hugged Paul before letting him go.

That was progress.

Yet now Paul worried about being separated from *her*. Even though Aliyah curled up by his side every night, Paul had nightmares where Aliyah slipped away, Aliyah having run off to an abandoned house where she burned, burned, burned...

"I'll live wherever Aliyah's happy," Paul demurred.

"Paul. *Paul*. Bad idea."

"...what? Why?"

"If you give up everything for your children's happiness, Paul, you can't teach them how to be happy."

"Oh, come on. You were the one who gave Aliyah that ludicrous speech on how she'd be alone forever..."

She thumped her breast with pride. "*I'm* bad cop here, Paul. You're good cop. *I* tell Aliyah the cold realities so she doesn't drown in your dreams. And... shit, I *want* you to prove me wrong. But... I'm lonelier than ever there. I'm trying, man. Because I love you. But a life without kissing, or fucking – that's empty, man. You need more than *agape* to function, you need *eros*." She eyed Paul, shrugged. "OK, maybe you don't. The only woman I've ever seen you make googly eyes at is your ex."

"Valentine, I…" Paul swallowed. "All you do is go to the swing clubs. You're just… fucking."

"I'd *like* love," she said wistfully. "But since my flux impaled the last guy I loved on a rusty pipe, a girl's gotta fill the void with something." She sighed, looking out the window. "Two bisexual firemen will do."

Rainbird drove through a decrepit industrial zone, a place filled with abandoned paper mills and businesses that had long vanished. Paul knew the areas well – 'mancers thrived in rotted homes that normal people didn't dare to visit.

It was dusk before they pulled up before a ramshackle mansion – a looming Victorian household peeled down to the rotted wood by years of neglect. The windows were boarded over with plywood, the sagging roof so denuded of tiles that even pigeons refused to roost there.

Stenciled across a boarded window in bright pink letters: "PAPER STREET SOAP COMPANY." Muscular workers dug ditches outside.

Valentine pressed her nose against the window, whistling low as she admired scores of filthy biceps. At first Paul thought they were landscapers – why would anyone tend to the lawn when the house was about to fall over? – but then he noted tarps stuck on sticks, rainwater barrels, stacks of glass signaling the beginnings of a greenhouse.

"Great," Paul said. "It's a military compound."

Valentine hopped out of the car. "Well, we know our bug-bomb-o-'mancer will be at the front of the line," and strode up to the house like she owned it. Paul voiced some feeble concerns about doing some reconnoitering; Valentine ignored him.

Rainbird coasted behind, rolling his cigar between his fingers, glancing uneasily at the burly men armed with shovels. Paul cruised to a halt, his attention caught by the way the men didn't react.

Paul limped up, approaching the workers with the caution of a hunter approached a deer. They kept digging holes as the light faded, not paying the slightest bit of attention to him. Or the setting sun. Or, in fact, anything but their shovels.

They were all young men, handsome as actors; their heads were shorn in tight cuts, their broken-nosed faces full of the fanatic's glazed admiration.

He walked in experimentally between two men picking up a glass pane. They bumped against him, knocking him off balance without so much as an apology; they didn't seem to register Paul's existence. Then they picked up the glass, threatening to bowl him over.

"They're mesmerized," Rainbird said.

"No." Paul touched them on the shoulders before smelling the 'mancy on his fingertips. "It's deeper. I don't think they exist."

"...what?"

"It's like Mrs Liu's cats. There are no lunchboxes or port-a-potties here. And these men are too... well, too perfect. They're extras on a Hollywood lot." Paul repressed the urge to try to unmake them. "Our 'mancer wants fanatics working for him, and like Mrs Liu I don't doubt he has a handful of real people mixed in with the lot, but... his 'mancy is filling in gaps."

"Creating people." Rainbird looked discomfited. "That's a whole new level of 'mancy."

"We'd better catch up with Valentine before she gets in over her head."

Valentine stood under the gabled porch, poking two men in pseudo-military uniforms who stood at attention, satchels at their feet. They waited outside the door as if they expected someone to come get them.

She flicked their noses; one flinched, the other didn't.

"Check this out, Paul!" She gave him a lopsided grin,

proud of her discovery. She poked the one who flinched. "PC." Then she wrapped her fingers around the other one's crotch, squeezing tight. He didn't move. "NPC."

"...What?"

"Game terminology," Valentine explained. "*This* dude's real. A player character. As witness!" When she knocked his cap off, he began to sweat. "But this one?" She dug her fingernails deeper into his testicles: no response. "A Non-Player Character. Our bug-bomb-o-'mancer made him up. He's set dressing."

"Yeah, we figured that out."

The capless, real man – a young white kid who couldn't have been older than twenty – bent over, intending to pick up his cap, then thought better of it.

"...is this part of the test?" he ventured.

Valentine rooted through his satchel. The kid started to protest, but thought better of that, too, baffled as Paul by Valentine's antics.

She tossed the items at the kid's face as she extracted them from his satchel. "One pair black boots. Two pair black socks. Two pair black pants. Two black shirts. And – there it is..." She held up a rubber-banded wad of cash as though it were a smoking gun. "Three hundred dollars in personal burial money."

"Valentine," Paul asked. "Do you know what the hell is going on?"

She grinned like a mudshark.

"I do. My sweet stars, Paul, this is a *delightful* psychosis." She rapped her knuckles on the door; her knocks boomed, as though the house was hollow. The kid shuffled his rumpled clothes around with his feet, unsure whether he was allowed to bend over to pick it up.

"Is this part of the test?"

"You have to determine your own level of commitment," Valentine shot back. The door rattled half open, held by another suspicious young military kid. He goggled at Valentine.

"I'm here for the club tonight." She winked, which looked odd on a one-eyed woman. "Me and my two friends. Not that, you know, we should have heard about it. But *you* know how boys gossip."

He looked down at her breasts, distracted. "I- I'm not sure whether that's–"

She gave him a disarming smile. "Is that in your rules? You got eight of them, last I checked. Don't think 'No women' is in there. This is cancer, right?"

"What? I..."

"God, you don't even get your own references." She pushed open the door, exasperated. "Look, kid, we got faces to punch, same as you. I'm willing to bet I've used my cock more than you've used yours, and I bought mine at Amazon. Is the club in progress?"

"...well, yeah, but..."

"Downstairs? In the shitty basement, filled with men's sweat?"

"I wouldn't–"

"My kinda action. I'm in." She pushed past him, all but daring him to tackle her. Paul apologized as he followed in Valentine's wake, walking into the mildewed stench.

Valentine shouldered past men – only men – who halted next to triple-decker bunk beds, who paused in filling up industrial drums with chemicals, who stopped rewiring sputtering electrical fixtures to stare at Valentine. She bumped them aside, headed through the maze of rooms towards the basement.

Pained cries echoed up the stairs, the wet smack of fists bruising flesh. Men cheered.

He's got an army here, Paul thought, feeling small as he limped along on his artificial limb, trying to keep up. Rainbird cruised behind him, arms held tight at his sides, puffing on the cigar.

Valentine charged down the basement stairs, as though she couldn't wait to see the show. The basement was body temperature, the heated stew smell of shirtless men crammed in to an airless place, laced with stale cigarette smoke and a sharp metallic blood scent. There had been rows of narrow windows facing the west, once, but they'd been boarded over to give people privacy.

The crowd downstairs, at least thirty shirtless men, fell silent as Valentine strode into view. Piles of shoes, socks, and shirts had been tossed into the corner, along with bloodied towels. Several beaten men cuddled each other, whispering reassurances.

And yet, Paul thought, that smell was strangely invigorating. Like a lion's den redolent with the meat scent of predator piss. Parts of you only came alive once you realized your next few moments would be brief, exciting, and possibly final.

The men in the arena had yet to notice Valentine. Two pudgy accountants grappled each other in a mockery of martial arts. One had smashed the other's head into a splintered support beam, but had rallied to kneel on his friend's chest, woozily punching his buddy's teeth out.

Valentine sized the shirtless men up like they were a buffet, eyeing them with such lust that they covered their nipples. They stopped cheering, uncertain; Paul realized they'd been confident this gladiator-style arena was a great idea, and it *had* been a great idea as long as nobody else passed judgment. Someone who found this amusing could sweep away their illusions.

Then their leader stepped out of the shadows.

He was bared to the waist, his finely muscled chest awash in a sheen of dried blood, a cigarette dangling from the corner of his mouth. His spiky hair was sweat-tousled yet somehow still model-perfect. He had a blackened eye, but it *did* look like makeup on him – the bruise on his tanned cheek accentuating his perfect cheekbones, forming a frame around a perfectly blue eye.

The 'mancer – for it was the 'mancer, no doubt – smiled, his crooked grin at odds with his hesitant fighters; he alone seemed content with Valentine's presence. He gave her a welcoming smile, an effect only slightly spoiled by bloodied teeth.

"Ever see the rabbits freeze underneath a hawk's shadow?" he said to his men, never peeling his admiring gaze away from Valentine. "We got a predator here, boys. And you are shitting pellets."

Valentine drew in a shallow breath at the 'mancer's sheer beauty. She dug her elbow into Paul's ribs. "He's got inguinal creases, Paul. *Inguinal creases.*"

"What in blazes is an inguinal crease?"

"It's the 'V' surrounding a six-pack ab that makes my panties disintegrate."

The 'mancer tapped the two fighting men, pulled them aside as if asking to cut in. They stopped, stunned at Valentine's presence, but then the crowd reached out to draw them in for manly hugs, slapping them on their sweaty backs, handing them towels.

The 'mancer stepped into the arena. The other men stepped back, waiting for his lead.

He winked at Valentine, his bruise-puffed eye barely managing the trick. "So what's your plan here, hotcakes?"

"You." Valentine pointed at him. Called him out. She tugged off her stiletto-heeled boots.

He threw his head back and laughed. "You've distilled self-hatred into self-destruction. We can help you to the next level. You know the rules?"

Valentine pulled her shirt over her head, tossed it at Paul. She unbuckled her bra and tossed that at Paul too, her ample breasts plopping out. Paul held her still-warm clothing in shock, unsure who to give it to – but Valentine didn't think twice about getting half naked before a room of strange men.

She stepped towards the 'mancer, brimming with glee.

"This is fight club. And if this is my first night at fight club…" She sighed happily, as if she'd found the home she'd been seeking all her life. "If it's my first night at fight club, I have to fight."

"Goddamned straight," he said, and punched her.

TWENTY-SIX
I am Jack's Clinical Insanity

Valentine caught the 'mancer's fist in her hand.

"You went for the ear," she said. "How predictable."

She kicked him hard in the balls. He went down grinning.

"Nobody ever seemed to do that in your little movie," she said, teasing – almost flirtatious. "It's almost like you forgot guys have testicles."

"What the fuck is this, Valentine?" Paul asked.

"It's a movie," she explained, grabbing the 'mancer by the hair, slamming his face into the dirt. "*Fight Club*. Had a boyfriend obsessed with the damn thing. Though not as obsessed as Tyler Durden here."

He grabbed one of her nipple rings, twisted it hard enough that she let go. Then he socked her in the face, sending her bouncing back against the support beam. "This isn't just *Fight Club*!" he said heatedly. "I am a Chuck Palahniomancer!"

"Oh, fuck off." She landed a roundhouse to his ribs. "There's nothing here from *Choke*, or *Survivor*, or any of Palahniuk's other books! It's just the movie! *You are a fuckin'* Fight-Club-*omancer!*"

He kneed her in the gut.

Paul watched them pound each other, feeling an odd exultation. This was psychotic, yet honest – not the hothouse flowers of Payne's Institute, but an organic insanity that blossomed in whatever goddamned direction it chose.

Rainbird kept his distance as the men whooped and hollered.

It started as an ordinary fight, but soon enough Paul felt 'mancy flickering between them as the bruises blossomed. Tyler kept laughing, even when she was beating him – *especially* when she was. He fought harder, bringing his combative 'mancy into play. Valentine simply kept pace with her own 'mancy – even though she could go *much* larger, given her 'mancy could draw upon every fighting game in existence.

Yet surprisingly, Valentine played fair, matching him equally. Paul had seen her transform into a fifty-foot-tall boss monster, with flailing tentacles. But she kept her 'mancy low, enduring all the blows he rained down to blacken her cheeks.

They had compatible 'mancies, Paul realized: Valentine's magic created cartoonish destruction, as did Tyler's. And as she got the upper hand on Tyler, rolling him over and kneeling on his arms to smash his face, Paul found himself looking away.

It wasn't the gore. It was the *intimacy*. They exchanged punches instead of kisses, but every blow was an exorcism, reducing each other to survival mode. Regrets? Smashed away with an elbow to your jaw. Inadequacies? How could you feel inadequate, when your body was shoved to its limits and still functioned so triumphantly? All her life, Paul realized, Valentine had retreated into Bowser's Castle alone, crawling with the itch of things she could not control. Paul had always thought she'd retreated there to find small victories to help her chase bigger ones.

But as he watched her slam Tyler's head into the bloodstained sawdust, Paul realized the Castle was where Valentine went to die, over and over again. She'd lost too often to allow herself the delusion of guaranteed victory. Instead, she fled to the Castle to find an ordeal so overwhelming, the luxury of self-pity would destroy her: you "won" in the Castle not through triumph, but by facing your blackest despair without holding back.

Tyler howled his approval as Valentine straddled him, smashed him, destroyed him. He was losing, but losing with every ounce of skill he had to offer.

Valentine had walked into this shabby basement, only to find herself standing inside someone else's castle. She punched with the accuracy of perfect love, him smiling up at her through bloodied teeth because he'd found someone who would never softpedal his flaws.

One by one, Tyler's men directed their attention elsewhere, surly jealousy on their faces.

Rainbird exhaled a cloud of black smoke. "Is this part of her mission?"

"I think she's, uh… welcoming him to the fold." Valentine began kissing Tyler, grinding her hips against him. "Yeah, that's super-welcoming."

"This is–"

A sound of impact, filtered through thick plywood. A cry of pain came from outside the boarded-over basement windows, followed by the distinctive sound of policemen calling for backup.

Tyler popped up, his face already half healed. "That'll be the punji stakes."

"Punji stakes?"

"Covered pits all around the house. Filled 'em with sharpened stakes. Vietnamese used to cover them in their own feces to punch their shit deep into soldiers' feet. Me, I put the stakes in point-down, so they have to choose between keeping their foot where I want it, or losing their toes."

Yowls of anguish. Tyler cupped his hands around his mouth. "*Wise choices! Wise choices, buddy!*"

Paul gasped. "You lined *traps* around your house?" Valentine echoed him, dreamier: "You lined traps around your *house*?"

Tyler ignored them. "Gentlemen! You are not a special snowflake! You are a bee, your stinger roped to your liver, dying for the sake of the hive! *Now get out there and show them what Project Mayhem can do!*" The fighters jogged upstairs, faces grim, as Tyler helped a battered Valentine to her feet.

"All right," Rainbird said. "Let's—"

The windows exploded inwards. Paul tumbled backwards, bleeding, as another hollow *boom* echoed throughout the basement. Several basketball-sized clusters flew in through the shattered window – and then exploded into a thousand ping pong-ball-sized things that looked vaguely like grenades, each made of a sticky red rubberized material. They bounced madly around the room, rocketing hard enough to daze Paul as they ricocheted off his skull. A few moments later, they were everywhere – rolling on the floor, stuck to the pillars, adhered to the walls.

"*Hey! My homeowner's insurance won't cover that!*" Tyler roared, just as a fusillade of rubber bullets caught him in the throat. He gagged, fell backwards.

Paul plucked a ball off the wall, rolled it between his fingers. They had serial numbers engraved in the small ridge around their equator.

Perfect. He worked best when given IDs.

He read one, activated his bureaucromancy to trace this unique identifier back to the armament factory that created it, to the production line it had rolled off of. He induced a bit of 'mancy to ensure this thing's quality control had gone slightly awry, so this particular whatever-it-was was a dud – and then pulled up the paperwork that led to its creation –

Patent #8,234,009 B2: An anti-'mancer grenade containing a microscopic chip of high-grade opal (2), surrounded by a set of P-wave sensors (5) to detect fine fractures caused by the presence of any non-Euclidean physics (a.k.a. "'mancy"), attached to a magnesium-based pyrotechnic charge that explodes upon fracture (7a), thus ensuring the safety of civilians while disabling any 'mancer resistance…

Paul traced that back to several other advanced variants

on 'mancy-sensing – the drones, small Roomba-sized jet-black devices, near-invisible at night, that could be flown across the city at night to detect 'mancy. The drones had been deployed last night in their first official tests, flying in complex patterns designed to overlap for maximum coverage. Any 'mancy-induced fracture in the drone's embedded opal – like, say, a crazy 'mancer filling his front yard with artificial men – would broadcast an alert...

"Time to get out." Rainbird conjured up the sheets of fire he'd used to teleport into Paul's apartment–

"*No! Don't use* – " Paul covered his face. As Rainbird summoned his 'mancy, the flashbangs around him detonated in a blinding explosion. Rainbird was catapulted backwards, head lolling. Unconscious or dead? Paul couldn't tell.

The only reason the cops weren't hauling Rainbird out of the basement was Tyler's punji stakes. Phosphorus-blinded, Paul saw dim shadows of confused Task Force members digging each other out of the punji traps, calling for backup.

Valentine grabbed him. She yelled something; Paul heard nothing but ringing. If the broken windows hadn't dissipated the explosion's force, Paul's eardrums would have burst.

Tyler gagged, vomited, grabbing his throat. "Guh! *That*'s new."

Paul realized: his eardrums *should* have burst. Just like rubber bullets should have ruptured Tyler's throat. Tyler had visions of a world where men could beat each other to bloodied pulps each night and still work the next morning. So his 'mancy had shielded them from harm.

A blinding spotlight swept across the room. Valentine dragged Paul to cover, rolling him over the carpet of anti-'mancer grenades. A booming voice, amplified so loud Paul heard it over his ringing ears, rumbled through the room.

"PSYCHO MANTIS," the voice said. "THIS IS DAVID GIABATTA, OF THE NEW YORK ANTI-'MANCER TASK FORCE. YOU HAVE SEEN OUR TECHNOLOGY. WE HAVE WEAPONS TRAINED ON YOU IN THE BASEMENT – ALL

FOUR OF YOU, INCLUDING THE UNCONSCIOUS ONE. AND WE WILL PROVE TO SMASH THAT WE CAN BETTER THEM."

Even at top volume, David sounded quite proud. "SURRENDER. AND YOU WON'T BE HURT. MUCH."

TWENTY-SEVEN
Quality Control

Valentine cupped her hands around Paul's ear. "*I've got half a plan, Paul,*" she shouted. "*Now it's your turn to pull a miracle out of your ass. Can you disable these fucking grenades?*"

Paul shook away the flashbangs' wooziness. Despite having survived several pitched battles, he never *liked* the chaos of combat.

"*Yeah,*" he said. The balls jittered at their feet as something tanklike rolled towards the house. He gestured towards Rainbird, who lay – either unconscious or dead, he couldn't tell – in a smoldering semicircle littered with fragments of detonated grenades. Several laser sights jittered across Rainbird's body, which lay between them and the stairs: Task Force members ready to fire in case someone else broke for safety.

"*You've gotta clear me a space!*" Paul hoped his voice didn't carry outside the basement. "*I'm lucky I didn't set off the ones around me when I analyzed it.*"

"*You trust me, Paul?*"

She was still naked from the waist up. Paul thought he'd probably get used to combat before he got used to her bare breasts.

But he trusted her.

"*All right.*" Valentine got out the Xbox controller she

always kept at her hip, then pulled Paul against her. *"If I'm not quick enough, this could be game over. Ready, Tyler?"*

Tyler grinned like a mudshark as she yanked him up against her body.

"Jump towards the stairs on the count of three."

He fucking hated how crippled his artificial limb and half-foot made him sometimes.

"One…"

If they died because he couldn't jump high enough…

"Two…"

He looked to Valentine. Her worried glance didn't give them good odds.

"Three."

They all leapt into the air, Paul less than the others. As they reached the zenith of their height, Valentine thumbed the controller's button and shouted *"Rocket jump!"*

A force-shield glimmered into existence below their feet.

It expanded as the grenades on the floor went off simultaneously, the shield dimming like polarized glass to protect them from the cacophony of thunder–

The explosion launched them across the room, the force raising them high like a rocket, far higher than nonlethal flashbangs should have been able to –Valentine's videogamemancy at work.

"FIRE!" The Task Force opened fire upon them, the laser sights zipping towards them – but Valentine interposed her force-shield between them. A blue bar appeared over her head, chipped away with each bullet, dwindling as the shield's effectiveness eroded.

"Up the stairs!" she yelled, shoving them out into the chaos aboveground. Tyler's men scurried to and fro, some already writhing in pain from rubber bullet hits, others tossing gas masks at each other, still others getting out guns.

Whatever else Tyler did, Paul thought, *he prepared these boys for war*.

There were blackened spaces, cleared of rubber balls, where the flashbangs had hit Tyler's magic pseudo-men and disintegrated them. Paul was surprised at how many real followers Tyler had. That still left thousands of flashbangs rolling around.

How much additional funding did David get? he wondered, dazed.

"*Into the garbage chute, flyboy!*" Valentine yelled, yanking Paul into the commissary, shoving him into a nearby pantry.

"This isn't a–"

"It's a *Star Wars* reference, Paul. They can't fire grenades into an enclosed space with no windows. *Shut them down.*"

More bullets – still rubber, but even rubber bullets could kill with a lucky shot – bounced off the shield, as did more explosions as Valentine's magic triggered more grenades. They fired through the walls; as promised, David had some high-tech scopes.

Thank God he wants to bring us in alive, Paul thought. *If he didn't want to show up SMASH, we'd all be dead.*

As if David had read his thoughts, another announcement blared from the speakers: "KEEP IN MIND I DON'T HAVE TO DEFEAT YOU. I JUST HAVE TO FORCE YOU TO GENERATE ENOUGH FLUX UNTIL YOUR OWN MAGIC DOES YOU IN. I REPEAT: GIVE UP."

If he got captured, Aliyah was as good as gone.

Valentine slammed the door. Paul crouched down in the pantry, shredded bags of pancake mix pouring down on his head, trying not to think about how low Valentine's shield was getting.

He had to defuse the grenades. And whatever other technology David had brought with him.

Paul remembered the serial number – he'd always been good with figures – and followed the trail back to its arms manufacturer, seeing a new venture capital corporation that specialized in anti-'mancer weaponry. He felt himself breaking opals – they had detectors, but given that every 'mancer had their own unique approach, nobody knew how to keep all of them out – yet Paul dove into the records.

The grenades were just the tip of David's technological

investment: they'd covered the front lawn with anti-'mancer mines. The cops had rubber bullets, nerve gas tranq darts, surplus military gear.

And worse: looking over the patents, Paul realized why the grenades were red rubber. That red was radioactive dye, microscopic shreds intended to embed themselves deep in the skin, so even if a 'mancer changed shape they'd still be identifiable through a Geiger counter. Paul, Valentine, Tyler and Rainbird – if Rainbird was still alive – were all marked.

He'd deal with that later.

"*That guy's a 'mancer?*" Tyler yelled from outside the door, incredulous.

"*He's doing 'mancy right now.*"

"*Fuck,*" Tyler said. "*That guy's the stealth bomber of magic.*"

And he was. His 'mancy was usually whisper-quiet, just rifling through files – nothing like Tyler's body-destroying violence or Rainbird's flaming holocausts.

This next move would be noisy.

A couple of lucky bullets punched through the door. "*Speed it up, Paul! I'm losing shield power!*"

It was all about quality control. Munitions factories had tight quality controls, designed to ensure duds didn't cost some poor soldier his life. There were best procedures, careful testing, all to ensure a 98 percent reliability rating. These explosives in particular were created in combination with specially trained Unimancers, brainwashed 'mancers who'd calibrate the opals with precise tests until they broke.

One out of every fifty grenades had been pulled randomly from the factory line, thrown into testing, a staggeringly expensive process: they needed full-on 'mancy and a 'mancer-safe explosive range.

Now, Paul thought. *What are the odds that out of the thirty thousand or so explosives saturating the campus, the remaining ones are duds?*

He pulled up all the records, the things that *could* go wrong with explosives – the magnesium, the potassium nitrate, the P-wave sensors, the opals. The temptation was to go after the opals, but the opals were hand-inspected before placement.

The P-wave sensors, however, were experimental electronics sourced from overseas. Where they had lesser anti-'mancer standards.

Paul reached back, collated the records of the tested grenades. They'd assigned each explosive serial numbers so they *could* be checked, but they'd inadvertently made it easier for Paul's 'mancy to work. He made a list of the properly tested grenades, then cross-referenced them with lists of successfully tested P-wave sensors, correlating so that anything that anyone had inspected would pass, but the rest would have manufacturing defects.

The P-wave sensors were sensitive. Too much impact during shipping could damage them. Yet the shipping containers had impact sensors affixed to them, little green labels that turned red if too many G-forces were applied in transit – but if Paul traced *those* back, he could relax the standards people had used to create the labels, causing defects in those too...

Slowly, Paul built a complex web, cascades of freak reactions and overlooked regulations so all the explosives that had not yet fired would *never* fire.

When he had built that complex network in his head, trembling with effort, he fished a small legal pad from his pocket and signed it into existence.

Nothing happened.

Yet of course, nothing *would* happen. The only difference is those explosives, once primed to fire, were theoretically inert. He'd have to do 'mancy and hope nothing detonated.

The flux slammed into him.

It was like he'd been plunged deep underwater at submarine depths, the bad luck squeezing him so hard he feared it'd burst his lungs...

It worked, he thought, glad despite the pain.

But the flux was insistent, almost self-flagellating: *you did this to save your own skin, didn't you?* He tried to tell it that he'd used 'mancy to selflessly protect Aliyah, but the truth was that David's forces terrified him...

The house.

It was flimsy at the best of times. Tanks rolled towards them.

This house could collapse.

The flux rushed out of him, seeking that dreadful future. Then Paul remembered:

The badge.

Payne's Samaritan Mutual badge.

He thrust his hand into his pocket – *keep these touching your skin at all times*, Payne had told him. Paul wished he'd listened. Was he too late? He examined the badge: instead of reading "Samaritan Mutual," as it had back at the office, instead engraved on its surface were four words:

Always Thank Your Benefactor.

Of course.

He squeezed the silver badge between his fingers and whispered: "Thank you, King." As more shots punched through Valentine's shields, he even managed gratitude.

The badge's surface – almost like a crown – grew more elaborate, twisting with crenellations. The grooves stiffened, forming miniscule inscribed boxes, fine letters, form numbers:

All the bureaucracy at Samaritan Mutual, packed into a space three inches across.

The badge grew heavy in Paul's hand. His 'mancy was tugged from off his chest, pulled towards an inescapable potency. Rules were writ into the badge's grooves, ones that held the weight of authority – a *literal* weight that called all the 'mancy in the area towards it, commanding it, calling the flux back.

Two eyes popped open on the badge. A pure blue.

Payne's eyes.

Come to me, the badge said in Payne's inexorable tones. The flux turned back like a dog called by its master, abandoning this foolish idea of collapsing the house, instead plunging into the maze of Payne's forged regulations.

The forms scissored back and forth as the flux poured in, the edges on the boxes glimmering like razors, sucking in this sticky tide of bad luck and slicing it up, dispersing it into small packets out across all the insurers who'd rendered themselves accountable to Payne.

Paul clutched the badge, shaking in gratitude as the flux dispersed. His bureaucromancy reached out to connect with the forms, as reflexive as a handshake, and Paul felt Payne deciding who got what: this claimant would get caught in a traffic jam, this claimant would get a cold, this claimant would discover himself erroneously overdrawn…

Payne's a busy man, Paul thought woozily.

Then the pantry's roof caved in, brought down by a thunderous boom.

"*Paul!*" Valentine yelled, yanking the door open. Her shield's meter was a ragged stub, dwindling under the unceasing hail of rubber bullets. "*You got it done?*"

"Yeah," Paul muttered, then realized Valentine couldn't hear him. "*Yes!*"

"Good. Go get 'em, space monkey."

Tyler stumbled past the shield, pushing past the bullets to head out the front door. His men, huddled underneath their bunk beds, craned their necks to watch as he staggered out onto the porch with raised hands.

"*We surrender!*" he cried.

TWENTY-EIGHT
Watch the World Burn

Valentine had reskinned them before they walked out onto the front lawn to surrender. Paul was back to being fat old Mr Galuschak, whereas Valentine was clad in the Psycho Mantis garb of gasmask and skin-tight leather gimp suit.

At David's orders, Tyler's half-naked men had filed out of the Paper Street house to lie on their bellies on the ground, lines of anti-'mancer mines propped before their noses.

They interlaced their hands behind their heads, face down. Tyler did it with such casual relaxation, he all but sunbathed in the spotlights.

The mines shouldn't work, Paul knew, but that didn't relax Paul as he lay down before them. Black-helmeted cops advanced upon them, grasping tasers in black-gloved fists; a fair number sat in back, medics cutting off their boots to examine their shredded legs.

David sat perched in an armored Humvee, surveying the scene with satisfaction.

"I thought your plan would involve something other than surrendering," Paul said bitterly.

Valentine held up a single finger. He'd given her that same signal, once, when they'd been held hostage: *This is step one.*

"HEADS DOWN!" David ordered, shouting into a

bullhorn. "ANY MOVEMENT WILL BE FIRED UPON!"

Paul thought of Aliyah. And trusted Valentine.

"For a 'mancer," Tyler observed, "You are *totally* risk-avoidant. How the hell are you gonna change the world if all you're doing is defending existing territory?"

Paul blinked. "You're out to change the world?"

"Aren't you?"

The cops approached cautiously, unhooking auto-injectors from their belts. Paul knew from scanning the munition records that each had a cocktail of drugs designed to destroy short-term memory so 'mancers literally wouldn't know where they were.

The first cop got to Tyler. Tyler rolled over, smiling, bare-chested, as though the cop was bringing him breakfast in bed.

"How much can you know about yourself if you've never been in a fight?" he asked, so offhandedly that only Paul detected the 'mancy radiating from his model-perfect abs. The question rankled. Paul bristled, and he wasn't even Tyler's target.

The cop paused, bristling. "We were just *in* a fight. And we kicked your ass."

Tyler chuckled. "No, no, no, Lenny. You went *hunting*. You got yourself a nice big .458 Winchester rifle with your 1.5x scope, and the nice hired hands set you up a blind so the lion couldn't see it coming, and you pulled the trigger when the safari guides told you to. But that doesn't make you a man. It makes you a tourist."

The cops hesitated, mesmerized by Tyler's words.

"We're not candy-asses," the cop muttered. "We're fucking cops, man."

"Then *act* like a cop, goddammit!" Tyler sprang to his feet. "Cops don't fucking hide behind shields and tanks! They whip out their goddamned batons and beat the shit out of people, mano a mano!"

Lenny Pirrazzini ripped off his helmet, revealing sweaty helmet-hair and his useless awful mustache. *Oh, Lenny*, Paul thought. *Not you again.*

Of course Lenny *would* be the most susceptible to Tyler's spiel.

"LENNY!" David shouted from a bullhorn. "PUT YOUR GEAR BACK ON!"

"Come on, Lenny." Tyler danced back and forth, snakelike. "Don't you wanna know what it's like to go toe-to-toe with a 'mancer? No equipment, no backup?"

Lenny cocked his head back and forth, bumping chests with Tyler.

"Are you calling me a coward?" he asked. The other cops crowded in close, ripped their helmets off, their bloodlust rising.

Tyler shrugged. "Well, I know Paul Tsabo killed two 'mancers with his bare hands." *Not quite accurate*, Paul thought, but outrage blossomed across Lenny's face regardless. "I mean, unless you think you're less of a man than a guy with only three limbs…"

Valentine made an embarrassed wince; Paul realized Tyler didn't even know who Paul was. Tyler used his 'mancy to pluck factoids out of the air, goading Lenny on–

Lenny punched Tyler in the face.

Tyler cracked his neck, gave that Brad Pitt smirk. Blood trickled from his nose. He shrugged.

"That the best you got?"

"*That's it!*" Lenny said, ripping off his armor, and the other cops piled on Tyler. Tyler's men leapt from the ground, punching whoever they could, the cops screaming incoherently and stripping naked and punching Tyler's men.

"*You can't talk about this!*" Tyler laughed as he elbowed Lenny's front teeth in. "*You promised you wouldn't talk about this!*"

The snipers, Paul thought, clambering to his feet. *They'll shoot us*. But no, even the snipers flung their rifles aside, running past a red-faced and shouting David, chest puffed with pride as they raced to take on a 'mancer with good old-fashioned pugilism. Cops with half cut-off boots, their feet still bleeding from the punji pits, shoved the medics aside to limp into the fight. The medics flung aside their scissors to tackle the cops, smashing their heads against the wheel wells.

Tyler's madness, Paul thought, terrified. *It's a virus. He's infected them with* Fight Club.

He turned to Valentine, ready to pull her away. She leaned against a cop car, covering her shy grin with one hand.

"Oh, how I *do* love to watch him work." She was lovestruck.

"So what do we do now?" Paul asked. "Just... run?"

"Tyler's on it. He's good at vanishing. He just has to handle the cops, and then–"

A gunshot rang out across the field. Tyler jerked back, shocked, blood fountaining from his shoulder; David perched atop the Humvee, clutching a sniper rifle.

"THAT ROUND'S HYDROSTATIC SHOCK SHOULD HAVE KILLED YOU," David said. "SMASH BE DAMNED, I WILL BLOW YOUR FUCKING HEAD OFF IF ANYONE THROWS ONE MORE PUNCH."

Tyler collapsed backwards into the arms of his men, who formed a protective circle around him. "No can do, David! In death, I get a name."

Paul *really* wished he'd seen that fucking movie.

David sighed, exasperated. "FINE. DEATH IT IS."

An explosion blew off the rear of the house.

"...THE FUCK?" David cried. The cops looked around, as if waking from a dream, touching the bruises on their faces with their fingertips – and then cried out as they saw the bright flames roaring up from the back yard, the smoke blotting out the moon.

"Huh," Tyler shrugged. "I guess someone got at the napalm tanks."

"You make *napalm*?" Valentine squeed.

I've been waiting all my life for some mysterious stranger to show up and involve me in an Adventure, Valentine had told him shortly after they'd first met, disappointed by Paul's cautious nature. *What'd I get? Minimum wage jobs*.

As Valentine flicked away the incoming shards of glass with her forcefield, Paul realized he might not survive Valentine's idea of Adventures.

Yet the fire engulfing the house moved too fast for napalm. The dilapidated siding went up quickly as matchheads, the rotted wood popping into sparks; the roof became an instant blaze with an oxygen-snuffing *whoof*, every shingle blazing like a gas oven being turned on. The windows turned a molten red before evaporating in a spray of atomized glass.

The cops, wisely, began to flee.

With a glimmer of 'mancy, Tyler pulled out sunglasses and a bag of popcorn.

By the time Paul turned around, the house itself – all three stories of Victorian architecture – had lifted into the air, rising off the foundation like a disintegrating rocket. The floors buckled into heaps of burnt timber and ash, the roof imploding, the chimney snapping in half and spraying out superheated brick – but a great flame vortex hauled tons of blazing architecture upwards even as the house collapsed, scooping the timber up in a roiling mass of white-hot kindling, crushing the home into a rough inferno that rose still higher into the sky.

And Rainbird rode that crumbling conflagration, his overcoat burning, one hand grasping what once had been a weathervane as he straddled the wreckage – as though he rode a cyclopean steed summoned straight from the fires of hell.

His burnt-tree mask's blazing eyeholes held no possibility of mercy.

"Too much evidence." Rainbird's voice was ominous as timber crackling. "Burn it all to cinders."

Rainbird gestured towards David – and the house rolled towards him, the fiery wreckage tumbling like balls inside a bingo machine, vomiting out scorched couches and twisted iron bedframes and smoking Persian rugs from the sky.

David squeezed his eyes shut as the debris bore down upon him in a ragged firestorm, a scourging fire sweeping across the landscape to show David the limitations of his pitiful authority.

The badge at Paul's hip shivered. Rainbird's monstrous flux poured into it – even spread out over thousands, it was more than the system could bear. The person who'd been scheduled to be caught in the traffic jam got upgraded to a fender bender, the person who would have had a cold now sprained an ankle, the overdrawn checking account metamorphosed into identity fraud...

A tsunami of fire soared over Paul, and Tyler, and the cops, threatening to broil them all. The policemen stopped running, fell to their knees, begging forgiveness...

"Valentine!" Paul yelled, *"We can't let him–"*

"On it." She grabbed the Xbox controller at her hip, thumbed the green X of its "On" button.

A burst of green energy radiated out from her, her potency matching Rainbird's, sweeping across the panicked cops as the fire sluiced through them, burning them.

They didn't burn.

The Humvees burned, the tires flaring smoke, the gas tanks rupturing. The ambulances melted in a grinding brushfire. The tanks were hurled so high into the sky they had hang time, a good three seconds before they plummeted back again, bursting into shreds of military hardware.

But the cops did not change.

Tiny green numbers flared over their heads – *hit points*, Paul knew – which dropped to zero as the attack took them. They dropped to the ground, unconscious. Rainbird engulfed them in angry firestorms, swept their bodies up into the air and shook them, chucked them at the ground – yet those hit points remained stubbornly at zero.

"It's a multiplayer co-op match," Valentine shouted up. *"Nobody dies here, Rainbird! They only respawn after a cooldown time."*

Tyler reached up and lit a fresh cigarette off of a burning

duvet whizzing overhead. "Oh my God, that girl twists my heart into a balloon animal."

The badge glowed as hot as Rainbird's fire; he dropped it. With Valentine and Rainbird clashing 'mancies draining into it, the flux shaded fatal – fender benders crumpling into head-on collisions, sprained ankles crushed into shattered femurs, identity fraud deepening into portfolio collapses…

This much 'mancy strained at the edges of reality; other realities longed to push through into ours. That was how Germany had been destroyed: a 'mancer fight had broached the other worlds and *things* had poured in to devour Earth's delicious reality.

Paul felt the air pulling apart, the struggle between Valentine and Rainbird punching holes into more hostile dimensions…

Rainbird fluttered down, surrounded by a fiery corona, hands twisted into claws. *"What are you doing, little girl?"*

Valentine held up her controller, which blazed with gamefire. *"Saving your dumb ass."*

"They've seen too much. This equipment will be reused against us. We need to burn the source – their expertise. Their leader. These men."

Valentine was red-faced. *"You fucking moron! Have you seen what happens when you kill a New York cop!? Kill one policeman, and New York will do anything to hunt us down!"*

Rainbird looked pained. *"We won't leave anyone to tell. Your papermancer will erase the digital evidence – the one thing he's good for – and this? Will be done."*

The burning building above them dropped precipitously: a threat. Valentine activated her shield, which glimmered around them: a counter-threat. Paul's Galuschak suit melted, his cheeks dribbling fake fat.

Worse, bulges appeared in the air around them. Something colorless squirmed, trying to wriggle through:

The buzzsects, Paul thought, horrified. He'd seen them, once. They were avatars of hunger. They ate laws of physics. They ate 'mancy. They were voracious for the taste of our good clean universe.

The artificial skin sloughed off his left arm, exposing his ever-bleeding wound. He'd stopped them once – but what would it cost him now?

What if he couldn't stop them, and New York became the next Germany?

"*Valentine! Broach imminent!*"

She grimaced; her skin was still laced with scars from the last demon invasion. "*If I drop it, he'll kill all the cops, Paul. Can we…*" She swallowed. "*Can we live with that?*"

"*Jesus fucked a donkey,*" Rainbird spat. "*This is war, you fools! War is fire! If you don't burn the ground so there's nothing left to take the flame, it spreads! Someone's going to die, and it's them – or it's us.*"

He lowered the wreckage more, resting its full weight on Valentine's shield. Green sparks coruscated through her as she fought to stave off Rainbird's power.

The air squirmed, tiny rips appearing, insectoid jaws nipping through.

Paul played with forms. Rainbird could lift houses up on flaming tornados. Rainbird could battle with fire whips, could beat Valentine at her own literal game–

What the hell could he do against that might?

"*You,*" Tyler said to Valentine, "overcomplicate things."

He socked Rainbird in the jaw. Rainbird tumbled over backwards, unconscious; the rubble dropped from the sky.

With a grunt, Valentine lifted up her shield like a gigantic dinner plate and tilted it, sliding the embers of the Paper Street home onto the empty lot next door.

Then she collapsed.

"Not everything needs 'mancy, sweetie," Tyler said, kissing her on the cheek. "Come on, let's go."

"Can't…" She looked around, dazed. "We can't leave Rainbird behind."

"*I* can. That guy's a douche. And we're, uh… well, we're running out of time."

He jerked his chin over towards the melted Humvee wrecks. Released from Valentine's spell, the cops were coming to.

"We gotta get Rainbird." Valentine grabbed at Rainbird weakly. "We have to."

"You got a choice," Tyler said. "Run with me now, or don't. Not trying to be impolite here, but I got a battalion of armed enforcers coming to."

He head-jerked again towards his men, who leapt over fences, evading the area. They'd had a plan to escape, Paul realized, and had enacted it while Rainbird had gone full-tilt – and Tyler watched them leave.

"Won't they stay to rescue you?" Paul asked.

"I taught them I'm no special snowflake. They wouldn't respect me if I asked for help. You in, or out?"

Aliyah. Rainbird knew about Aliyah. If they left him behind, he'd get captured by SMASH and everything Rainbird knew would lead the government right to his daughter's door.

"...I'm out."

Tyler clapped Paul on the shoulder. "Good luck, man. Take care of her. She *is* a special snowflake."

He ran for the fences.

"Wait!" Valentine cried, reaching after him. She collapsed onto the scorched lawn, exhausted.

Paul tugged her to her feet. "Go *Grand Theft Auto*, Val. Get us out of here."

"No deal." She gestured at the strained sky above them, otherworldly dimensions threatening to push through. "One glimmer of 'mancy, and *they* get access."

The air behind her rippled like smeared glass. The air thrummed with the low hum of buzzsects gnawing at the laws of physics.

"Do you remember those things eating you alive?" She swallowed. "I do."

David raised his head, weary. "The 'mancers. They're still here." Then: "*Get* them, you fools!"

"They aren't the ones we should be getting," Lenny protested. "They stopped that idiot from burning us."

A thin grumble of assent.

"*'Mancy. Is. Illegal.*" David gathered strength from that single, idiotic statement. "Any able-bodied man who doesn't move to get them will be brought up on charges."

Like zombies, exhausted and naked and bruised, the cops stumbled to their feet to converge on Paul and Valentine. They patted the ground, dazed, looking for any weapons they could find. Their batons and guns had been swept clean – but they picked up twisted chunks of incinerated patrol cars to hammer the 'mancers into submission.

Not a one of them recognized the signs of a broach.

Paul looked around, realizing the bind they were in. The last time he'd healed a broach, he'd done it while SMASH had been occupied by Valentine's attack. And SMASH were trained 'mancers with a respectable fear of extradimensional incursions. But now? David led the Task Force, an egomaniac who barely understood 'mancy. If anyone distracted Paul while he tried to mend reality, the broach might worm itself in so deep that America's best efforts might not be able to push it back.

No, Paul thought. *I can do this. I can–*

There was a sizzling noise as his arm dripped fresh blood onto the cinder-covered ground, as if to remind him what had happened the last time he thought he could push back an extradimensional incursion.

He sagged. Once again, he was calculating Imani-odds – unwilling to risk global destruction to fix an immediate problem…

He looked around. What could they do without 'mancy? Rainbird, a large man, was unconscious. Paul was not a strong man, and Valentine wasn't big on endurance; they might be able to drag Rainbird a block or two before the cops caught up.

Paul ticked off the options on his fingers. "We've got… no 'mancy. No equipment. Aside from this phone."

"We're about to die, and you're making lists?"

Paul looked hurt. "You know it's how I cope with stress."

Valentine heaved Rainbird over her shoulders in a

fireman's carry; her knees buckled, and Rainbird tumbled down her back, landing face-first in the smoldering soil. "Fuck, Paul, I don't know – *call* somebody."

"Who would I–?"

The phone rang.

Paul squinted at the name on the phone. He held it to his ear, baffled. "…Oscar?"

"Your friendly neighborhood drug distributor," Oscar demurred. "I have agents stationed nearby. Did you want a ride? Oh, never mind, I'll assume you do. How much would you estimate this purchases me in Flex?"

"A lifetime's supply," Paul said, feeling a wave of gratitude as a minivan screeched onto the street, two men in ski masks tumbling out.

"Good to see you again, Mr Tsabo." K-Dash gave Paul a merry wink as he fired a burst from his automatic rifle, forcing the incoming cops to dive for cover.

"Did you bring donuts?" Paul asked.

K-Dash gave an exaggerated gesture of failure. "We ate them all, sir. On stakeout duty, watching you. But I promise I'll get you a nice fresh baker's dozen on the way back home."

Paul felt a strange sense of reunion; he'd *missed* his bodyguards.

Quaysean and Valentine hugged before chucking Rainbird into the back seat. K-Dash fired over the cops' heads, warning them away. The cops shouted for reinforcements, but all the electrical equipment in the area had melted.

They piled into the van and Quaysean pulled out, driving maniacally through the back streets, screeching around corners. Paul hadn't known Quaysean was such an expert driver – but then again, Oscar wouldn't have assigned them to watch over him if they weren't truly skilled.

"They know what your car looks like," Paul said. "And they have 'mancy-sensing drones…"

Quaysean flashed him a toothy smile. "We got that covered, Mr Tsabo. Don't you worry about a thing. Want a sip of my coffee?"

Despite himself, Paul relaxed.

They screeched into an old repair shop, where a battered SUV waited in a shadowy garage. A pleasant blonde woman sat in the front, the perfect soccer mom; a small white kid in a baseball cap sat next to her.

"In the back, Ms DiGriz." K-Dash opened the door for her. "Not so fast, Mr Tsabo – you have to authorize something first."

He handed Paul a legal pad, then nodded to another gang member. A wiry black kid leapt into the front seat of the van that had picked them up.

Quaysean handed the kid an old McDonald's cup brimming with Flex – Paul's Flex – spilling over with clear crystals glimmering with pure, captured 'mancy. The kid, eager, gobbled a handful and then jittered as the energy coursed through him.

A request popped up on the legal pad:

The party of the first part would like authorization to use your Flex to speed like a madman and/or evade the cops on a wild, nonfatal drive through New York.

Paul looked up at Quaysean with new respect. Quaysean tipped his cap. "We *have* thought this through, Mr S. Oscar's a little protective of his investments."

Paul signed it. The wiry black kid pumped his fist and stomped on the accelerator pedal, screeching out of the repair shop. Paul knew from past experience with Gargunza's men that their Flex trips rapidly became the stuff of legend; Oscar had snapped up a kid willing to trade a ten-year jail sentence to ride wild on Paul's stolen 'mancy.

Quaysean quietly pushed Rainbird into the SUV's trunk, then climbed in. "They'll chase him. He's got all your markers – Valentine's crazy *Grand Theft Auto*-style car chases in the van she was last seen in, shattering opals in every drone overhead for miles around. By the time they realize their mistake, we'll be long gone."

Paul jerked his chin towards the soccer mom. "And your driver…?"

"Put a nice white lady in the driver's seat and she never gets pulled over," Quaysean said. "My advice would be to take a nap in the back, after you talk to Mr Oscar. If I don't miss my guess, you're going to need all your energy to deal with Mr Payne."

Paul smiled. "How much do you know?"

"Did you want to say 'thank you' first?"

Paul pumped Quaysean's hand. "Thank you, Quaysean. *Thank* you."

Quaysean bobbed his head, blushing. "Glad to be of service, Mr Tsabo. Now let's get you some donuts. You've got a deal to broker back at the Institute."

They knew about the Institute. Paul shivered.

TWENTY-NINE
Losing Limbs

Paul had to wash up before he met with Payne. But Aliyah waited in his office. She was a little girl, sitting expectantly on his desk.

Paul was glad; he'd worried she'd wear that scarred warrior's skin all the time.

"You got hurt," she said.

For a disorienting moment Aliyah looked like a tiny Imani, waiting coldly for him to come back from late nights at the office.

Except Aliyah wasn't angry.

She was upset her daddy had lied to her again.

And Paul *had* been trying to hide things from Aliyah. He'd snuck in so she wouldn't see him covered in bruises, his clothes scorched, his hair choked with soot. He hadn't wanted her to know how close he'd come to dying.

"I got away," Paul offered.

She frowned, then leapt off the bed to hug him, pressing her face to his belly. "You can't leave, Daddy. Ever."

"Sweetie, I have things to do—"

"No. It's not *safe* out there. You have to *stay here*, where nobody's trying to kill us." She kicked his titanium shin. "You keep losing fights. You keep losing limbs. I'm going to lose *you*."

"You won't–"

"Shh." She pressed up against him. It was as though she was trying to commit him to memory, storing this moment against some awful future where her daddy had died. "This place is perfect, Daddy. Can't you see?"

Paul imagined himself as one of Payne's hothouse flowers, holed up among the filing cabinets as he handled Payne's infrastructure for him. Forgetting to wash. His natural shyness growing like a cancer, eroding his ability to speak to people.

Outside was violence and uncertainty; inside was the slow withering of safety. Paul understood, for the first time, why Valentine wanted to leave.

I still have to talk to Payne, Paul thought, pulling away from Aliyah to go shower.

"Hey!" Aliyah yelled, furious. "You can't leave!"

"I have to convince Mr Payne that we *can* stay," Paul told her, and turned on the hot water.

THIRTY
Doubt Truth to be a Liar, But Never Doubt I Love

Payne loomed over Paul like a drill sergeant, bellowing, seeming to fill the entirety of the conference room.

"How in blazes did they track you back to *here*?"

"*The party of the first part may, at any time, use the drug to locate the party of the second part no matter where he may be,*" Paul quoted. "That was our deal. Oscar wanted to ensure I couldn't skip out on my responsibilities."

"And you *accepted* that?"

"It seemed an appropriate thing to ask for in a business deal. And it wasn't like I had a lot of choice. He'd deduced the truth about me."

Payne turned away from Paul, fuming. "So a great 'mancer became a drug manufacturer. Working for a mundane."

"*Hey*. I'm not the only Flex maker here. My clear, backlash-free Flex was only legendary because people had seen it before. Back in the 1960s. When Samaritan Mutual was *founded.*" Payne turned, outraged. "Or was I supposed to believe you made your fortune selling insurance?"

"I wasn't propping up some penny-ante drug dealer, Paul! I was building an empire! An empire to *protect* 'mancers! 'Mancers who, you may recall, are endangered thanks to your poor judgment!"

This place is perfect, Daddy. Payne was right; they'd almost lost this glorious retreat. He imagined Aliyah's happiness turning to screams as SMASH agents rained anti-'mancer grenades on the place, drugged them, carried them off.

But he'd be damned if he took responsibility for what wasn't his fault. Payne had done that back at Samaritan Mutual: he'd scream at people until he found a scapegoat.

Aliyah's life was at stake, again, and once again Payne was blaming anyone else but himself.

"This was not *my* fuckup," Paul said. "If Rainbird had gone in alone, he'd be tagged and bagged. Those devices knocked him the hell out, and *I* disabled them. So let's not blame *me* for overwhelming forces – forces that, thanks to Oscar's help, we escaped."

"You shouldn't have *needed* this criminal's help! I've heard Rainbird's report. You could have cleansed the issue!"

Paul remembered how terrified the cops had looked as Rainbird's firestorm had swept in on them, humiliated men about to die. "*Cleansed*?"

Payne waved the problem away. "They're *mundanes*, Paul."

"So was *I*!"

Payne plopped into a chair.

"Oh, Paul." He squeezed the bridge of his nose. "I knew it'd come to this. I'd hoped you'd see necessity, but… I see it's time to break open an old wound."

He took Paul's hand. His touch had the coolness of an old man with poor circulation.

"Paul, I know you've always resented me for… well, what happened with Aliyah."

"You mean when she was dying and you tried to fire me to avoid paying her claims?"

"*No.*" Payne's certainty made Paul's doubt waver. "As long as she was dying, I paid. That was the contract we had. Note that not one claim to save that beautiful girl's life was refused. You may not believe me, but I said prayers. I'm glad she lived."

"Funny, given that you looked for every excuse to shortchange her."

Payne stiffened. "I authorized the best care in the best burn ward in New York City. That's what I *agreed* to, Paul. You paid me cash, and if something went wrong, I looked after you. I owed you. As I owe protection to all my clients."

"And yet you hunted for ways to weasel out of my claims."

"That, too, the contract. You're a... a bureaucromancer. You understand the power of agreements. If someone wants my money, is it not my right to verify they kept to their terms?" Payne sighed, as though this conversation was already spiraling out of control. "When your daughter was dying, I authorized every expenditure. That was what I promised to do – and I keep my promises. But you – you wanted more. That's understandable, Paul, as a father. You wanted to make her pretty again. But those million-dollar surgeries weren't part of our bargain."

"That was my daughter's *face* you were denying."

"Believe me, Paul, I looked at her photos every time I denied a claim. I owed you that. And you know what I saw? My darling sisters. Lisa, and Anna."

Paul sat, puzzled. Payne blinked back a tear.

"This world is a harsh place, Paul. *That* is what the broach taught me. My mother had to make a choice between saving me, or my sisters, or those filthy buzzsects would have devoured us all. And... she saved me.

"Watching them die, Paul, I..." He looked away. "What happened to them was worse than death. That's when I realized: this world is not filled with enough kindness to save everyone. *Someone* must decide who lives and who dies. And my mother, she... She couldn't. She hung herself once I was safe in America."

Paul wasn't sure what to say. "I'm... I'm sorry."

"I'm not asking for your sympathy, Paul. I am, in fact, asking for the exact opposite of sympathy. For if I paid out my money to all the folks who tugged on my heartstrings, well... I couldn't afford *this*."

Payne flicked on a security monitor; Aliyah rolled in a tumble of Mrs Liu's magical cats.

She could have been abducted by SMASH. They could have lost everything.

But could he have watched those cops scream until their throats roasted? He knew those men. He imagined Lenny's mother grieving, unsure who'd killed her son because Paul had wiped all the evidence away...

...he understood why Payne's mother had killed herself. Not that he could condone it – leaving a small boy alone in the world seemed like the cruelest thing to do – but Payne had opened a window opened into the guilt his mother had endured.

Payne nodded. "I now have twenty 'mancers to look after. Yes, I denied your daughter's coverage. Yes, I injured thousands yesterday, dispersing your flux. Yes, I would murder – and it *is* murder – a squadron of police to protect them. Because *someone* must be strong enough to make terrible choices, Paul. That is what a king does."

"The king of New York," Paul muttered.

Payne squeezed Paul's hands. "And this drug dealer – I'm sure he wants the Flex. You're right. I distributed my own drugs, back in the day. I even built my own laboratory. But once we give it to him, well... my experience with dealers tells me they always escalate. He'll want more."

"I don't think he will." The look Payne gave him made Paul feel naïve. "He's... a businessman. His brother always wanted more, and got killed for that. I think Oscar is... well, reasonable. We can deal with him."

"Yet the man refuses to meet with us." Payne flicked another monitor on, showing K-Dash and Quaysean sitting in the atrium underneath Rainbird's baleful gaze. Rainbird kept burning off his left hand, making it regrow, making them squirm. "He sends minions."

"Would you blame him? He doesn't want you to know where he is, any more than you wanted him to know where *you* were. And the man's avoided the cops for years – we're just one more authority to circumvent."

"Can't you track him–"

"I tried. Even if I felt like having you sic Rainbird on him, he's using burner phones, dropping them quicker than I can find them. He's off the Internet. He's got long experience ducking government surveillance. What about your other 'mancers?"

Payne scowled. "Useless for practical missions. Hothouse flowers."

"Look, what he wants is Flex. Give him Flex. You said you had a laboratory–"

"*I will not be beholden to a criminal!*"

Payne looked ready to strangle him at that moment. Paul changed tactics.

"With all due respect, sir, you don't have a choice. We can't find him. But if you work with him, he could be a great ally. He's hunted by the cops, too. He could help us make this place safer. And don't you want to be safer, with New York City's new anti-'mancer hardware?"

Payne sniffed. "You're romanticizing the man, Tsabo. He's more of a murderer than I am."

"Maybe. But weren't you the one who said we had to make hard choices?"

Payne pushed his hands through his white mane of hair. He turned to the security monitors, flipping through them – looking at Mrs Vinere the masquomancer, the bookiemancer in his sports-related enclave, a high shot of the atrium. Looking over all he owned.

Then he switched back to Aliyah, playing with Mrs Liu's cats. And Mrs Liu's cats, as they always did in Aliyah's presence, did far stranger things – in this case, singing "Rum Tum Tugger" as Mrs Liu clapped along.

Mrs Liu looked thrilled. And as Payne panned back to the atrium, he saw the 'mancers lining up, waiting to play with Aliyah – a community united by their love of Paul's daughter.

Payne clasped calloused hands behind his back. "You know, Paul," he said, his voice heavy with disappointment, "When I found you, I thought I'd found the answer to my prayers. Someone to carry on my legacy. And to my surprise, your daughter is the leader."

He left the room.

THIRTY-ONE
Her Side of the Mountain

Paul paced in the entry hall of the fake school he'd created, waiting for Imani to show up. He'd planned all the details, knowing what would comfort Imani: he nodded to the friendly security guard who would scan Imani's credentials, check her against a list of authorized visitors, issue her a temporary badge. The guard, an actress who'd been told she was participating in a reality show – which helped explain all the hidden cameras – gave him a jaunty little salute.

The LisAnna Foundation For Children's Post-Traumatic Stress Disorder was well-lit, with freshly painted yellow walls – they had to be freshly painted, they'd only started refinishing the place last week – and thumbtack boards covered with construction-paper turkeys spelling out "WHAT'S AUTUMN MEAN TO YOU?" There were red lockers and benches and water fountains at kid height. There were stairs leading up to the dorms, which Imani would not have access to – but if she snuck up there, she'd find a nurse's buzzer on every wall and a teddy bear on every pillow.

Paul had never considered himself a good liar. But surrounded by his faked institution, he had to admit he had a talent.

So why did walking around inside this fabrication make his skin crawl?

This was just another layer to prevent David and Imani from questioning their daughter's increasingly odd behavior. And still, Paul felt jittery…

He peered out through the glass doors, looking at the parking lot covered with dead leaves, itching for Imani to show up.

He almost hoped she'd see through it. He'd never liked fooling his ex-wife, and this – this was too much.

"She's late." Payne consulted his pocketwatch. "Is that unusual? She seemed fastidious."

He peered out into the lot again. "Maybe she hit a traffic jam. She's not used to driving."

"Maybe she's decided she doesn't want to come."

"She'd call. And… she doesn't give up like that."

Payne trailed his fingers along the alphabet stickers lining the walls. "But you have to admit, Paul. It'd be easier if she left us alone. She, and her husband…"

Paul almost yelled at the old man about how "easier" didn't mean "better," but Imani screeched into the parking lot.

She got out of her pearl-gray Tesla, looking flustered, snatching her bag off the passenger seat. She had her phone in her right hand – then pitched it into the car before storming up to the Foundation's front door.

By the time Imani burst into the lobby, Payne had disappeared. Imani breezed past Paul, slapped her driver's license on the security guard's desk. "Imani Dawson, here to see Aliyah Tsabo-Dawson. Sorry I'm late."

"Imani, are you–"

She flung up her hands, almost smacking Paul in the nose. "I'm fine, Paul. Just – don't touch me."

She got her badge from the guard, who gave Paul an *Is this supposed to happen?* look before Imani charged down the hallway. Paul trailed behind, realizing Imani didn't know where she was going.

Wherever she went, she'd find a simulation of a working school. But he wasn't concerned about Imani seeing through the illusion; he was concerned about Imani.

She got halfway down the corridor, past the fake gymnasium, before she slumped on a bench to run her hands through her curled hair.

"I'm sorry. Can we… sit down for a moment?"

"Of course."

Paul thought silence might make things better. But Imani seemed to get tenser as the minutes dragged by, clenching and unclenching her fingers like she was strangling leprechauns.

"Is everything… OK?" Paul asked.

"Of *course* it is! It's *wonderful*! I… Oh, fuck, Paul, I'm sorry. This isn't your fault."

"…David?"

She rubbed a tense spot in her forehead; Paul suppressed an absurd urge to rub her shoulders. "Let's just say there's not quite enough time in the day to be a securities lawyer, a mother, and a loving wife. Especially when the mother aspect requires twice-a-week trips to upstate New York."

Paul thought of how stressed David must have been. Paul had ignored the calls from reporters, asking the Task Force's ex-leader what he'd thought about David's job – but even though Paul had refused to dogpile on David, the Paper Street battle hadn't gone over well in the headlines. Millions of dollars of hardware, vaporized. Nobody dead, thankfully, but still a rout.

And Paul had been glad to see rumors the 'mancers had acted to protect the cops. Buried on the back pages, naturally. But a rumor.

He realized Imani was looking at him, while Paul calculated political costs. He should say something.

"So… an argument."

"*The* argument. Ninety minutes of accusations. I'm lucky I didn't get pulled over." She fished a compact out of her purse to check her eyes. They were swollen from tears. "And all the time, he's telling me how I don't need to be driving all the way out to Hudson, we need to concentrate on us, Paul's on it, let Paul deal with it, concentrate on being a lawyer…"

Paul did a double-take. "He wants you to quit being a *mother*?"

Imani sighed, as if the last thing she felt like doing was defending David. "I know you two have never gotten along, but… believe it or not, David's deeply protective of me. Anything that makes me unhappy becomes his enemy."

Paul remembered the way David had chewed him out for making Imani believe she was a bad mother. "Oh, I've seen that at work."

"And, well, Aliyah hasn't exactly been a source of joy lately, what with the barred windows and the swearing and the sneaking out. We're either guarding Aliyah, or regaining strength for her next visit. He thinks she's a toxic influence in my life – and he thinks once she's gone, I'll go back to drinking champagne with my friends at fundraisers."

"Jesus. So David thinks he can fire a kid the way you'd fire an employee?"

"But I'm *not* giving up on Aliyah!" She blotted her eyes with a handkerchief. "She can push me away all she wants. That's how daughters work. She's angry, and traumatized, but… she needs her mother."

You have to admit, it'd be easier if she left us alone.

Aliyah's life was at stake. So was Paul's. All the 'mancers in the Institute.

It *would* be a lot easier if Imani didn't come snooping around.

"You're right," Paul said. "She needs you. You ready?"

"Gimme a minute."

Imani washed her face in the water fountain, reapplied her eye shadow. She rummaged around in her purse, patted something inside as if she drew strength from it.

"Let's do this."

"Good. She'll be happy to see you."

Paul led her down to the playroom, a lovely playspace with paint-stained tables piled high with crafts projects, cubby holes filled with construction paper, and a padded floor where Aliyah and several children her age laughed and played tag.

Aliyah's schoolmates were also actors. But Aliyah laughed for real, letting out long shrieks of happiness, dodging the other kids.

Aliyah had forgotten to pretend-play and just... played.

The illusion was so complete that for a moment Paul saw her as an ordinary little girl, playing with companions. No, not ordinary: accepted. For a moment, he'd opened a window to a world where 'mancers and mundanes could play together.

Paul felt a full-body, triumphant shiver. Aliyah hadn't played with the kids at the old school, because she'd been terrified her 'mancy would squirt out. But now she'd been training with Rainbird and the Institute 'mancers, she had much better control.

And Payne's money helped; if Aliyah did anything odd, all these children were paid to be quiet. That boosted her confidence.

Then Aliyah saw her mother, and flinched.

A small boy tagged Aliyah; Aliyah didn't even notice. She stumbled to a halt, muscles tensed in preparation to flee, her hands unconsciously reaching out towards Imani. The other hired students came to a stumbling halt, unsure what to do now the kid in charge had decided the game was over. A handful, sensing Aliyah's fear, glanced uncertainly in Imani's direction.

Imani approached Aliyah as though petting a feral cat. She, too, reached out – but did not dare touch Aliyah. Instead, she crouched down.

"Hey, baby."

Aliyah puffed out her cheeks, an aborted tantrum. "... hey."

"I'm sorry I haven't visited in so long, sweetie. I brought a special story. Do you want me to read to you?"

Aliyah swung her arms back and forth, then looked at the floor and muttered.

"What was that, baby?"

"*I said yes!*"

The other kids recoiled from Aliyah's anger, exchanging uneasy glances. But Imani smiled, grateful her daughter was talking to her.

"Will you show me to the reading room?"

Aliyah thrust her hand into her mother's with such force that for a moment, Paul thought Aliyah had punched Imani. But Aliyah stormed ahead, tugging Imani, moving at a rapid clip.

Paul bolted away from them, headed for the security center, not wanting to miss a thing.

He scanned his security badge at the red door. Payne and Valentine waited in a plush recording room filled with monitors and various controls to flick through the Foundation's hidden camera feeds.

"It's not right, watching a girl and her mother." Valentine crunched down on a Cheeto with disgust. "I fucking hate that icebox bitch, and even *I* think she should have some privacy with her kid."

Payne adjusted a dial, bringing up the sound as Aliyah and Imani approached the lounge. "Aliyah is still an inexperienced 'mancer. If something goes wrong, and Aliyah *does* lose her temper in a magical way, I assure you we'll regret *not* knowing about it much more."

Valentine tossed a Cheeto at Payne. "Imani's not gonna suspect a damn thing. I'm super-young for a 'mancer, and I'm twenty-seven. Even if something weird happens, she's not gonna think an eight year-old kid's doing 'mancy."

"Well, I believe in taking no chances."

"Says the guy letting the *Fight Club*-omancer run amuck in town."

Payne scowled, tensing. Valentine had been increasingly snotty since she'd met Tyler – tuning in to the local news channels in hopes he'd show up, endlessly rewatching *Fight Club*, her tastes drifting towards beat-'em-up games. Payne refused to authorize any search for Tyler, however, deeming the man a suicidal menace.

The Institute was designed to wall 'mancers off from danger. Valentine thrived on a steady diet of danger. And Tyler could provide that.

"I'm not a fan of all this surveillance either, Valentine," Paul said, wrestling the conversation back to Aliyah and Imani. "But... I'm trying to figure out how to help Aliyah."

"Why don't you *ask* the kid?"

"Have *you* gotten her to talk about anything she didn't want to?"

Valentine licked her finger, checking off an imaginary point in the air. "OK, granted. Kid's not big on sharing. But I'm not sure Big Brother is the way to go, here."

"Neither am I." But Paul didn't look away as Payne brought up Imani and Aliyah's feed.

The visiting room was designed to be comfortable enough to keep Imani there. So it was appointed with all the amenities: a comfortable couch, a fridge with Imani and Aliyah's favorite drinks, a television. But no videogames.

Aliyah curled up into her mother's arms – lying stiffly, like a doll. Imani pulled out a faded book from her pocketbook. It was tabbed with Post-It notes. Payne zoomed in to focus on the title: *My Side of the Mountain*.

"When I was young, my Mommy read me this story," Imani said. "I didn't get it at the time. But... I think maybe you will."

Valentine rolled her eye. "Oh, yeah, *this'll* go well. Our little ADD princess is gonna listen to a frickin' *story*?"

Paul leaned in closer. "You might be surprised."

And as he watched Imani open the book as Aliyah snuggled up against her, Paul realized how little he knew about Imani and Aliyah's interactions these days. There had been a time when Imani had read Aliyah to sleep after Paul had gotten Aliyah ready for bed. Paul always sat in the corner, wrapped up in the sense of the three of them as a unit, closing his eyes and floating along with Imani's voice as she read *Goodnight Moon* or *The Giving Tree* or *The Little Engine That Could*.

Now? He had no clue what Imani did to put Aliyah to bed these days. He felt a powerful longing for everything he'd lost in the divorce. For Payne, watching them provided protection, safeguarding Aliyah in case things spiraled out of control.

But for Paul? Payne had opened yet another window to what might have been, one where they were still together as a family. He couldn't help but peer through.

Imani started reading, her voice dusky, comforting. "'I am on my mountain in a tree home that people have passed without ever knowing that I am here…'"

And consulting the book with great reverence, she told a story about a girl named Sam, who'd run away from home to live in the woods, and was now freezing to death in a snowstorm.

"I think I read this, once," Payne said, frowning. "But… Sam is a–"

"*Sssh.*" Valentine waved her hands to silence him. She hunched forward, attention focused on the screen. "I wanna hear what happens next."

Payne turned to Paul. "…Sam was a boy, wasn't he?"

"That's what all the Post-It notes are for." Paul felt such fierce pride for his ex-wife that it hurt. "She rewrote Sam to be a girl. Because she thinks Aliyah would react better to a girl protagonist. And she… I think she's abridged the whole thing herself, so she can read it all in an evening…"

"*Shhh.*" Valentine elbowed Payne aside to turn up the volume.

And as Imani read each succeeding chapter, her voice as perfect a narration as you could ask for, Aliyah relaxed into her mother's arms. Aliyah grabbed her mother's free arm, pulled it around her like a blanket. She lay underneath the book cover, refusing to move up to where she could read the words along with her mother.

Paul knew why: *Mommy* read the words.

Aliyah's vivid imagination was why she'd become a videogamemancer at such a young age – while other children would have focused on beating the game, Aliyah had imagined worlds beyond what Mario had shown her. And her imagination had been Imani's gift, showing Aliyah the power of story.

Long before she had lost herself in videogames, Aliyah had lost herself in her mother's words.

And so as Imani told the story of Sam, and how Sam made all her animal friends in the winter, the falcons and weasels and raccoons, Aliyah shivered from imaginary cold. She giggled as the animals stole Sam's provisions, then mouthed "yes" as Sam stole two dead deer from the local hunters. And she tensed up as Sam's mother found her in the wilderness, having finally tracked down her runaway daughter after reading newspaper articles about the "wild girl of the wilderness."

Then, instead of hauling her daughter back home, Sam's mother decided to come live with Sam. She brought the family – Sam's dad, her brothers and sisters – so Sam would have company in her lonely wilderness life.

Aliyah relaxed, sighing.

"That's how much I love you, sweetie," Imani said, closing the book. "No matter what you do, you'll never be alone. Maybe I won't understand why you do it, but I'll always find you. And I'll live with you. Wherever you are."

Aliyah nodded once, content – then, as she considered what that meant, a look of betrayal flashed across her face.

She slapped the book out of her mother's hands.

A crackle of 'mancy filled the air.

Payne stabbed a red button. Security guards bolted from their stations.

"You will *never* find my home!" Aliyah screamed, taking a step towards Imani as though she wanted to punch her, then clutched her fists to her chest. "We're safe there! I finally have friends, and all you'd do is *kill us*! Kill us *all*!"

Imani looked as though she'd been gut-punched. "Aliyah, I want to–"

"You want me dead! You want Daddy dead! You and

David – stupid, stupid David! Get out! *Get out*!"

A shimmer of 'mancy shorted out the fluorescent lights overhead – but the security guards burst in through the doors, distracting Imani. They acted like counsellors, telling her Aliyah was quite upset and it was several hours past her appointment, and it was time to leave.

Imani sagged in their arms, looking utterly defeated. She let them escort her off the premises, as the guards sympathized and told her that parents often upset the children with PTSD, it's really the therapists who know how to handle it, and Imani got in the car and sat there stunned for a full five minutes before driving away in a daze.

Paul didn't talk to her. He was too busy holding Aliyah, who sobbed into his shirt, wailing for a mother who she'd trusted for just a bit too long.

THIRTY-TWO
The Fire, and What the Fire Burns

"You almost got Daddy *killed*!"

Aliyah felt guilty as she dunked Rainbird into the cauldron of molten iron again, blistering flesh from bones. She didn't like hurting people, even people like Rainbird – and she especially didn't like hurting people who had nothing to do with why she was angry. Aliyah was still mad that Mommy had tricked her, using that stupid book to pretend Mommy was ready to protect her, when her stupid boyfriend had almost killed Daddy.

She'd believed Mommy. Even now, she wanted Mommy hugs so bad she ached for them, and every time she felt that stupid *stupid* need, she shoved Rainbird's disintegrating body back into the lava.

Rainbird never minded. He always smiled as she boiled his eyeballs, dragged him along the burning catwalk, dunked him in the cauldron.

That smile made her madder. He smiled like they were friends, and they *weren't* friends, she was just *learning* stuff from him, and so she pushed his head underneath the red-hot pig iron until his cheeks melted and his teeth turned black.

Rainbird's smile held secrets, and she would beat him until the secrets fell out.

"Enough," he burbled.

Aliyah pushed him down further. "You lied! You didn't protect my *father*!"

"*Enough!*"

A volcano drove Aliyah back. She wore her Kratos skin, which should have protected her – it was from *God of War*, a Rated-M-For-Mature game Rainbird had let her play. Rainbird brought her all the most violent videogames – "So you can learn new magics," he'd said – and Aliyah loved Kratos the most. Kratos killed everyone with his big curved daggers. He killed titans, he killed gods, he killed anyone. He never felt remorse.

He didn't fear fire.

But Aliyah did. She hated that weakness. Whenever Rainbird shot flames at her, she clenched herself so as not to wet her pants.

"I cannot save a man from his bad impulses." Rainbird's flesh grew back as he pulled himself up onto a slotted catwalk. "I *had* him safe. We could have escaped. But he endangered himself. You know that."

Aliyah wanted to try to hit Rainbird again, but... Rainbird was right. Daddy pulled his punches. He'd stopped her from hurting the policemen at the garage, and she hadn't *wanted* to hurt policemen, but....

Daddy would rather die than hurt people.

That shouldn't feel like a weakness, but it was.

She had her daddy's weakness, and that's why she needed Rainbird. Rainbird had no weakness. He was all strength, and maybe strength was scary. Rainbird didn't seem to care about anything but fire, and occasionally her. He made her sick to her stomach, but Aliyah had decided Rainbird was like medicine: something awful to be endured to make her stronger.

"It's time you worked, little girl," Rainbird said. "We all must pitch in to safeguard this place. Mr Payne needs you to find someone."

He went over to his safe, the only place in his lair that

didn't burn, to pull out a photo. It showed a small man in a nice white suit and Panama hat, walking with a cane.

"That's Oscar," Aliyah said. "That's Daddy's…"

She trailed off, shamed because she wanted to say "boss."

"Your father's *old* boss," Rainbird said. "Only a 'mancer should lead another 'mancer."

Secretly she agreed, but Rainbird couldn't trash-talk Daddy. "Daddy owes Oscar *money*."

"What are debts, to those such as us?" He reached into the safe, produced a handful of burning twenties, flicked the ashes aside. "Now. Find Oscar. He is hiding from us."

She looked down at the photo. She'd never liked Oscar. Oscar reminded her of when she thought 'mancy was scary, back when she'd shrieked when Daddy did magic. She didn't like that time at all.

"…how?"

Rainbird looked puzzled. "I believe your Aunt Valentine found her last target by making him a… what did you call it… a 'quest item.'"

"Oh!" That was what she loved about 'mancy: there were always new ways to use your powers. Daddy taught her that. And the Institute was a wonderful school where Mrs Vinere taught her about masks and she taught Mrs Vinere how masks worked in videogames. Juan the bookiemancer taught her the mathematical formulas that determined whether a Pokemon got trapped.

This was how the world *should* work, Aliyah thought. Not a world that treated magic like a crime, but a world where her special powers were *beloved*.

She spread her hands open. A radar screen popped out between her palms, complete with a glowing dot to show Oscar's location.

"Perfect," Rainbird said. And though Aliyah hated the way she thirsted for Rainbird's approval, she glowed with pride. She liked it because mean ol' Rainbird wouldn't do anything nice just because he thought he should. Daddy showered her with praise for stupid stuff, gushing over little kiddie accomplishments, but only a grown-up's work would satisfy Rainbird.

It was like Rainbird saw something she could be, and was shaping her. Which made her uncomfortable sometimes. But Daddy made her uncomfortable, too. He said he wanted her to be whatever made her happy, and Aliyah didn't know what happy was these days.

Valentine used to be the person who told Aliyah what made her happy. But Valentine hated this place so much that Aliyah being happy here started arguments. Aliyah couldn't understand why Valentine didn't like this place, but Valentine wanted a boy with a cute butt and *that* was disgusting.

"All right," Rainbird said. "Mr Payne has given us our orders. Let's go get him."

"We're not going to...?" Aliyah couldn't say the word "kill." She thought about killing a lot. She played Rainbird's murder games like they were real. Sometimes the people in them *became* real as she played, but Aliyah only had killed one person and her 'mancy couldn't make anything she couldn't imagine. So in the end they all burned like Anathema had, weeping for mercy as they fell from a window before they splattered apart on the pavement, and then Aliyah shuddered and turned off the game.

"Today, we send him a message." He sniffed, then added: "It'll protect your father."

They got into a limousine. It was creepy leaving the Institute this late, and even creepier leaving when there were almost no cars on the road, just a dead flat space between times when people were awake.

The dot on her radar glowed as Rainbird steered the car through the freeways, towards Oscar. The dot grew bigger. Aliyah squirmed in her seat, hating this silence.

"How will this protect my father?"

He puffed on his cigar. It smelled like burning bodies. "The same way I would have protected my father. By walling off his worst instincts."

Aliyah turned to face him. Rainbird never spoke about anything but the present. She hadn't thought he had a past.

Rainbird grinned. "We lived in a small village. We'd heard armies were coming. But my father, he was like yours. He believed in *talking*. 'We have all lived here all our lives,' he said. 'We have had our differences. No one needs to resort to violence.'

"Then the armies came. Boys, like me. Nine, ten years-old. All the men had been killed in battle, you see, but they needed someone to keep up the war. And these boys, they couldn't be convinced. They shot my father for daring to speak up. Then they shot my mother. Then they told me I was a soldier."

Aliyah clapped her hands over her mouth. How could Rainbird speak so calmly? She couldn't even say "Anathema stabbed Daddy."

Rainbird followed the dot into a sleazy motel's parking lot, pulling into a parking space at the back. "They beat me whenever I cried. They needed people killed, and either I'd kill the people they needed killed or they'd kick me to death. And I was scared, like you, little Aliyah. Scared all the time."

Maybe we do need to kill people, Daddy had said. *The question is, do you want to be the person who does that?*

"So how did you…"

Rainbird pointed towards the two men sharing a cigarette, watching for anyone who approached where Oscar slept. "Get us there."

Aliyah had learned from Valentine how to play stealth games, and Rainbird had let her play all the *Assassin's Creed*s, games where she snuck up and slit men's throats. She fiddled with her Nintendo DS, and Oscar's guards in the car became dim automata, with glowing green cones marking their line of sight. The cones swept back and forth.

"I got good at killing," Rainbird said, cocking his head in admiration at Aliyah's work. "But while the other boys forgot their villages, took on the army as their new family,

I burned to escape. And one day, we fought in an old hotel, another battle against the United Front, and... it caught fire. We couldn't escape. And as the roof collapsed upon us, I realized: fire didn't care. Fire never cared. I must *be* the fire, and as they burned alive I was burned to life."

His eyes gleamed like banked coals. Aliyah remembered her own flame, the firestorm welling up inside when Anathema had hurt her father, the scarring fires pouring out to consume someone else...

She'd been glad when she'd killed Anathema. So glad. And she'd tried hard to hold on to that ephemeral joy, but had been weighted down by all sorts of questions of who got to kill and why and her daddy telling her nobody should kill and yet she had killed, a part of her had liked it, and a part of her felt like throwing up all the time...

Rainbird smiled. And that smile did hold a secret, yes; once he'd held that teeter-totter feeling of excitement and sickness, but he'd left the sickness behind to kill whoever walked in his path.

Aliyah trembled. She wasn't sure she wanted to learn this lesson.

Then she thought of Anathema, stabbing her father. Of the policemen, tying him up.

Maybe we do need to kill people.

He would have died twice if she hadn't saved him, and what would happen if she couldn't kill and Daddy took a bullet to the head?

"I don't..." Aliyah struggled to find the right words. "I don't see how this protects my father."

"Let me show you."

Do you want to be the person who does that?

"I can't kill now," Aliyah protested.

Rainbird ignored her, sauntering past the green cones, melting the lock on the motel room. Aliyah trailed behind, walking in to discover a sleeping Oscar in his motel bed, curled up in silk pajamas, small and vulnerable.

He *was* small and vulnerable. Enspelled by her stealth

game, Oscar would not wake up. They could stab him, and he would die as an insta-kill; those were the game's rules.

But Rainbird loomed over the bed, relishing the power of knowing he could end Oscar's life at any moment.

"What are…" Aliyah remembered to whisper. "What are you doing?"

"Who is this?" Rainbird flicked his fingers towards Oscar's snoring form.

"He's Oscar."

"No. What kind of person is he?"

"…Daddy's boss?"

"No."

"I don't *know*." Aliyah was frustrated enough to stab Rainbird again.

Rainbird held up a finger. "What I learned when my fellow soldiers died was, there are two things in this world: the fire, and what the fire burns. And when you are the fire… it is *your job* to burn. There is no shame in burning kindling. It's who you are, and who they are."

"That's disgusting."

"It is true. But look at you, Aliyah: you have turned these men into puppets for your amusement. For you, it is not the fire."

He knelt down, tapping her chest. She slapped his hand away. He grinned that secret-storing grin at her.

"You…" He frowned, struggling to remember a term he'd heard elsewhere. "…are the player character. And these…" He swept his hand around to encompass the guards tick-tocking mechanically back and forth. "These aren't people. They are NPCs."

She looked down at Oscar. Rainbird was right. Oscar wasn't a man, any more: he was a mission. Something you'd never feel bad about killing, because he'd been placed there for your amusement.

Maybe we do need to kill people.

These aren't people. They are NPCs.

Rainbird took out his phone to photograph Oscar's

sleeping form. Taking all the photos right up against Oscar's nose, as though to highlight how stupid and helpless he was.

Aliyah stood by his side, watching.

THIRTY-THREE
You Don't Bring Me Donuts Anymore

Payne spread open an old, brittle map across his desk, tracing mountains with gnarled fingertips. He located a spot marked with a neat blue "X."

"I can offer you my old Flex laboratory," Payne said. "It's far out in the high hills, where no one thinks to look. I haven't used it in decades, so it'll take my men a few days to get the equipment back in order. But – it served me well, and it'll serve you well."

Payne drummed his fingers on his desk, contemplating his next words.

"The question is, Paul... do you *need* a Flex lab?"

Paul steeled himself. He'd been expecting pushback from Payne.

"What would you suggest, sir?"

Payne shrugged, in that noncommittal way people did when they offered to do terrible things. "Rainbird gives us... more options... to handle these drug-seeking blackmailers."

"I thought you said we couldn't find Oscar."

Payne gave Paul a cheerful wink. "I have resources. You don't have to be beholden to mundanes, Paul."

And what Paul wanted to say was so bizarre he couldn't form the words:

You never brought me donuts.

Which was the strangest reason Paul had heard of not to murder someone, but it rang true. He might not be buddies with K-Dash and Quaysean, given that hard wall of "Oscar might order me to kill you some day" that stood between them, but... they'd discovered Paul's sweet tooth, and had brought donuts to the Flex brews. They'd given him coffee.

Whereas Payne had given him infinitely more than a $9.99 box of donuts, but... Payne hadn't asked Paul what office he'd want; he'd just made one for him. Paul couldn't shake off that uncomfortable feeling Payne viewed him as an extension of his own needs, and...

...the donuts K-Dash and Quaysean brought didn't feel like attempts to curry Paul's favor. They had the scent of organic kindness, of nice things people did for folks they liked.

Paul had never seen Payne eat a donut. The man lived on black coffee and vitamins. And he never offered any to anyone else.

"It's... complicated, sir." And once again, Paul found that "sir" tacked on to an otherwise innocuous sentence, the subjugation bubbling up unwanted.

Payne let loose a disappointed wheeze.

"Paul. I understand. Men get attached to people who stand their ground next to them. But... they're not your friends."

"They saved my life."

"They saved an investment. That doesn't make them your allies."

But Payne hadn't seen the childlike grin on Quaysean's face when he'd watched Paul do 'mancy. He hadn't seen the way that Quaysean and K-Dash had, after a few Flex-brewing sessions, quietly held hands and given Paul a forthright look that said *This is who we are, and I'm trusting you*. He hadn't seen the raw joy as K-Dash had hugged Valentine.

It was business, yes. But you could mix business and friendship.

More importantly, you couldn't mix bureaucracy and murder. Oh, Paul had explored enough to know there were forms lurking in CIA files that *could* request death. But that wasn't the bureaucracy he had fallen in love with. The bureaucracy he knew helped people; it didn't send fiery hitmen to incinerate them.

"I'd rather give him the Flex, sir. It's easier."

Payne clenched his fists. "Paul, I'm not saying it's *good* to kill people. But if we don't, we are at the mercy of organized crime."

"Oscar's crime is *so* organized, I'm certain K-Dash and Quaysean are the only other people who can identify us. If more people knew, they would have tried to leverage me. Trust me, I saw it when his brother kidnapped me – everyone's hungry for Flex."

"Paul, I..." He buried his face in his hands. "Squeamish men cannot lead."

"I don't like killing."

"*Nobody likes killing!*" Payne pounded the map. "I am trying *very hard* to respect your authority, Paul. But I am now beholden to an unknown crime syndicate with uncertain roots, and your squeamishness during the Paper Street incident means we still have David Giabatta working to track you down. Forty years of experience tells me these are *not* wise decisions. These are not designed to *minimize* risk."

"*I* think they are. Oscar's worried about Valentine taking him out for years. If he dies, I'm pretty sure he has leaked information ready to go."

Payne snorted, seeing through the lie. "'Pretty' sure."

"Yes."

"Yet he's never mentioned this post-mortem threat to you."

"Why would he? If I knew, I'd work to defuse it."

"So you don't want to exterminate the biggest leak to our safehouse, based on... a *hunch*."

"He and I think alike."

"*You* are not a crime overlord. *You* could barely keep two 'mancers at heel. And as such, I will *beg* you to reconsider, because the sooner we can burn Oscar Gargunza's bones to ash and bury that particular threat vector, the safer we will all be."

Payne hunched over the desk, doing his best to stare Paul down. If Paul refused, Payne would order a hit on Oscar anyway...

"*Found him!*"

Valentine burst through the door, applying mascara with one hand, hiking up her bandolier with the other.

"We *got* him, Paul! Hang on, I gotta..." She fiddled with the security monitors, then gave up and grabbed for her Xbox controller. Several newscasts flickered across the screen, showing New York's tungsten-yellow streets flickering with a skyscraper on fire.

No, wait – not "a" skyscraper.

The skyscraper where David Giabatta held office for the New York Task Force.

And it wasn't on fire, exactly. Only half the facing windows were aflame, as though there had been *very careful* explosions ...

"Is that a gigantic 'V' written in destruction across the skyscraper?" Payne asked, peering closer.

Valentine did a girlish pirouette. "Isn't that *romantic*?"

"That is..." Paul shivered, thinking how this would play out in tomorrow's headlines. "That's insane! It's taking a huge risk, calling out David! And he left your initial up there as a billboard-sized clue–"

More explosions. Windows mirroring the other side of the building detonated, showering glass down upon the cops who'd cordoned off the area.

"Now it's a 'W'." Valentine scratched her chin. "What's *that* mean?"

"This isn't even *Fight Club*!" Paul shouted, apoplectic. "This is *Say Anything* with terrorism! I sat through that awful movie, and Tyler Durden wasn't doing all this just to get some girl's attention!"

"Kinda the way it worked out for him, though."

"That's not the point! That movie was about brutal cynicism! He's... *inaccurate*!"

"And bureaucracy isn't about making the world better, Paul. We 'mancers pick and choose from our source material. I got me a *Fight-Club*-o-'mancer who skews romantic."

"You have no 'mancer at all, Ms DiGriz," Payne interjected. "You'll stand down."

"What?"

"We rescue 'mancers who are willing to play ball; we are *not* rescuing this boy from his own poor decisions. We've taken too many chances."

"But..." Valentine scrambled for rationales. "He knows my name. My first name, anyway. He knows Paul's name. If he gets captured..."

"He won't. I've seen his kind before. He's another anarchomancer in modern clothing." Payne said the word "modern" with a moue of distaste. "He's halfway towards killing himself already, and he'd die before anyone hauled him in. And if *we* ushered him into the fold, he'd not play well by our rules."

"We can't let him die!"

"What we *cannot* do," Payne said, "Is risk twenty 'mancers to save one idiotic boy."

"But it is a *cute* boy... wait, that won't work on you. Tyler is a *potent* boy."

"He's powerful, I grant you that. He's also hell-bent on self-destruction. I too watched the film. He won't get the happy ending he thinks he will."

"But I–"

"Leave to help him, Ms DiGriz, and you'll be on your own. It's high time you chose which side you're on."

"Which *side*?!?" Paul barely held back Valentine as she leapt for Payne, fingers crooked to claw his eyes out. "This is a fucking 'mancer, you emaciated scarecrow! You're the asshole forever telling us you're saving these precious flowers!"

"I'm also the one telling Mr Tsabo that a ruler makes tough decisions. It's my money. It's my Institute. It's my risk pool. I have been quite generous with my resources – and between you, the Task Force, and this overly informed crime syndicate, I have taken more chances than I can bear. This additional hazard is off-limits. Do you understand me?"

Valentine's voice was low and poisonous. "Oh, I get you."

Payne sneered. "You little reptile. You–" He stopped, massaged his forehead. "*You* talk some sense into her, Paul. You understand what's at stake. Your position. Your daughter's future. *Talk* to her."

He stormed out, back stiffened.

Valentine clasped her hands together in prayer, shook them at him. "*Pleeeeeease*, Paul."

Paul shrank back in his chair, leery of the things she could talk him into. "Valentine…"

Valentine saw Paul's uncertainty. She flattened her palm between her breasts, as though massaging her aching heart.

"Look." Her voice cracked. "I gave up a lot to be here. Because I love you."

Her weakness always terrified Paul. He thought of her as so strong, he forgot she could break. "Don't…"

"No, Paul. You don't understand. You've got Aliyah to cuddle up with at night. You hardly ever left your apartment. A stack of forms, that's like Disneyland for you. You didn't lose anything, being transplanted here."

"That's not true."

"No. It *is*. But for me, I gave up so much already. When I killed Raphael, I–"

"You didn't kill him, Valentine. That was…"

"My flux did it, Paul. It killed him because I loved him, that insensitive little shit, and that was the proof I should never have a boyfriend. My love is a chambered bullet, waiting to fucking kill the next motherfucker who opens up to me. So I moved in next door to you, and it wasn't terrible because you're my best fucking friend, but I started hitting the swing clubs because sometimes that was the only way I could get a fucking *hug*, and I…"

Her tears smeared her mascara. She swatted her cheeks, then waved at the screens. "*That*, Paul. That's a guy who's interested in me, someone who can maybe take the punches I give – and if I don't go at least *try* to look for him then I might as well lie down in a grave and pull the dirt over my fucking head, because what the fuck am I living for if I can't love somebody?"

"Valentine, I…." Paul took her hand. "You deserve love. You *do*. You're…"

"Say it."

"You're my best friend, too."

She sniffled. "I kinda needed to hear that right now."

Paul's eyes stung with tears. "But I don't know how much leeway I have with Mr Payne. He's pissed. He's *right* to be pissed. And if he kicks us out, then Aliyah loses all this support, all this training…"

"I get that, Paul. I *do*. But…" She trembled, afraid to say what came next. "Don't I deserve to have somebody for me?"

Paul stared over at the burning office building, seeing more cops screeching in as news helicopters swarmed around. It would be dangerous. And Payne was right; Tyler would not fit in any better here than Valentine.

But what good was being second-in-command at the Institute, if he couldn't use that power to help his friends? What kind of friend was he if he condemned Valentine to living among antisocial 'mancers, sexless?

"Oh, God," he muttered. "This is such a mistake."

"That's how you *always* say yes!" Valentine squealed, and tackle-hugged him.

THIRTY-FOUR
Finding the Bomb

Doing magic, Paul had discovered, involved lots of driving.

Valentine could have opened up a portal, but she'd already generated enough flux *Metal Gear Solid*-ing her way out of the Institute. So she drove a stolen car while Paul did research on his laptop.

She mashed the accelerator to the floor, headlights zooming through blackness, even though neither were quite sure where to go yet. And she would not shut up.

"This is like a first date test," she babbled. "All I got is an initial. If I can find him with a single letter, well, then we're meant to be, aren't we?"

Paul grunted noncommittally.

"A muttered affirmation does not signal approval of my love life, Paul."

"Sorry. I'm researching."

"Can't you just..." She signed an imaginary piece of paper, Paul's literal signature move.

"I'd have to use Payne's access," he explained. "Besides, much of what the munitions companies do is public record, if you know where to look. What did you call it when you tracked me down online? Googlemancy?"

"Googlemancy."

"Well, I'm Googling."

She thumped the steering wheel. "Good times, Paul. It's you and me, on our own again, investigating. That feels good. Clean."

Except it didn't, not to Paul. He stroked Payne's badge, feeling its chill ridges; without Payne's authorization, it was just a chunk of dead metal, unable to drain away flux's danger. Valentine did a little booty-dance in her seat, enthused – but Paul felt as though he'd stepped away from Samaritan Mutual's protection to search for a lunatic who he didn't even like.

"All right, I've got the address," he said, pulling it up. "We're not too far from it, anyway. They're international companies, so they have to be delivering *somewhere* within the Port Authority. If you look at the companies David's contracted with, the anti-'mancer munitions usually deliver to the Newark-Elizabeth port…"

"'W' for Warehouse."

"This is a slender lead, Valentine. I wouldn't get too excited."

The parking lot to the port was sprawling; even at three in the morning, every inch of asphalt was packed with cars, because cargo arrived at all hours. This, Paul knew, was where New York and New Jersey's cargo landed, stacked on ships trundling in from all continents, constant tides of merchandise to be unloaded.

They pulled over before they got to the parking lot's gate, so Paul could 'mancy up the appropriate credentials using his legal pad. But as they presented their badges, the guard noted Valentine's eyepatch.

The guard leaned out of his booth, pushing his face through their car window.

"Do they call you Valentine?" he asked. He spoke with a zealot's slightly hypnotized cadence.

"Who wants to know?"

He tapped the bruise on his bandaged cheekbone, winking conspiratorially. "Tyler's been waiting for you."

Valentine punched Paul in the shoulder. "You see? *True love*. I can read this guy like a book."

"Well, yeah," Paul said. "That book is *Fight Club*."

"Pull over to the far side," said the guard. "Walk to the west side entry. Someone from Project Mayhem will meet you there."

The guard pulled his hat down, slouching back into his booth. Paul leaned over, feeling the mild embarrassment of having to repeat your order when the drive-through clerk didn't hear you. "Has Tyler already–"

"The first rule of Project Mayhem," the guard recited serenely, "is that you don't ask questions about Project Mayhem."

Valentine stomped on the gas and parked, as though humiliated by Paul's questions. They looked over the miles of orange and black corrugated steel shipping containers, stacked into towers for as far as the eye could see – a massive, moving maze that changed as cranes sorted through the containers to find the one they needed. Workers wearing orange safety vests and hard hats moved along, marking inventory off on touchpads.

The Port Harbor was city-sized, and needed to be. Anything shipped by boat ended up here. Nobody, not even the most diligent bureaucrats, could catalogue everything in these cargo holds – there wasn't the manpower to verify what all these massive crates held, so stashed in with legitimate shipments were drugs and illicit arms and God knew what else.

"Whoah." Valentine whistled. "That's a lot of shipping."

"$256.8 billion dollars in commerce over the last financial year," Paul noted.

"Well, aren't *you* the Harper's Index of our little social circle."

A scruffy Polish guy met them at the entryway, squinting through bruised, swollen eyes. He handed them each a hard hat, an orange reflective vest, and a dockworker's uniform. They changed into them, then walked into the battered steel labyrinth. Forklifts whizzed around corners; quivering shipping containers blocked out the light as the cranes hauled them high into the sky.

"Do you know what Tyler intends to–" Paul began.

"The second rule of Project Mayhem is that you don't ask

questions about Project Mayhem."

Paul probed the guy with 'mancy to verify he hadn't been formed from Tyler's obsessions. But as far as he could tell, their guide was very real. Tyler had been gaining support among the dockworkers.

"*Paul!*" Valentine drew her index finger across her throat. "*Totes* rude to verify someone's reality."

"They don't ask questions, they don't have any knowledge, they just follow orders–"

The guard coughed. "The fifth rule of Project Mayhem is that you have to trust Tyler Durden."

"See?" Valentine said, as though that solved everything. He hunched over to follow their guide between two rusted shipping containers.

"*V!*"

Tyler hailed them from the top of a large, rusted shipping container, feet dangling off the edge as he kicked the corrugated steel sides, smoking a cigarette. A group of dockworkers had gathered below him, looking up at him with adoration, shuffling from foot to foot as though they couldn't wait for the party to begin.

The container sat in an impromptu battered asphalt courtyard, walled off by the careful placement of other shipping containers. Tyler had wanted privacy, and the dockworkers made it happen.

Their efficiency should have reassured Paul. But this had a cultlike flavor; the waiting dockworkers, the seclusion, all smacked of ceremony.

Tyler jumped down from the container to meet Valentine – then panicked as he realized he'd leapt down eight feet. He landed awkwardly, scuffing his hands. His men rushed forward to pick him up; he smacked them away, covering his face, making incoherently embarrassed noises.

Valentine pushed the Project Mayhem members aside to kneel down, taking Tyler's hands in hers tenderly. He gave a perfunctory struggle, but Valentine held his wrists, refusing to let him push her away.

"It's OK," she whispered. A cryptic smile bloomed across her face, as though she'd been expecting this moment. "It's OK."

He let her peel his hands away. Tyler's face had changed. He still wore Brad Pitt's handsome features, but his eyes held the scared terror of an insignificant accountant toiling at Samaritan Mutual, a chubby man who'd gone home to one too many single-serving TV dinners.

He offered that fear to her belligerently, tilting his chin as though he expected her to punch the vulnerability from his body–

–but instead, Valentine kissed him chastely on the lips.

He nodded when she was done, as though a ritual had somehow been completed. And when he brushed back his hair, his eyes had snapped back to the old Tyler.

"Hey," Tyler said, slipping on his sunglasses. "No hard feelings about the abandonment, right?"

"You offered, I declined."

"We got a nice little firebomb in here." Tyler thumped the shipping container a little too hard, adopting a swagger.

"This container holds all the latest anti-'mancer technology shipped over from Israeli factories. They're super-sensitive to 'mancy. So pretty much anything we do will cause a massive explosion." He winked at Valentine, who clasped her hands together in pride. "I mean, how do you feel about casting spells together? Because that last fight, well, it hung high in the rafters of *my* life."

"Are you fucking *crazy*!?"

Tyler's men stepped back as Paul limped forward, looking to Tyler for orders. Tyler, nonplussed, took a long draw off his cigarette.

"Is any 'mancy really sane, Paul?" he replied.

"I cannot believe you used 'mancy to taunt David Giabatta. The city's terrified of 'mancers after we damn near wiped out the Task Force–"

"No, we *saved* the Task Force," Tyler said calmly. "It was your firebird freak who almost killed them."

"Regardless – we have a law enforcement organization that keeps the far deadlier SMASH out of New York, and after everything we've gone through, you're *amping* the pressure on them? To... to go on a *date*?"

"Whoah!" Tyler held his hands up, wiggling his fingers as if to show there was nothing up his sleeve. "Not a scrap of 'mancy in *that* operation, Paul. Just hard-working Project Mayhem members, using all the improvised explosives mankind has to offer."

"And how many of those hard-working members were real?"

Tyler stubbed out his cigarette. "What do you mean?"

"Jesus. He doesn't even realize what he's doing. He wants to be the center of attention so badly he'll conjure up associates..."

Valentine stepped in between them. "Ix-nay on the akefay udesday talk, Paul. Bad for morale if half their team dissolves into a puddle of soap fat."

"This isn't a *team*! A team has a goal! All Tyler wants to do is... well, it's *mayhem*!"

"No." Tyler corrected Paul with the firm confidence of a man holding a royal flush. "What I *want* to do is take any organization who thinks brainwashing 'mancers is valid, and show them they can't fight organized resistance." He jerked his thumb towards the dockworkers. "This is the organized resistance."

"And then what? The Task Force falls, SMASH comes to town, and – what? You beat up the military until the 'mancers are all free?"

Tyler smirked – a strangely sympathetic grin. "So how's that paperwork thing working out for you?"

Paul would have punched Tyler if that didn't fuel Tyler's magic. Instead, he trembled with rage. Because Tyler was right: with all his access to bureaucratic power, the most Paul had done was piggyback on someone else's safe space.

He *should* have been able to do more. For Aliyah. For Valentine. For everybody. And yet this upstart 'mancer, with his movie-stolen good looks and reliance on chaos, claimed to have a better plan than Paul.

He turned to Valentine for support. She refused to meet his gaze.

"Your problem," said Tyler, "is that *you* are afraid to let everything crumble. You can't make an omelet without breaking a few eggs, Paul!"

"Those omelets are *people*, Tyler. People are going to die. They're going to die because your showdown feeds the newspapers with all the bad-'mancer headlines they can get!"

Tyler flung his arms wide. "Fuck that! People are dying right now! The only difference is they're dying in classic, well-worn ways! I'm not afraid to look people in the eye and tell them their spilled blood is what oils the gears of change. Am, I fellas?"

He whirled to face the dockworkers. They cheered: "We have to trust Tyler Durden! We have to trust Tyler Durden!"

Tyler puffed up, drinking strength from their applause. Which enraged Paul, because Tyler Durden wasn't even this guy's true name; he'd erased his records to obscure his unimpressive past.

"You're following a movie!" Paul cried. "All you cinemancers are flawed! You're seeking a happy ending, but real life doesn't have credits!"

"This isn't about happy endings, Paul. It's about *meaning*. These guys go to a useless job, go home, buy expensive shit, feeling like the same organic sludge. They are meaningless. In creating change, they infuse their anonymous lives with meaning. They will *die* to attain relevance. They can help *me* live."

"You are not Tyler Durden." Paul's voice was hoarse with anger. "Tyler had no ego. *You* are a nebbish seeking glory. *You* are a fucking cult leader."

"And you are ineffective."

"Enough!"

Tyler cringed as Valentine clicked the green "X" on her game controller. The shipping container made a muffled *whoof* sound, its battered sides crumpling outwards as Valentine's 'mancy triggered all the opal chips inside the anti-'mancer munitions. The container rocked, spurting smoke, tilted to fall on its side with an echoing *boom*.

Valentine made a gazelle-like leap to the top, an effect marginally spoiled by the sproinging Mario "bounce" sound effect that accompanied her. She straddled the smoldering container, addressing the crowd.

Tyler gazed up at her, lovestruck as a pimply teenager.

"Paul," she barked. "If we have a goddamned chance to sabotage these anti-'mancer technologies, we take it. And Tyler..." She trailed off, biting her lip. "*Jesus*, you're good-looking."

He winked.

"Tyler, we've been making a difference. It's just... small. And corporate as fuck. Will you come with us? To help make it better for the 'mancers we have?" Sirens blared as the container's explosion reached the ears of the Port security. "Before all the cops converge on our position?"

"You'd be surprised at how many cops understand *some* 'mancers are looking out for their wellbeing." But Tyler gestured for his men to scatter, then reached up to help Valentine down. She muffled a smile with her fingertips, blushing – then interlaced her fingers with his, holding hands.

"Come on." She rushed past Paul, dashing towards the car. "We gotta get him back to the Institute."

Valentine looked alive, her eyes wide with adrenaline excitement. She tugged Tyler, who stared at Valentine with a goofy grin that said he couldn't believe his own luck.

Paul straggled behind them, limping clumsily, mapping his next move. He didn't want Tyler Durden mixing with Samaritan Mutual again, not at all. Paul wondered how long it'd be before Tyler ruined everything at the Institute. Days, at most.

But once Valentine had promised to show Tyler Durden around, Paul was sure it would have taken warfare to stop them from going.

THIRTY-FIVE
The Last of Us

Paul woke to Valentine's screams.

He rolled off his bed – Aliyah wasn't there. But something hammered at the walls of the Institute, a pulsing earthquake that caused files to rain down from his shelves.

Dazed, he broke for the door – and remembered, too late, that his right foot no longer existed. He had, as usual, put his artificial leg in the recharging station before he went to bed, giving his stump skin time to breathe, and in his panic he forgot he was crippled.

His face impacted against hardwood floor. Blood flew.

Something slammed into the Institute again, so hard that Paul heard the creak of beams torqueing. The chandelier in the ceiling dipped, swaying precipitously. Valentine shrieked, a full-throated howl.

A low-bass growl, feral and terrifying, matched her screams.

Where was Aliyah?

What was attacking them?

He grabbed for his artificial leg, slid it over his stump, locked it into place. His other foot, the one missing four toes, didn't grab the floor any more – you never realized how much toes kept your balance until a spear-wielding maniac severed them – so he hunted his orthotic boot, tugged that on. All the while the thumping continued, a deep booming sound echoing from every surface, now accompanied by screams from the atrium.

Paul darted out into the lobby's marble floor, seeing the confused 'mancers gathered around the door to Valentine's room: Natasha the culinomancer, Juan the bookiemancer, Idena the origamimancer. They stood frozen, terrified as rabbits, unsure what to do.

But the thumping quickened in pace, rising in pitch, headed towards some dreadful crescendo.

"*Kick in the door!*" he shouted.

Mrs Vinere, wearing an elaborately-colored parrot mask, stared at Paul. "You don't have a mask," she muttered, twiddling her thumbs. "You can't be out here without a mask."

"Yes," the plushiemancer said, hugging a fuzzy pony to his chest. "You have to go inside."

"I said *kick in the door!*"

"The staff will see you!"

"The whole place is going to come down!" Valentine let loose a lung-emptying howl. "Get the fucking door down before someone gets hurt!"

Payne's 'mancers shuffled their feet, panicked by new and unknown factors.

"Oh, goddammit–" Paul rushed for the door, remembering his policeman's training – kick next to the lock, brace your back foot for maximum impact – and lashed out. But the springy coiled surface of his artificial foot bounced off harmlessly.

"*Someone help!*" Paul cried. The 'mancers milled about. Valentine's howl trailed away. The pounding stopped.

The door to Valentine's room exploded.

Paul flinched; Rainbird emerged from his room's fiery cavern, hands smoking, storming towards Valentine's apartment. Aliyah trailed behind him, looking shamed, even through her angry old-man tattoo-mask and chained daggers.

Paul would ask about that later. He leapt through the splintered doorway, eyes watering from the smoke. "*Valentine!*" he yelled, so panicked he forgot to use her code name. "*Valentine!*"

Valentine lay naked on her bed. Leather straps were wrapped around her hips, securing a wagging pink dildo to her crotch.

Tyler Durden, bathed in a post-sex sweat sheen, laid face-down next to her, goggle-eyed with gratitude.

"Say it?" he asked.

"I won't," Valentine replied, lighting up a cigarette. "It's a stupid line."

"Please. It's what *she* says. In the movie."

"Oh, all right." She rolled her eye good-naturedly. "'I haven't been fucked like that since grade school.'"

Valentine passed him the cigarette, then noticed Paul. "Hey, Paul, what's up?" she chirped, reaching down to unbuckle her strap-on. "Sorry about the noise. Tyler thought he'd show me some moves. I got to show him some."

Tyler closed his eyes, practically melting into the bed. His cynical sneer had melted away, his brawny limbs slack, as though Valentine's domination had lifted some great burden from him.

Paul fishmouthed, speechless.

"What's up?" She chucked her strap-on into the corner. Then noticed Rainbird shoving the hothouse 'mancers aside, Payne roaring to know what was going on here.

"Ooh," she muttered. "My bad."

"All right, so I made a mistake," Valentine said.

Payne had shuffled Valentine and Paul off to the meeting room while he calmed the Institute's 'mancers down, then ordered the contractors to gauge the extent of the damage. Even now, the monitors in the room were cracked, their camera views skewed.

"A *mistake*?!" Paul spluttered.

"I don't know if you've *had* sex since you got 'manceritized

– but if you had, you'd see how hard it is to keep that shit bottled up. 'Mancy isn't something you do, it's who you *are*. And if you're not paying attention… it leaks out." She poured herself a glass of water, offered one to Tyler. "That was great fucking sex, and we lost control. Kinda what sex does. But now we know we fuck earthquakes, unless we rein it in." She stifled a grin with her fingertips. "Which is actually kinda hot…"

"You almost collapsed the whole Institute!"

"I *said* I was sorry."

"And it's not just the Institute – the Task Force is bringing in new equipment all the time! What if a drone had flown overhead? You could have exposed us all!"

Tyler chuckled. "Not much of a loss. This place is like a shopping mall where they sell dysfunctional people."

"*Tyler!*" Valentine said.

"Get the fuck out," Paul hissed. "Before I sic Rainbird on you."

Tyler made an exaggerated "We got a badass over here" gesture, and headed for the door. Paul slammed it behind him.

By the time he turned back around, Valentine was fuming.

"Is *that* how it's going to be, Paul?" she asked. "Rainbird, the guy who almost fucking murdered you? *He's* your new consigliere?"

"And *that's* your new boyfriend? The guy who just said people deserved to die?"

"He's prone to hyperbole, Paul – but there's truth curled up in here. You wouldn't invite anyone here to a party, and you know it."

"This isn't a party. It is a *refuge*. And you endangered us all, including my daughter."

She flicked her fingers, as though swatting a mosquito. "OK, I made a mistake–"

"*A* mistake?"

"Yes. One mistake. An expensive mistake, sure, but the

one thing Payne has flying around in great numbers is money..."

"You don't wear the mask," Paul said, ticking off Valentine's sins on her fingers. "You wreck your room out of petulance. You toss Cheetos at the guy who *owns* the place, for God's sake!"

"I don't wear the mask *he wants* me to." Valentine shifted to her hooded Alex Mercer form. "But I'm not fucking stupid, Paul. I hide my real face from the staff. I get the need for secrecy."

"You destroyed thousands of dollars of videogame equipment!"

"Terribly sorry – I thought it was *my room*. To decorate as *I pleased*. I didn't realize I had to check what flair was permitted in *my living quarters*."

Paul felt a terrible confusion welling up inside. "And you threw–"

"Yes, yes, I threw Cheetos at Old Creepy's head. That's my *real* crime here, isn't it? I don't fucking bend the knee. But you know what? I stayed here because you asked me to, and I did what I could to make it comfortable. But if it wasn't the sex, I bet dimes to dollars Payne would *still* get his panties in a wad about something."

"It's Payne's money," Paul pleaded. "Like it or not, if we don't keep him happy then he kicks us out. And if we lose this place, then Aliyah can't–"

"Why the fuck is she wearing a *God of War* skin?"

"...a what?"

Valentine leaned forward. "*God. Of. War.* The bloodiest fucking game the PlayStation has to offer. She's dressing like a psycho who punches Hercules' face in! This place is toxic, Paul! You and I, we..."

Her voice dropped to a whisper.

"We have to get out."

And for a moment, Paul was tempted.

Then, on the monitors, he saw Tyler Durden bumping chests with Rainbird, Payne rushing in to break them up.

"To go where, Valentine?" he asked. "Your boyfriend can't even get out the door without getting into another scuffle. What are we going to do, go punch the government until they fucking leave us alone?"

"Maybe! Paul, sometimes you have to lose everything to be who you really are! *Tyler* understands that. *I* get that. But you…" She shook her head. "You've been playing it so safe with Aliyah for so long, you can't see how all this safety is hurting her."

He slapped his palms on the conference table. "*I am protecting my kid the best way I know how!*"

"You are screaming way too much these days, Paul. I can't tell if that's a good sign or a bad sign."

He squeezed his temples, feeling the mad pulse of things spiraling out of control. "It's a bad sign."

"This is a bad place."

"It *isn't*, Valentine. It just… it needs some fixing. And you…"

He closed his eyes, not wanting to say what came next.

"You're part of the problem."

Valentine made a tiny wheezing noise.

"If it was just you, I'd work with you. But your boyfriend – Tyler – he should have known to keep you in line. That sex was too much, you should have–"

"*Pardon* me?"

Valentine kicked a chair aside, rising to her feet.

"Nobody keeps me in line, Paul. I *am* my line. Tyler likes queuing up with me, because we are *simpatico*. Even our 'mancy laces together – a lot better than yours and mine. And he's right about needing to change, Paul. You? You've been frozen since… well, since I met you."

She hocked a green loogie onto the table, then thought better and flicked an imaginary button. The table split in two.

"You want to choose those freaks as her parents over me? Fine. *Fine*. I'll be back in ten years to see the mess you've made of her!"

"You won't last ten *days*!" Paul shouted. "Once the Task Force gets dissolved, SMASH will *crush* you!"

"See this?" She showed Paul the back of her hand. "I'll bitch-slap them back to Washington. And when I'm done, you'll thank me for making New York a safer place."

Paul sagged. "Please, Valentine," he whispered. "Don't do this. They'll kill you."

Her voice trembled with rage and sorrow. "It's better than curling up here to die."

They glared at each other, eyes watering. Their lips twitched as they tried on words of forgiveness, words they couldn't quite force past their pride.

Valentine brushed off the hem of her skirt.

"Have a nice life, Paul." She closed the door quietly behind her, which was somehow worse; he'd seen Valentine's rage before, but her cold disappointment sapped his confidence. Why was Aliyah dressing like a war god? What crimes had Valentine really committed?

He bolted into the hallway – but Payne blocked his way, scowling, the ceiling creaking ominously overhead. Valentine had almost collapsed the Institute in her lust – leaving Aliyah homeless again, all these 'mancers and their pretty, defenseless magic crushed under steel beams.

Where would he live, if not here?

How could he protect his daughter without Payne's assistance?

You need to understand, Valentine had said. *What you have now? Me and your Dad to talk to? This is the most social support you'll ever get.*

Aliyah had looked so beaten then.

She looked happier. Surrounded by 'mancer friends. Trained by other 'mancers. Protected by Payne's risk pool. Here, she could grow up to be someone strong, not another SMASH statistic…

Was it worth losing his best friend?

He took another step towards Valentine. Payne intercepted him. "Choose," Payne said.

Something tore open inside Paul: the faint hope he
might be happy, some day. No, he *didn't* like it here, playing
by Payne's rules. After all these years, he found himself back
in the same situation he'd been in when Aliyah had gotten
burned: working at Payne's abeyance, sacrificing whatever
he could to protect his daughter.

Payne glared, his king mask regal, unforgiving.

Paul sank to his knees.

"I'm sorry, sir," he whispered.

Payne stood silently, letting Paul repeat himself until he
could apologize without choking on the words.

THIRTY-SIX
Victory Poses

Aliyah didn't miss Valentine. Did not miss her at all.

Why should she? She had all the videogames in the world. Shelves and shelves of them. All the bloody-killer games that Valentine told her a little girl shouldn't play, a million billion systems with games to fit whatever mood she had, and Aliyah wasn't any lonelier, because stupid Valentine wouldn't play those videogames with her anyway. All Valentine wanted to play was the same stupid Mario games they'd bought with their money, talking about how the "lifestyle" – whatever that was – involved *working* for your rewards.

Then Valentine had bumped parts with some stupid boy and almost collapsed the house.

Stupid, stupid Valentine.

Rainbird had told her they were better off without Valentine; Aliyah had broken his jaw. That was what Rainbird was good for: hitting. You could hit him as much as you wanted and he'd never stop smiling.

But still, the Institute felt *different* without Valentine in it, even if she and Valentine hadn't been talking much. Now everybody wanted to play with Aliyah. Mrs Vinere kept coming by with her masks, and that ori-something-mancer wanted Aliyah to help fold paper better, and they all

thanked her *so much* for helping make their 'mancy stronger
– and yet without Valentine curled up in her wrecked room,
door cracked to peer out into the lobby to see Aliyah…

…it was like nobody was keeping score.

It was like Aliyah was just winning, all the time, and that
was crazy.

She wanted to talk to Daddy, but Daddy was a bad idea
these days. She could feel people getting mad whenever she
got near Daddy – the man who'd been stupid enough to
sneak that *Fight-Club*-o-'mancer into the Institute, the man
who let drug dealers into the place. Aliyah still pretended
to sleep with him until he drifted off, because she had to
protect her daddy, but…

Rainbird had said her daddy was acting like an NPC,
these days.

She should have hurt Rainbird for saying that, but she
didn't.

Aliyah hated this mood. She went to the racks, started
yanking games at random. They were fresh from the factory
– hadn't that shrinkwrap scent brought her joy once? – and
Aliyah grabbed them, shucked them, stuffed the disc into
her Xbox without even looking at the label.

There should have been triumph. It was way past her
bedtime, she was playing all the games, sneaking past
clumsy old Daddy, and why was this not working?

She kept playing, sometimes ejecting the disc before
the splash screen had finished loading, sometimes getting
through the tutorial before screaming and switching to
something else.

Then she grabbed a gift-wrapped box.

Aliyah was so used to getting gifts from Mr Payne these
days that she nearly opened it reflexively. But this gift didn't
have Mr Payne's crisp edges and neatly tied bows. This gift
was sheathed in crumpled newspaper comics, taped crudely.

Aliyah weighed it in her hands.

She opened the note on it:

Don't let your yesterdays make your tomorrows, kid.

– Valentine

Then she peeled off the paper, placing it carefully to one side.

Valentine's last gift was, of course, a game.

Aliyah brightened. A *bloody* game. An older game called *Watch Dogs*, some *Grand Theft Auto* knockoff, but…

Valentine never let her play *GTA*.

Valentine thought Aliyah was ready for Mature games.

She hugged the disc to her chest.

Victory.

THIRTY-SEVEN
Know Your Role

By the time they drove to Aliyah's appointment a week later, Paul's status was reflected in the limousine's seating arrangement.

Payne got in first, as he always did – the Samaritan Industries' CEO wouldn't suffer anything else. But now Aliyah was ushered in second, the Institute's favorite girl, and when she leaped into the car she found the week's newest videogames, gift-wrapped and waiting.

Rainbird got in third, bumping Paul aside with his shoulder. And then Paul, almost an afterthought, slid into the back.

Aliyah still curled up next to him. She always did. But it seemed increasingly as though she stood watch out of duty. She'd been furious at the damage Valentine had done, yet paradoxically she'd resented Paul for making Aunt Valentine leave. When he'd tried to talk to her about it, she'd gotten angrier and angrier about Daddy leaving the Institute unattended, eventually getting so flustered that Payne had to promise that no, her daddy was *not* leaving Mr Payne's protection.

So Paul's refuge had become a house arrest. All the hothouse 'mancers blamed him for the sex-induced earthquake. They were too socially awkward to confront him; they simply avoided him like a bad luck charm. Payne showed up with the morning paperwork for Paul to look through, hunting through atypical patterns in the claims reports for evidence of 'mancy – but he dumped the files onto Paul's desk, told Paul what to hunt for, and left.

Rainbird peering through Paul's door, a smirk curled around his cigar.

Paul endured this, because Aliyah seemed happier than ever. Something had changed; whereas before, she'd been reticent to use her 'mancy lest she hurt someone with it, now she practiced in great gouts in the lobby, leaving the ever-beleaguered cleanup crews to fix her work. She was more comfortable in her 'mancy, having left some nebulous worry behind.

He thought about showing Aliyah's newfound comfort with 'mancy to Valentine, to demonstrate the correctness of staying, then remembered he wasn't talking to Valentine any more.

"I don't like seeing Mommy," Aliyah said. "It's not safe."

Paul started to answer – but Payne spoke first, as though he'd forgotten Paul might have a worthwhile opinion.

"We need your mother on our side, Aliyah." He indulged her whininess with a patriarchal air. "So you must be nice. If she wants to visit you twice a week, well, that's a small price to pay to stay in such a wonderful land as the Institute."

"But she could find the Institute," Aliyah fretted. "I could just call her."

"We've built a separate school for her to visit, it's forty minutes away. And she must see you in person, Aliyah; it's only right that a mother spend time with her daughter."

"I thought you said it would be easier if Imani left us alone."

Paul's words were like a small bomb detonating in the confines of the car. Aliyah whirled on him, aghast that her stupid father had dared to speak up again. Rainbird made a clucking noise with his tongue, and when he caught Aliyah's gaze he rolled his eyes.

Paul felt a clammy chill.

Payne took a long time to form his reply.

"In the wake of all the *disastrous* events that have befallen us as of late," Payne opined, the weight he placed on the word "disastrous" leaving no doubt as to whom he blamed, "I have decided the wisest approach is diplomacy, for the time being. Our best bet is to be so kind to Aliyah's mother that she will do anything to keep her daughter with us."

Payne sipped at a cut crystal glass, contemplating whether to continue talking to Paul. Then he added: "This is why I have decided you will, in fact, brew Flex for Mr Gargunza. We may deal with his ilk later on, but with so much upheaval, it is best to calm whatever waters we have at our disposal."

He glared at Paul with barely concealed rage. Paul cringed, feeling the pressure to say something:

"It's quite kind," Paul offered, "to spend so much money on a false school for Aliyah."

Payne gave a miniscule headshake. "Aliyah is the Institute's crown jewel. She makes our 'mancers stronger. She learns the correct lessons about harmony. She is our future."

Left unsaid: *And you are not.* But that was all right: Aliyah was happy. She unwrapped more videogames, squealing with joy as she held the wrapping paper up to the window and watched the highway winds suck them out.

She shouldn't toss wrapping paper out the window.

He'd discuss it later with her. In private.

The limo pulled up in front of the LisAnna Foundation. Aliyah leapt out.

"My bought friends are here!" she squealed. "I'm gonna make 'em play dodgeball!"

That terminology was concerning. He'd talk to her about that, too. But it was a relief, at least, to see Aliyah so eager to have friends to play with – even if they were, as Aliyah correctly noted, paid actors.

But actors could still enjoy themselves, couldn't they?

Valentine had read him articles on sex workers, whether Paul had wanted to hear them or not – Valentine read whatever she found interesting out loud. And Valentine had known an ungodly amount of sex workers; she said they often enjoyed time with their clients. Maybe that's how kid actors worked. Maybe these kids liked spending time with Aliyah, and this was in some way a healthy relationship.

God, he missed Valentine.

They went into the lobby to wait for Imani. Rainbird cornered him, squeezing Paul's shoulder perhaps a bit too hard.

"Mr Payne will be taking the lead in today's interaction," Rainbird told him, blowing smoke in Paul's face. "Don't interrupt."

"I won't."

"That would be a surprising behavioral change."

Rainbird bared his teeth at him, then breathed flame until his gums sizzled.

Paul looked away.

He was looking forward to at least seeing Imani, stalkery as that felt. She was the closest thing he had left to a friend these days. Asking her to lunch was out of the question, at least not until he was out of Payne's doghouse, but... seeing her would make him feel better.

Though his anticipation at how much better he'd feel highlighted how lonely he was.

Her Tesla pulled into the parking lot.

Two people were in it.

David had come along.

Paul fought back terror – *he knows!* – which wasn't helped by the tense-shouldered way Imani got out of the car without looking back. But then Paul realized:

If David had come all the way out here with Imani, that must mean Imani and David were reconciling.

Paul leaned against the wall, smiling.

He supposed their renewed relationship should have saddened him, given the torch he still carried for Imani, but... he'd never wanted company in misery. No matter how terrible things got for Paul, it always made him buck up to see someone else thriving.

And if Imani could rekindle her relationship with David... He'd been too busy to think about her marital woes, but the idea that maybe Imani might salvage her marriage with David was a balm to him. She'd hated the idea of her first divorce: Imani prided herself on executing Great Plans perfectly, and so for her their divorce had been a humiliating display. Her *second* marriage tanking must have felt like a needle to her eye.

But David had accompanied her, lending support on what had to have been a grueling trip – off to have her psychologically imbalanced daughter yell at her – which meant things were going all right for *someone*.

He moved to greet her. Rainbird yanked him back, heating up his fingertips until Paul yelped.

"Not your show, little man."

Imani stormed in through the door. Paul was glad to see she'd left David in the car – she doubtlessly remembered how deeply Aliyah loathed David, and how much it would upset Aliyah to see him here.

Payne moved to intercept her. He must have used Mrs Vinere's masqueromancy, because instead of being a septuagenarian ex-Marine with a buzz-cut, he was instead a late-fifties Hispanic man with tight black curls. But he still moved with Payne's titan-of-the-industry cocksurety.

Imani cocked her head, trying to recall where they'd met.

"Ms Dawson," Payne said, cheerfully. "I'm Mr Jimenez, principal of the LisAnna Foundation For Children's Post-Traumatic Stress Disorder. It's time to consult over Aliyah's progress. Do you have a few moments before you spend some time with your daughter?"

"You're not Jimenez." Imani looked troubled. "That's not your name."

"I'm afraid it is." Payne tapped his badge with forced jollity. "Look me up. I've worked here for years, Ms Dawson."

She took a step back, scanning him from head to toe. "I *know* we've met." Buried in her voice was the clear implication she hadn't enjoyed it much, either.

"I apologize for not meeting with you before, but... there's no need for hostility. We here at the LisAnna Foundation want what's best for Aliyah. May we discuss her recent breakthroughs?"

She turned to Paul. "*We* can, sure. Paul is Aliyah's parent, too. We should *both* be in that meeting."

It was a rallying cry Paul hadn't expected to hear. Imani had tried to parent separately, after the divorce, blaming Paul for the way Aliyah had nearly burned to death in his apartment. She'd taken Aliyah aside and raised her according to separate rules in the weeks she had custody, as though parenting was a sport and she would beat her ex-husband.

They'd treated their two houses as separate armed camps – furtively trading notes, but never allowing access to how they treated Aliyah when they were alone. Paul couldn't share Aliyah's 'mancy, of course. But Imani had enabled his secrecy by letting her nights with Aliyah become black boxes, where currying gossip from Aliyah became the only communication method.

For the first time, Imani had acknowledged they had to help Aliyah together.

"Yes," Paul said. "I–"

Payne/Jimenez cleared his throat.

Not your show, little man, Rainbird had said.

Paul clenched his fists so hard his fingernails dug furrows into his palm.

"....I've already had my meeting with Mr Jimenez," Paul said.

Imani drummed her fingertips on her hip, looking as though Paul had let her down once again. "Fine," she huffed. "Let's discuss how to make my girl's life easier."

Payne escorted her down the hall, attempting to take her arm; she shook him off. She vanished from view, along with the chance at a more cooperative form of parenting.

"Good boy." Rainbird patted Paul on the head and moved away.

Aliyah, Paul reminded himself. *You're doing this for Aliyah.*

He could have gone to the security room to watch Payne try to charm Imani, he supposed, but it would have made him mad regardless whether Imani reacted well or poorly. So he paced in the school's entryway, burning off his anger.

His phone rang. He picked up.

"Hey, Mr 'Mancer Killer!" Lenny sounded three beers to the wind. "You hear anything about the Task Force?"

"What about it?"

"Am I gonna have a job next week?"

Paul looked out at David, still sitting in the passenger seat, smoking a cigarette. "...what?"

"Rumor is we're gonna get shitcanned, Paul. Mayor's bringing the federal troops in again. I figured if anyone had any inside information, it's you."

Lenny's hero worship grated on Paul more than ever. "Sorry, Lenny, I got nothing. I've been concentrating on Aliyah."

"Sure, sure," Lenny said, distracted. "Listen, that's... not why I called. You know about 'mancers, right?"

Paul choked back a bitter laugh. "A little."

"Can they be... nice?"

David got out of the car, looking around anxiously.

"Of course they can, Lenny," Paul said. "They're people."

"I thought they were all obsessed. Crazy focused."

Paul peered out of the double-glass doorway, trying to listen to Lenny and pay attention to David as David sauntered around the grounds. David's suit was rumpled, his hair half combed. His fresh young model's face had dark rings under the eyes.

Why was David sneaking around?

"Obsession's tricky, Lenny. You can be obsessed with good things, too. Why are you asking?"

Lenny took an infuriatingly long time to answer, but

Paul didn't feel comfortable hanging up on him yet. Even though David walked around the parking lot's perimeter, shielding his eyes to look through the school's windows.

Paul heard Lenny pound down another can of beer.

"...I think the King of New York saved my life."

Paul almost snapped back, *The King didn't save your life, Lenny. I did.* But then he remembered *he'd* claimed to be the King of New York, back when he was trying to get Lenny to free him.

"Why do you think that?"

"The same old Polish dude was there at the showdown last week, and I swear to God, Paul – he argued not to kill us. Just like I swear he'd talked the videogamemancer out of swallowing us up with black holes. And it's not just me, I've... I've talked with the other boys. They heard it, too. Is it..." Lenny swigged more beer. "You know 'mancers better than anyone. Is it possible one is on our side?"

David crept up the pathway to the front doors, looking furtive.

"Gotta go, Lenny. I'll call you later." Paul hung up, then stepped out before David could investigate further. "Anything I can help you with, David?"

David's expression twitched between uncertainty and a welcoming smile, like a neon sign flickering on. Eventually the old charm plastered itself across David's face – but something wheedlingly desperate remained.

"Paul!" He grasped Paul's hand and pumped it. "Good to see you. Who'd have thought I'd run into you here?"

"...where else would you run into me?"

"Of course, of course." He chuckled, a high-pitched keen. "Listen, Paul, I just... there were no hard feelings. You know. About... that."

Paul almost said, *There were absolutely hard feelings. You shot rubber bullets at me.* But then he realized David must be referring to firing him from the Task Force.

"I guess," Paul said.

"The thing is, you did a hell of a job setting that up. And

it was… necessary, don't you think? Creating something a little more tailored for New York's needs than SMASH?"

"I don't want to reminisce about the good old days, David."

"Sure, sure." David was suspiciously agreeable. "I thought you might be proud of your legacy, is all. You having started up the team and all."

"What's going on here, David?"

David ran his hand through his thick black hair. "… listen, Paul. I need a favor."

"A *favor*?"

"Things are… well, the mayor's sunk massive funds into the Task Force, and the results? Hell, you've seen the headlines. Our equipment is wrecked. But we've got *one* lead. I think the guy who rented that garage for Psycho Mantis, well… I think he's a paperwork-mancer."

Paul's blood froze. David registered Paul's shock and nodded, as though everything was going to plan.

"Oh, yeah. I knew *that* would get your attention, Paul. Knowing how much *you* hate 'mancers. And I can't think of anyone better suited to track this motherfucker than you. Except I've been following it, and the paper trail leads all the way back to SMASH, and… well, if SMASH figures out they've got a paperwork-mancer hiding in their midst, then they get the credit, and everything we've worked for gets shut down. We need to show SMASH they're compromised, so we can keep it going. So what do you say? Can you help do what you do best?"

"…you didn't come here to support Imani."

"What?" David laughed, a little too uproariously.

Paul pushed closer to David. "You tagged along in the sole hopes of catching *me*. You don't give a shit about Imani or Aliyah."

When Paul heard his words echoing back at him from the courtyard, he realized he was screaming. Windows flew open. David backed away.

"I'm not stopping her from wasting her time on some

crazy kid, Paul." He looked baffled. "But New York's safety is at stake. You trust those schmucks to do a better job than us?"

"You have *a wife*! You have a *wonderful* fucking wife who you're *alienating*, who is doing her *damnedest* to try to support your pathetic ass *and* her troubled daughter at the same time, and you... you ride with her to a stressful counseling session to *play politics*?"

David looked baffled. "Some things are more important than family, Paul."

Paul decked him.

Or tried to, anyway. Paul had always been scrawny. He let loose in a wild swing that clipped David's chin.

David clutched his face, astonished. Paul stared down at his fist, stunned to be so out of control.

But Imani – he'd been so happy for her....

David's face reddened, and struck back – a hard blow to Paul's gut that took the wind out of him. Paul tumbled forward; David kneed him in the face.

"You stupid *fuck*!" David cried, punching Paul's neck. "You gave me a useless fucking department to work with, *asshole*!" Paul struggled to fight back but David grabbed him in a headlock, dragged him back to the parking lot...

Then Rainbird tackled David to the ground, hauled him away. Paul's blurred vision could just make out Aliyah, watching him with a funereal solemnity, shaking her head as once again, someone needed to rescue him.

It would have been easier for Paul to black out. But he had to shuffle back into the school.

"Don't look at me," he murmured through swollen lips. Aliyah didn't take her eyes off him. Nor did Payne, who glared with dripping malice.

Only Imani had the decency to look away.

THIRTY-EIGHT
Shattered Servants

"Mr Payne has a mission for you, Aliyah," Rainbird said. Aliyah thumbed the "pause" button on her game so he wouldn't see.

"Gimme a minute. I gotta save."

"Pause it. This is important."

"*I gotta save!*" she yelled. "*Get out!*"

Rainbird gave her that maddening smirk and exited.

Aliyah relaxed. She didn't need to save; she just didn't want Rainbird to see what she was playing. She took the card off her lap, the one she always put there when she played *Watch Dogs*:

Don't let your yesterdays make your tomorrows, kid.

– Valentine

She stashed the card in a *My Little Pony* game box, then slid the *Watch Dogs* disc in with it, hiding the game among the hundreds of kid-friendly games lined up in her room. And as she did, she had a thought – a thought that, in her head, sounded like a much older version of herself, someone as old as Valentine, speaking kindly but without mercy:

You hide Valentine from Rainbird. You hide Rainbird from Daddy. You hide everything from Mommy.

Maybe you should talk to someone.

Aliyah felt a wild urge to talk to Daddy, to tell Daddy

how she was scared to kill again and how she *didn't* want to be the person who does all the killing, and all the sick guilt she felt over hitting Rainbird all the time...

...but all Daddy did was make things worse. He drove Aunt Valentine away, and he almost let loose the Institute's secret, and Rainbird could have made them all safe except that stupid Daddy didn't want any cops killed.

You're afraid Daddy will hate you, that older voice said. *You're afraid if you show him what a murderer you are, he won't love you.*

What about Mommy?

Mommy wants to kill you.

"*Shut up!*" Aliyah screamed, grabbing her Nintendo DS. She hated the Nintendo DS. It was a baby game, meant for stupid kids, yet she couldn't do 'mancy without it.

She wasn't a kid. She was a *videogamemancer*. She could hurt people. Lots of people.

Rainbird waited for her in the lobby. "Mr Payne has acquired a name." He thrust a form into her hands, with a single name typed neatly: *Lucas Cournoyer*. "Find this man."

Aliyah fired up her quest map – which was now CtOS, the map you used in *Watch Dogs*.

Aliyah didn't like *Watch Dogs* much.

At first she had. Valentine's game was like every *Grand Theft Auto* knock-off – you were a dude with a gun running around a city, jacking cars, running over all the pedestrians. She laughed. But then she realized *Watch Dogs* had one difference:

All the pedestrians had names.

You had to look the names up with CtOS, but there they were: Ethan Fitzimmons, Doris Shaftsbury, Helen Tomlinson, Luis Damilo. They each had little dollar signs telling you how much they made, so you could hack into their bank accounts, but...

...there were also little facts about them.

Not much. "HIV positive." "Illegal immigrant." "Illiterate." Barely a sentence. Just enough for Aliyah to wonder who these people might be, if they didn't exist for her to kill.

Because when she killed them, the names blanked out. You couldn't know anything about a corpse, and now when Aliyah saw a body in *Watch Dogs'* streets she wondered what she could have learned about that person.

Rainbird had been driving for an hour, tracking down the name on the paper with Aliyah's help, before Aliyah finally asked. "Who is this?"

Rainbird sighed in a plume of superheated smoke. "That is Oscar Gargunza's most well-supplied enemy. Mr Payne had to sort through many conflicting reports to find it."

"Why?"

Rainbird removed his cigar from his mouth, the closest he came to expressing surprise. "Don't question Mr Payne. I may explain things to you, but Mr Payne's authority is not to be trifled with."

"*Duh*. Now tell me."

"A good soldier never fights someone head-on when he can enlist someone else to do the dying for him. We impress upon Mr Cournoyer that we can find his enemy for him, and *he* will do the work for us."

"So Oscar goes away."

"Yes."

That was good. And bad. Oscar made Daddy do stupid things. And Mr Payne hated, hated, *hated* Oscar. Everything would be fine if it wasn't for Oscar, at least as far as Mr Payne was concerned.

But someone would have to kill Oscar to make him go away. Aliyah knew that much. Oscar didn't let things go. He was almost as obsessed as 'mancers.

"You are not to tell your father," Rainbird snapped. "This is our secret. We are meeting to see if Mr Cournoyer is willing to serve as our executioner. Do you understand?"

Maybe you should talk to someone.

"*Duh*," Aliyah repeated. That twist of guilt, floating in her stomach.

That guilt made her want to hit someone *so bad*.

They pulled up across the street from a compound. Aliyah knew the word "compound" because Rainbird had made her play violent military games. This place could have been pulled straight from a *Call of Duty* level; a barbed-wire fence surrounding a warehouse with all the windows blocked over, with guards walking around out front. They weren't *obvious* guards, pretending to be guys having a smoke, but they watched Rainbird's car roll up like they were ready to shoot.

"He's checking his shipment's quality control." Rainbird pulled on his fiery mask, gave her one of Payne's risk-control badges. "All his guards are here."

Aliyah clasped the badge against her chest like Rainbird taught her, muttered thanks to Mr Payne. "What do you want me to do?"

"They're NPCs." Rainbird poked his cigar in their direction. The guards headed towards their car, reaching into their jackets. "Get violent."

He wanted her to go nuts.

She *liked* going nuts.

Aliyah kicked the car door off its hinges, bowling the guards over. A handful dodged, unloading their guns at her – but Aliyah emerged as Kratos, the God of War himself, the bullets sparking off the Hell-forged chains wrapped around her wrists. She flicked her hand and the curved daggers lashed out, smashing them in the gut, knocking them back into the fence so hard the chain links crumpled around them.

Rainbird fought back.

These guys were *tissue paper*.

Aliyah ran up to the front gate, which was locked, and after a brief QuickTime event where buttons flashed into existence over her head, she yanked the gate off.

Rainbird trailed behind her, taking contented puffs on his cigar.

More guards rushed out, firing machine guns at her, but her 'mancy was strong and all the flux poured into Mr

Payne's badge, and it felt so *good* to see the men scared of her, running away as she bashed them again, and it was OK to hurt them because these weren't people, they were NPCs.

The pathway led her to the target: Lucas Cournoyer, a pudgy French man in a fine suit, surrounded by three burly men. They huddled around a crate of fine white powder – *that's what cocaine looks like*, Aliyah thought – and she flicked the bodyguards' bullets away before punching them through the walls.

"Good work, Hotplate," said Rainbird, picking his way along the twitching bodies.

"Who- Who are you?" said Lucas Cournoyer, peering out from behind a crate.

"I'm a friend," Rainbird said jovially – though even Aliyah flinched when his burning-tree mask crackled open in a rough-knotted smile. "We have common enemies. *Your* enemies, however, have 'mancy. I've taken some photographs of Mr Gargunza to show you how easy it would be for us to remove your opponents for you… but we'd need something in exchange. Shall we talk?"

Mr Cournoyer was pretty slick, Aliyah thought; he nodded, once, then bowed to invite Rainbird back to his office for wine and negotiations. Aliyah followed, but Rainbird stopped her.

"These are *private* negotiations," Rainbird told her. "What I discuss with Mr Cournoyer is between him and our leader."

"But I–"

"You know this is how you keep a righteous man safe: by keeping him far away from unpleasant truths." Rainbird looked around at the groaning guards. "Don't fall to your father's weakness; stay here and ensure no one causes trouble."

Aliyah wanted to sneak-listen in on Rainbird. But Rainbird always knew when she was coming. And Daddy was in enough trouble with Payne.

That's when she noticed all the blood.

In the games, the bodies vanished when you stopped paying attention to them. But the guards here – they coughed, bit back screams. The men she'd tossed through the walls lay limp on the other side, their limbs twisted into painful angles, the people well enough limping over to them to try to help. They struggled to breathe through broken ribs.

These are NPCs, Aliyah reminded herself, trying not to look them in the eye as the remaining guards dragged the unconscious ones away from her, as though she was some terrible, terrible thing.

She'd wanted to be a threat.

Why was being scary so awful?

There was one guard, a slim black man, whose chest hitched. She reached out, grasping the CToS from *Watch Dogs* to get more information on him:

Malik "Pee Wee" Reles:
  - Got into gangbanging to pay for his Gramma's nursing home bills
  - Goes to night school in the hopes of getting out of the game
  - Major: Accounting
  - Survival Prognosis: 35%

Aliyah looked at the tiny man bleeding to death on the floor. He looked back at her, eyes wet with terror – terror of her, terror of dying, terror of what would happen to his Gramma without him.

"You're an NPC." Aliyah clapped her hands over her face. "You're an *NPC*."

Do you want to be the person who does that?

Maybe you should talk to someone.

THIRTY-NINE
Deadly Loyalties

Paul woke, as he always did, to Aliyah curled up next to him.

She twitched in her sleep, whimpering; he held her against his chest to calm her down. After everything he'd done to her, he was still grateful his presence comforted her.

And she'd been clingy lately. She refused to go to sleep until he did, then slept far later than him. Which wasn't what he thought of as "normal" when it came to eight year-old girls.

But what was normal? She was a 'mancer. She was a burn victim. She'd killed someone in self-defense. Payne's therapists assured him Aliyah's behavior was normal, and this clinginess was just a phase, but... how would they know? As far as Paul knew, Aliyah was unique in all the world.

He *did* know he had to calm an increasing number of nightmares. Even though she went to bed when he did, she slept in far later, sometimes until noon. And even then she stole Red Bulls from the vending machines to stay awake.

Was doing 'mancy with all the other hothouse 'mancers that draining?

He'd tracked her sleeping patterns, a suspicion he disliked in himself. He knew she sometimes snuck off to play videogames while he slept – that much he'd figured out from the night Valentine had woken them all. Doubtlessly Aliyah had stolen violent videogames from Valentine's room, which was where she'd picked up that awful *God of War* skin.

Maybe that was where the nightmares came from. He'd looked through her games. He'd thrown all the bad ones out and lectured Aliyah, who remained stone-faced.

In her sleep, though, Aliyah's face flickered between terror and deep concern.

Paul held her tighter. She seemed reluctant to be with him in public, refusing to hold his hand – who could blame her? He was the Institute's pariah – yet in private, she drank up his embraces, never letting him go.

He pushed his nose into her tangled hair, smelling her little-girl scent.

His phone buzzed, reminding him the meeting with Mr Payne was in an hour, so Paul darted off to shave and put on a nice suit. But by the time he knotted his tie, Payne rapped upon his office door.

"All right, Paul," Payne said, strangely jovial. "I've confirmed the hematite is in place. Your laboratory's all set." He handed Paul a typed-out sheet of directions and a faded map. "Get this done, and you'll be back before dinner."

Paul glanced back towards Aliyah. "Just another few moments, Mr Payne – I need to get Aliyah ready–"

Payne clucked his tongue. "Paul, *Paul*. I thought we'd decided not to bring your daughter to your immensely dangerous drug manufacturing sessions. Do you *want* to expose her to stray flux?"

"She gets upset when I leave her–"

"And you're beholden to a *child*? Tell me, Paul, who is the authority figure here?" He thumped Paul's breast pocket. "We've got professionals here to look over her. All our 'mancers are with her. I'll be with her."

"You, sir? I thought you'd be coming–"

"I have no need to relive past history. I brewed my

legendary Flex there, back in the day – 'clear as a pane,' they said – but I serve no purpose putting myself near the danger of a drug brewing today. Why, you don't need backup, do you, Paul?"

Paul felt the heat rushing to his face, his bruises throbbing. He remembered Rainbird pulling David off him, the humiliation of assistance that only a handicapped man could feel so thoroughly.

"No, sir. I can do this on my own."

Though he felt a pang of loss; he'd never brewed drugs without Valentine.

"Good man," Payne said. "The biggest danger you'll face is boredom, I'm afraid. I drove to those foothills many a time, Paul, always a tedious sojourn; the mountains swallowed up the radio signals. Had to sing my own tunes on the way out."

"Well, we have iPods now, sir."

Payne's cheeks flushed. "Quite right. Quite right. Pop off, get it done, and return with a batch of drugs to satisfy this Oscar fellow for a time. Come on, let's get you to your car."

"Just a moment, sir." He tapped his artificial leg. "I have to get the car charger for this."

Payne grimaced, as Paul thought he might; most people got embarrassed whenever Paul drew attention to his disability. "Oh. Yes. Go do what you need to."

Paul went back inside, closing the door – and, more importantly, keeping Payne out of his bedroom. Payne's trust in Paul these days was thin; Payne had arrived early to watch Paul's preparations.

Doubtless Payne would have disapproved of indulging Aliyah's fears.

Paul stroked his daughter's hair. Aliyah relaxed, her nightmares passed. When she woke, maybe Payne's professionals could treat the separation anxiety she'd express when she woke up to find her daddy gone.

But Payne be damned, he wanted Aliyah not to panic in the first place.

Paul tucked the map underneath her pillow, scribbling a note: "I'll be right here. If I don't answer your calls, it's because there's no cell phone reception out in the hills. Back by dinner. XXOO, Daddy."

"You ready, Paul?"

"Yes, Mr Payne," said Paul, starting the long drive out to brew himself a big batch of magical drugs.

FORTY

The First Thing That Goes Wrong for the King

K-Dash and Quaysean curled up in the hotel bed, hands on each other's bare hips.

Their lovemaking had been predictably explosive. That was something they'd counted on ever since the first time they'd laid eyes on each other – seconds after they met, they both knew they were meant to fuck. Though it had taken a few months of sizing each other up before they allowed that to happen. Revealing yourself as gay in the gangs they ran in had a cost – more fistfights, more disrespect. So they both made sure they were on the same page.

And when they fucked, it had been carnal magic. Each worshipping the other's hard muscular body, reveling in each other's firm grips, propelling each other to pleasure.

But what neither had counted on was the tenderness.

They cuddled every night, stroking skin, taking pleasure in this gift of vulnerability. Other gangbangers in Oscar's crew spent their earnings on huge televisions, flashy cars, chunky gold jewelry; K-Dash and Quaysean made secret reservations in the best hotels.

The hotels were their addiction, escaping the constant chest-bumping gang lifestyle to go places nobody expected you to throw down. They'd all but given up their apartment, letting their friends crash there rent-free, luxuriating in the freedom of waking each morning to a scrubbed bathtub and freshly laundered sheets.

Quaysean's phone rang. Not his real phone; the burner phone Oscar contacted them on. Quaysean slapped K-Dash's stomach to wake him up, then answered the call.

"Yeah?"

"*Yo, man, you OK?*"

Quaysean covered the phone and mouthed: *Not Oscar.* K-Dash leapt to his feet, threw his holster on.

"We're fine," Quaysean said. The worried phone-voice was Li'l Deets, Oscar's probable second-in-command. Oscar's hierarchy was nebulous at best, as he had found giving people explicit org charts encouraged internecine warfare – but Deets was high on the list. Deets resented having to check in with Quaysean and K-Dash, because Quaysean and K-Dash were the only people who Oscar had entrusted the 'mancy-fueled wing of his organization to. "Should we be fine?"

"You should be dead."

Quaysean leapt to his feet. K-Dash tossed him his pistol. "That a threat, or a signal?"

"Your fuckin' apartment burned down an hour ago, man. Oscar's hotel burnt down, too. Oscar is ashes."

"…dammit." Quaysean swiped his index finger across his throat: *Oscar.* K-Dash raised his eyebrows and mouthed: *Did Paul do it?* Quaysean shook his head – *not enough information.*

"Maybe he's not dead." Little Deets sounded angry enough to pick a fight. "You tell me. I know nothin' about 'mancy, but two buildings burnt down sounds the fuck like magic to me."

"We're rushing to no conclusions."

"*Rush?* Oscar had all the connections! And you want to–"

"Here's what you're gonna do," Quaysean told him. "You're gonna check with your inside men with all our rivals: the Balaguers, the Cournoyers, the Ortiz contigent. You work your angles; we'll work ours. Then, once we got all the info we can get, we'll sort it out for you."

"Motherfucker, I don't know anything about magic! You share! This ain't the time to keep your turf!"

"Fool, I didn't ask you about 'mancy. Now do your fuckin' job."

Quaysean hung up. K-Dash packed their clothes in their suitcase, then they headed out for breakfast. Both knew if that psycho Rainbird was on the warpath, their best bet would be to stay in public.

K-Dash sipped his coffee, muttering: "It's a hit."

"A stupid one," Quaysean agreed.

"Dude looked up our apartment address from our records, saw some Hispanic dudes curled on the bed, said 'must be them'."

"And burned it."

They both frowned: *That doesn't sound like Paul.*

They liked Paul. Paul hadn't had to share his 'mancy with them, but he always let them watch. Paul gave them goofy grins whenever he caught them holding hands, encouraging their romance. Paul tried to get his daughter to warm up to them. Little things, stupid things maybe – but it was enough that K-Dash and Quaysean didn't want to think him capable of a putting out a hit.

But Paul had been working with that Payne dude, and Payne was pretty damn cold.

They ate eggs while they waited for Li'l Deets to call them back.

"I got your damn info," Li'l Deets snapped. "It's fuckin' Cournoyer. Word on the street is he's moving to get his own 'mancy. Some massive hit's going down this afternoon. Half his boys are in the hospital, the other piled into a van headed to upstate New York. Now will you tell me what the hell is happening?"

"They're gonna kill our 'mancer." Quaysean hung up again.

K-Dash was first into the bathroom, but they both piled into the stall together. K-Dash got out the salt shaker of Flex they had left, snorted a pinch – all they needed to locate

Paul, according to the letter of Paul's contract. Paul had intended for only Oscar to find him, but realistically anyone with a snootful of Paul's contractually restricted Flex could track him down.

K-Dash's eyes glowed, literally *glowed*, in a way that Quaysean found quite arousing. "He's in upstate New York, all right."

"His phone's going right to voicemail."

"No signal out there."

They pondered their options. Paul wasn't critical to Oscar's operations; he was significant juice, no doubt, saving Oscar's men from accidents that might lead to drug busts, but they'd gotten by without Flex before and could do so again.

Slightly more troublesome was what their place in the new organization would be. They'd already pissed off Li'l Deets. But if they dropped everything, went back to conference with Deets, they'd be fine.

But Paul was a friend.

"He has a daughter," K-Dash said, concerned.

"And Valentine."

"Maybe Valentine's gone already. Payne didn't like her. I think this is Payne pulling up stakes. He *really* didn't like us being involved."

"So Payne gets Oscar's biggest enemy to put a hit on Paul."

"Who sucks at guns."

"And is miles away from help."

"And then Payne gets to blame Paul's death and ours on a rival gang, which probably plays pretty well in his organization."

Quaysean already knew what they would do, foolish as it was, as one of many reasons he loved K-Dash was K-Dash's irrational loyalty. Few men had watched K-Dash and Quaysean kiss, and Quaysean doubted that Paul knew what an honor that was to witness their affection, but that didn't fucking matter.

"He's hours away," Quaysean objected. "Even if we drove top speed, we'd never get there in time."

K-Dash flipped through his notepad, the one that held the contract Paul had signed to activate his Flex. He tapped the words.

The party of the first part would like authorization to use your Flex to speed like a madman... on a wild, nonfatal drive through New York.

"I love you," Quaysean said.

They kissed. K-Dash's tongue vibrated with the electric tang of 'mancy.

FORTY-ONE
The Second Thing That Goes Wrong for the King

Mr Payne was right about one thing, Paul thought. *This sure is a boring drive*.

He'd cranked up his best 1990s hip-hop, but the scenery was tedious: a lone highway snaking among forest-covered mountains. The exits held paltry little places, towns too small for even a Denny's to survive; just a diner of uncertain origins and a grubby gas station that closed at nine in the evening.

Paul consulted his notes to find the proper exit; the mountains were so high, his GPS was dead weight here. The roads eroded from asphalt into pebbled dirt, curving around deep woods to deposit Paul at his destination:

Mr Payne's drug laboratory.

It didn't look like a drug lab, but then again Paul had enough experience to know that Flex labs that *looked* like drug labs got busted quick. This shuttered-down gas station would have been antiquated in the 1960s – back in the days when selling candy bars was advanced marketing, and no self-respecting gas station wouldn't change your oil and fill your tires. There was a bay big enough for one car to pull into – or would have been, if it hadn't been tacked over with plywood.

It was an absurd place for a gas station, but Payne had

never intended for it to be successful as a gas station.

Paul pulled around the two holes out front where the pumps had once been, parking the car in the back. A sturdy door was locked with three separate padlocks, to keep the local kids out of mischief.

Paul unlocked them, feeling desolation.

He clicked on the lightswitch – fluorescents flickered on. He'd entered by the cash register area, where once someone had rung up gas sales – a tiny alcove barely big enough for five or six people to wait in line, assuming five or six people had ever gathered here simultaneously.

There was a thick hardwood counter the cashier had once stood behind – a solid chunk of rain-darkened maple. Paul had little doubt the original owner had built it himself, and would have been proud to see it survive all these years.

Probably would have been saddened by the plywood over the broken windows, though.

Paul walked through the swinging door to the garage, seeing the usual accoutrements installed by Payne's handymen – the desk with fresh legal pads, the alembics, the hematite.

What he did not expect to see was his daughter, crying.

"...Aliyah?" He scooped her up in a hug. She grabbed him tight, crying harder; his entrance had triggered a cascade of emotions.

She crawled with flux. She must have gained it fast-travelling here – and that weighty flux-load indicated she felt guilty about coming here, so guilty the universe amplified her self-hatred. Despite that, her bad luck had yet to cause the roof to collapse on her head, which made Paul happy; Rainbird, creepy Rainbird, had taught her to control her flux.

"Malik Reles," she said. "Look him up."

"What?"

"*Malik Reles*, Daddy! You can find anyone! You have to find him and see if he's OK!"

"Sweetie, I... I'm about to brew some Flex. I can't afford

any bad luck going into this. Can it wait for later?"

"*I need to know!*"

Paul suppressed a groan. Aliyah was so wound up, the only way to calm her down would be concession. And while he usually drew firm lines whenever Aliyah threw a tantrum, maybe telling her what she asked for might reveal the cause of her concern.

He unpacked a fresh Bic pen from the stockpile, scrawled requests for information on a legal pad.

"Does he live in New York, sweetie?"

"I think so."

Fortunately, it was a fairly unique name, so Paul could narrow his requests down. He whistled with relief when the legal pad morphed into a hospital record, not a death certificate.

"He's not OK," Paul grimaced. "Records say he fell off a dock. He broke his skull, and has internal bleeding. They've…" Paul tried to think of a better way to put it, but Aliyah would know if he lied. "They've put in an induced coma – a super-sleep – while they try to figure out how to fix him."

Her cheeks were raw with tears. "Will they?"

"Honey, I'm a bureaucromancer, not a doctor. And the doctors don't know. Though the prognosis, it's… it's not good." He sat her on the desk, wiped her nose with his handkerchief. "Now. Why?"

Aliyah cried into her hands.

"Aliyah." Paul tried to sound reassuring. "It's OK."

Her sniffles stopped. She hitched in a deep, shuddering breath, like she was about to jump off the diving board for the first time, squeezing her eyes shut. Then she opened them, staring earnestly at Paul:

"Do you think I should have killed Anathema?"

It's finally coming out, Paul thought, glancing at the bag of hematite. *I wouldn't have chosen today to lance this wound, but… this is good.*

"Sweetie." Paul took her hands in his. "You didn't have any choice."

Her forehead furrowed in frustration. "But *should* I have killed her?"

"If there was another way for you to stop Anathema, you would have done it. She was... she liked hurting people. She thought killing was how people proved they were *better* than other people. And you didn't even know you had 'mancy then. I don't think you could... I don't think you had a better way, sweetie."

She punched him in the chest, furious. "*That's not what I'm asking!*"

"What, you want to know whether – whether I thought Anathema deserved to die?"

"Yes!" she said, exasperated.

"*Nobody* deserves to die, sweetie."

"*She* did. She hurt people. You said she liked it. And she... she made it so the only way I could stop her from stabbing you was to kill her. You said so! So she deserved it."

Paul shook his head. "Sweetie, it's... maybe we have to kill sometimes. But killing, it... it hurts our heart. You know that. You feel bad, don't you?"

She slammed her fists against her knees. "*No.*"

"So if you don't feel bad, what do you feel?"

"I'm mad at *you!*"

"Why me?"

"Because you tell me killing is wrong! You tell me it's what bad people do! And then you don't kill *anyone*, and they come back again and again with bigger guns, and you make it so other people have to hurt people to protect *you!*"

She couldn't breathe fast enough to keep up with her anger. Paul reached out to hug her; she slapped him away. But when he backed away to give her more space, Aliyah clasped his hand to her face, rubbing her cheek against his palm.

"And I *liked* it," she whispered. "I *liked* hurting people. Except now maybe I don't and you're making me hurt them to save you and that makes *you* a bad man, Daddy, you're a *bad man...*"

What the hell did Aliyah do? Paul wondered.

Tires crunched on the gravel outside.

"And nobody loved Anathema!" She flailed at him. "Nobody's going to love me because you made me hurt people, and I'm just as bad as her, I'm just as bad as her..."

The tires could wait a moment. As could the people getting out of the cars outside. He grabbed her hands.

"You listen here, sweetie," he told her. "I will always love you. You know why you're not bad as her? Because you want to be good. And even if you were as bad as her, you are my daughter and I will never *ever* leave you."

That's when the bullets ripped through the plywood window, smashing into Paul's skull.

FORTY-TWO
Aliyah's Auto-Save

Gunfire meant "videogames" to Aliyah.

That saved her father.

If 'mancy had been a spell she activated, then the bullets would have blown Paul's brains into wet clumps. But her 'mancy was merely how Aliyah viewed the world, and she'd never witnessed anyone being shot for real.

So when she saw her daddy getting shot, Aliyah instinctively gave him a health bar.

That did *not*, however, stop her father's blood from splattering across her face – that happened in videogames. Her scream burbled to a premature halt as she recognized the taste in her mouth.

He was bleeding. The bullets had punched holes through his clothing.

Daddy just died.

Aliyah felt that cold, too-thin separation between what *could* have happened and what *did* happen.

He's alive no he's alive

No he died he was dead right now you saved him

And all the fears she'd never allowed herself surged out – going into Daddy's room at the Institute to see his empty bed, his fake foot's charging stand forever empty – Aliyah threw up a force field to stop the next fusillade as Daddy tumbled to the ground, unconscious.

You lost Daddy

No he's here he's right here

He got shot and died he died but you saved him

And then the flux slammed into her like a plane crash, bad luck pouring into her looking for a worst fear to come true and they were still shooting and any bullet could kill her daddy any of them God Daddy was so *fragile*

Get him to the counter. Get him behind the hard wood.

That was the older Aliyah, the one that told her to talk to someone. Aliyah focused on those words. If she thought about anything else, the flux would surge in and make Daddy dead, so she focused on feeling Daddy's ankles in her hands, one warm and bony and the other cold titanium, ignoring the bullets chipping away at the forcefield as the gunmen yelled in confusion.

Why had she left Mr Payne's badge back at home? Because she knew Mr Payne would be angry if she went to go see Daddy, and Mr Payne could track her with that wherever she went, and now she wished she had and

The flux squeezed tighter, demanding all the good things she'd done get evened out.

Don't think about Daddy

Bullets chipped off the hardwood. Plywood splinters stuck in her skin. She hated being a little girl, but she *wasn't* the God of War now, she was someone with a dying Daddy who didn't know what to do.

"*Someone help!*" she yelled.

Tires, screeching. Surprised shouts. A heavy *thud* and a *bang* as a car plowed through the crowd of people outside. Several men yelling in startled anguish as they were efficiently assassinated.

Aliyah huddled up next to her father, pummeled by flux, trying not to think about the men, or Daddy, or anything. As long as she kept her mind blank, nothing would happen.

Someone kicked in the back door, guns at the ready.

Daddy's work friends. The men who kissed when they

thought no one was watching. Except they looked mean, now, the kind of men who even Rainbird feared.

Don't look at them, Aliyah thought. *Don't look at them, think of nothing…*

One of them – she wished she could remember his name – punched his boyfriend in the shoulder and jerked his chin towards Aliyah.

"Holy shit," one – K-Sean? – said. "It's his *daughter*."

The other one – Quay-dash? – gave her a great relieved Disney Prince smile. "Oh my God, little one, I'm so glad we got to you in time."

"We gotta get her out of here."

She cradled her father's head. "He's *hurt*!"

K-Sean nodded, as if to acknowledge how bad this was; Aliyah felt relief. She'd been too tense for tears – but now she saw how scared K-Sean and Quaydash were and that was proof how scary this had all been, and she let loose volcanic tears.

Quaydash hesitated, reaching out to comfort her with one quivering hand while he squeezed his gun grip in the other, and Aliyah knew why: he was good with bullets, not so good with kids. Just like Valentine.

She realized how foolish she'd been to hate mundanes. 'Mancy didn't make you good or bad – it was love that made the difference. And these two men still cared about her even though she'd thrown their donuts in the sewer…

She loved them. She loved them more than she ever believed she *could* love a mundane.

The flux surged down that love, sensing its chance.

"*No!*" she cried, yanking her hand back, but it was too late.

K-Dash and Quaysean flinched – and then a stream of fire poured in through the doorway, shoving them back against the plywood, separating them, their dark hair going up like matchheads. Aliyah muffled her screams as their clothing burned off, their tribal tattoos blossoming to blacken their skin, revealing exposed muscle, then charred bone.

They didn't even look at her as they died. They brought their guns up to fire at their murderer, their last thoughts of protecting Aliyah – but the guns turned red-hot in their hands, exploded.

When the flame ceased, the two men were ashen smears.

"*Aliyah!*" Rainbird screamed. "You do *not* leave Mr Payne's Institute without permission! What were you thinking? Oscar's men could have shot you! You're lucky I got here in time to save you!

"I swear," Rainbird muttered. "You're as irresponsible as your father."

Her bad luck was Rainbird's good luck. Her flux had led him straight to her, just in time to kill K-Dash and Quaysean. Aliyah looked down at Daddy, wiped fake videogame blood off his skin.

K-Dash and Quaysean had died so Daddy could live.

Then she thought nothing at all as she drifted away.

FORTY-THREE
There Should Have Come a Cold Funeral

The room was dimly lit, funereal; all Paul could see at first was the soft white curtains drawn around him.

Then he noticed the people standing around him, gripping the rails of his hospital bed: Mrs Vinere, the masqueromancer, wearing a taut mask depicting concern. Juan the bookiemancer peered at Paul's heart monitor, ticking off Paul's vital signs in his notepad. Idena took the scrap paper Juan tore off his pad, folded the stained yellow paper into pure-white lilies.

And at the foot of his bed, looking down with the gravity of a coroner, stood Mr Payne.

"Once again, I have rescued you from your bad choices."

Payne didn't sound angry, as he had in the past: his deep voice rang with sorrow. What had happened? Why was Paul here? Last he remembered, he had arrived at the laboratory.

Paul moved to sit up; his clothes were stiff. He probed his shirt with his fingers, felt crusted blood ringed around holes in the fabric–

Aliyah–

He leapt out of bed – but the 'mancers moved as one, pressing him against the mattress, comforting him with their touch.

"Your daughter is traumatized," Payne said gravely. "She

watched her father die. Oh, her 'mancy reversed death's flow – she's such a strong one, that girl – but she may as well have watched your brains hit the wall. Rainbird is looking after her."

"But who–"

Payne closed his eyes, inhaling through his nostrils. "Your partner Oscar. For whatever reason, he decided you were a threat."

"No – he wouldn't..."

Paul batted away wispy memories of K-Dash and Quaysean bursting through the door, guns in hand.

Payne smiled ruefully. "Your faith in them speaks well of you, Paul. But therein lies your weakness." He leaned in, as if revealing a dreadful secret: "You are very, very bad at understanding who your friends are."

"Quaysean and K-Dash wouldn't..." He remembered them burning, their bodies twitching as their muscles shrank and roasted under Rainbird's fire. He remembered Aliyah screaming for help. They *had* been there, guns in hand, his shirt riddled with bulletholes.

What had he done to his daughter?

Paul began to weep.

Payne squeezed Paul's shoulder. "I wish I could allow your grief, Paul. But though I have tried with all my strength to interpose myself between you and your unwise decisions, the psychological damage you have inflicted upon your daughter is the least of our problems."

The 'mancers clutched his hospital bed rails, bracing for a storm.

"What else?"

"David Giabatta is no longer the Task Force chief," Payne said. "It has been dissolved. You could have strengthened his position to keep SMASH out – but instead, you engaged in pugilism. Now the mayor has petitioned SMASH for assistance; shock troops are inbound."

"But Valentine and Tyler–"

"Will be overwhelmed by government forces. They

learned their lesson with Anathema – SMASH will send in everything to exterminate this threat. I've extended an offer of protection to the two of them, as I would any 'mancer, but…" Payne frowned with distaste; Paul could only imagine what Valentine had said to him. "They prefer death to dependence."

"We have to–"

"*Paul.*" Payne spoke in the hushed tones of a man performing an intervention. "Have you learned no lesson? They're not your friends. You've put your faith into so many poor bets, Paul. And I'd teach you… but it's too late to learn."

"You can't save them?"

Payne grasped Paul's hand in his chill fingers. "Paul," he said, choking up. "I can't save *you*."

As Paul looked at the sad procession of 'mancers, he had the bizarre impression of attending his own wake.

"What do you mean you can't save me?"

Payne squeezed Paul's hand tightly enough to hurt. "Think it *through*, Paul. The mayor has handed the Task Force's files to SMASH."

Stupid. He was so *stupid*, to punch David instead of forging alliances. David had followed Paul's paper trail from Galuschak's Garage for weeks, all the way back to where Payne and Paul had buried it in SMASH's files. David would rather let a 'mancer go than share credit with SMASH…

But now SMASH had David's files.

They'd find out he'd assisted Psycho Mantis.

"No, please!" Paul grasped Payne's lapels. "Sir, with your experience we can bury this deeper…"

Payne took no pleasure in peeling Paul's hands off his suit.

"I can't help you, Paul. If I intervene, well, I give them a trail that leads them back… well, here." He waved at the 'mancers; Paul imagined each falling helplessly to military SMASH teams. "And even if I could suppress the information, those files are but one lead."

"One?"

"You've been so tragically clumsy, Paul." Payne's voice was thick with sympathy. "Your... compatriot... is in love with this Tyler Durden – a man who commits suicide at the end of the film."

"That's not the way it ends," Paul objected. "He abandons his Tyler Durden persona to become–"

"He shoots himself in the *mouth*, Paul! Only narrative foofaraw keeps *his* brains inside his skull! And so I *assure* you, they *will* fight to the death. And what happens when they find Valentine's body in the battle's aftermath? Your best friend? With her one eye and videogame tattoos?"

"But I–"

"Paul. You *will* get caught. You've made poor decisions. And... you are hurting *her*."

Payne flicked on a monitor showing Aliyah, hugging her knees on her Super Mario-sheeted bed, rocking back and forth. Rainbird stood guard next to her; Aliyah shivered.

"You might keep her secret for a little while longer, Paul. But how much damage have you inflicted upon this poor child? You burned her in your apartment, Paul. You forced her to murder for your protection. You made her save you from a splattery death, Paul, and then she watched as Rainbird burned people you attempted to convince her were her *friends*.

"How long, Paul?" Payne clasped his hands together, imploring Paul. "How long will you torment this girl before you recognize you are *bad* for her?"

The guilt was so great, the tears crystallized inside him.

"What..."

A 'mancer handed Paul a glass of water. It was a kind gesture, the first he'd seen them make. Aliyah's influence, her sociableness, had made them better – then he realized what he'd done to Aliyah, and the water turned to dust in his throat.

"What would you have me do? Kill myself to hide your secrets?"

Payne drew back the curtains, revealing the body on the steel mortician's table. The skull was bullet-shattered, the face an unthinkable ruin.

But the bare stump on the right leg, the amputated toes on the left – those were clear markers.

"In a sense, Paul," Payne whispered. "In a sense, yes."

Paul was grateful Rainbird had left. He didn't need more of Rainbird's sneering judgment.

Aliyah's suffering was judgment enough.

She hugged her knees on the bed, the burn scars on her face darker. Aliyah's once-bright eyes had dimmed, her gaze hollowed out.

Her Nintendo DS sat dead by her side, which scared Paul more than anything; Aliyah was so deep in shock that not even Mario could not soothe her.

Paul wanted to scoop her up in his arms, but Aliyah was all tension, a trap ready to spring.

He'd done this. Him, and his foolish trust.

It was better this way.

"Aliyah." He squeezed her ankle. He'd always squeezed her ankle. It had been the only part of her he could touch during her skin grafts.

She didn't answer.

"Sweetie. I…" He swallowed. "Daddy has to go away."

He thought of the body the 'mancers had shown him. *This is what Aliyah does for them*, Payne had said. *Mrs Vinere could only do masks before. But with Aliyah's support, she grows stronger.*

And so Mrs Vinere had copied Paul's body. To be discovered. To all the world, Paul would be dead – and even when SMASH unearthed him, they'd think Valentine was the 'mancer. Who would suspect two videogamemancers, let alone a girl who was almost nine?

But the body… It had been like seeing his own future. His stump scars. His scrawny belly, unbreathing. His wet lump of brain, nestled like a lopsided egg yolk inside his shattered skull.

He'd thought *this is what Aliyah saw*.

That was when he had vowed to leave.

"I have to fake my own death," he said. "It's... it's complicated. Mr Payne will explain it to you. And I don't want to say that so soon after you saw what you did, sweetie, I know it was terrible, but..."

The words curdled in his throat. "Terrible" was what you said when someone lost their job. What did you say when a girl in third grade saw her daddy shot to death, then had to do awful magics to save him?

"I don't... I don't want to leave," Paul tried again. "But they'll find you if I stay. They'll... they'll *hurt* you, Aliyah. And Mr Payne has promised to look after you. Mommy will keep you at the Institute, I know she will. She will never leave you, no matter what. And..."

Aliyah kept staring into space.

"You'll be safe here," he continued. "That's all I ever wanted for you, Aliyah. Just... a place where you can grow up. And be..."

Paul stopped, frozen by revelation. Whatever she would be, he'd never see that. He realized she'd never been just a child to him – she'd been an arc soaring out into time and space, a point on a long line stretching out beyond adulthood. Never Aliyah the eight year-old, but Aliyah the nine year-old, Aliyah the fashion-conscious teenager, Aliyah the arrogant twenty year-old ready to conquer the world, all those potentials Aliyahs wrapped up in one unspooling truth.

Now he would never see any of that.

He would never hear her tell him about this boy she met, and know before she knew that she loved him.

He would never be there to hug her when her first boyfriend didn't work out.

He would never get to see her cleverness be tempered with wisdom, never get to see what wild and worldbreaking 'mancy she would accomplish.

He would never get to see what she packed with her to

take to college, and what she left behind at her house as childish things.

He would never get to see her fall in true love, as he had with her mother, never hold her arm as he walked her down the aisle, never watch her sneak a drink before she was twenty-one, never get to argue politics with her, and never never never and Paul was dying.

He was already dead. He'd seen himself on the slab. But now he saw the futures he walked away from, and it killed him all over again.

"I don't want to go. But do you... do you understand how much I love you? That if I could give anything else up, I would?"

"They died for you."

The words were a whisper. "...what?"

Aliyah whirled on him, from blank to furious in no time at all. "They *died* because of you! They died because of *me*! And you made me... you made me..."

"Sweetie, I made you what?"

"*Get away!*" She launched herself at him, clawing at him, kicking. "*Get away from me! You're weak! You're a bad man! You make me do bad things!*"

"Please don't. Please." But she scratched him hard enough to draw blood – no 'mancy, just a child's wordless fury, and before Paul could say anything the orderlies came in, whispering apologies as they escorted Paul from the room.

The last Paul saw of his daughter was Aliyah, kicking at the orderlies, as Rainbird shoved them aside to imprison her in a hug.

Payne was kind enough to give Paul a limousine ride back to Westchester.

"You know what you have to do, Paul," Payne said. "I don't envy you. But I do admire you, for what it's worth."

"I'll miss her."

"Of course you will." He patted Paul's leg affectionately.

"I'm glad to see you're finally able to make the hard choices, Paul. Few fathers would be willing to sacrifice themselves so. But a good leader shields those they've vowed to protect."

I'm shielding her, he thought. *Not leaving. Shielding.*

"We'll take good care of her. Don't you worry about that."

"I won't." He should worry, Paul knew. But he didn't. He felt the numbness of stumbling up before the firing squad, realizing all his options had evaporated.

Get away from me, Aliyah had said. She didn't mean it. She'd miss him. She'd come to regret those words, in time. He wished he could help her.

But he couldn't stay.

The limousine pulled up before an alleyway squeezed between an Italian joint and a diner. Seeing that alley again dug up an old ache – the walls were bare brick now, the once-dry alleyway plumed with dishwashing-machine steam. But there were plenty of trashbags heaped high for Paul to slither in.

"The body should be discovered soon," Payne told him. "And then… well, I wish you luck."

Paul stumbled out, drunk with despair. It was late, and the night would get colder; the autumn air had the chill scent of dead leaves, a frosty bite that nipped chunks from his lungs. He crawled into the bags, his artificial foot snagging on the plastic, making as quiet a bed as he could among the garbage.

One 'mancer had died here already.

Come morning, it would be two.

And Paul tuned in as the changes started to cascade across the bureaucratic web. That first police report of a dead body. Matching Paul's wallet to his body's distinguishing marks. The first identification of Paulos Costa Tsabo as the deceased.

Payne had been kind. To keep Aliyah's secret hidden, to keep her safe, Paul had to die. Yet Paul could kill himself for real – or he could take Payne's offer, sever all ties by annihilating any connection he had to this world.

He hated leaving Aliyah. If he didn't go, SMASH would brainwash her, annihilate everything he loved about her. And Payne would protect her. He had the resources, so much more wisdom....

The moon fled the sky as Paul watched the death certificate file. He reached out to accelerate the process. He sent tendrils of bureaucratic magic out, finding his tax records, his social security records, his SMASH files, marking them all: *dead, dead, dead.*

Paul shrank as his body decayed – not his physical form, but the body of records Paul viewed as himself. Automated routines recategorized Paul Tsabo, shifted him from "living" to "dead"; interest rates stopped accumulating for him, billing routines shut down.

He had not thought of himself as a man in years. He was a collection of records.

Paul filed a thousand graves to bury himself.

His tether to his beloved bureaucromancy ebbed away. This was right, this was correct; if he did any 'mancy SMASH would find him, if he left any trail then Aliyah would find him.

He bore down, one last burst of 'mancy. And as he annihilated his magic, he thought maybe Payne hadn't been kind. It would have been easier to chew his wrists open: he watched himself evaporate into nothingness, insisting to his beloved system that he was no one.

Maybe he deserved this eternal half-life for placing Aliyah in such danger.

His magic dwindled. His sense of self dwindled. He nestled deeper into the garbage, feeling things crawl across him, realizing the nameless held no power, the nameless had no existence.

FORTY-FOUR

Come morning, he was no one.

Part III

Mr Kamikaze / Mrs DNA

FORTY-FIVE
Every Piece Sacrificed

When Aliyah felt hungry enough to get some food, she discovered they had taken her Nintendo.

She uncurled her legs; fierce cramps shot up her thighs. Her recent memories were slurred – people had asked her questions, but parsing words into thoughts seemed like too much trouble, so she'd let the sounds slide through her brain. She remembered yelling at Daddy, remembered seeing K-Dash and Quaysean sizzle like hamburgers on a grill, remembered…

Rainbird had killed K-Dash and Quaysean.

She'd saved Daddy.

She needed to hold Daddy for a while. She'd been angry at him, and it was *OK* to be angry, but now she needed to tell Daddy why she was sad.

She hopped off the bed, wincing – her stomach hurt, how long had it been since she'd eaten? – and wandered over to get a sandwich.

Rainbird knocked on her door. "Mr Payne has a mission for you."

"Where's Daddy?"

Rainbird drew in a luxurious puff on his cigar, bolstering himself for a fight. "Your father left."

A vague memory floated to the top: yelling at Daddy

for him to get out.

He wouldn't *really* leave her, though.

But as she pulled at the memory, trying to recall what had happened, Daddy looked serious. More serious than she'd ever seen him. Daddy was…

…he hadn't cried, had he?

Her stomach cramped up. Daddy didn't cry.

"*Where's Daddy?*"

"I told you, girl. He left. He's not coming back. We have an important task."

"*Where's Daddy!?*"

Rainbird clucked his tongue. "Don't change your mind, girl. I heard you wailing at him to get out. You wanted me to teach you how to have no regrets? Start here."

She punched him in the groin, where he'd taught her to. Rainbird squeezed his cigar so hard the ember popped off; with a glance, he got it smoking again.

"I'm warning you, Aliyah. Mr Payne needs your services, and needs them now. Time is of the essence."

"*I don't care about stupid Mr Payne!*"

Aliyah's head rebounded off the shelves of cartridges before she realized what happened. He'd hit her just hard enough to get her attention; that exactness of how much pain he had doled out scared Aliyah.

He kneeled before her. "Mr Payne has safeguarded you, and you will *not* disrespect him. Your father has abandoned you. You will never see him again. And without this–" He waggled her Nintendo DS in the air "–you are an ordinary child."

"*Give it!*" Aliyah lunged for her Nintendo, like Rainbird had taught her.

He slapped her backwards.

"This is no game, Aliyah." The embers in his cheeks glowed, a banked fury. "You will apologize to Mr Payne."

"I *won't!*"

Rainbird rolled up his sleeves, preparing for an extensive beating. Fear shot down Aliyah's spine. "I am not your father, Aliyah. I am here to teach you how this world works. And when you are standing in his seat of power... you *will* show Mr Payne His due respect."

Aliyah thrust her chin forwards, as if to say something. Rainbird shifted, ready to meet insolence with violence.

It burned, not saying "no." But Aliyah had to play nice until she got her Nintendo DS. Then she would show Rainbird who deserved respect.

"...I'm sorry."

He tossed a risk control badge at her. "Say it the way He wants you to."

Aliyah wanted to throw the badge in his face, but that would get her another beating. She clasped it to her chest, the thick silver ridges feeling like blades against her skin.

"...Thank you," she said through gritted teeth. "...King."

The badge grew warm, pulsating, sucking vital energy. She dropped it with revulsion – but Rainbird caught the badge before it hit the ground, shoved her back against the hard wire racks, brought his fiery cigar so close to her eye that her eyelashes sizzled.

"You will never drop this again." He clipped it to her shirt. "You will carry it with you at all times. After you almost died sneaking out on us to visit your father, we will track you."

He deposited a sandwich into her hands. "Now eat. You'll need strength."

Aliyah hated herself for following orders, but she was starving. Rainbird sat as content as a cat across from her, taking gentle puffs on his cigar.

"I'm going to need my Nintendo if you want me to find anyone," she said through a mouthful of turkey.

Rainbird gave her a wan smile. "I need no help to *find* our target. You could find him yourself if I gave you his name."

"His name?"

"Finish your sandwich. Some tasks call for full bellies."

Now she wasn't hungry. But she ate. When she finished,

he took the wrapper, lit it, then set fire to the wall.

Sweat prickled across Aliyah's face – well, some of it anyway. Her skin grafts didn't sweat. Aliyah remembered lying helpless on the carpet, feeling the heat roast her cheeks....

She'd never had that fear as a 'mancer. 'Mancers played with fire.

But without her Nintendo DS, she wasn't a 'mancer. She was a little girl.

Little girls got burned.

Rainbird swept his hands across the flames, spreading them further, pushing them open. "This won't hurt you," he said, seeming a little wounded. "You are a girl of fire. Remember, Aliyah – *you* came to *us*. Seeking to shed your remorse. You brought the 'mancers together – made them a community."

He drew back blistered stumps, the fire devouring the wall – and then kneeled before Aliyah, almost in genuflection.

"Payne is old," Rainbird told her. "Payne will pass. But His empire will not fall. You, Aliyah – *you* will keep the Peregrine Institute going."

"But I don't want–"

"This isn't about what you want any more, Aliyah." Fresh bones squirmed from his wrists, unfolding like snakes, raw new skin embracing them. "You're poisoned by your father's weakness. But soon, you will have no more regrets."

He breathed onto the wall of fire, and it puffed inwards in an ashen skirl, blossoming into a portal. A cool black dot danced among myriad sparks, a shimmering pathway snaking through the inferno.

Aliyah held her own breath; despite all her fears, the flames beckoned her, urging her towards some great mystery on the other side.

"Step inside, and find the place where all regrets wither."

Aliyah took a step towards the wall, feeling the high buzz she associated with painkillers. A luxurious rapture waited beyond, if she could brave the flames. The hair on her arms sizzled as she stepped in, knowing to place a foot wrong on this path meant tumbling into a never-ending inferno...

And she emerged from a conflagration, stumbling into her bedroom.

Her ceiling was aflame. But her bed was still made, her toy chest pushed against the wall, the shelves holding Mommy's comforting books.

David was tied to Mommy's good kitchen chair.

David's face oozed with blisters, his scalp streaked with burnt hair. He struggled against the ropes, making pathetic whimpering noises through the handkerchief duct-taped into his mouth, begging help from whoever had come through the flames – then saw Aliyah, and froze.

"He knows," said Rainbird, emerging from the flames.

"What is this?"

Rainbird turned David's chair to face Aliyah, showing him off. "A stupid politician."

David made angry noises. Rainbird poked a hole through his cheek.

"Stop that!" Aliyah screamed. Rainbird ignored her, grabbing David's hair, sneering at him.

"*Someone* stole the files from the Task Force before he left the office, didn't he?" Rainbird purred. "*Someone* didn't want SMASH getting credit for the bust he'd tried so hard to make – wanted it so badly he committed a federal crime. And then he called in a favor from someone else he *very* much didn't want to owe favors to, to fetch the records from SMASH – why not, he was washed up anyway – and found the 'mancer behind Galuschak Garage."

"...Daddy?"

"Mr Paul Tsabo." Rainbird smirked. "And then Mr Giabatta here recognized your videogame obsessions, understanding how you snuck out of a room with no windows..."

"He knows." Aliyah flattened herself against the wall, imagining what would come next: SMASH hauling her off to the brainwashing camp in Arizona, scrubbing her memories to make her a weapon...

"Don't worry." Rainbird smacked David's head. "He didn't tell anybody."

"*Why?*"

"This is the fun part: *he* recommended your Daddy for the Task Force."

"That makes no sense."

"It does if you think like a mundane, Aliyah! If David outed your father as a 'mancer, to admit his own stepdaughter was a 'mancer and he just... didn't... know, then David would be the laughingstock of New York! If he'd called the mayor right away, we'd have been outed in a heartbeat – but no. He *thought* about it. Long enough for Mr Payne to be alerted someone had accessed the files he owned in SMASH's system. Long enough for me to kidnap him."

"Why are you *telling* me this?"

"Because, Aliyah, to kill people properly you must first understand how they come to deserve their own deaths." Rainbird patted David, like a pet.

She remembered K-Dash, Quaysean, curling up in the flames, their bones cooking. "*No.*"

"You killed once, in self-defense." Rainbird moved towards her, the flames above them growing hotter. "Now it's time you murdered."

"No!" she yelled, but her hair caught fire and she batted it out and it was all she could do not to scream like a stupid little girl.

"We need him dead. And we need it to look like Valentine killed him. Then it looks like Valentine assassinated the Task Force executives. Then SMASH kills Valentine and her movie-star lover, and everyone's questions are answered – and we are *safe*, Aliyah."

"*I won't let anyone kill Valentine!*" Aliyah yelled, and the fire portal above her whooshed, billowing the smell of burning carpet and oh God she was six years old again and back at her daddy's place and everything was on fire.

"This is the way of things, Aliyah. My soldiers made me slit my friend's throat. You have it so much easier. All you must do is kill a man you despise."

"*Just let him g–*" She coughed, the smoke peppery in her lungs.

"If you free him, he will turn you in – and we'll kill *you* before that happens, Aliyah."

"I'm going to take over!" Her tears steamed on her cheeks. "You can't hurt me!"

"Every piece must be sacrificed to save the King," Rainbird said sorrowfully.

"Daddy won't kill! So I won't–" Another fire blast, this one hot enough to scald her skin, and Aliyah remembered the pain of the nurses pulling the dead flesh off the roots of her muscles, and even though they'd knocked her out with painkillers she still woke up and screamed–

"Your father would not kill, and he was useless. The only power one has comes from killing. And you *will* kill David, Aliyah, or I will fry you."

He thrust the Nintendo DS into her hands. "Raise one hand against me," he whispered, "And I will incinerate you one limb at a time. I have killed hundreds of 'mancers for Mr Payne. Do not throw yourself on that pyre."

Aliyah grasped the Nintendo. The room burned around her, so hot it sucked the moisture from her eyes.

David pleaded for his life, his words muffled.

When she'd dreamed of the best thing that could happen to Mommy, that thing was David disappearing. David yelled at Mommy. David didn't love anyone. David wanted to brainwash them...

Maybe we do need to kill them.

Do you want to be the person who does that?

And oh God, now Daddy was gone she realized she did not want to be the person who did that, that killing Anathema had been almost more than she could bear and it wasn't Daddy's fault the world made people kill, he'd tried to protect her from men like Rainbird.

I don't want to do grown-up magic any more, she thought. *I want my childhood magic back...*

"Choose, Aliyah." And the flames ate her hair and she gripped the Nintendo and summoned her biggest magic and hurled bright blue fire straight at David.

Unseen forces hauled him into the air, chair still dangling from his legs; the air crumpled around him. David was pulled inwards, into a black hole, folded into pieces, the wood splintering...

David screamed.

And when the flames lifted, all that was left of David was a small pile of ropes.

Aliyah fell to her knees, sobbing, begging forgiveness.

"I am glad you showed your loyalty." Rainbird knelt next to her, stroking the singed remnants of her hair. "You asked me how to have no regret, Aliyah. The answer is simple: you do terrible things over and over again, until the regret falls away."

Aliyah never stopped crying as Rainbird plucked the Nintendo from her hands and brought her home.

FORTY-SIX
The Kindly Ones

Imani couldn't believe Paul was dead, even as she attended his funeral.

The sheer size of Paul's funeral seemed designed to impress upon Imani how her ex-husband was gone; she'd had to change the church location once she realized how many people would be attending. She'd switched from a small funeral home to a massive cathedral with high-vaulted walls and dark wood benches and a place for reporters to sit as long as they promised not to take photos.

She organized the service, because no one was left to do it. Reporters had asked for a morning funeral, so they could make the evening news. Officers had asked to do a three-volley salute in tribute to Paul, which required permits to be filed. And during the whole complicated process, she kept thinking *oh, I should get Paul to help, Paul would love setting all this up*, then remembered Paul was dead.

OK. She was no slouch at organizing things herself.

That was, she supposed, one of many reasons they'd fallen in love.

Crowds parted as she approached the casket, teeming well-wishers who'd never known Paul – they knew THE MAN WHO'D KILLED THREE 'MANCERS from the headlines. They recognized her as his ex-wife, reaching out to touch her, as though she were a reliquary for Paul's legend.

She shrugged them off. They'd been quick enough to pillory him, back when Paul had led the Task Force. But now the anarchomancers had shown how toothless David's Task Force was. Now that the mayor had closed up shop to cede power to SMASH, people thought better of old Paul. Paul had never said a bad word about David in public, never tried to hog the limelight, had merely retreated to live a quiet life to protect his daughter.

And then a 'mancer had murdered him.

She strode up to the coffin to say her goodbyes, the first in a long line. The former Task Force had turned out to pay Paul their respects, as had the cops, as had a surprising amount of people who Paul had helped at Samaritan. Strangers pulled her aside, explaining how Paul had pulled strings to get their claims through.

Imani smiled; Paul had always tried to do right by people. One more reason she'd fallen in love with him.

He couldn't be dead.

But here she was, kneeling before the black shiny casket. It had been a closed-casket ceremony; the mortician, a wispy blonde with a cane and tastefully purple eyebrows, had informed Imani that Paul's face could not be reconstructed for the open-casket funeral she'd wanted. The mortician hadn't wanted to be so blunt about the extent of Paul's damage, but Imani wasn't one for dodging hard truths, and so had gotten it out of her.

Imani felt a mad urge to fling open the casket; she half expected to find it stuffed full of Samaritan Mutual forms. But she didn't. She had to play the grieving ex-wife today, and while she longed to go mad she had always excelled at playing to expectations.

She did run her fingers along the lid, though.

She did not cry. She *would* not cry in front of strangers.

After Imani had said what goodbyes she could muster, she went back to take her place in the reception line. She *was* the reception line. She longed to hold Aliyah's hand, to feel her daughter's warmth – but even though Aliyah had begged to come to the funeral, the therapists at The LisAnna Foundation For Children's Post-Traumatic Stress Disorder had advised against it. Aliyah had been having serious regressions, they told her; new environments might cause a breakdown.

Looking around, Imani regretted the decision. Why should Paul's daughter, the one thing he lived for the most in all his life, not see how many people had loved him? Imani didn't trust the therapists there; she'd questioned too many "expert witnesses" bought and sold by corporate masters. There was something oily in the way those men agreed with whatever she said, yet found some jargon-laden way to explain why her instincts were wrong.

But Paul had chosen the LisAnna Foundation personally, and countermanding his last decision seemed disrespectful. Imani had researched the alternatives, of course, but the LisAnna Foundation had by far the best reviews; Paul would not have settled for anything but the most sterling treatment for their daughter.

And Aliyah was in deep trouble, Imani knew; she'd upped her visits to three times a week even before Paul had passed on, trying to figure out why Aliyah grew cold and violent.

"Do you ever think the good ones lost?" said an officer, sliding into place next to her.

Imani frowned; the man had a wispy, ill-fitting mustache, and his skin exuded the cinnamon reek of Axe body spray. But he'd slicked his hair down for the funeral, and his expectant gaze told her she'd met him somewhere before… Lenny. Lenny Pirrazzini was the man's name. One of Paul's officers.

"What do you mean the 'good ones' lost?"

"The 'mancers." His breath was hot with booze.

"There *are* no good 'mancers," she shot back.

Lenny shook his head. "That's not what Paul thought."

Imani stiffened. That didn't sound like Paul. Paul had been hell-bent on hunting down 'mancers; he'd gone after that stupid illustromancer alone because he wanted the bust, which had damn near killed him. Even hobbled, he took a job at Samaritan Mutual so he could turn 'mancers over to SMASH.

Some days, Imani had wondered if all that was left of Paul was hatred for 'mancers. He never talked about them.

"'Mancers burned my child." She kept her voice even; she was very good at keeping her voice even. "They crushed my husband's leg. They cost us our marriage. And now..." She gestured towards the casket, that damned sleek capsule, so shiny there couldn't be a body inside.

"And a 'mancer saved me from burning. Twice." Lenny bobbed his head. "I don't mean to offend you, Ms Dawson, it's just... it felt to me like there was a war between two kinds of 'mancers in this town. One was on Paul's side. And the other..."

He shook his head, realizing his foolishness. "Shit, I'm sorry Ms Dawson. Sorry about Paul. And, well, your husband."

Oh, yes. *That*.

Imani felt a guilty shock; she supposed she should be frantic at David's disappearance. But her relationship with David had crumbled ever since he'd carried her across the honeymoon suite. She'd gone seeking Paul's opposite, someone handsome and physically strong and ambitious – and she had found his mirror image, in a way. Paul's love was accepting but diffuse, trusting in Imani's ability to find her own happiness: even during the best days of their marriage, sometimes she felt like Paul wasn't standing by her side but instead was watching coolly from a distance. Whereas David carried a deeply combative love, treating anything that affected Imani's moods like it was an enemy to be destroyed. And after years of patiently enduring Paul's post-traumatic withdrawal, having someone tell her *fuck* that guy, let's go dance until you're happy, well...

...she would have loved anyone who told her it was OK to care for herself.

But *Paul* would have never called Aliyah an ungrateful bitch. *Paul* never would have told Imani how she'd raised that damn kid all wrong, that Aliyah needed to learn how to show respect, that they could get back to normal by clamping down on Aliyah.

Yet when things had started to go sour on the Task Force, David had treated Aliyah like she was responsible for all his troubles. "Everything was great until that damn kid got burned," he'd said. Like Aliyah had *asked* to almost die. She'd never forgiven David for that.

She worried for David, but realistically she'd been about to kick him out anyway. It had been exhausting, listening to his anger at everything that got in his way. She wanted him to be *safe*, but... in that abstract sense.

In truth, him being gone was a relief, and if that made her a bad person, so be it. She didn't want him dead – which, to be honest, he likely was, because if a 'mancer had killed Paul Tsabo and now David Giabatta had vanished, then someone was targeting the Task Force to send a message.

What message? Who knew? SMASH would find out. And after bobbling the ball on Anathema – after Paul had shown them up – the federal forces were hell-bent on taking down Psycho Mantis. Army 'mancer troops rolled in in massive numbers, ready to destroy.

It felt to me like there was a war between two kinds of 'mancers in this town, Lenny had said. *One was on Paul's side*.

She frowned.

But New York *had* grown a little darker since Paul had stepped down. Everyone knew someone who'd been in a car accident, or broken their leg; even the stock market had collapsed. The very clouds rained bad luck down onto New York.

Imani shook those thoughts away to greet people, thanking them for sharing their stories of Paul. She was unflaggingly polite, calling upon all her charm-school lessons.

But she looked at that casket in between each visitor. Wondering.

"Yes," Imani said, after the crowds had gone. "I need to see him."

The pixielike mortician blanched, her pale skin growing even paler. "The body – your ex-husband – is not in good condition, Ms Dawson."

"I've watched surgeons strip the flesh from my daughter's face, Ms Ratcliff. I watched her struggle for breath, positive she would die before her seventh birthday. I can see my ex-husband's corpse, and you will show him to me."

This was not technically true, as she had no legal right to view the body. Still, Imani spoke calmly, as though this were a done deal, and the only thing to be gained by protesting was hours' worth of frustrating debate.

The mortician squeezed her cane nervously, then required Imani to sign a form indemnifying the funeral home from potential emotional distress. Which seemed fitting.

Once the signatures were complete, the mortician swung the lid open.

Imani allowed herself one gasp. They hadn't had her identify him, because his face was shattered. Yet Paul's medical records were so well-known he would have been impossible to misidentify. His head was wrapped in Saran Wrap to hold its remnants together, his body wrapped in plastic to prevent leakage. She saw his stump, rimmed with red callous from where he jammed it into his artificial foot. Paul's half-severed toes, unwelcome new additions.

"That's not him," Imani muttered. But she had no reason to believe that.

"What's that, Ms Dawson?"

"Nothing."

Maybe she was going mad.

•••

She drove out to the LisAnna Foundation, rejuvenating her spirits with a large iced coffee from Dunkin' Donuts. The day's events had exhausted her. But she would not leave Aliyah alone on the day of her daddy's funeral, even if it meant three hours of driving.

Imani pulled into the parking lot, glad to arrive before the sun set.

Please, let Aliyah be in a good mood today, she prayed to no god in particular.

She could never predict Aliyah's moods. One day, Aliyah would be flinging books at her, her face flushed black with anger, yelling "You want to kill me!" And another day Aliyah would be sweet, settling in as Imani read her yet another classic book – Imani had started choosing classic stories with no mothers or fathers in them, like Pippi Longstocking or *The Phantom Tollbooth* – and Aliyah would drink her words up.

The therapists suggested Aliyah might be schizophrenic, or borderline autistic, or some other lifelong syndrome.

Imani believed, with the irrationality she believed that Paul wasn't dead, that if she could reach Aliyah she could heal her. The lightning stroke. Just one revelation, and all would be well.

The therapists, and in particular repellent old Mr Jimenez, chuckled and said this was unhelpful thinking. *Hollywood* thinking. There was no miracle cure for your daughter, they'd said – just iceberg progress, two steps forward, three steps back.

To Imani, though, Aliyah felt like a festering wound. Once that wound was lanced…

…alas, it wouldn't be today. Not on the day of her daddy's funeral. Imani envied Aliyah's closeness with Paul, maybe even missed that connection to her ex-husband himself, but today Aliyah would be devastated.

She got her visitor's badge from the security guard, let them escort her to Aliyah's room. "She's not playing with the other kids today," the guard said.

Aliyah was curled up on the couch, hugging her knees. But Imani had learned she couldn't sweep Aliyah up in a hug nowadays – she had to sit next to Aliyah, let Aliyah come to her on her own terms.

She sat down.

Aliyah inched closer.

And Aliyah looked *older*. Her once-bright eyes had hollows. Her mouth, so carefully reconstructed after the fire, sagged at the edges. She moved like a beaten pet.

Imani's arms itched to engulf Aliyah in a great big Mommy hug and squeeze her until the tears flowed.

Instead, she took out a book from her purse. "Today's book is *The Borrowers*," she said. "It's... a little weird, but I thought you might like it..."

"Can we go outside?" Aliyah whispered.

"...what?"

"Can we go for a walk?" She put her mouth to Imani's ear. "It's nice out. I just... want to walk." She looked at the ceiling as though there was something there, but Imani saw no spiders.

Imani breathed easier. Aliyah hadn't wanted to go outside since she'd started attending the school.

"Let me check with Mr Jimenez."

"No." Aliyah trembled. "No, you *can't*."

"Sweetie, the grounds are locked. I can't just take you out, I have to get permission."

"But he won't..." She sagged, disappointed. "OK."

By the time she exited the room, Mr Jimenez walked briskly down the corridor, looking agitated. She got his attention. There was something familiar about Jimenez, a sour authoritarian aura; it drove Imani crazy, pinpointing where she'd met him, because normally she was good with faces.

"Excuse me, sir."

Jimenez bowed. "Can I help you, Ms Dawson?"

"Aliyah has requested to go outdoors for a walk. I'd like to take my daughter on a stroll around the grounds. Would you open the back gates for me?"

"Oh, no. No, no, no, no." Imani loathed the fussy way Jimenez snapped off his denial. "Aliyah is not well. You know what today is?"

"I just came from his funeral," she snapped. "I believe I have an idea."

"Yes, of course." He headbobbed a rather unconvincing apology. "But Aliyah has been *very* unstable as of late, and our grounds, you see, they don't have proper monitoring. We don't let patients walk outside."

"A grievous omission, I'd think. The outdoors is critical to children's development."

"But these are... they're *different* children, Ms Dawson," he protested. "And the escape risk–"

"Is minimal, given that I run 10ks every other weekend. I think I can outpace a small girl who, for the first time since she arrived, wants to go for a walk with her *mother*."

"Of course, of course. If you'll hold while I get an orderly to escort you–"

"I didn't ask for an escort." Imani unveiled that razor-lined smile she'd perfected in boardrooms. "I want some time alone with my child."

"But she could overreact! Violently!"

"In which case I will carry her back in a way that ensures she does not hurt herself. Or is that a problem, Mr Jimenez?"

"Of course, no, no. No. It's not." He seethed quietly.

Good. She liked putting a pin in this prick. Aliyah beamed at her while Jimenez went out and opened the gates for them, and Imani drank in that happy sensation of feeling like a hero to her daughter.

She took Aliyah's hand and led her out onto the great grass lawn. The entire school was ringed by large stone walls and a southerly thatch of trees, as you'd expect at an Institute far out in the boondocks.

Aliyah's feet crunched on dead leaves as she plodded away from the school, putting as much distance between it and her as she could. Imani trailed behind, letting Aliyah guide her.

And when Aliyah got to the far woods, she dropped to her knees and began to cry.

Oh, crap, Imani thought shamefully. *Maybe she wasn't prepared to go outside*. She usually didn't countermand the people she'd hired. Why did Mr Jimenez get up her snoot so much?

But she waved off the orderlies stepping out of the Foundation doorways – then put her arms around Aliyah.

"I'm a bad person," Aliyah whispered, with the air of a dreadful confession.

"You're *not*, sweetie."

"I *am*."

Imani turned her daughter to face her. "Sweetie, you could never do anything so bad that I wouldn't love you."

Aliyah cried harder. Wrong thing to say, apparently. "What if I killed someone?"

Imani hesitated. "Why do you... you couldn't–"

"I did, Mommy. I'm a *murderer*. I killed the bad 'mancer, and Daddy warned me I didn't want to be that kind of person, and I thought I was, but I *wasn't*..."

"Sweetie, your *Daddy* killed the 'mancer."

"Daddy doesn't kill anyone. I thought that was bad, but it wasn't. I was too selfish, I didn't appreciate Daddy, and he left..."

"He didn't 'leave', sweetie. He's..." She debated how to approach things here, decided honesty was best. "He's dead. And *that's not your fault*."

"He's not dead."

Aliyah said it with such casual force that Imani believed her.

"And I killed Anathema." Aliyah sobbed so hard, her words would have been incoherent to anyone else. "I'm a murderer, and a mean girl, and I am the worst thing in the world to you. You want me dead. You've always wanted me dead. And now I'm in a place where I'd *rather* be dead, so I'm telling you, and I wish I didn't have to..."

"*I don't want you dead!*" Imani's voice sent birds scattering.

"Sweetie, I don't know why you think I want you dead. You keep saying that, but there is no force on Earth that would make me hurt you. Why do you keep saying that?"

Aliyah brought her head back in a hard sniffle, turning to face her mother. "Because I'm a 'mancer."

Imani stopped breathing. Her arms stiffened around her daughter, her brow furrowing in confusion. She gave Aliyah a hard stare, uncertain who this thing was in her embrace.

Aliyah shivered in her mother's arms, squeezing her eyes shut, not wanting to watch what came next.

Then Imani breathed again – a puff of surprise. A joyous grin touched her lips, as though after a long time, she was finally, utterly, in on the joke.

"Why, that explains *everything*," she said, and when she hugged Aliyah to show her nothing had changed, Aliyah pressed her whole body into her like she had back in the old days, trusting her, that wound lanced once and for all.

FORTY-SEVEN
Imani vs the 'Mancers

"So... did you have a good conversation?" Mr Jimenez asked as Imani brought Aliyah back to the school gate. His voice was light. But as they had walked back across the green, Imani had noted every staff member lining up along the windows, watching them.

I have to leave you here, Imani said, after Aliyah had explained everything. *Because if I try to take you away, they will kill me. The only way we can survive is to pretend nothing has changed. Do you understand?*

Aliyah nodded. *But you'll find Daddy?*

I know where he is. And Aliyah had trusted her, even though Imani was guessing where Paul had fled, and wasn't sure this "Rainbird" character hadn't killed him.

But she knew how corporate executives worked. If Imani grew too troublesome, they'd need Paul back to sign custody over to them. No good CEO would destroy a resource when they could leave them on hold.

Imani handed Aliyah off to an orderly. Aliyah sobbed, as Imani had instructed: *Cry like you're terrified*, she'd said. *Mommy* will *come back for you.*

Aliyah wailed as the orderly hauled her away.

"I'm sorry to ask, Ms Dawson," Jimenez said, creeping closer. Payne. That was *Payne*, the cheap bastard. "But it's useful for us to know what Aliyah is talking about. If you wouldn't mind sharing...?"

A threat, cloaked in a request. If she balked, Rainbird would burn her.

But Payne was no different than Imani's executive clients. Every CEO thought they could read their lawyer's emotions. And every lawyer knew if your CEO saw any hint of disgust at their money-grubbing, sociopathic behavior, you'd be out of a job.

Try my poker face, Imani thought, giving Payne a rueful half smile.

"She's..." Imani sighed. "She refuses to acknowledge her father is dead. I tried not to contradict her, because she got angry whenever I tried to explain how death works, but... she's not dealing well with this, is she?"

As she turned the question back to the so-called authorities, Payne relaxed.

"She's not," Payne assured her. "Did she say anything else?"

"She's developed all these crazy fantasies about murdering people. She thinks... she thinks she burns people alive. Probably leftover survivor's guilt from the apartment fire. And..." She covered her eyes, sniffling. "Forgive me. It's... hard to listen to her. I tried to be supportive, but..."

Payne took the bait, sliding into his caregiver mode. He put his arm around her shoulders.

"There, there, Ms Dawson. It's always tough when a small child loses her grip on reality."

"Of course. Maybe I shouldn't..."

"Oh, it speaks well of you to come here, Ms Dawson. But between your ex-husband's death and your husband's disappearance, well... you must take care of yourself. Let the professionals take care of Aliyah. That's what we're paid to do."

"Maybe you're right," Imani allowed, thinking, *I will take care of all of you.*

But first, I have to get Paul.

FORTY-EIGHT
The Illustromancer's Legacy

Imani hadn't remembered the exact location of the alley Paul would have retreated to. Googling old headlines made her heart race. She'd never forgotten that phone call.

Your husband, Mrs Tsabo – he tracked down the 'mancer. Alone.

Imani had felt the world slow to a halt then, an avalanche of loss threatening to bury her in grief. *Is he...*

No, no, he's alive, the officer had told her, his voice suffused with wonder. *In critical condition, but alive. Something magical attacked him before he shot the bitch dead, but... But his ankle's crushed. They... they can't save his foot.*

That grief avalanche roared past, leaving Imani elated. On some level, she'd never expected Paul to survive. Once Paul dug into a case, he would not let it go – and Paul had taken out every book in the library on Titian, the illustromancer's obsession, spreading them out upon the bedsheets so he could gaze upon the paintings for hours.

She'd never understood why this case had seized him above all others.

But Paul had taken to wandering around in his off-duty hours, squinting as he tried to see New York through the illustromancer's eyes. And while Imani found Paul's single-minded devotion charming – he'd outwooed her suitors in

346

college, doggedly remaining while she'd dated enough men to realize how special Paul was – this 'mancer obsession had filled her with dread.

She'd wanted to tell him to stop, but… shutting that down would have shut down a vital part of her husband. *This would pass*, she told herself. *Once he finds her, he'll call in SMASH*.

But of course he hadn't.

Of course he'd tried to arrest her singlehandedly.

And for a moment, suspended in that pause between two sentences from an awkward cop, Paul had been dead. Now he was alive again, and she didn't care about his deformity – he was still hers.

He had died, and come back.

Except Paul had never recovered. He'd withdrawn. Like Aliyah, she'd known he kept *some* secret, perhaps even from himself – but Aliyah came by her stubbornness honestly. Paul brimmed with self-hatred, so Imani tried to explain how 'mancers were walking rips in reality, shooting them was a kindness…

She'd tried so hard to pull him out of the mire of his self-loathing. Then she'd sought comfort in someone else's arms – and in the aftermath of David, some days she wondered if she'd chosen a lover who was Paul's polar opposite in an attempt to goad Paul back into caring about *something*.

Now, as she walked into the alleyway where the illustromancer had set up shop – she'd seen the pictures where that poor deranged woman had plastered the walls with Titian posters, in the back alley of what once had been a frame shop – she knew why Paul pursued the magic, and realized how toxic her 'mancer-hating statements had been.

"Paul."

She spoke confidently, feeling she could will Paul into being here.

No answer. The alley was dark. The Italian restaurant flanking this alley had closed for the night, though the diner next door was still open.

Something skittered over the garbage bags in the dumpster.

"Paul," she said: louder, angrier. The man had cost her a good marriage with his damn closed-mouthedness. He *owed* her a discussion.

Still no answer.

"*Paul!*" she yelled. She leapt into the dumpster, not caring about her $500 Donna Karan scarf....

...and there he was. He stared up with unseeing eyes, pale. She couldn't recall seeing Paul with so much as a five o'clock shadow – but a ragged beard had grown on him, like lichen.

She was so grateful she wanted to punch him.

He blinked, as if fearing her an illusion. "...Imani?"

"Paul."

"...no. I'm... not him. I pulled myself down from the stars. I'm..." He closed his eyes, sank back down into the dumpster. "I'm nobody."

"Are you the man who married me? Are you the father of Aliyah Tsabo-Dawson, our child?"

He looked stunned. "Yes."

"Then you're somebody." She reached down for him. "Come back."

Imani went next door to fetch Paul a meal from the diner, which got some looks – her fine Zac Posen suit was smeared with dumpster gravy – but she returned as soon as possible.

"Here," she said. "Coffee is love."

Paul cupped his diner coffee as though he was huddled over a campfire. Imani found the gesture endearing – so endearing she reached over and took his hands.

"So... you know?" he asked, blinking owlishly.

"Yes."

"How?"

"Aliyah told me."

He squinted. "And you're... OK with this?"

She whistled, low and long.

"I don't know if 'OK' is the right word, Paul. It... makes *sense*. I'll figure out how OK I am with it later, but right now I feel relieved. I can start fixing things."

He grimaced. "I... thought you'd turn us in."

"I would have."

Paul gave her a weary grin. "I always loved the way you never bullshit me."

"When this whole thing started, I would have thought, 'Well, we need professionals to handle this,' and called in SMASH, and been surprised as all hell when I never saw my daughter again. But I've seen how hard you tried to keep it from me. I saw how suppressing who you are ate you both up. And – well, watching David work, I don't think all that much of the professionals these days, either."

"David's no professional." Paul sipped his coffee and made a bitter face. "He's a politician."

"At least he's alive."

Paul cocked his head. "What?"

"Aliyah," Imani explained. "She didn't kill him."

Paul's glare was a look of such cold fury that she repressed an animal instinct to run from that uncompromising gaze.

"*What did they do to Aliyah?*" Paul's eyes refocused on a distant spot beyond her.

No; his eyes *glowed*.

Like most people, Imani had never witnessed 'mancy. Paul's eyes had gone the glossy black of a CRT screen. Tiny green letters scrolled up from underneath his eyelids, in thick block fonts.

Paul's eyes were windows to all the information in the world. Imani shrank back; her husband's gaze was bottomless, merciless. Paul was a channel to petabytes of information, scouring Payne's records, and she could drown in that data.

And yet... there was something beautiful about that power. For the first time, she understood why Paul had tracked down that illustromancer, had wanted to warm his hands by her magic's bright fire...

"They... they tried to make Aliyah kill David," Imani volunteered. "But she didn't. She just–"

Imani laughed. His magic was glorious. Now she understood why he'd locked Aliyah away – this 'mancy was too noisy, the SMASH teams would see them, they'd haul them to the Refactor...

"She locked David in a Pokeball, Paul!" Imani spoke quickly, trying to gain his attention. "Think of how clever our daughter is, Paul. They thought they could make her murder, but instead she balled David up and he... he rolled underneath her bed..."

"*Payne*," Paul whispered.

Wet papers pulled themselves off the alleyway's muck, lurching broken-backed towards Paul – old meal checks, delivery receipts, shredded credit card receipts knotting back together in attempts to please their master. Old tax forms dove out of the dumpster.

The forms loved Paul so much they came to life and genuflected before him. *This is what he saw when he saw the illustromancer*, she thought. *Something both beautiful and terrible*.

Paul knotted his hands into fists.

Hairs stiffened on Imani's neck. Force waves emanated out from Paul, and she realized how much Paul had been holding back all along – not just his 'mancy, but a righteous anger he had pent up for far too long.

Imani felt Paul reaching out to computers across the globe, accessing forms, shoving the information through levels of bureaucracy. Bits flipped in computerized records; forms spontaneously shredded themselves, leaving layers of confetti.

Paul had been dead, now he was alive. Any good bureaucracy had forms to reverse clerical errors – and when they didn't, Paul spun the paperwork himself, creating new procedures. And while it would have normally taken weeks for the changes to seep back through the records, Paul rammed through the changes instantly, reverting tax records, insurance forms, the files in SMASH.

Undoing all his mistakes.

When he was done, the papers at his feet applauded in dry crumpling noises.

Paul lifted his head to the sky.

"Payne!" he cried.

And the forms around him disintegrated. For miles around, the ink on every credit card signature unlooped, forming the same word – PAYNE – before disintegrating into tangled coils.

Every dot matrix printer in New York City clacked to life, hammering on the paper furiously until the page was battered solid black.

"*Payne!*" Paul bellowed, and the files in every filing cabinet in New York thrashed like wild animals, battering at their steel cages, maddened by some unknowable force.

Paul's fury was like a storm sweeping down on the men who had enslaved their daughter. Imani took his hand, feeling his 'mancy flow through her – surfing Paul's devotion to Aliyah, Paul's rage, Paul's commitment, his beliefs so strong the universe itself stepped aside rather than face this glorious madman down.

She flung her arms out and howled mad laughter, realizing the man she had loved had returned to her at last.

FORTY-NINE
Lightning Loves Thunder

"Incoming." Tyler had kept watch while Valentine tried to eke out some sleep.

Valentine groaned, shrugging off the pile of pee-stained towels she'd been using as blankets. They'd been running from abandoned house to abandoned house – God, Tyler had a fucking radar for shitholes to end all shitholes – kicking bums out to live in their refuse, trying to stay ahead of SMASH.

Not that Valentine had particularly high standards for living, but at least she'd kept the bedbugs out, never worried about stepping on used needles. Now she couldn't sleep, because no matter where they went, SMASH tracked them down.

Her only consolation was Tyler's phenomenal sex. But it seemed increasingly likely that would end, too.

She grabbed the Nintendo DS from Tyler's hands. "God*dammit*, Tyler," she muttered, looking at the glowing green readout fanning out from the screen, reading the incoming troop positions. "With these readings, you should have warned me twenty minutes ago."

"These readings are a bunch of dots," he said, combing his spiky hair with his fingers.

"You were not ready, player one," she grumbled, knowing he was right. Tyler was good at long-term planning, but

SMASH hadn't allowed them time. The SMASH troops, brainwashed 'mancers except for their commanders, had stormed into New York City, using their Unimancy to track down magic.

"So how bad is it?" Tyler asked, shrugging on his red leather jacket and lighting up a cigarette.

"Bad." The SMASH troops had snuck into place as they always did. If it wasn't for Valentine's videogamemancy, she never would have seen them coming – SMASH troops acted like one organism. If one saw you, *all* saw you. As long as they had one stealth expert on the team, *all* were stealth experts. You heard them coming when they smashed through your windows.

They were close. Too close.

Valentine brought up the map, looking for exit routes. This felt like a videogame marathon competition: fighting past her sleep-deprived muzziness to make the correct strategic decisions, reflexes failing, pressure rising.

"They've got eyes in the sky." She pointed to whirling icons that signified choppers. "If we run for it, they'll know."

"How the hell do they keep *finding* us?"

Valentine sighed. Unlike Valentine, who could turn off her games for a while, Tyler *was* his 'mancy – much as it pained her to admit it, his chiseled abs and Brad Pitt-handsome face radiated 'mancy. She could abandon him to save herself, but...

She'd abandoned one friend already, and it had all but killed her.

"Can't Portal my way out this time," she muttered, watching the soldiers set up around their position, having learned from Valentine's past escapes. "Maybe I could go all Dig-Dug and tunnel into the ground, but..."

Tyler chewed on his cigarette. "The flux."

SMASH's Unimancers couldn't quite do countermagic. Yet a hundred identical magic-imbued soldiers *could* firm reality's beliefs, increasing everyone else's flux backlash a hundredfold.

"That's a long way to dig," Valentine mused. "Tunnels collapse."

"*They* don't have flux," Tyler said bitterly.

"They get bad luck, same as any 'mancer. They're distributing it to other soldiers. Like Payne. Whereas *our* bad luck gives them another coincidence to take advantage of…"

"If only we had someone like Paul."

She whirled on him, ready to yell – he knew not to bring up Paul around her – but Tyler's face was caught halfway between the badass Tyler Durden he pretended to be and the timid accountant he'd once been. Which was why she loved him. If all she'd seen was badass Tyler, well, she'd shrugged off lots of badass idiots. She loved his vulnerability.

And Paul.

Goddammit, she missed Paul.

He peered out of the cracked basement window. "You got a clever escape plan? I'm fresh out."

She closed down the games radar. "No. They've got us cornered. We gotta fight."

He cracked his knuckles. "This is it: ground zero. Would you like to say a few words to mark the occasion?"

Valentine ignored the way he quoted that fucking movie again, and instead grabbed his cheeks, bringing him nose-to-nose with her. "We do *not* surrender." She lifted up the gun she'd shoved into her skirt. "We carry Aliyah in our heads. And we do *not* let those brainwashed bastards take her. Their goal is to capture; death is our escape."

"On a long enough timeline, the survival rate for everyone drops to zero."

She thwacked him. "*Stop fucking quoting.*"

He looked so wounded, so afraid to disappoint her, that she kissed him. He melted into her kiss, just another confused boy with issues to work out, having armored himself in butch philosophies because he was such soft, soft Jell-O inside.

Valentine wondered if she'd ever get over falling for men

who needed her to save them.

Then she looked at the hundred soldiers waiting outside, and realized: no, she wouldn't.

She gripped her Xbox controller. "Why are they hesitating?" she asked Tyler. His 'mancy wavered, shaken by death fears no true Tyler Durden would have. "They're in position. But maybe if we hit them hard, we have a chance. Go on three... two... one..."

Her phone buzzed.

She arm-barred Tyler, stopping him before he dove out the window. She flashed her cracked iPhone at him, which had a text from a number she couldn't identify:

You can always find me in the maze.

"Well, that's cryptic," Tyler said.

"To *you*, maybe," Valentine grinned, cracking open her DS.

"What are you—"

She pressed her finger to his lips. "Shh, baby. Mommy's working."

She fired up *Mario*. This would have to be a perfect speed-run: she had no time to get to Paul's level. Once she did, and SMASH detected the surge in 'mancy, they would come in no matter what happened.

She smacked her lips. She'd kill for a Red Bull.

She fired Mario across the landscape, running as fast as Mario's stubby little legs would carry him, taking advantage of every glitch. Jump, jump, hunch into the fourth pipe, hit the flag to Zone 1-2. Ricochet jump off the turtle, jump through the ceiling, warp to Zone 4....

God, she loved a challenge.

"Their eyes are glowing," Tyler reported. "The SMASH team. They're staring into space."

"Do you tap Stradivarius on the shoulder during his concerts? Shut up and—"

But Lakitu's stupid cloud-camera hurled a spiked egg at her, and she blocked out the impending SMASH invasion to duck under it, running to Paul, clean jump over the piranha plants, into World 4-2 and towards Paul.

"Goddammit, Paul," Valentine muttered. "Why'd we decide your castle was in World 8-2?"

The soldiers had paused for some reason, giving her precious time – but she couldn't count on their inactivity. She had to hop in pixel-perfect jumps across needle-like peaks, where any fall meant game over...

There. The dark blue bricks of Bowser's castle.

Paul waited there, extending his hand from the screen, pushing his fingers through the clear plastic. Which was crazy; he was no videogamemancer, but somehow he bridged the gap between their 'mancies.

Paul's world vibrated with deadlines and demands, a place where everything fit into a neat box, and if it didn't fit then he would build a box to fit it. Slipping into his magic felt like putting on a paper straightjacket.

But with it also came the scent of freshly washed towels, and clean floors, and safety.

She'd missed those. Even if she wasn't entirely comfortable with that 'mancy, she now realized someone had to do it, and that someone was Paul.

The soldiers outside snapped to attention, sensing the surge in 'mancy. They fired through the window...

"Gotcha," Paul said. His grip was sure and strong. She grabbed Tyler's hand, and as rubber bullets bounced into the basement Paul tugged them through the Nintendo....

To land in an oppressively tidy apartment. Valentine had always thought Paul had been a little retentive when it came to his place, but this looked like Martha Stewart's masturbatory fantasies. They plopped down on an autumn-brown leather couch, three magazines positioned on a freshly wiped glass table, a pitcher of iced tea on a tray.

It took Valentine a moment to recognize Paul, who leaned against a black-flecked marble counter, huffing with effort. He'd grown an unappetizing unshaven drunkard's look. His stained suit looked like the paper placemat underneath an unappealing diner meal. His titanium foot was the only thing that made him look like – well, Paul.

But he also looked somehow… *comfortable*. She couldn't quite articulate the sensation – but Paul had always seemed allergic to his own personality, vibrating with indecision. Yet moth-eaten and battered, Paul seemed more relaxed than ever.

She stormed up to him. "Say it," she said belligerently.

He gave her a wan smile. "I was wrong."

"Now say the better thing."

"…and you were right."

"Now say the sweetest thing of all."

Paul rolled his eyes good-naturedly. "And I'll never doubt you again."

"Hug it out," Valentine said, sweeping Paul up in a huge twirling embrace, the kind she knew made Tyler a little jealous. Let him be jealous. Paul was her friend, even if his awkward hugs were like being crushed by a praying mantis.

"How the hell did you do videogamemancy?" she said, squeezing him tightly. "I mean, we showed you, but… that's *way* outside your comfort zone. The flux on that's gotta be *crushing* you."

"All I have to do is convince the universe the world is better if I save my daughter from Payne, and the flux dissipates. I can do *that* without blinking."

"You righteous sonofabitch! *You found another loophole!*"

Someone coughed politely. Imani. Paul's frosty ex. Which explained the too-clean apartment. She pierced Valentine with a jealous gaze.

Valentine stopped, not quite releasing Paul.

"Are you two…." she whispered.

"We're concerned parents," Paul demurred… but Valentine saw the blush darkening beneath his stubble. "She called in a threat to SMASH for you, to buy us time. Claimed I was magically altering their records, had set them up to attack two innocent people in a basement."

"Wait – SMASH knows you're a bureaucromancer?"

"When I undid all the records marking me as dead, I… I

was noisy. Everyone knows, now."

Valentine ticked off her first positive checkmark in Imani's favor. "And they *believed* you when an anonymous tip called in to warn them about the mysterious bureaucromancer?"

"As a lawyer, I can be very convincing." Imani bestowed upon Valentine the politest of possible smiles. "And in light of recent disasters, every government agency's sensitive about catching bad PR."

"Great. Well, look, Mrs Tsabo, I'm totally gonna Bechdel it up with you after this is over, but now we gotta discuss Payne before he kills us."

Imani blinked, her distaste clear. She shot Paul a quizzical look. "Can you translate her for me, please?"

Paul shrugged, goofily content. "I catch about fifty percent of her on a good day."

"I'm talking about kicking Payne's ass," Valentine said.

"...What the fuck is *wrong* with you people?"

Tyler paced in the living room, plunging his hands into his hair, looking more like Edward Norton than Brad Pitt.

"Jesus, we barely escaped SMASH!" Tyler spluttered. "Not 'fought' or 'beat,' mind you: *escaped*. The government is *still* hunting us. They know all our tricks. And unless things have changed, we have a multibillionaire executive with his own private psycho pyromancer murderer, who can do all the 'mancy they want and spread their bad luck out across thousands of clients, whereas every act of magic *we* do hands a critical advantage to the bad guys. You're acting like being friends again has *fixed* everything, and... and things don't work that way!"

Valentine made a raspberry with her armpit. "...for *you*, maybe."

"It's OK, Valentine." Paul limped forward to handle a hyperventilating Tyler. "Tyler, I want you to listen to me."

"OK..."

"My eyes are open."

Tyler did a double-take at Paul quoting his own movie to him, then examined Paul's face for doubt. SMASH's havoc had eroded Tyler's faith, but Paul's experiences had lent him certainty.

Certainty was a deadly weapon in a 'mancer's hands.

"You don't need to worry, Tyler... because I'm a bureaucrat. That means I'll utilize all my resources – and yes, that means everyone has a purpose." Paul poured himself a glass of iced tea, drank it deep. "I'll even give Project Mayhem a purpose."

"But... but Project Mayhem *has* a purpose," Tyler protested. "Mine."

"Not anymore."

Tyler tensed, as if preparing to punch Paul, then his tension drained away. Valentine knew this was for the best; Tyler liked playing leader, but she knew from the way he curled up trembling in her arms that he hated the responsibility.

Valentine raised her hand eagerly, as though hoping to be picked first in gym class. "Is my purpose to kick Rainbird's fiery little ass?"

Paul cocked fingerguns in her direction.

Valentine clapped her hands together and danced.

FIFTY
Not a Game, But Murder

Valentine had led weary soldiers through wartime Germany, she'd investigated toppled castles as a Templar knight, crept deep into underwater palaces ripped apart by libertarian civil wars. Videogames were fundamentally warfare; Valentine mused she'd spent most days wandering through wrecked places strewn with dead bodies.

But as she stepped into the Institute's burning wreckage, she realized videogames never told the full truth.

She covered her nose as the smell hit her – the sweet barbecue scent of roasted human bodies. Videogame heroes never sweated, but here the ashes turned into a salty paste on her skin. She staggered down the burning hallways, trying not to look at the flaming piles of what used to be 'mancers.

He'd killed everyone.

Worse, he *intended* her to be scared. His flames whispered how he would rape her with fire, spitroast her over a slow flame, boil the fluids in her eyeballs.

And Valentine would creep around a corner to discover Natasha the culinomancer's body rotating on a white-hot spike, lacquered in barbecue sauce, her face carved. She kicked in the door to the changing room to discover a hundred still-burning plushie dolls, incinerated when they'd rushed to protect the plushiemancer, the plushiemancer slumped against a wall with his eyes steaming.

She'd wanted to face down Rainbird, she reminded herself. Yet he chipped away at her certainty – and if a 'mancer wasn't certain, she was doomed.

A flame licked her head, sizzling hair away.

She hated how his psych-out techniques were working.

"I've beat *Resident Evil* on game-plus, asshole!" She hoped she sounded more confident than she felt. "I buried *Silent Hill*, destroyed *Dead Space*! I know what a trip to the boss level looks like. And you're behind…"

She exuded videogame power, splintered the atrium door open.

"…this door," she said.

The atrium's trees burned, their branches waving like shrieking victims. Rainbird's room had spilled out molten lava, oozing thick tendrils through the marble floor, lighting up the atrium with a hideous orange light. The 'mancers' rooms had been turned into pyres.

Rainbird had moved his throne of knotted rebar out to the atrium, planting it on the remains of the service desk.

Of course he sat on it, gloating.

Of *course* he did.

"Aunt Valentine!" Aliyah cried, handcuffed to the throne. Valentine grinned, because this stupid fuck had done the dumbass thing of hauling Aliyah out to see her Aunt Valentine burn. Except that reminded Valentine who she'd come here to protect. Even though the air was superheated with the stench of burning metal, Valentine felt strength pouring into her.

Rainbird smiled, his teeth a gate for the furnace inside.

"Where is your papermancer?" he asked. "What plans does he have to defeat me?"

"No plan." Valentine cracked her knuckles. "I'm just the wrecking ball."

She stepped carefully over Mrs Vinere's burnt bones.

"Did you have to fucking kill them?" Valentine asked.

"They were *people*, you asshole. Not evidence to be ditched when the feds got close."

"They gave us nothing. They should expect nothing in return."

"They should have kicked your ass to the curb long ago."

Rainbird stepped down from his rebar chair, circling Valentine. The scent of 'mancy filled the air, like stormclouds pregnant with lightning. "They would fail. I've killed hundreds of 'mancers."

Valentine stepped over broken glass, keeping him at a careful distance. "People like me."

Rainbird shrugged, as though their deaths weren't worth considering. His hands blazed with fire, shifting, probing Valentine's defenses for weakness. "We offered the rebels safe haven. They wanted a different way."

"*That's* why New York's been so quiet, you insane motherfucker. You slaughtered the ones who didn't fit into your little petting zoo."

"It was a good plan!" Rainbird made a feint; Valentine didn't bite. "I should have incinerated the papermancer on the spot when I realized he knew who we were..."

"Ah, but you're not a real fire now, are you?" Valentine shot back. "*Real* flame burns whatever it touches. *You* were terrified to displease your master. You're an enslaved candle...."

"*Enough!*"

Rainbird lifted his hands, and a torrent of lava plunged down through the broken windows overhead–

Except Valentine slid across the floor on a sheet of ice towards Rainbird, crouched low, one foot pointed straight at Rainbird's feet as she shot towards him like a speed skater. She smashed into his ankles, popping him high into the air.

"*You can't*–" he roared, flailing as he tumbled backwards.

But Valentine ignored him, and, summoning a great globe of ice between her palms, shoved it in Rainbird's direction. The snowball hit him, iceflakes hissing into the lava around him – but it froze him in midair as though he were a paused movie. His body was rimed with a blue frost-sheen, suspended above the ground as if designed to defy gravity.

Valentine's crinoline skirt melted away to reveal a blue ninja's outfit, her mouth and nose covered by a mask, a bandana tied around her head.

A deep announcer's voice boomed out of nowhere: "Sub-Zero."

"Welcome to my fighting game, motherfucker," Valentine said, screaming *"Mortal Kombat!"* before uppercutting Rainbird high into the air.

Rainbird arced up, dazed, and Valentine launched herself at him with a spinning flip-kick, catching him in the mouth. She slammed him up against a pillar, and when he tried to slip past she swept his legs out from under him again, then roundhouse-elbowed him when he got up.

Aliyah cheered.

"Enough!" He sank his fingers into the pillar. The building shook, magma moving deep underground as Rainbird's anger sank into the roots of the earth, the pillar toppling towards Valentine. She rolled away, landing on her backside.

"You think you can defeat *me*!?" Rainbird roared, stalking forward. "I've slaughtered 'mancers for years! I know all your foolish tricks. I know your–"

A slippery pool of ice bloomed beneath Rainbird's feet, and he did an awkward dance as he avoided falling flat on his ass. Valentine smashed her foot into his jaw.

"You don't even know not to walk into a Ground Freeze!" she sneered. "That's *Mortal Kombat* 101!"

She caught him under the chin with a double-fisted uppercut – launching him through the ceiling, sending him high into the night sky before he landed with a lung-emptying *whoof* on the roof. Valentine leapt up after him, bursting through in a spray of debris.

"Fine," Rainbird said, clasping his badge. It glowed, siphoning his flux away. "You want to play games? Even games fear the firelord."

He leaned over and vomited a spear of fire straight into Valentine's gut. It knocked her backwards, sending her tumbling towards the roof's edge. She patted out the flames on her gi, panicked.

"Hey, *that* move's not in the book!"

Rainbird rose into the air in a corona of flame. "This is not a game, you one-eyed fool. This is murder."

Valentine did a high flip-kick to try to catch him in the face again; Rainbird caught her ankle, smashed her into the ground. She rolled away as Rainbird punched down hard enough to send shockwaves of force, sent Valentine flying.

Before she could regain her footing, Rainbird had landed on her, pinning her to the ground. Valentine plunged ice knives into his leg; they hissed into boiling water. She formed an ice clone of herself, rolling out from under him; he reached back with a knotted fire-whip and slammed her back into place. She broke his nose with a well-placed palm strike, but Rainbird broke her cheek, shattered her shoulder, rammed her head into the buckled ground.

"Did you think you could defeat me?" He loomed over her, his broken nose dribbling blood onto her face.

Valentine coughed. "Wasn't my plan, no."

"You said you had no plan."

"Aunt Valentine lies a lot," said Aliyah.

Valentine craned her neck to look over at tiny Aliyah, standing in a perfect warrior's stance behind Rainbird, her pale old-man's face tattooed with a streak of red:

The God of War.

The thick chain looped around his neck, yanking him off Valentine. Aliyah clutched her Nintendo DS, filling with magical force – and then heaved, sending Rainbird on a high arc overhead, the chain straining, before smashing him face-first into the cracked roof. Aliyah pulled him back, Hulk-smashing him in every direction, grinning like a girl at her birthday party.

"Thank you for sneaking me the Nintendo, Daddy!" Aliyah said gleefully, sending Rainbird's body into the roof again and again and again. "Best present ever!"

"Gah!" Rainbird said, melting the chain – he catapulted off the end, sailing high into the night, then caught himself on a cloud of fire. "Where is the papermancer! *Where is he*!?"

"You pay attention to me!" Aliyah yelled, snapping her other chain out and dragging him back down to earth. "Remember? Your special project?!"

She smashed Rainbird through an air conditioning unit. Aliyah advanced upon him, flicking her knives in his direction, gashing his scarred skin.

"You said the only power one has comes from killing," she told him. "Maybe the only power *worth* having comes from caring!"

"Maybe it's just fucking *power*, little girl!" he screamed, incinerating her knives. He bore down upon her as she kicked at him. She caught him a high hard one right to the groin, but Rainbird inhaled to fill his torso with healing flame.

"This isn't about goodness," Rainbird told her, forcing Aliyah back against the roof. "It isn't about righteousness. It's about who has the power to destroy."

Aliyah smashed her palm into his throat.

Rainbird backhanded Aliyah hard; she landed dazed, her Nintendo DS spinning across the rooftop. Rainbird spat broken teeth, turning to Valentine.

"Two 'mancers. And neither could defeat me."

"Didn't expect to," Valentine said. "Paul promised me I could get my licks in first."

"Who, then? Who will defeat me now?"

Valentine turned to look at the scrawny, filthy man climbing over the edge of the roof. A man dressed in what once had been a nice suit, once-neatly-combed hair askew, heaving himself up the ladder on his artificial foot.

"That'd be Paul," Valentine said serenely.

Rainbird choked out a disbelieving laugh – but then realized:

Paul was not afraid of him.

Paul still looked more like a mugged accountant than an avatar of destruction. But as Paul adjusted his tie to face down Rainbird, he radiated indomitability.

Paul held up a manila folder, brandishing it before him like a shield.

"On September 14th, 1993," Paul said, "The Red Cross diagnosed you with severe spinal scoliosis. They gave you a TLSO back brace, which you wore for the next two years. In 1997, UNICEF gave you another back brace for final adjustments."

Rainbird shook his head, unimpressed. "So?"

"Not anymore."

Paul ripped the medical files in half.

Rainbird's back convulsed as something was torn from him – a timeline of safety and healing sundered, bones curving painfully into new shapes. He lunged forwards, but his left leg went numb as his spine pinched around now-deadened nerves–

He tumbled to the ground, years of muscle memory stolen.

But his twisted body still coursed with flame.

"I'll burn y–"

"In 1996, Doctors Without Borders prescribed a course of primaquine and intravenous fluids to treat your malaria." Paul said, his voice chillingly calm. "That didn't happen, either."

He ripped the medical files in half again, and Rainbird's body convulsed, gnawed at itself, his ribs popping out as what had once been a treated case of malaria turned into a recurrent case that had chewed young Rainbird's body for years.

"I'll devour you," Rainbird said. "You won't–"

Paul knelt over Rainbird's body, now twisted with sores. He held up one record: a UNICEF Child Protection Section report.

"I'm not sure what happens if I tear this," Paul said conversationally. "It's the task force who helped demobilize the child soldier squad you worked for. The local workers who pretended you weren't a 'mancer because they hoped you might recover in America. The ones who handed you over to Payne, thinking him a kindly benefactor." Paul waggled the paper, looking at it with genuine curiosity. "If I undo this, what happens? Do you wind up back in Sierra Leone? Or would you be dead on the spot, executed for your crimes?"

Rainbird fell silent, beaten.

"Aliyah," Paul said. "Come here."

Aliyah's *God of War* outfit melted away, leaving a guilty child. Paul placed the Nintendo DS in her hands solemnly, then stepped away, leaving her to face Rainbird.

"You got a rough deal, Aliyah," he told her. "A lot of bad things will happen to you. People want to kill or brainwash or control you, all for reasons you had no choice in. That's not your fault.

"And you're right. We do have to be strong – strong enough to fight our enemies.

"But killing people doesn't make you strong, Aliyah. Rainbird can do it. Any moron with a knife can do it. Killing is literally the easiest way to solve a problem. Just throw anyone who disagrees with you in a grave. And..." Paul gestured down at the burning bodies in the atrium, conveying with a gesture how effective Rainbird's plan would have been if Paul hadn't stopped him. "The shame is, killing people *works*. More often than we'd care to admit."

Aliyah hugged her Nintendo against her chest. "Why are you telling me this, Daddy?"

"Because I love you, kid. I'll love you no matter what you become. But Anathema gave you too much power, too soon. I can't stop you from doing things anymore. For better or for worse, you've got to make your own choices – and whatever you become, I'll stay with you. So."

Paul drew in a deep breath.

"Should we kill Rainbird?"

Aliyah gave a weird little laugh, thinking he'd made a

Daddy joke – then turned her Nintendo DS over and over again in her hands. It flickered with gamefire, sprouting knives, rattling like an uneasy Pandora's box.

"He killed all my friends," she said, nodding towards the atrium where all the 'mancers' bodies laid, sprawled and smoking. "He didn't just murder them, Daddy – he made them *suffer*."

"Yes."

"He would have killed Aunt Valentine," Aliyah continued.

"Yes."

"And…" Aliyah wiped tears away, frustrated. "If we leave him alive, he might kill people *again*."

Paul gave her a rueful head bob, acknowledging all the Daddy wisdom in the world held no good solution. "Yes."

"He doesn't deserve to live," Aliyah said, her Nintendo DS growling like a living thing in her hands. "He was crazy, and Mr Payne made him crazier. Someone has to stop him. Someone has to make him pay for what he did. Except we can't give him to SMASH because he knows – he knows us, and then he'll turn us in, so there's not even a *jail* for bad men like him…"

"Like I said, sweetheart. Killing works. More than any of us would care to admit. Maybe he does need killing." Paul's voice broke. "The question is, do you want to be the person who does that?"

Her Nintendo DS curled into a wicked dagger – the God of War's preferred weapon. Rainbird made mewling noises, struggling to get away; Paul stepped on his neck, pinning him to the rooftop.

Aliyah brought the dagger up and down, a smooth arc between its tip and Rainbird's burning heart, measuring just how easy it would be to remove Rainbird from this earth.

She snarled, her face flickering between the murderous God of War and Aliyah, heartbroken and pure. Then Aliyah washed away, and the God of War whirled to face Paul – not Aliyah-sized, but a giant man, all her rage personified, her daggers dropping gore to the earth.

"What if I *am* this?" she roared, her breath charnel, something hideous burning and twisting underneath her ribs. *"What if I'm a killer like Rainbird?"*

Paul reached up to cup the God of War's scarred cheek.

"Then I'll still love you," Paul said.

"Daddy!" the God of War cried, all her heartbreak set loose at last. And as Paul scooped her up in his arms she shrank, becoming Aliyah, becoming a forlorn girl who had no good solutions but now knew the bad ones.

"Come on, V," Paul said, and they left Rainbird, trembling, on the rooftop.

FIFTY-ONE
Cold Mercy

Rainbird writhed on the heated tarmac, plotting revenge. His knobbed spine pushed waves of pain up a body he no longer recognized. His weakened muscles were atrophied mockeries.

But deep within him, he still felt it: that fiery flicker.

His body could be rehabilitated.

His flame could be restoked.

"It will take months," Rainbird swore, crawling towards the rooftop ladder. "Perhaps years. But I *will* track you down, papermancer, and I *will* show your daughter the error of mercy–"

"Yeah, about that," said Valentine.

Rainbird made a choked noise, scrambling backwards; Valentine shrugged and walked forward. She looked resigned, as though checking into work at a job she didn't like.

"You see, some guys, you beat 'em and they go, 'Well, that guy was more talented than me, good for him.' And they give it up. But *other* guys – well, they think the whole universe was created to hand them victory. And guys like that are fucking dangerous, because no matter how honestly you beat them, they feel cheated. So they never quit. They come back to stab you in your sleep."

"Paul doesn't kill!" Rainbird cried. "He wouldn't–"

Valentine knelt down, patted Rainbird on the head. "I know. That's sweet of him. And I will do anything – anything, Rainbird – to keep my family from making those hard choices. Are we clear?"

"But I–"

"This isn't personal."

Rainbird shrieked as Valentine morphed into Sub-Zero form, grasped him, frost blossoming over his stiffening body. She lifted his ice-encased corpse over her head and brought it down over her knee, shattering Rainbird into a thousand chunks.

That announcer's voice boomed overhead again. "FLAWLESS VICTORY," it said. "FATALITY."

Valentine sighed and kicked the pieces into the gaping hole where the atrium's overhead window had once been. She hissed as she wrenched her broken shoulder back into place, watching as Rainbird's remains char-broiled in the cooling lava streams.

"I hate killing," she said, to no one in particular, then vanished into darkness.

FIFTY-TWO
Unmask the Tyrant

Paul pressed the silver button in Payne's elevator. The elevator shuddered, checking with its master, and then rose.

A good sign, Paul thought.

He was alone, carrying nothing but a briefcase. Payne might have had his security guards escort Paul off the premises, a contingency for which Paul hadn't planned – but having his intermediaries shoo Paul away didn't seem Payne's style. Payne loved gloating, disdained the impersonal touch.

So Paul walked into Lawrence Payne's green-tinted lobby, the eternal Samaritan Mutual logo engraved in tasteful gold. It was well after midnight, but the old man never left.

The secretary still wore her form-revealing red dress – but whereas before she'd all but ignored Paul's existence, now her smile was a freeze-dried mockery.

Oh yes, Paul thought. *You know I'm a 'mancer now. Everyone does.*

Paul paused by her desk. "You should leave."

"Mr Payne has not authorized–"

"I realize he is your boss. Yet things are about to get quite bad in there. It would be best if you left."

She nodded, but her fingertip crept towards the security button.

"Don't you dare leave, Ms Pennywinkle," Payne's rich voice said. "Mr Tsabo will do no violence to you, nor anyone. It's not his style. Though do shut the door after him; we men need our privacy."

Payne sat at his desk, looking joyous at the sight of Paul. His smile was so broad that for a moment, Paul thought that Rainbird wasn't defeated, that the Institute wasn't in smoking ruins, that Payne hadn't just ordered his hothouse 'mancers killed.

His wide office window looked over New York City, allotting Payne a vast view of the town he ruled.

"You're looking a little worse for wear these days, Paul," Payne said, welcoming Paul in.

"Funny; I don't care as much about appearances as I used to."

"I felt you probing through my records the other day," Payne said, pouring a glass of Scotch. "I may not be able to keep you out – but I hope you don't think you can alter my files without me noticing."

"I wouldn't. But then again, that's your 'mancy's nature, isn't it?"

A dreadful playfulness. "Why, whatever do you mean, Paul?"

"You're no bureaucromancer."

He swigged down his drink, shuddering. "Of *course* not. Slave to a thousand procedures. Held responsible to committees. I'd never tether myself to such frippery."

"Then what do you call yourself?"

"You know who I am: the King of New York."

"Say your 'mancy's name."

"If you must hear it, fine," Payne snapped. "I am an *authorimancer*. I am the monarch of my domain. Nothing happens within Samaritan Mutual that falls beneath my notice – because I make my underlings do paperwork for me. And you, Paul, with your petty little mind – you should have been perfect to carry on my tradition!"

"That's not what bureaucracy is."

"Oh, but it is. Little functionaries never question the laws put into place by wiser men, Paul. Empires have run for centuries after their greatest leaders died, their noble policies carried on by tedious administrators. I thought I had someone who might carry on my grand work for generations, Paul. Instead, I got *you*."

"Bureaucracy isn't how tyrants hold sway over lesser men," Paul said. "It's how the public holds men with too much power accountable."

Payne waved off Paul's remarks. "Either of us could open up the history books to prove our point, Paul. That's not how this works. It's about what we believe. And I assure you, the world needs men like me."

"Murderers?"

"People *will* die, Paul. The best you can hope for is a compassionate man, making the decisions for them – someone strong enough not to break. My mother, *she* broke. She couldn't live, watching my sisters fall to the broach. So what did she do? She condemned her son to a living hell, abandoning him in a madhouse city overflowing with magical refugees – the ghettos a maze of 'mancer wars, packed with deadly conflicts, a *war zone*!"

The old man's pride made Paul sick. "So you took power. And cleansed the city of anyone who disagreed with you."

"I *saved* the city, Paul." Payne spoke as though he couldn't believe he had to make this argument. "After watching Anathema tear this town apart, I thought you of all people would understand how bad a 'mancer war would be. But no; you threw aside *years'* worth of valuable experience for mere sentiment!"

"Sentiment? We're talking murder! You slaughtered those poor 'mancers to hide your trail!"

Payne's fingers tightened around his glass. "That's a choice you backed me into, Paul. And I regret having to make that order. They were beautiful. Worthless, impotent..." He guzzled another Scotch, looking dimly sad, like a man who'd had to put his dog to sleep. "But oh, so beautiful."

"No. They could have been powerful. You starved them."

"Starved them?" Payne spluttered. "I spent millions *outfitting* them! There are many crimes you can lay at my door, Paul, but the 'mancers I sheltered? I encouraged those poor doomed beauties."

"You locked them away. You encouraged isolation. And... even now, Payne, you can't see it? You can't see why every obsessive nut doesn't become a 'mancer?"

"Do tell."

"*People*, Payne. 'Mancers are only as powerful as the people they care about. And you – you put them in a zoo, you encouraged them to pay tribute to you and not talk to each other. They dwindled into shadows..."

Payne made a small *hmpf*ing noise. "I thought Aliyah was the key."

"She was. Because they loved her. And through her, began to interact with each other." Paul sighed. "Then you cut them short."

"Interesting." Payne made a *comme ci, comme ça* wave with his palm. "Well, I'll do better next time. Thanks for your advice."

Paul gritted his teeth. "There'll be no next time."

"No, no, no," Payne tut-tutted him. "This is corporate America, Paul. Shut down one branch, we open up another subsidiary with the same people under a different name. Rainbird didn't kill the staffers – they got paid vacation. As soon as you've left town, I'll reopen shop."

"Left *town*?"

Payne poured himself another Scotch. "We're at a stalemate, Paul. We can't turn each other into SMASH; we both have too much knowledge. Sure, SMASH knows you're a bureaucromancer... but do you want me to reveal all your weaknesses? And as for me, I don't have the firepower left to kill you now. So seeing as you're helpless to stop me, it's time I help you."

"Oh?"

"Don't mock me, you little turd. My authorimancy lets

me know everything I touch. I know where every ounce of hematite goes, if I care to track it down. I know my every file, and I'll know if you change anything. I know my every employee, and they are contractually bound. Should you convince one to change sides, my risk pool will destroy them. Or did you think I kept the Institute a secret with a good dental plan?"

"That's monstrous."

He reached across the desk to pinch Paul's cheek. "You're a nice little man, Paul. You have such bold notions of right and wrong, yet are too timid to make any real changes. So here's your safe bet: I outfit you with a nice new false identity, let you slither off somewhere else to do whatever good you see fit there."

"And what will you do?"

"What I've done before: import some other psychologically damaged enforcer from someplace where 'mancy runs a little wilder. People like Rainbird are a dime a dozen, if you know where to look. And then, once I've got backing, I'll round up the 'mancers in New York again. I'll find *someone* to carry on in my name."

"And if Valentine tears your heart out?"

"I took a page from your paranoia, Paul. I have records on you ready to release in the event of my death. Should Valentine decide to kill me, every newspaper in the world will know all I know. Think you can keep your daughter safe from SMASH then?"

"The alternative is leaving New York's 'mancers as lambs for your slaughter."

"*I* kept those poor hothouse flowers safe. *You* ruined them."

Paul's shoulders slumped. "And the people you had Rainbird murder because they didn't fit your standards? Did they not count?"

Payne hunched forward. "Necessary sacrifices."

"You're a madman. I thought maybe… maybe even now, we could talk it out. But there's nothing to be done."

"So you'll leave?"

"No," Paul said, opening the briefcase. "I'm sorry."

He reached in to pull out an Xbox controller. On the sides, written in paint, were four words:

FOR K-DASH. FOR QUAYSEAN.

Payne's eyes flew wide open as he lunged across the desk, looking to knock the controller from Paul's hands – but Paul thumbed the Start Button. A wave of 'mancy burst out from the controller, a signal wave that rippled the air, shoved Payne backwards – and then the window blew outwards.

The 'mancy rippled across New York's star-dappled darkness, radiating out across the streets in the spokes of an expanding circle. As it passed over the skyscrapers, explosions went up in its wake – a crumbling building here, a burst of flames there. Not every building:

Just the ones Samaritan Mutual had insured against 'mancy.

"*What did you do*?" Payne asked, clutching his chest. As an authorimancer, each act of destruction to Payne's safewarded properties were a blow to his heart.

And Paul remembered back to when he'd had Valentine fire up her "quest item" to find a stray bag of hematite buried in a long-abandoned Flex lab in Connecticut.

He remembered driving all the way out to Pennsylvania's woods to brew the biggest batch of Flex he'd ever made, then speeding off as the flux-dumped earthquake echoed across the Appalachians.

Paul remembered meeting with Imani, who had pored over the insurance contracts Payne had set up with his clients. "Are you sure Payne would cover this if we blew up these buildings?" Paul had asked, and Imani had given him that shark-toothed lawyer's grin: "If he refused to cover it, they'd sue him for every dime they could get."

Paul remembered meeting with Valentine, who had shown him the new game she'd created, hooking *Sim City* into *Civilization* into a war game, so she could map each of Project Mayhem's members, coordinating their efforts to set off bombs upon Paul's start-button command.

He remembered meeting with the Project Mayhem members – a surprising number of 'mancy fans who longed to be in the proximity of Tyler's beat-'em-up magic. They stood in a warehouse as Tyler handed over the reins of power. He remembered explaining the bombs themselves had to be quite mundane – but he had something to ensure this operation went off without a hitch. And Tyler's men had applauded, loving being part of something that would make the city safer for 'mancers.

Paul thought of what Tyler had told him:

Only by creating change can they infuse their anonymous lives with meaning, Tyler had told him. *They will die to attain relevance.*

And Paul thought, *if they'll die for reasons as dumb as Tyler's, then there have to be men who'll fight for good causes.*

"You thought I'd try to alter your records," Paul said. "I'm beyond that now."

The debris smoke billowed out as each Project Mayhem-targeted site imploded.

"You're as big a monster as I am," Payne whispered. "How many men did you just kill to get your revenge?"

"None. Or don't you feel the 'mancy?"

Paul ran his finger down an imaginary line in the air; it felt like pudding slithering out of the way. The air in Payne's office – across all of New York – had thickened in the wake of a titanic act of magic.

I'm going to give you all Flex, Paul had told Project Mayhem. *This is distilled 'mancy. You will use this to ensure nothing interferes with you setting off the bombs. But more importantly, you will use it to create incredible coincidences, ensuring no one gets hurt. You will use this Flex to guarantee that major projects get cancelled so no one is working late, that all the skeleton crews working the night shift fall ill, that all the overnight janitors are on their smoke break when the shit goes down. Are we clear?*

Yes Mr Tsabo sir! they had shouted, taking the Flex from his hands with the reverent air of men attending communion.

"You were supposed to be a bureaucromancer!" Payne snarled. "Not a terrorist!"

"Ask a Republican," Paul said. "We're practically the same thing."

"This won't work," Payne said, increasingly frantic. "I'll deny the claims because they're 'mancy–"

"Funny thing is, after Anathema attacked the town, your biggest customers decided they needed magical coverage after all."

"*I* have insurance against this! Bankruptcy insurance! I'll–"

"You didn't *own* those claims," Paul said, feeling the thrill of walling off Payne's objections. "So I doubt you noticed when those agreements vanished from the files of the people protecting you."

"I'll refuse to pay!"

"You might," Paul said, locking the final piece into place. "But you are an *authorimancer*, Mr Payne. Your kingly powers derive from protection. The 'mancers gave you nothing but adoration, so you cut them short. But your clients – why, you've made written agreements to look after them. And truly – what kind of a king can't repay what he's promised to protect?"

Payne dropped his Scotch. It warbled a bit as it plunged through an air congealing with 'mancy, buzzsects pushing through.

Payne's Scotch tumbler shattering was music to Paul.

"I suppose you've thought of the business owners who'll go bankrupt as a result of this? All the people thrown out of work? All those people you, as a compassionate bureaucromancer, are supposed to *care* about?"

"Better than you starting another murder cult."

"Well played, Paul." Payne gave him one single, cold bow. "I guess you *have* learned to make the tough decisions."

"Thank you."

"It'll take years for this to wind its way through the courts, of course. I'll have to devote all my energy to fighting this.

I wouldn't have the time to start another Institute, not with as few years as I have left–"

"Well, you're pushing eighty, I'm sure you'll die before perpetuating further evil– "

"–but there's another way."

Paul gave Payne a raised eyebrow, feigning surprise. "Oh?"

Payne's eyes flared a cerulean blue. A glimmering crown of pure 'mancy arced across his brow. Payne's wrinkles pulled tight as he straightened to reveal his true archetype of the Deathless King.

"*I've learned some tricks from you, Mr Tsabo.*" Payne's voice acquired a theatrical boom that would have driven most men to their knees. "*You backdate. You can rewrite history with your forms to change the past.*"

"I wouldn't," Paul said, cheerily conversational. "I really wouldn't."

The air flexed around Payne as he drew upon the power he'd stored throughout the offices of Samaritan Mutual. Filing cabinets exploded. Cubicles imploded as Payne sucked the energy of years of unhappy wage-slaves doing his bidding.

Payne's secretary, quite reasonably, fled.

"*And so I will steal your trick to undo you,*" Payne said. "*I'll go back in time to send the police to the Appalachians – they'll shoot your pathetic Flex lab full of holes…*"

Paul poured himself Payne's scotch, ignoring the light show. "I didn't tell you I set up shop in the Appalachians," Paul said, with the air of a man making small talk. "How'd you know?"

"*I know everything in my building!*" Payne swelled into a bronze muscular sculpture of a man, shrugging through the ceiling. "*Anyone who sets foot in my domain now reveals all their secrets!*"

"Then you see what's about to happen?"

The air convulsed, physics stretched to its limits by competing versions of reality – and Payne looked down at it, his mouth wide in silent horror, as a slit tugged open in the air before him, ripping open a portal to a darker universe.

Flylike buzzsaws boiled out.

"*Broach!*" Payne yelled, stumbling back, his once-deep voice distorted to a trembling wail. "*Broach! Broach! Brooooooaaaaaccch!*"

The buzzsects ignored Paul, homing in on the man enwebbed in spells.

Payne screamed, squeezing bolts of pure 'mancy from the air – which had all the effectiveness of waving meat in the face of hungry wolves. The buzzsects swarmed in around the bolts, devoured them, gulping up the 'mancy and shitting out empty space – not blank space, *empty* space, the absence of a void, as they chewed up Payne's 'mancy and excreted their home dimension, building bridges to this place…

"No!" Payne cried, swatting at them; with each swat, they gnawed trails through his arms, devouring the color of his skin, devouring the integrity of his muscles, devouring the texture of his bones. "*Lisa! Anna! Mother!*"

But the buzzsects paid him no attention, as they burrowed under his flesh and gobbled the time from his heart, wolfing down the laws that kept cause and effect linked, trapping Payne to relive endless horrors in a micro-universe without closure….

Within minutes, Payne was a seething miasma of conflicting dimensions, his coherency devoured.

The thing that had been Payne bulged, ready to birth new swarms…

"None of that." Paul squeezed his ever-bleeding wound to draw their attention.

The buzzsects champed serrated jaws. They launched themselves at Paul, gobbling down the laws of gravity as they went, eating the concept of numbers, gulping the notion of subatomic bonds until atoms warped into new and unearthly shapes.

That's not the way things work, Paul thought. The universe he knew was a set of bureaucratic laws, followed precisely – when a single electron circled a single nucleus, it acted according to standards. On Earth, gravity pulled things down at the rate of 9.81 meters a second. Numbers went one, two, three….

Paul knew the laws of physics. He cherished them – rigid order, making a home safe for people. He believed in them strongly enough that his magic didn't weaken the world's rules – it *enforced* them.

And who administered petty laws better than a bureaucrat?

The buzzsects hissed, retreating as Paul sewed up the broach. He'd done this once before, back when Valentine and a weakened SMASH team had fought each other to a standstill – but he'd been timid back then. Paul had told himself he couldn't risk the broach spiraling out of control.

And it was a valid fear: even the best SMASH teams feared a broach. Triggering one on purpose was insane, gave a hostile dimension a toehold–

But that fear, he now realized, was the failure state of bureaucracy: a hidebound organization that suppressed change. He should have trusted Imani, trusted he'd find another way if Imani had turned Aliyah in, trusted his own instincts about Payne. But he'd confused stability for safety, and as much as he hated Tyler, Paul had to admit Project Mayhem had a point:

Stop trying to control everything and just let go.

Filled with confidence, Paul closed the gap, walled off the buzzsects, forcing them back home.

But just before he sealed the broach on this alien dimension, he heard the droning coalesce into a chilling voice that burrowed into the moistest parts of his brain:

We remember you.

Paul leaned against the desk. He wasn't sure he'd be able to sleep tonight, knowing whatever was on the other side of our universe had marked him. That was assuming, of course, he could evade the SMASH teams – but they wouldn't be using their Unimancy to track anyone down. Because after Valentine and Tyler got done, there would be enough magical strain in New York that nobody sane would cast a spell for weeks.

But there were still two things to do:

First, Paul thumbed the "Emergency" button underneath Payne's desk, signaling to anyone left to evacuate the building. Just in case they hadn't gotten the message from the file cabinets exploding and the building quaking.

Then he kissed the Xbox controller, swept Payne's papers off the blotter. He reached into the briefcase and laid mementoes upon Payne's desk: a charred origami unicorn, a cracked mask taken from Mrs Vinere's apartment, a sheaf of number-scrawled pages from Juan the bookiemancer.

Then he placed the controller carefully in the center. He touched one side – K-Dash – and the other – Quaysean.

It seemed fitting.

"Thanks, guys," Paul said, and limped out of the building.

FIFTY-THREE
Where is my Mind?

Tyler and Valentine had taken their places high in an office building across from Samaritan Mutual. They stood before a large glass window, in an unfinished floor, affording them a perfect view of Samaritan Mutual's towering high-rise. They had turned off the lights, so the only illumination came from the burning skyscrapers.

Tyler chewed his nails, excited.

"Are you sure we should do this, baby?" Valentine asked, her broken shoulder still in a sling. "With so much 'mancy boiling around us, we might cause another broach..."

"Please, Valentine," Tyler said. He didn't look like Brad Pitt any more, not since they'd started dating – but Valentine had fallen in love with the man, not the face. "I *need* this."

"Of course you do," she sighed, lovestruck. "Say when."

Tyler leaned over to press the "play" button on a cassette player. The Pixies poured out of the speakers, a slow-driving slurry of pounding drums and ghostly vocals, playing "Where Is My Mind?"

He grabbed a gun and eased it into his mouth. He had practiced this shot for months, Valentine knew. Still, that made pulling the trigger no easier.

His mouth filled with the acrid taste of cordite. His teeth shattered.

But the bullet blew a hole through his cheek, just like the narrator had done at the finale of *Fight Club*.

"*Nnnh!*" Tyler cried, shuddering. He clasped his palm to his face, letting the pain flow through him – and then bright-eyed, turned to take Valentine's hand.

Tyler looked out the window at the Samaritan Mutual office building, holding his breath as though he'd been waiting for something all his life.

He squeezed her hand. Valentine snapped her fingers – and explosions burst out of Samaritan Mutual's windows, the building lurching to one side, crumbling, falling, the entire thing collapsing just like the credit card companies tumbling in the final shot of the movie.

Tyler turned to Valentine.

"You met me at a very strange time in my life," he told her.

Valentine smiled.

FIFTY-FOUR
Three Weeks Later

The church basement had the comfortable feel of an old leather boot: well-worn, a little antiquated, suited to its clientele. The pastor had set out a battered steel coffee pot on a wide folding table, complete with stacks of pink saccharine packets and powdered coffee creamer. It burbled as it heated up, almost ready for the 7:00 meeting.

Paul had brought a big tray of Dunkin' Donuts. Which was a little sad; he'd hoped Kit would bring the donuts, but Kit's flight had been delayed. Which was a shame, since Kit selling his home to go on the road with them seemed like the final step in this crazy scheme, but...

He'd have to give his talk tonight without his oldest friend to back him up.

Former Project Mayhem members set up folding chairs on the scuffed linoleum tiles. They all wore guns underneath their jackets, but thankfully this town was in a hunting region, and nobody thought much of a concealed carry. Paul hoped they wouldn't need to use them.

He examined the posterboard, which was covered with local events – grief support groups every Tuesday, addiction clinics Thursday, cancer survivors Saturdays, the space rented from the church to pretty much anyone who needed a space to chat. The pastor had assured them anonymity was guaranteed, except he always kept the confessional booths open upstairs in case anyone wanted to talk – and so nobody thought much of the "Friends of Paul" meeting slotted in for Friday.

Paul looked out over the empty chairs: he hoped people would show up tonight.

Check that: he hoped people who didn't want to kill him showed up tonight.

"Don't worry," the man who once had been Tyler Durden said. "I've been to lots of these meetings. Nobody shows up early. They'll come."

"Thanks, uh…." Paul couldn't remember Tyler's new name. But Tyler's cockiness was gone, his spiked hair replaced by a trucker's cap, his angular face softer. The men still came to him for advice, and Tyler was surprisingly competent, though he often deferred to Paul. He whistled contentedly, then kissed Valentine on the cheek before he went off to set up the lectern.

"So he's… not magical anymore?" Paul asked.

"Three weeks, and I haven't felt a glimmer," Valentine said.

"I didn't think you could, you know, *stop* being a 'mancer."

Valentine adjusted the sling on her broken shoulder, not wincing; instead, she watched who-once-had-been-Tyler set up the lectern, smiling dreamily. "It's like you said, Paul: he was a cinemancer. People who love movies seek endings. And once he got what he wanted, his need to do 'mancy… evaporated."

"I thought he'd want to, I don't know, take over the city or something."

"That's one interpretation of *Fight Club*. The other is that it's about a very sad boy who found his girl. He just needed to be important to somebody, and, well…." Valentine blew a heart-shaped bubble of pink bubblegum. "He's my world."

"But why isn't he Tyler Durden anymore?"

"That name doesn't fit," Valentine shrugged, then tugged

at her sling; she hated being restrained. "And he didn't want to go back to being a schlubby insurance agent again, so he chose a new one."

"What's his new name again? I can never remember."

Valentine gave Paul the rueful grin of a woman who adored her lover's silliest quirks. "His name is Robert Paulson."

"Valentine!" Imani said. "I need to double-check something with you."

Imani was dressed far too nicely for the church, wearing a ruffled fur coat that made her look like a model slumming on location, but she was so spectacular Paul couldn't help but admire her. She didn't glance up from Aliyah's Nintendo DS, waving both Valentine and Paul peremptorily over to one of the couches.

Aliyah squatted on the couch, concentrating on the double screens.

Valentine rolled her eye. "Don't say 'please' or anything, Mrs Tsabo," she muttered. "Juuuust order us around like peons…" But by the time she got over to Aliyah, Valentine said, perhaps a bit too brightly, "Yes, Mrs Tsabo?"

Imani was so caught up in deciphering the icons spread across the radar map on the Nintendo that she didn't register the slight. She pointed to a vector graphic that looked like two stars joined at the hip. "What's that?"

Valentine peered in. "…two policemen on patrol. In a… yeah, a squad car."

Imani got out a small legal pad, drew the tip of her manicured nail down a line of hand-drawn charts. "Icons with angles indicate an outside authority we need to be aware of." Imani peered up at Valentine for confirmation. "Circled icons indicate people travelling in a ground vehicle."

Valentine raised her eyebrows. "Very good for a woman who doesn't play videogames."

"Didn't."

"Pardon?"

"I didn't play videogames. Now I have reasons." Imani turned to Aliyah. "Now, Aliyah, you told me those policemen were walking."

"I thought they were!" Aliyah protested. "They were going slow!"

"If they're police in cars, they could be driving slowly to case the area." She waved a former Project Mayhem participant away from setting up the chairs. "It's probably nothing, but can you check upstairs?"

The Project Mayhem man nodded. Imani hadn't been able to go back to her job as a corporate lawyer, now they were on the lam, but she'd taken to running operations here with a crisp efficiency. "Sure thing, Mrs Tsabo."

She frowned. "I'm *not* Mrs Tsabo. I'm Ms Dawson." She blew a brief kiss in Paul's direction. "No offense, love."

The man jogged upstairs, passing the guards tasked with patting down everyone to ensure nobody had their cell phone during the discussion. Paul felt grateful that many of Project Mayhem's members had stayed on with him; having gotten a taste of 'mancy, they thought the government's laws were cruel, and had agreed to help out. It felt weird, having unpaid volunteers working for him in their spare time, but also somehow correct.

Imani planted her finger on Aliyah's screen. "Now, sweetie, if you're going to warn us when SMASH troops are inbound, you have to know the game better than Aunt Valentine. I'm going to point at each of these icons, and you're going to tell me what they are."

"But M*ooo*mmmm…."

"If ifs and buts were candy and nuts…" Imani recited.

"…we'd all have a merry Christmas." Despite her mock outrage, Aliyah snuggled up to her mother, relishing the group activity. Imani poked at the crowd of incoming icons trickling into the church, quizzing Aliyah on what each one represented, rewarding correct answers with a squeeze and kiss.

●●●

Aliyah had turned nine last week. She still had nightmares – after everything she'd been through at the Institute, that would be too much to ask for – but despite living in a stolen van, despite constantly watching for incoming SMASH teams, despite the endless disguises and Kit not arriving yet, Aliyah had what she wanted:

A loving family.

And that, Paul thought, would have to be enough.

"Come on, chief," Valentine said, eyeing the new members on the screen. "Looks like you got a full house for your talk. Let's pull you into the back before you get swarmed with well-wishers."

She pushed him into an old-fashioned bathroom with a vending machine that sold combs and hair gel. Paul flipped through his notecards, debating for the thousandth time whether he'd arranged his speech in the right order, then put them away. His suit was damp with flopsweat; if he looked out at the people who came before it was time to talk, he'd break down.

Valentine peered out the bathroom door, eyeing Imani's teaching. "She's no better at videogames than you are," she groused. "But she's devoted."

"You really don't like her, do you?" Paul asked, worried.

"She's not my favorite person, Paul. She's bossy and uncreative. But I don't have to get your attraction, any more than you have to get what Robert is to me; I just have to respect it." She smacked her lips, debating whether to continue. "And she's teaching Aliyah to be *precise*, Paul. Imani's upped that kid's 'mancy game. Soon she'll reskin herself to pass as some other kid and stay that way all day."

"Then we can send her to school," Paul said. "The kid deserves a third-grade class and a good game of dodgeball."

"Yup." Valentine wiped sweat off her forehead. "So have you and Imani, uh…" She poked her finger though the circle of thumb and middle finger.

Paul's weary look stopped her. "Is that all you ever think about?"

"No, but I'd like to confirm you think about that *ever*."

Paul took a moment to peer out at his ex-wife again, feeling the keenness of a crush that had never ever abated. "We were hoping to get her divorced first," he admitted. "But I don't know if that'll happen."

"She won't fuck you until she's divorced?"

"She said she made a big mistake, cheating on her last husband," Paul said ruefully. "She's never functioned well without closure."

"You two are made for each other."

"She's been sleeping in the bed next to me at night. I'm pretty sure we're gonna get together in… that way… soon."

"Are you *blushing*, Paul?"

He turned away. "*No!*"

"Paul and Imani, sittin' in a tree – K-I-S-S-I-N-G…"

"*Shut. Up.*" He punched her, lightly, on her good arm. Then: "Thanks for asking, though."

He hugged her, taking care to avoid her broken shoulder. She squeezed back, then whispered in his ear. "You're gonna do great, Paul. I know you're nervous, but… they came because they *didn't* believe the headlines. You tell 'em the truth, and…"

"…and?"

"Well, I don't know what'll happen." Valentine straightened Paul's tie inexpertly. "But whatever falls out, it's not the same old bullshit. So it's worth a shot."

"You and Imani never bullshit me," Paul said. "*That's* what you have in common."

"Never compare two women, Paul. This is the surest way to bring disharmony into a stupid man's lifestyle. Anyway, get your rear into gear. It's time." And she shoved him out into the room before he could argue.

The murmur of people talking cut off as Paul entered the room. Paul recognized a few faces: Lenny Pirrazzini, arms crossed as though this had better be good, sitting with a couple of other Task Force staffers. Paul knew exactly how many regulations they'd broken to be here. A couple of

K-Dash and Quaysean's tattooed buddies, looking around as though the cops might swoop in on them. A few ex-clients from Samaritan Mutual. And Paul noticed reporters, asking for permission before they broke out the microphones.

But mostly, the crowd was strangers – people who'd heard through whispered channels that the 'mancer who'd terrorized New York would be speaking here tonight. They'd snuck here, thinking the truth was worth the risk.

Paul walked through the punishing silence, feeling the weight of their attention settle upon him. He reached into his vest to finger the notecards – he'd read every book on speechmaking he could find–

And as he spread his talking points out across the lectern's tilted surface, they slid to the floor.

"*Go Daddy!*" Aliyah yelled, pumping her fist, and the room laughed.

They all knew Aliyah, Paul realized. Everyone here had read a thousand profiles on the grade-school 'mancer – news articles compiled through interviews with her old teachers, from Payne's former employees, from her physical therapists and even her old schoolmates.

But they didn't know Aliyah like *he* knew her.

That was what was important.

Paul swept the remaining notecards off the lectern.

"So," Paul said. "You want to hear about 'mancy."

The crowd murmured assent.

"My magic is bureaucracy. The *good* kind of bureaucracy. The kind that keeps the government accountable to the people. Except… I wasn't accountable. I was so worried about protecting my daughter, that when the time came, I hid who I was, just like any tyrant.

"But that's not who I am. And that – that let things fester.

"So I'm going to tell you a story tonight. I'll tell you what happens when the government forces 'mancers to choose between state-mandated brainwashing or a criminal career. I'll tell you about Mr Lawrence Payne, a man who thrived in the absence of government supervision, and the things that happen when you allow 'mancers to prey upon each other. And at the end, I'll ask you to reconsider the current laws, and urge you to get your government to change it."

Paul spoke, his words growing stronger. Some were revolted by 'mancy's danger, and a few older European refugees stormed out in disgust when Paul spoke of his first broach.

But others nodded sympathetically, leaning in. They glanced at Aliyah, as if imagining what they might do if they had to protect their child from government troops. Aliyah waved merrily before Imani forced her back to monitoring the game-radar.

Paul remembered what Aliyah had asked the night before, when they had tucked her into the bed at the apartment he had rented using magical credentials and a fresh videogame skin.

What if they don't believe you? Aliyah had asked. *What if we put ourselves in all this danger, running from SMASH all our lives, and nobody listens?*

All we can do is tell the truth, sweetie, Paul had said. *Tell it as loud as we can.*

Aliyah had cuddled up to him, and clenched her fist defiantly, as if to say *I can be loud*.

And as Paul approached the end of his story, he looked out over the audience. Some had screwed up their faces in confusion, while others had leaned back in their chairs and tuned out, whereas still others wore grim expressions, knowing what they'd do once they left.

"Any questions?" Paul asked.

ACKNOWLEDGMENTS

"I now present an act," says Daffy Duck, stepping out onto the stage, "that no other performer has ever dared to execute!" And Daffy then proceeds to drink a gallon of gasoline, a bottle of nitroglycerin, a bullhorn of gunpowder, and a goodly swig of uranium-238.

He lights a match: *boom*. And for the first time in his entire life, Daffy transcends his audience, gets the applause he so desperately needs, even has Bugs Bunny cheering: "That's terrific, Daffy! They want more!"

But Daffy is dead, an angel floating up to heaven. "I know, I know," he says. "But I can only do it once!"

And *that's* how I felt about writing the sequel to *Flex*.

In case you're new here, *Flex* was the end result of twenty-five years of effort and seven failed novels. It took all I had just to get it published. So when they told me, "See that? Well, do it again," well, I will admit to needing some emergency laundry services amidst my smallclothes.

Because *Flex* was, as I noted in the acknowledgments then, my "gimme" book in that my hardcore fans were guaranteed to buy it. Many of you lovely folks followed me over from my blog and my Twitter account and my FetLife account to purchase Ferrett's Debut Novel – but as any good bibliophile knows, there's a very wide gap sitting between "purchased" and "got around to reading," and an even wider one between "read" and "loved." It could well have been that I got The Shrug, as people flicked through some pages and wandered off.

And yet as the initial reviews came in, it turned out many of you loved the book on its own merits, and *did* want a sequel to *Flex*. I became a Real Boy! (Or, at least, a Real Author, as opposed to the Popular-Blogger-Slumming-As-Fictioneer that I'd been playing at for so many years.)

And so to ensure I didn't disappoint, I enlisted an army of beta readers to help me:

I gave Dr Natasha Lewis Harrington, who works clinically with children, a writeup on Aliyah's psychological condition, and had her translate it into the formal language of an assessment report. She wrote a lot more; I edited down. Sorry! It was good stuff!

Heather Ratcliff, aka "MortuaryReport," provided consulting on funerals. As a reward, she makes a cameo appearance in this book as the funeral director. Unlike John Lennon, she can legitimately say that she buried Paul.

Daniel Starr, aka "The reason Europe is now a wasteland," convinced me I needed to have better reasons why the Institute was hunting 'mancers. I made some up.

Miranda Suri gave me some excellent advice on how to amplify Paul's borderline PTSD with the buzzsects more believable.

John Dale Beety's breathless "holy shit" live-critiques of the action sequences helped me remember what not to cut – which, in many ways, is more important than knowing what *to* cut.

Josh Morrey reminded me to keep the pressure on when the book transitioned from "Paul is being hunted" to "Paul is being courted."

Elise Tobler stayed brilliantly on my case to justify why Paul and Valentine were at odds with each other.

Meg Taylor reminded me to explain why Paul had to die, which is a chronic failure of mine in beta drafts: I have reasons why characters do things, very good reasons, and then forget to tell you about them.

Bill Ferris hadn't read the first book, and so helpfully highlighted all the places where I'd forgotten to properly explain bits to new readers.

Raven Black had problems with Paul's oft-contradictory philosophy on killing. Which I took as evidence that I was doing it right. Real people contain multitudes.

Richard Adler was a man I met back when I worked for Borders, and I know he has immaculate tastes when it comes to science fiction, and so when he *liked The Flux*, that gave me strength to churn through some tougher edits.

Carolyn VanEseltine reminded me to explain better why Paul had gained strength and confidence at the end, thus bolstering the story arc.

Christina C Russell found Paul to be a sad-sack parent, and was grievously annoyed by my gratuitous Stephen King-style usage of name brands. I fixed one, refuse to fix the other. OfficeMax and Dunkin' Donuts *all the way*.

Yet a confession: while I felt the pressure of satisfying you all, I also didn't want to let down Rebecca.

Rebecca Alison Meyer, for those of you who don't know, was the inspiration for Aliyah – my surly little spitfire, the only kid I know who completely got the concept of sarcasm at the age of three. When I looked at a blank page and said, "Why would Paul love his daughter enough that he would die for her?", I thought of Rebecca – then four, but even then possessed of the snarkiness of a fifty year-old comedian.

I sold *Flex* on the day Rebecca's brain cancer was diagnosed as terminal.

I wrote the sequel while sitting Shiva with her parents.

Our Little Spark is gone – but in Paul's journey here, I tried to capture the love I felt for her. I don't know if I succeeded. But if you feel moved to find out more about Rebecca, you can go to Rebecca's Gift at *rebeccasgift.org* – and if you wanted to donate a few dollars to the charity they've set up in her name while you were there, well, I wouldn't mind at all.

OK, just a few more people to thank, and I promise I'll

shuffle off. I'll be back in a year for *Fix*, book three of The 'Mancer Chronicles, which I vow *will* finally reveal what's happening in Europe. Evidently, if you casually decimate a whole continent off-screen, people want more details! Who knew?

Thanks, again, to my Mom and Dad and my Uncle Tommy, who raised me as a glorious triumvirate. (For the record, Tommy was Valentine.) Thanks to Carolyn Meyer, whose oft-rebellious but good-natured showdowns with her parents inspired some of the conflictual scenes in this book – and thanks to Kat and Eric, her parents, for supporting and loving me. Thanks to Angie Rush, my, er, best friend.

Thanks to everyone I thanked in the first book, and if you haven't read the first book, thanks for going back and reading that as soon as you finished this one, *as I'm sure you're doing*.

Thanks to the Angry Roboteers: Mike Underwood was Fan #1 of *Flex* and has ably supported it enough to encourage me to write this sequel, Penny Reeve and Caroline Lambe promoted it, Marc Gascoigne and Phil Jourdan edited the crap out of it, Steven M-R wrapped it all up in a lovely Valentine bow. Look at it! It's here in your hands right now because of them! Wow!

And above all, thanks to everyone who bought *Flex*, and everyone who talked about it. Your reviews, tweets, and face-to-face recommendations are why this is here today. I hope, *hope*, this sequel is reward enough.

Yet as always, there is one person who I couldn't have done this without. When I ran out of ideas, she would get off the couch whenever I said, "Mind going for a plot-walk with me?" When I despaired, she fed me strength. When I wrote badly, she bashed me with loving excoriations. She is the light I steer by, the beauty that pries me out of bed when depression smashes me down, the even-keeled sensibility that anchors me when I'd float off on tides of stupidity.

I love you, Gini.

Arf.